The Brains Trust

❀ ❀ ❀

ALSO BY R. G. TUGWELL

❀ ❀ ❀

THE BRAINS
TRUST

by R. G. Tugwell

❀ ❀ ❀

The Viking Press

NEW YORK

VIKING COMPASS EDITION
Issued in 1969 by The Viking Press, Inc.
625 Madison Avenue, New York, N.Y. 10022

Distributed in Canada by
The Macmillan Company of Canada Limited

Library of Congress catalog card number: 68-16079

Printed in U.S.A.

Acknowledgment is made with thanks to Raymond Moley for permission to quote from *After Seven Years,* Copyright 1939, © 1967 by Raymond Moley.

To ROBERT MAYNARD HUTCHINS,
who has always been interested in brains, though
not necessarily those written about in this book,
and not necessarily, ever, with approval of their
operations

Acknowledgment

When the manuscript of this book was substantially complete, it was read by Elliot Rosen, Associate Professor of History at Rutgers University. He had just finished helping Raymond Moley in the writing of *The First New Deal,* published in 1966, and was thus familiar with the materials saved from the period of our service with Roosevelt. The subject matter of that book was not, like mine, the summer of 1932; it began, rather than ended, with the November election; but there was much in it of use to me. This note is my thanks for Professor Rosen's co-operation.

Acting for the publishers, Malcolm Cowley, an associate on *The New Republic* in still earlier days than are written about here, helped in preparing the book for publication. The effort he gave to it was much beyond any reasonable expectation. To him, too, my thanks.

Contents

The Brains Trust

MEMBERS

RAYMOND MOLEY

Born in Beria, Ohio, in 1886.

Educated at Baldwin-Wallace and Oberlin Colleges and at Columbia University.

In 1932, professor of government at Barnard College of Columbia University.

In 1928, had been introduced to Roosevelt at Democratic campaign headquarters during the Smith campaign, by Louis McHenry Howe, then secretary of the National Crime Commission.

In 1930, had drafted a model for a state parole system at the Governor's request. During the next year, was assistant to Samuel Seabury during the hearings of the charges against T. C. T. Crain, Tammany District Attorney in New York (actually, Moley was Governor Roosevelt's representative).

In 1932, was a member of the commission to revise the administration of justice in New York. In early spring, was preparing a statement to be issued by the Governor on the occasion of Sheriff Thomas M. Farley's dismissal, then imminent.

Author of *Lessons in American Citizenship; Lessons in Democracy; Parties, Politics, and People; Politics and Criminal Prosecution; Our Criminal Courts;* and *Tribunes of the People.*

ADOLF A. BERLE, JR.

Born in Boston, Massachusetts, in 1895.

Educated at Harvard College and the Harvard University School of Law.

In 1932, professor of law at the Columbia University Law School.

Author of *Studies in the Law of Corporations; Cases and Materials in the Law of Corporations;* and *The Modern Corporation and Private Property* (with Gardiner Means) (still unpublished in 1932).

R. G. TUGWELL

Born in Sinclairville, New York (Chautauqua County), in 1891.

Educated at Buffalo and the University of Pennsylvania.

In 1932, professor of economics at Columbia University.

Author of *The Economic Basis of Public Interest; American Economic Life and the Means of its Improvement* (with others); *Industry's Coming of Age; The Trend of Economics* (with others); and *The Industrial Discipline and the Governmental Arts* (still unpublished in 1932).

FOUNDERS

SAMUEL I. ROSENMAN

Born in San Antonio, Texas, in 1896.

Educated at Columbia College and the Columbia University Law School.

In 1932, appointed Justice, New York State Supreme Court.

Counsel to the Governor, 1928–1932.

Member of the New York State legislature, 1922–1926.

Bill-drafting commissioner, 1926–1928.

D. BASIL O'CONNOR

Born in Taunton, Massachusetts, in 1892.

Educated at Dartmouth College and the Harvard University School of Law.

In 1932, law partner of Roosevelt. The partnership had been formed in 1925 when Roosevelt left his partnership with Langdon Marvin. O'Connor's sort of practice gave much more scope to Roosevelt's penchant for business ventures, sometimes of adventurous sorts. O'Connor was a shrewd brake on Roosevelt's chance-taking.

ASSOCIATES

ROBERT K. STRAUS

Born in New York City in 1905.

Educated at Harvard College and the Harvard University Graduate School of Business.

In 1932, assistant executive director, New York State Temporary Relief Administration.

HUGH JOHNSON

Born at Fort Scott, Kansas, in 1882.

Educated at the United States Military Academy and the University of California (A.B., 1915; J.D., 1916).

Vice-president and counsel, Moline Plow Company (resigned in 1929).

In 1932, employed by Bernard M. Baruch.

Author of many stories and essays: *Williams at West Point; Williams in Service,* etc.

CHARLES WILLIAM TAUSSIG

Born in New York City in 1896.

In 1932, president of the American Molasses Company and the Sucrest Corporation.

Author of *The Book of the Radio;* and *Rum, Romance, and Rebellion.*

Since 1932

Moley, Berle, and the author have gone on since 1932 to occupy other positions and add considerably to their lists of writings. Rosenman and O'Connor have continued to be prominent lawyers, but, besides, Rosenman has been assistant to two Presidents (Truman as well as Roosevelt), has edited the thirteen volumes of Roosevelt's papers, and has written *Working with Roosevelt* (New York, 1952). O'Connor first created the Warm Springs Foundation and oversaw the modernization of its facilities. He had much to do with the elimination of poliomyelitis, Roosevelt's crippling disease. He later became President of the National Foundation for attacking other crippling diseases.

Moley wrote *After Seven Years* (New York, 1939) and *The First New Deal* (New York, 1967)—recollections of his service with Roosevelt. The author wrote *The Democratic Roosevelt* (New York, 1956), a biography; and *FDR: Architect of an Era* (New York, 1967) for younger readers; and, as well, other studies of Roosevelt, his associates, and the New Deal, published in various journals.

Johnson and Taussig have died. Straus, for some years, was occupied in various New Deal posts. He now lives in Los Angeles and publishes the *San Fernando Sun*.

A Brief Chronology

Before April

Amassing of delegates for Roosevelt by Howe and Farley—a majority but not two-thirds.

Quarrels of the progressives with Hoover about relief, public works, and planning measures.

Establishment of the Reconstruction Finance Corporation (Feb. 2).

Moley's work with Roosevelt on the administration of justice and, in February, on preparations for the removal of Sheriff Thomas A. Farley.

Rosenman's and/or Moley's suggestion for a study group.

April

My visit with Moley; then with Rosenman and O'Connor; then with Roosevelt.

Subsequent sessions at the Governor's mansion; those present: Moley, Rosenman, and O'Connor.

The "Forgotten Man" speech (April 7).

The acquisition of Berle.

The "Concert of Interests" address at Jefferson Day Dinner in St. Paul, Minnesota, under Olson's auspices (April 18).

May

Intensified discussions and study of national problems, often from memoranda prepared by Berle, by myself, or by others.

Roosevelt's recreational visit to Warm Springs, Georgia.

Address at Oglethorpe University, Atlanta (May 22).

Return to Albany.

Nomination of Norman Thomas by the Socialist Convention (May 23).

Maneuvering for the Convention.

Descent on Washington of the Bonus Army.

June

Continuation of discussions; visits of experts, mostly shepherded by us.

Preparation of acceptance speech.

Rise of Democrats' confidence; imminence of the Convention.

Republican Convention in Chicago (June 14).

Passage of the Patman Bonus Bill (June 15).

Talks with Wallace and Wilson in Chicago; the Domestic Allotment scheme.

Start of the Democratic Convention (June 27).

The deal with Hearst to make Garner Vice-President in exchange for Texas and California votes (June 30).

July

Roosevelt's flight to Chicago and the acceptance.

Return to Albany and celebrations of the nomination.

Voyage of the *Mystic II* up the Atlantic coast.

Addition of General Johnson to the Brains Trust.

Planning for the active campaign and worries about Tammany and the Walker case.

Passage by the Congress of the Relief and Reconstruction Act (July 21).

Passage of the Federal Home Loan Act (July 22).

Establishing of Brains Trust headquarters at the Roosevelt Hotel in New York.

Dispersal of the Bonus Marchers, Washington (July 28–29).

Radio address on the Platform (July 30).

August

Preparation of materials to be used by Moley in writing speeches for the Western trip.

Campaign address at Columbus, Ohio, on failures of the Hoover administration.

Hague's party convocation at Sea Girt, N.J., and speech on ending prohibition (Aug. 27).

Hearings in Albany on charges against Walker.

September

The flight abroad of Walker (Sept. 1), making dismissal unnecessary.

The Western trip:

Address on the Farm Problem at Topeka (Sept. 14).

Address on the Railroad Problem at Salt Lake City (Sept. 17).

Tariff speech at Seattle (Sept. 20).

Power Yardstick speech at Portland (Sept. 21).

Commonwealth Club speech at San Francisco (Sept. 23).

Address on Agriculture and Tariffs at Sioux City (Sept. 29).

October

Campaigning and shorter trips to the Midwest and South:

Radio Address to Business and Professional Men's League (Oct. 6).

Address on the Federal Budget at Pittsburgh (Oct. 19).

Addresses on Farm Problems at Springfield and St. Louis (Oct. 21).

Attack on Republican leadership at Baltimore (Oct. 25).

Speech on Unemployment and Planning at Boston (Oct. 31).

Hoover's speech warning that "grass will grow in the streets" if Roosevelt should be elected.

November

Final speeches in New York City (Nov. 3 and 5).

Election (Nov. 8): Roosevelt nearly 28 million; Hoover under 16 million.

INTRODUCTION

❦ ❦ ❦

H istorians have made the events of spring and summer in 1932 well enough known. Several have written about them, and others doubtless will. Also, those who had some part in the proceedings have reported their recollections, their impressions, and their afterthoughts.* They do not agree on all matters, even some important ones; but it is understood, or it should be, that recollections are subject to discount, and also that disparities are not necessarily evidence of attempts to deceive.

Those who have read such accounts will have gathered that it was a time when the nation was in paradoxical trouble—rich in ability, poor in performance—and that the prevalent suffering may have tended to distort sight and hearing. When a revolution was talked of and dissolution seemed possible, it was not a time to be keeping notes for the instruction of posterity. Besides, if the others were like me, it did not occur to them until afterward that what they individually did or said had a significance warranting record.

In such matters, we were innocents; how innocent, I hesitate to admit; I was, after all, forty-one years old, and Raymond Moley was forty-six. It was not until Ray and I, almost a year later, were

* Especially Raymond Moley, James A. Farley, Samuel I. Rosenman, Flynn, Eleanor Roosevelt, and Frances Perkins.

having a disagreeable conversation with the then Secretary of State, Henry L. Stimson, backed by an assistant named Bundy, that the term *aide mémoire* took on any intimation of utility for me. Stimson threatened us with one, and obviously the prospect of some future scholar leafing through the files and discovering how a Secretary of State had felt about us was meant to be intimidating. It would give us pause, as I am sure he would say. Someone who had dealings with Stimson about that time said of him that he was the only man he had ever observed who could look pompous sitting down. His pomposity was on display that day, and it was so well supported by Bundy that we wondered if the Stimson back did not have an essential Bundy stiffening. It could well have taken two for such remarkable certitude.

I am afraid the threat gave both of us amusement rather than pause, but then we were not subject to bureaucratic discipline. Descending the steps of the old State, War, and Navy Building in the spring sunshine, we spoke about it. Ray remarked, as by now he had done many times since he had known that he would soon occupy an office there, that Washington was going to be different from Albany—unpleasantly different.

He had various ways of saying this, some of them picturesque but all of them deprecating. I had another reaction; I was impressed in spite of myself. I concealed it from Ray. But I had noted in Roosevelt an accustomed acceptance of formality. It was hidden by his politician's ease, but I already suspected that deference to formality was more natural to him than the ease. Behind both there was another Roosevelt I had studied earnestly. In view of his seven years (1913–1920) as Assistant Secretary of the Navy, nearly twice as long as the four of his governorship in Albany, it seemed certain that he must have a sophistication we lacked. He would move into office with experienced smoothness. *He* would know what an *aide mémoire* was; he must have read— and written—many of them. It was appalling, really, that we had not done more than make a few notes for our own use. We doubtless should have been making elegant justifications for some time past.

That account of Stimson's, with Bundy's clipped to it, does now repose in the files, I presume, and tells the incident as he would like it told. I have only recollection for support. I wish now I had the backing of many more notes than the infrequent ones I made and kept.

Some thirty-five years after that spring it is obvious to me, as it seems not to have been to some others, that there are risks. By that I mean that during the intervening years my recollections have been affected by what continued to happen. It will be impossible, no matter how I try, to recapture precisely the moods and excitements of 1932; consequently, what I report may be regarded with skepticism. Thinking it over, I have decided just the same to go ahead, hoping it may be granted to me that I mean well. It may even be that perspective will illuminate many occurrences that, if one may judge from the general interest, seem to have grown rather than diminished in significance.

While those summer months were passing, we had not fully realized how sharp a bend in history was being rounded. It can be seen now that old wrongs had broken through the concealment of the then establishment, that old mistakes and neglects were demanding their consequences, and that the victims of a careless competitive system had reached the full stretch of their tolerance. We talked about this tension. At some moments I thought Roosevelt saw how radical a reconstruction was called for; at others I guessed that he would temporize as the transition was made. I was right in this last. The New Deal was a mild medicine.

In his place another leader, say Bob La Follette or Floyd Olson, might have attempted more than would have been accepted. Being one of this breed, I was always urging more than the elders would swallow. I think now that I was too impetuous. I also think, however, that Roosevelt erred too—on the minimal side. He could have emerged from the orthodox progressive chrysalis and led us into a new world. He chose rather rickety repairs for an old one.

I really believe myself to have been proved right in wanting to reach our known potential more quickly; but that was his responsibility. What he did is still not being assessed at its worth in comparison with what might have been done, because what he did seemed so startling to those who were used to looking backward. He seems heroic to those who measure him by his predecessor, but that is because they cannot accept his amazing resemblance to Hoover—under a contrasting mask. They do not realize that both saw the same light and both followed it. Hoover had wanted—and had said clearly enough that he wanted—nearly all the changes now brought under the New Deal label. Some of them he was unable to achieve because he was obstructed by the Democrats who came into control of the Congress at the mid-term elections in 1930 and behaved in dog-in-the-manger fashion. Others his Republican traditionalist colleagues would not countenance. So not much was done; he was marked for exile, and Roosevelt could carry on. But it *was* a carrying on, not a reconstruction.

If now an observer brings himself to look beyond the year of action and through the haze of hope that so fortunately hid the facts of failure, he must see that the Roosevelt measures were really pitiful patches on agencies he ought to have abandoned forthwith when leadership was conferred on him in such unstinted measure. I thought then he could have, and I now think he could have. The full tragedy of his turning away was measured in later troubles. Unless I am mistaken, painful reorganizations are still to be gone through. The compulsion this time is not cold and hunger; it is a rising revolution of technology, which demands even more insistently the institutions of great management. Those institutions ought to have been perfected in thirty years of experience, instead of being smothered in the tangles of a system more accurately called a nonsystem.

What I have to add to what has already been said is in this strain. It is, in distressing part, an account of actual frustration as success in the election materialized, of unjustified euphoria, of half measures that seemed sufficient only in contrast to none at all. Others have not seen it that way, so I must make my own interpretation. If my account is a gloss on events that are by now historic stereotypes, it is not because those events did not happen, but because I see them differently. I must be forgiven if I seem to retell old tales. Their moral, at least, is not what is usually concluded.

The verdict of my own generation, and pretty generally the verdict of the generations since, is that Roosevelt rose to the demands of 1932. It seems still to be accepted, moreover, that he did so magnificently. I grant the magnificence, because that implies style, *élan,* assurance, all that sort of thing. I do not grant now, and I did not then, that this implies adequacy, prescience, all *that* sort of thing. It had glamour but not substance. It was not enough.

It is quite clear, in the train of events, that he had purposes beyond those he disclosed in the campaign and in communications with the Democratic elders. Certainly he meant to give the nation a system of security for all; he meant also to establish an organization for international government. These were not even mentioned (in public; they were discussed privately), and this, as will be seen, seemed to me mistaken. When the party elders took him for their candidate, there was an understanding. He kept within their terms of reference. After he became President he went further, or tried to, but then *he* was frustrated, and that, I think, was because his campaign had been so muted at their insistence.

A public that could not be asked to approve Social Security or an organization for keeping the peace could not be expected to accept economic discipline and the substitution of duty for privilege. A later President would tell Americans that they must ask not what the country could do for them but what they could do for the country. Roosevelt told them nothing so impolitic. He kept saying the country ought to do more for them—make business better, provide more benefits—but there was no call to men's creative impulses or to their resources of courage. Later there would be a long campaign to prepare for war in defense of democracy, but in 1932 there was no such use of his talents to organize unity within our own borders.

Perhaps it was not the time for such urgings; men were licked, beaten down by a monstrous enemy they could neither see nor hear. The depression was like Poe's contracting room. Roosevelt the President was a giant who hunched his shoulders and pushed the walls outward again or at least held them motionless. It seemed as much as any man could do. But he did move; he blocked the machinery of contraction by assuring men's incomes, opening sources of credit, conferring rights to bargain, and so on. The power in men to escape, to break down walls and build new systems of collective living, had not been appealed to; and when it was all over, the establishment was more solidly planted than ever. Its functions had not been nationalized nor had its elite been disciplined.

Much of what should have been done would thus remain to be done when Roosevelt was through. In saying this, I risk dissent not only from outsiders but also from one of our number, apparently, although I thought the imminence of collectivism as apparent to him as it was to me. This seems not to have been so. A long time afterward Adolf Berle wrote: "Steadily, it seems to me, Roosevelt chose as much of the ideas and measures we presented to him as he believed he could translate into reality." *

This, I would say, ignores Roosevelt's conclusion that much of what we presented *ought* not to be turned into reality. If he had been free to lead Americans into a collective economy with all its necessary appurtenances, would he have chosen to do so? As we shall see, there were moments in the spring and summer I write of when it seemed he would have chosen this course, but they passed like shadows. In the record there is only one collectivist address, with a few other tentative suggestions looking in that direction; and to set over against this thin showing there are many atomistic ones. Most of the reformist promises were intended to punish businessmen for being dishonest rather than to arrange for co-operation in the public interest.

I shall say more about this, but let me quote Adolf further and more specifically. "I have little patience," he says, "with those liberals who thought he 'let them down,' because he did not go all out for their measures." I do not take this as meant for me because I accepted my assignments at the time and did my best with them;

---

* This quotation and those that follow are from Adolf A. Berle's review in *The New Republic*, March 7, 1964, of Bernard Sternsher, *Tugwell and the New Deal* (Rutgers, N.J.: Rutgers University Press, 1964).

my reservations were shared only with our inner circle. We were not required to say that what we contributed was offered without any reservations; Roosevelt knew well enough that we could not have done that. But who were we when the elders sat monumental and watchful all around the horizon? The decisions were his to make and not ours to question (after having had our say). Adolf puts it this way:

> He, not they, best knew what could be achieved. Certainly he, far better than they, could estimate the greatest common divisor of effective opinion in the Congress and in the United States. No one understood better than he the differences between "education"—preparing possibilities for tomorrow—and political action—designed to achieve tangible results today. In the grim business of separating today's possibility from dreams later to be achieved, friendship . . . never can and never should control the statesman.

If this distinction of Adolf's is to be accepted, although I do not see it as valid, it would mean that our questions at the time were concerned with what was to be put off until tomorrow. As it turned out, what was accepted for the campaign was a credible promise of banking reform and a vague one of relief for the unemployed and the farmers. These were immensely important objectives; but certainly all of us wanted more substantial achievements.

There were times, however, when budget-balancing seemed to be the central policy, and there were others when our plea for restored purchasing power had some recognition. Concerning what might be done about the depression there was no agreement. We were on the side of those who would collectivize. But we were always making such concessions to others that our proposals fell into the background. It was so much more dramatic to lash the bankers than to suggest a new system of banking, or to blame the middlemen than to say that producers would have to accept some discipline themselves.

Adolf does not associate himself, now, with my urgings in 1932; perhaps he did not then; but if not, there were crooks in his logic, and I do not recall that his clear mind ever tolerated deviations:

. . . it is fair to say that Tugwell's bent toward collectivism went beyond Roosevelt's own philosophy, and certainly far beyond the philosophy of at least nine-tenths of the United States. The country was not ready to accept economic planning and direct action in the measure Tugwell then wanted, though it clearly is on the verge of adopting such planning today.

But wasn't it right, after all, to have pressed for a start in this direction? Adolf seems to admit as much:

In the year 1964, the forces generated by the New Deal have about accomplished their potential. Yet in the light of results, and comparing the situation today with that in 1933, it is impossible to deny that a great advance in American welfare was scored. Equally it is impossible to deny that the American economic system now permits, and social morality demands, a huge advance of comparable proportions. . . . this requires a far greater measure of forward social planning, a capacity to use new resources of technology to a degree thus far undreamed, and larger visions of the content of life than those dominating the hopes of the Roosevelt Age. This is as it should be. The new generation should begin where we left off.

Adolf forgets. He had those dreams then, and at more than seventy he is still one of that younger generation. He gives Roosevelt too much credit and himself not enough.

Actually, Adolf and I were usually on the same side, but with different equipment. He was a student of corporate law and practice. I was a student of economic life, much impressed by an immense productive potential that the system was failing to release.

Ray's is a different case entirely. If I have been asked once, I have been asked a thousand times since the New Deal days, "What happened to Ray Moley?" The answer has to be, although it is never understood as I mean it, and is unsatisfactory to questioners, "Nothing happened to him."

I once had occasion to say something like this to Roosevelt himself. It was in the spring of 1935, at the time when I was working with him most intimately. A statement had to be written about something or other, and we were discussing it across his cluttered desk upstairs in the White House. I remarked that it was at times like these that we had need of Ray. "Yes," he said, "but Ray has joined the fat cats."

What he referred to was the editorship of *Today* and Ray's receivership of the St. Regis Hotel, one of Vincent Astor's properties. Obviously, he said, Ray had been taken into the Baruch circle. I objected. I reminded Roosevelt that even after Ray's immolation in the wreck of the London Economic Conference, he had gone on making himself useful around the White House. He must have drafted a dozen or more speeches in 1934; I knew because I had helped with some of them. I said to Roosevelt a little severely that Ray was no longer called upon. He acknowledged that this might be so, but said that Ray seemed to have interests now that were not exactly in accord with his own.

This conversation went on for some time and was once or twice renewed. Before it ended I said the real trouble was that Hull was unhappy when Ray was around. That was why he wasn't sent for any more. He had made the mistake of precipitating a showdown with his political superior. Roosevelt took it all right. He even remarked that if I had trouble with Henry Wallace, who was my superior, I had better keep it quiet. He went on to admit that very possibly it was not Ray's fault that he had been so humiliated. Hull considered that Ray had injured his dignity in London, and since he was the father superior of the party, and Ray had no standing in it, Ray must be sent into the desert.

If Ray had found new friends, I said, it was among a group of fellow exiles; most of those he associated with now would like to be sharing the White House power. I went on to say that I had watched the game being played between Baruch and himself. It resembled nothing so much as a kind of dance. Baruch was always tiptoeing around and being smiled at, but he was never given anything. He was always available in his Carlton Hotel apartment, and most days he could be interviewed from the bench he occupied in Lafayette Park—a sage just beyond the White House fence, waiting patiently to be of service. His men—George Peek, Hugh Johnson, and others—were called on; but not he. He was always being given just enough to keep him quiet.

Roosevelt said that I seemed to have found out about Baruch. I said that after my licking in the liquor-control affair I had reason to respect his power. He leaned over the desk to tell me that Baruch owned—he used the word—sixty congressmen. That, he said, was power around Washington. He said he didn't know himself why this effort was made and this control established. That could be speculated about. But those sixty congressmen had to be kept in line.

I ventured further, since he seemed to allow it. Did he think Baruch would ever forgive him for not making him Secretary of State in the first place?

He said that didn't matter. Actually there never had been any direct talk about an appointment. On the contrary, Baruch had always protested that he didn't want any office. It was only necessary to take him at his word.

They both knew, however, and if Ray had been added to those under obligation to Baruch, it might be because there was fellow feeling. Ray's hurt was as deep as Baruch's. Roosevelt remarked that Ray was a fellow who needed his hand held often; he repeated this comment on other occasions, I thought with real regret.

As time passed, Ray and I, neither of us losing in the least the regard for each other we had developed in 1932, saw things more and more differently. Finally he came to consider himself the prophet of a new conservatism and I continued to be a planner, a collectivist, even if only an academic one. Also, I never lost my awe of the presidential person. Our occupations almost never brought Ray and myself together, and we never had occasion to find out whether we were still talking about the same thing with somewhat different emphasis.

What follows is drawn from my colleagues' accounts, my own and their notes, and sometimes from my recollection of transactions that seem more significant now than they once did. These are precisely as trustworthy as most recollections. Historians have a discouraging lack of respect for such evidence, but then I have lost some respect for historians, or rather I have concluded that their views are very often views and not actually history.

It will be obvious that I have taken liberties. I have reported conversations that took place at times and places I cannot now specify. If I insist that they did nevertheless take place—if not in the words I have used, then in others amounting to the same thing —it is because that is the best I can do. I have the choice of doing this or of letting the exchanges drift into the oblivion that has shrouded most presidential conversations since the invention of the telephone.

Mr. Kahn, who was for years the custodian at the Roosevelt Library in Hyde Park, has told me that he was often asked—and custodians may still be asked, for all I know—what became of the transcripts taken in the booth where conversations between Roosevelt and his visitors were recorded. That booth was rumored to have been just beneath the presidential desk and to have been serviced by hidden microphones among the scattered souvenirs and gadgets there. Historians, he said, yearn so earnestly for such recordings that they refuse to believe they are mythical. It is frustrating to accept that most of what so important a man said, and what was said to him, has disappeared and cannot even be guessed at with any show of authenticity. Mr. Kahn disliked telling historians that they could never hope for such a trove and must do the best they could with the bales and boxes of official papers that exist. These do no more than they are known to do. Often Roosevelt signed but did not write them; he may have known their contents when they were signed, but perhaps only casually. Some of them were not even signed by him, even when his signature is plain on the paper. How that was done is known well enough. A good many of us knew about it at the time. It was necessary in the circumstances.

These historical difficulties do not prove that what I report here is true. I am sorry about that. Naturally, anyone who chooses not to accept what I say is at liberty to do so. But I have taken the alternative of not letting what seems to me important slip into limbo rather than that of keeping it all to myself. This may be mistaken, but it is the choice I have made.

One more thing: there has been some debate among us about

when we should say the work of the Brains Trust ended. The campaign of 1932 was such a success that some of the credit attached to us; this came as much from those who feared the Roosevelt policies as from those who were pleased by what he had promised. There was a natural rush of all those who would like to share the Roosevelt power, and their elbowings soon promised to be a harassment. For this reason, and because we had no interests of our own to push, Roosevelt continued to make use of us until the inauguration in March of 1933. But the old group fell apart. Adolf Berle was less frequently called on; Hugh Johnson disappeared (until he was called back to run NRA); Sam Rosenman was absorbed into the judicial system of New York; and Doc O'Connor, who was on call, was not closely involved in the new jobs there were to do.*

After election, Ray and I had entirely new duties. President Hoover hoped to involve his successor in international affairs that were rapidly approaching a crisis. Foreign nations were asking forgiveness of their debts, and there was a question of moratoria. The arrangements for a forthcoming World Economic Conference were pending; discussions were going on in Geneva to set up an agenda and to fix a time and place for the meeting. On all such matters, after serious and prolonged discussion among us, Roosevelt found it impossible to accept Hoover's suggestions, and this meant putting everything off until after the inauguration. Then the new President would have a cabinet and could deal with the Congress from the White House. Besides, as winter turned into spring, there was a new crisis in economic affairs. This time American financial institutions were deeply involved. There was a mounting panic as

---

* Kieran's name for us (the Brains Trust) came to have a kind of generic connotation. In *The New York Times* index (under "F. D. Roosevelt: advisers") as many references to the term can be found in 1936 as in 1933. But by that time, or even earlier, it had been expanded to include not only all university people in Washington but all those who might be called intellectuals. There was, indeed, a very lively exchange between attackers and defenders. This engaged such formidable persons as H. L. Mencken against and Nicholas Murray Butler for, surely as strange a pairing as can be imagined.

March approached, and it had to be dealt with in emergency fashion as the new administration took office.

During most of that time Roosevelt as president-elect kept all his volunteer advisers at a formal distance, seeing and talking with many people of all sorts but giving none of them much encouragement. His cabinet choices were not known very long before the inauguration; in fact, his nominees were not told of their selection many days before they were to assume office.

During this whole period of pressure and tension, Ray was the individual most depended upon for assistance in the many confidential matters that crowded in on Roosevelt. I was his second. We were helped by Robert K. Straus and John Dalton, and occasionally by Charles Taussig; it was also a time when others—Henry Morgenthau and Felix Frankfurter, for instance—were poking around a good deal and were allowed on occasion to carry out particular missions—as when Morgenthau traveled from one to another of the farm leaders and sent home reports of their attitudes. Adolf was sent for occasionally, but his association was no longer so regular as it had been in the spring and summer of 1932.

During this time, because so much depended on Roosevelt's intentions and because many of those who wanted dreadfully to be accepted by him were frustrated, we began to be talked about more than we had been during the campaign. The term "Brains Trust" really got its currency then. But Ray insists, and I am inclined to agree, that the Brains Trust ended its life at election time. What Ray and I had to do after that was of a different nature; it was more consequential because Roosevelt was now the president-elect, and it was more confidential because there was more prying; but there were just the two of us who were entrusted with anything and everything as the weeks of winter dragged by and the disappointments of that spring sapped people's resistance to misery.

This is why the events of the interval between election and inauguration seem now to us ones of a different order.

The work of the Brains Trust ended, we think, on election day in November 1932. And this book ends at that point too. There is much to be said about the succeeding period; Ray has written about it in books prepared with meticulous care, *After Seven Years* (1939) and *The First New Deal* (1966); I less extensively. But that period is not encroached on here.

The Brains Trust

To the Nomination

CHAPTER I

Concerning the Name

❧ ❧ ❧

Making only slight allowance for the vagaries of recollection, I feel safe in saying that in the late afternoon of September 5, 1932, James M. Kieran, staff correspondent of *The New York Times,* would have been sweating over his typewriter in Poughkeepsie's Nelson House. Kieran was covering Roosevelt, then at Hyde Park, a few miles to the north. The temperature was in the high eighties and the sweating was no joke; but it had been a good day, climaxed by an interview with Bernard M. Baruch, party angel and beneficiary. Since he had belonged to the stop-Roosevelt coalition right up to the nomination in July, a story about his coming to Hyde Park ought to rate page one.

The Republicans had won the last three campaigns, and just this sort of rift had contributed to the Democrats' defeat. Right now Smith was still sore from his beating, and other Tammanyites were alienated by the recent forced resignation of Mayor Walker. The tendency to party strife might still be active. So Baruch, who had just come back from a month in Europe, was doubly welcome to Roosevelt; his visit was a hopeful sign of healing.

There had been a picnic at Val Kill cottage, Mrs. Roosevelt's craft factory, now becoming a favorite gathering place because it was on a back road and secluded. Especially on a summer day, the

3

woods and fields around her retreat were a change from the tram-
pled lawns and crowding political delegations at Springwood, the
big house on the highway. Kieran had been enjoying one perquisite
of covering Roosevelt: reporters were treated as part of the family.
This was nice for them, but it did make their editors doubt their
complete detachment, and so was not quite the boon it might have
been.

This suspicion existed, but actually it hardly affected Kieran. He
mostly reported mere daily doings—voluminously, for the vora-
cious *Times*—and he had no license to speculate. The think pieces
were beyond his scope. Except in unusual circumstances, he hadn't
even a by-line. James Hagerty and Arthur Krock, who did, had
been enlarging all that week on the Walker case. Walker's humiliation, just recently made complete by his spectacular flight to Europe, was certain, they thought, to damage Roosevelt's chances.
John Curry, the grand sachem, would be plotting revenge if he followed the usual Tammany course. The pundits were writing
grandly, and at inordinate length, about Tammany's captive votes
and repercussions spreading through the party. Roosevelt's campaign organization would be weakened. New York City might even
be lost. Kieran's indicated duty was to write about the candidate's
doings, not his plans or his prospects; but the Baruch interview
was of Hagerty or Krock importance, and neither was around.

Baruch had spoken that day about Roosevelt's "family" and
"history"; these, he had said, guaranteed devotion to the nation's
institutions. No one with such a background, he had gone on,
could be a "radical," as some people were saying. Only Republicans and disappointed friends of Smith were saying anything of the
sort, and Baruch himself had been one of that persuasion two
months back; but Kieran, mindful of his modest status, had re-
frained from asking how long Baruch himself had held so favorable an opinion of the candidate. He merely inquired modestly if
Smith too could be expected to go along. Yes, said Baruch, Smith
would; he was a good party man.

This might dispose of the Tammany holdback which the seers
had been predicting rather hopefully all summer, and it might

make a considerable difference to Roosevelt's chances. It really made much more prestigious copy than the usual daily chronicle.

Kieran had gone on to describe the setting. There was a swimming pool at the cottage; and Mrs. Roosevelt, driving Baruch about the estate in her runabout—something of considerable significance—had caught the correspondents in their bathing suits. She had called to them from the driveway and as they came up had introduced her guest. They had rushed for copy paper and had stood around thus informally, asking questions and taking notes.

This was most of it, but there was still that cataloguing to do. So Kieran wrote:

> Professor Raymond Moley of Columbia, Adolf Berle, and John William Taussig, who belong to a small group known as the "brains department," which aids the Executive in gathering data for speeches, were guests at the picnic also. They are assembling material for the Executive's use on the western swing on which Professor Moley will accompany him.

There followed finally the itinerary of the impending trip to the Pacific Coast.

The Kieran story did make page one next day (without a by-line), but the minor problem bothering him had not been solved to his satisfaction. The locution "brains department" was not quite what he wanted.

On September 9 he had another account to write. The lead this time was the news that James A. Farley would accompany Roosevelt on the forthcoming trip. Since Farley was now chairman of the Democratic National Committee, this was not a sensational revelation, and the story was printed obscurely on page nine, column six. But the detailing had to go on, and presently there was this— another try:

> Professor Raymond Moley of Columbia University will be another in the group. He is recognized as the chief of the "brains trust."

Thus the "brains trust" was launched, on an inside page of *The New York Times* on a slow Monday in September. The other reporters knew a natural when they saw one, and they followed Kieran's lead. They balked at the plural "brains" at first, and their copyreaders were even more resistant. But Kieran kept on repeating, and his right to patent was gradually recognized: "brains trust" it was. Before long it acquired capitals and lost its quotation marks, and thus it passed into the language, the copyreaders revolting at every opportunity and trying to force a return to the singular.

Was it the original invention that, from this sequence, it would appear to have been? Perhaps not; at least Sam Rosenman, in *Working with Roosevelt,* written years later (1952), said:

> News of our activities had spread among Roosevelt's friends and associates, although the general public had heard little or nothing of it. Howe [Louis McHenry Howe] knew all about it by this time, and he did not like the idea. One day, in conversation with the Governor, he referred to the group as "your brains trust." Shortly thereafter on a day when we were expected at Hyde Park for a conference, the Governor told the newspapermen that a group was coming up to see him. Although Howe's reference to us had been derisive, the Governor, in talking with the newspapermen, referred to the group by the same term, "brains trust." One of the reporters used the phrase in his news articles next day—and it stuck. . . .

This was on Sam's own authority and without other support. But Louis may indeed have been the originator. If he was, the intention was undoubtedly derisive. He considered Roosevelt's career his own creation. He was exclusive and jealous, and he was especially jealous of Sam Rosenman, whose association with the Governor had become altogether too close. What is lacking is the testimony of Kieran, who later acknowledged authorship but said nothing one way or the other about origin. He was a reporter, it is true, and it could well be that the words were ones he recalled, not ones he invented. Sam's story is the only reason for doubting his claim, and even that would leave him with a certain credit for acuteness.

Although he was still a junior correspondent, Kieran was ahead of all the old hands, except Ernest Lindley, in recognizing us. His discovery of the Brains Trust may have helped him to get ahead. He did not move on to Washington with Roosevelt, as some others did, but he became Mayor La Guardia's press officer and was extremely useful to that thorny character.

It could be shown that he was not always accurate; he sometimes misspelled and sometimes called people by the wrong names—for instance, the Taussig he spoke of on September 6 was not *John* William, but *Charles* William. But he was now allowed a by-line occasionally, and in the Sunday *Times* of November 20, after the election, he had a prominent, signed piece called "The Cabinet Roosevelt Already Has."

He began this article in essay rather than reportorial style, referring to a famous historian, Philip Guedalla, who had chided his fellow professionals for repeating themselves. Said Kieran, so do the political campaigns the historians write about. There are the same red-fire parades, the same pledges, the same pomp and circumstance. But, he went on, behind the histrionics there are sometimes trusted groups of men who disobey the rule of imitation:

> Franklin Delano Roosevelt goes to the White House next March with a unique gallery of associates who have labored as prompters far from the footlights. One or two of them have been pushed down stage for a bow now and then. But their real work has been in the informal talks at a picnic, in the heated exchanges of a council of war, in the idle argumentation over a small dinner.

If Kieran was not entirely trustworthy about detail, he knew well enough what had been going on out of public sight in Albany, Hyde Park, and New York City. He proceeded to list the individuals involved. But here he found the spread of interest rather too much for his space. What he gave was chiefly a miscellaneous listing of old-time Democratic senators, New York politicians, and big-money supporters, but he also mentioned the Brains Trust. This last he now wrote of confidently as something understood from the mere name:

> There is Louis McHenry Howe, known as the "head man"; there is James A. Farley, the Democratic National Chairman;

there is Henry Morgenthau Jr., former Conservation Commissioner. There is Samuel I. Rosenman, legislative expert and political buffer, who formed the Brains Trust; and there is Raymond Moley, the Brains Trust head, professor at Columbia,
expert on public law, tireless worker and chief aide of the Governor on the final draft of public statements.

There are other members of the Trust: A. A. Berle, another
Columbia Professor, and R. G. Tugwell, still another man from
Columbia. There is a General Hugh Johnson. He is what is
called the "man" of Bernard Mannes Baruch, financier, on
whom Governor Roosevelt has relied for considerable guidance
in past months.

The last paragraph ran:

. . . Mr. Rosenman had inaugurated the Brains Trust led by
Professor Moley. As far back as last May the little corps which
arranged data for the Governor came into being. It gradually
assumed more importance. How much of the body will continue
is of course conjecture. On men like Bernard Baruch, Owen D.
Young, and Colonel House, Mr. Roosevelt relies greatly, but of
those in the personal gallery who have worked for months,
some of them for years, in direct touch with him, some, at least
will carry on in Washington.

Along with everyone else, Kieran found it hard to believe that
Colonel House, Owen D. Young, Joseph P. Kennedy, Bernard
Baruch, and other such elders and large contributors were not to
be in the cabinet. They were the grand panjandrums of the party;
Roosevelt owed them preferment; they were entitled to share his
power.

This was a strictly New York interpretation. Not to speak of
others, it left out the legislators—Senators Cordell Hull, Carter
Glass, Key Pittman, Tom Walsh, James F. Byrnes, and Claude
Swanson—four of whom would be asked to serve. (Walsh died before he could take office as attorney general, and Glass, suspecting
Roosevelt's orthodoxy, refused.) These were the real holders of
the party's seals. Roosevelt knew it, even if the New York newsmen did not.

Kieran, close to the scene of action, knew a good deal more
than he told; he did not feel free, for instance, to say what the

Brains Trust was for. When he wrote that its members "prepared data," he was following the polite stereotype. He knew that they wrote speeches, answered communications, and prepared public statements, and that Roosevelt's part in these, if major as to policy, was minor as to composition. But this was best kept a sort of trade secret. Also, our more important functions of orienting, informing, and setting up a dialogue were regarded either as not worth mentioning or as services to a statesman that ought not to be revealed.

As to beginnings, Kieran's November account had the group "organized" by Rosenman but "led" by Moley. This version was becoming accepted, and it was annoying to Ray. Sam was willing to take the credit everyone seemed ready to allot him, but Ray was determined to see the record corrected.

What Sam said (in *Working with Roosevelt*) was that the idea of such a group had occurred to him because of worry about the new activities being undertaken by the Governor. Since the candidacy had come into the open on January 22, he had necessarily been involved in larger affairs than those of New York State, and he often had to make comments on them. Besides, the economy "seemed to be going to pieces before our eyes," and the reasons for this were not apparent. There followed a conversation, circumstantially reported. Rosenman told the Governor one evening that they needed some "up-to-date information" and some ideas about what could clear up the "trouble spots." The campaign was about to start, and unless something was done he would be "in an awful fix."

Roosevelt was interested, so Sam indicated that he himself had a definite notion of the sort of people they ought to get together. The big financiers, the industrialists, and the national political leaders had not produced anything constructive to "solve the mess we are in . . . so why not go to the universities?"

Roosevelt, according to Sam, was reluctant. After all, his first interest was in being nominated and elected, and he was "not sure whether this kind of group would help or hinder." Only after some hesitation, and some questioning about just what such helpers

would actually do, did he give consent to going ahead. Sam offered
to talk with Ray. "He believes in your . . . objectives," he told
Roosevelt, "and he has a clear and forceful style of writing." Being
a university professor himself, Ray could suggest others. But Sam
was not sure, as he wheeled the crippled man to his bedroom after
this evening exchange, that he was convinced: Roosevelt said, according to Sam, that they'd have to keep the whole thing pretty
quiet. If it got into the papers too soon, it might be unfortunate.

So, by Sam's account, there was "thus born a peculiar institution in political life, and a new phrase in American political jar-
gon: The Brain Trust."

He used the singular; in 1952, when *Working with Roosevelt*
was published, he was still among the few who refused to use the
plural. At the end of the paragraph telling of Louis Howe's sardonic remark was this sentence: "The 's' of 'brains' was soon
dropped and the phrase Brain Trust continued to be applied to advisers of the President even after the original group had been completely disbanded."

But Lindley of *The New York Herald Tribune,* writing in 1933
(in *Scribner's Magazine*), had been quite clear that this was not
the case:

> The phrase "brains trust" was invented by James Kieran of *The
> New York Times.* . . . Most of his colleagues at first resisted
> the expression but Roosevelt soon began to use it, and it slowly
> made its way into the public vocabulary. It was brains trust,
> and still is in Roosevelt's circle, despite the mass rebellion of
> newspaper and magazine copy readers against the plural form of
> brain.

So much for the name. The group's beginning is rather more important, after all, and as to this Ray flatly contradicts Sam's version. In *After Seven Years* (pages 8–9), he says of Sam that he
was like the lady who, smacking the champagne bottle on the
prow, "has the illusion that she is causing the ship to slide down
the ways." Ray points out that by then he had been working for
several years with and for the Governor. Why should they need an
intermediary? During the late winter, when Roosevelt had become

acutely aware of his need to review and explore national affairs, he had spoken to Ray about it. The thing was in the air, and "Sam was not the man to stand in the way of the inevitable." Besides, Ray noted, Sam had a boyish love of Columbia that gave the university's professors stature in his eyes. The account finishes:

> Finally, when Sam announced one mid-March evening with the air of one who makes a tremendous discovery, that Roosevelt needed expert, professional advice on national issues, and that we ought to get some people together to assist him, he made it easy for me to encourage the notion that he was the originator of the happy idea. To have said that it had occupied my thoughts every waking hour since Roosevelt's pre-Bar Association speech (mid-February) would have been unkind. . . .
>
> And so Sam, too, was won—convinced, with the passing of time, that he had plucked me from academic obscurity, washed me, pitted me, and dished me up on a silver platter to the Governor.

I cannot assist those who may try to resolve this Rosenman-Moley dispute. I came into things shortly afterward—but afterward. I have heard longer and livelier arguments on both sides than can be documented, but they only sharpened the curiously detailed nature of the differing claims. Roosevelt might have cleared it up, but no one ever asked him to, and probably he would not have thought it mattered anyway.

CHAPTER II

Matriculation

🏵 🏵 🏵

R aymond Moley and I lived in adjoining apartment houses on Morningside Heights in New York City. The houses fronted on Claremont Avenue, and we met there on a morning in March 1932. Frigid drafts were blowing up from the river, lifting papers and whirling dust in the doorways and around the corners. The sun, nevertheless, had drawn mothers and small children, so bundled they could hardly move, into the less windy spots. Such a congregation eddied about us as we greeted each other.

Ray evidently had something on his mind. At least, he stopped me to ask if we could have a talk, and I must have asked what about; but he was vague about the subject. Noisy children and turned-up collars could well account for not prolonging a parley on the street; still, he seemed markedly reticent. We did go off by our-selves, anyway, a little later, and then he told me that he was "put-ting together some material" for Governor Roosevelt, who, as I must know, was a presidential possibility. He wasn't getting much light on some problems that were bothering him, such as what could be done about the persistent depression. There seemed to be a special interest too, Ray said, in the heated-up farmers out west. They were outraged by Republican neglect and obviously open to persuasion if reasonable promises of relief could be made.

We discussed the farm problem first. Their troubles, I said, were obviously involved with the country-wide depression. It was not generally realized, however, that their economic difficulties had begun as far back as 1921 and had prepared the way for the more widespread difficulties of 1929 and since. Still, theirs was a special problem, and what must be found was a reasonable explanation of the depression and its refusal to improve. He had made some inquiries, he said, and had got no satisfaction at all. Perhaps he was asking the wrong questions. One thing was sure—he had nothing of any use to a man in Roosevelt's position. He had heard that I had some ideas, and he would like to hear about them. Others he had talked to either spoke a language he did not understand or, when he did understand, seemed to offer nothing really explanatory.

Whom had he asked? Some of the economists in the School of Business at Columbia, but also some bankers and others downtown. What did the economists say? They were very learned about the business cycle and talked a good deal—as the businessmen did too—about "confidence" and "stimulation." They wanted what they called "the structure" supported; that, it seemed, would "restore confidence." They talked about the "profitless prosperity" of the years before 1929, saying that the lack of profits had discouraged expansion even before the onset of the later distress. The continuing paralysis was accounted for by the lack of prospects for anything better. But what had caused the whole thing? There was a phrase he heard a good deal, but, thinking it over, he found it more evasive than explanatory: this was the "aftermath of war." That was reaching quite a way back; "aftermath" must be a very loose word.

What did they suggest as a way to get going again? Mostly they dwelt, he said, on confidence. Confidence, they kept saying, leads to enlargement—by this they seemed to mean investment; investment starts up heavy industry, making a market for primary materials; this creates employment, and the employed then become consumers. It seemed too involved to him, he said; besides, he didn't see anything to prevent them from getting going again right away if they had confidence in each other. They could not have any fear of the Republicans in Washington. Hoover had no intention of frightening anyone. It must be that they actually didn't believe what they were saying. Confidence must be a more complex condition than just the atmosphere surrounding business.

I asked what they said about government; did they want something done that was not now being done? What, for instance, did they say about relief and public works? Or did they think recovery could begin without any such governmental action?

It was granted, he said, that forced spending starts some activity. But it has to be paid for. This means higher taxes, and if there was one thing they all agreed on, it was that the way to establish confidence was for the government to economize. Their biggest worry was the unbalanced budget. They talked all the time about *reducing* expenditures, not increasing them. This seemed to preclude public works. There was a kind of paradox involved.

This was about it. There must be some way out, but what was it? I suggested that he may have consulted the wrong economists, the ones who had provided the businessmen's ideas. I had no way of knowing Roosevelt's thinking—if he had done any—about these matters, but if he depended on the advice of the economists he was most likely to see, or of the bankers and businessmen who were managing things, he would be no better off than Hoover. Or than Ray was himself after his preliminary explorations among the wiseacres.

Ray encouraged enlargement; in fact, he pumped. But I needed no encouragement, and soon I was positively spouting. I said that since we were obviously equipped to produce an abundance of goods, there couldn't be any really good reason for not producing them. I went on to remind him that we had invented scientific management and thus made poverty and paralysis even more absurd. Then too, we had explored the business cycle until it was known that much could be done to curb its wilder rushes upward and downward. Add to all this that we had made business management into a profession, and the present situation became a fantasy.

I went on: as for physical equipment, we had more miles of roads and railways, more automobiles, more telephones, more power capacity than all the rest of the nations put together.

A few years ago our factories, machines, mines, and crop-land had been working smoothly, producing food and fiber for most of the Western world. For three years now, activity had slowed down until some industries were almost at a stop. Thirteen million men (more or less, probably more), a horrifying percentage of the work force, were unemployed; factories were running part-time, and the fires were out in most of the steel mills (steel production stood at about fifteen per cent of capacity); mines were closed; long rows of empty railway cars stood on sidings, clusters of ships were tied up at anchorages, and farmers were adding to a surplus of agricultural products that was already of smothering size.

I could have gone on with this catalogue and doubtless would have—I was full of the subject—but Ray was impatient. He knew the results well enough, he said; what he wanted to know was what could be done about them. He did let me explain that I took this paralysis somewhat personally. I was a Wharton School product. I had studied the efficiency movement and had even written a book called *Industry's Coming of Age*. In it I had said that industry was maturing, that we could look forward to an age of affluence as power and machines increased our productivity. I had miscalculated as to time by assuming that the rapid advances of the recent past would continue. We should have been moving year by year to higher levels. There would be checks; but the business cycle had had thorough study, and we knew how to keep the system running and how to get it going again when it slowed down. None of this knowledge was actually being applied. I was compelled to admit that there were those who simply would not do what had to be done.

Ray said he had an impression of bewilderment. Could it be that there was a conspiracy about it? He didn't think so. It seemed that many different measures were being tried, but events moved too fast for the remedies to have any effect. Probably all this talk about economy in government and balanced budgets was believed in sincerely enough. But it might be so strongly supported just because it required nothing of businessmen themselves.

I told him that, however it was arrived at, this theory called for precisely the opposite of what needed to be done. Balanced budgets were fine, but did not have to be balanced every year. At the moment the budget had to be *un*balanced.

What businessmen did not seem to realize was that their first need was customers with incomes to spend; the rest could come afterward. The indispensable purchasing power was ordinarily provided by the pay people got from their work. What was wrong was that they were not working and not getting any pay. The government had to create income—the federal government, the only one that could create it. Incomes would make customers; customers would start the factories; factories that were running required banking, railway, insurance, and other services. When the whole apparatus was in operation it created its own customers. Then balanced budgets could be thought of. But first there had to be a start—jobs, relief, benefits, anything to make customers of people.

Roosevelt had been doing something of the sort. I hadn't kept track very closely, but from what I knew it seemed to me that his instincts had started him in the right direction. He had been helping the unemployed rather than weeping about missed dividends. He had been giving relief—such relief as one state could give by itself—out of public funds instead of relying, as Hoover did, on appeals to private philanthropy. What he had done was probably undertaken for the wrong reason—for a charitable one—but if it had been big enough, it might have had the right effect. He had discovered that no state could find enough funds for the purpose. The depression had been too long and too severe.

We returned to agriculture. Roosevelt, I said, had shown all along an awareness that the farmers were in deep trouble. I knew this because I had been giving some special study to the problem. I had watched his efforts. The farmers' depression had started with falling wheat and cotton prices as far back as 1921, and all during the speculators' "new era" rural problems had got worse. Finally the sickness had spread to industry, and then to finance. So Roosevelt had been right in paying special attention to agriculture. I was not sure that he regarded the farmers' problems as being closely related to the general ones of depression; I thought not. He had a special feeling for the farmers. But did he see that farmers' incomes, like those of the unemployed, had to be raised as a recovery measure?

Ray thought I was probably correct in guessing that, mainly, Roosevelt had had a simple desire to relieve human misery and perhaps had resented the unfairness of letting the workers and the farmers carry the heaviest burden of hard times; but it was interesting that I should think it was something to build on for recovery.

He pointed out that Roosevelt's efforts had been favorably commented on. But not, I said, by business people or bankers, and not by economists; doubtless the unemployed were grateful, but they were inarticulate; no one knew what they thought. Anyway it seemed that more had been undertaken than could be carried through. I was hearing criticism of the insufficiency of the state's efforts.

We agreed, as we talked further, that the paralysis was by now getting into the fabric of the system. This was shown by the bankruptcy rate among small and even medium-sized businesses and by the foreclosures of mortgages on homes and farms, as well as by the swelling numbers of the unemployed. According to rules derived from experience in former depressions, deflation should by now have run its course and an upturn should have begun, but nothing of the sort had happened. I thought I could explain why. It was because this time the weight of accumulated debt was so heavy, and because assets were so thoroughly frozen. Nothing could lift the weight or thaw the frost but an infusion of buying power, and this was denied by Republican policy.

Roosevelt did not really have a different view of policy, but he had more human sympathy. He saw that such a situation could not continue. Something would crack. Millions of people were destitute.

They would not stay that way peacefully until the slow processes of deflation were completed.

Roosevelt had at least provided aid for the unemployed, and he had done so even when it had to be paid for out of bond issues. Many taxpayers had been offended, but it had brought some needed decency into a situation characterized by shocking neglect. Even if what he could do had been fractional compared with the need, it was a correct beginning. It could be built on. But only if he knew that the objective was as much recovery as assistance, and only if federal resources could be used.

At about this point we adjourned for that time. Ray wanted a couple of others to hear the rest of it, he said, and I would only have to repeat. He wanted me to say to them just what I had said to him. He mentioned Sam Rosenman and Doc O'Connor.

Who were *they?* (I had never heard of either.) Sam, he said, was Counsel to the Governor, but he was something more than the title implied. It was he who, until Ray began to do it, had drafted statements and speeches. Sam had begun that during the first governorship campaign in 1928. Doc was a lawyer, nominally Roosevelt's partner, except that Roosevelt had never really practiced much. Doc's present involvement was hard to describe. He was around a good deal; he sat in on strategy meetings, criticized, and did odd jobs when he was asked. Also he helped to keep things straight.

This last, Ray said, had become an urgent matter in Albany. As the number of delegates to the convention who were pledged to Roosevelt increased, the concourse of political hopefuls, would-be assistants, and those anxious to give advice useful to themselves, all converging on Albany, had grown to unmanageable size. The Democrats were smelling victory, and none of them wanted to be left out when the favors were distributed. There were many who had to be seen, but many could be put off. The separation was not easy, and there was no organization. The Executive Mansion would soon be a shambles from basement to attic. It was getting worse day by day, and what was important was in danger of being submerged in trivia.

Besides, Roosevelt was governor of a state badly wounded by the depression, and its affairs had to be looked after. At the same time he had to consider what his situation would be if presently he should become the Democratic presidential candidate. For one thing, he would have to talk and talk and talk. He could not avoid saying something that would commit him to action. Sam and Doc were worried about what it could be. Not only were they open to suggestion; they were anxious for some light. First, Ray said, they would have to be sold . . .

On me? I asked, bristling a little. Now look, he said, he'd been through this himself. He could be as touchy as any other professor, but about this he was willing to give or take almost anything to get in on it. If this was going to be a campaign for the presidency, an enormous audience would be reached. Whether Roosevelt was elected or not, he'd be talking to the whole country. Was he going to educate them or fool them? Was he going to be made a little more competent, or was he going to repeat what he would be asked to say by the people who saw him most often? Was he going to be an alternative to Hoover or a kind of blurred copy?

I really needed very little persuasion. The truth is that I felt myself deeply involved in the strangulation of the economy. Those who had the power to lead were not taking the reasonable way out. And this was the only opening I had had—besides talking and writing—to a means of doing anything about it.

The evening with Sam and Doc was successful. Ray sat and listened after giving me a start. He fondled his pipe; he seldom smoked it, but he played with it a lot. We all knew what we were there for, and I marshaled, again, the array of facts and theories I had worked out. They listened closely until I finished, then looked at each other.

Sam said the Governor would have to hear what I had to say. It made sense, and it was the first time he'd heard it all put together in a package. Doc agreed. Damned if he didn't think it was good politics too, he said. It would make some people madder than hell, but they were bound to be mad anyway. So that didn't matter.

He turned to Ray, saying that this guy was really radical, wasn't he? Obviously he wasn't troubled about it. Ray said I was like him. We were progressives.

I observed that there were several different breeds of progressives. I was not even sure where I belonged any more.

Ray said he was the Van Hise kind. What was I?

I had thought of myself as a Wharton School kind; the Taylor Society kind. I was East; he was Midwest. But I had read Van Hise too—and I knew what he meant. We were really agreed.

But this was academic talk. Doc said he guessed it was no more radical, anyway, than the times called for. They sure called for something different.

I liked them; they evidently liked me. That liking helped, and it went on helping during the months to come.

First Night in Albany

❀ ❀ ❀

Mrs. Roosevelt began it at the dinner table in the Executive Mansion. I had been introduced, with one of her husband's wide gestures, as a Columbia professor, but a few of her gently probing questions had exposed my Chautauqua County origin. She wanted to know if we were farmers. I said that I had grown up in a small town and that the Tugwells had an interest in farming; also we had a fruit and dairy place on the edge of our village in Niagara County. Yes, I guessed we were farmers, although our living didn't depend on it. My father was a businessman.

She asked me if I knew about the Tompkins County land-retirement experiment, planned and carried out by the School of Agriculture at Cornell. I did, and I spoke well of it. She was especially interested in the resettlement of families who could no longer make a living on their hill farms in competition with more productive areas. They had been reduced, most of them, to destitution.

This led to an argument that was to go on and on, for she at once enlarged the possibilities to include similar resettlement of the urban unemployed, and I objected. It was one thing to establish practiced farmers on more productive land; but city workers, I argued, would be lost and probably unhappy. Didn't she know that farming was a complicated occupation? And that city people were likely to be unsuited to life on a farm?

The Governor interjected, a little testily, that at least those who were resettled would have something to eat, and this was more than they were sure of as things stood.

Not, I said, unless they could grow it. I doubted if most of them could.

It was obvious that a copiously flowing emotional spring had been exposed. It could hardly be contained in one conversation; besides, I was familiar with the illusions involved. Diversion seemed in order: I suggested that not only such depressed areas were troubled; other farmers, recently prosperous, were in distress. The depression, usually thought of as industrial, had begun with agriculture and would not be cured until some general remedy had been found. The retirement of submarginal land and the resettlement of its farmers was important, but it would not contribute to general agricultural recovery.

The exploration of this idea carried us through dinner and continued in the big living room. There the discussion developed more in the way Ray had intended. He was a little uneasy at first, seeing that my views about agriculture did not run with those of the Roosevelts; and anyway, this seemed to him hardly relevant to the main issue.

When we were settled, Roosevelt took the first turn. He was talking, with gestures, as he wheeled himself to another chair and made the shift to it without help. It occurred to me, watching the neat transfer, that the talking was calculated. His crippled legs must have led to the invention of many such diversions, finally become unconscious.

Now Roosevelt asked about the connection between agriculture and the general problem. He said—what I had been told he had learned by experience—that one state could do very little by itself to relieve unemployment. Neither, he said, could it do much about the wider agricultural problems—surpluses, low prices, foreclosures, and all the rest. A state could help with tax favors, better roads, advice from extension agents, but the present trouble was not reached by such measures.

I joined in to say that city and farm people I had talked to were being drawn together by the recognition of their common problems. It was slow and painful, but in the Congress, for instance, one of the farmers' best friends was Fiorello La Guardia. He had made innumerable speeches on the theme of mutuality. And it must be said that his New York City constituents seemed to understand.

I hesitated to expand on this to Roosevelt, realizing he was well enough aware of it. But there logically followed, I felt, other more involved observations, and since I was encouraged, I went on to these.

The decade of the booming twenties, I reminded him, had followed a vast war expansion. During the war competition had been adjourned, and both resources and management had been marshaled and pooled. Competition had given way to co-operation, and the antitrust laws had been ignored. The resulting increase in productivity was immense. But only after the Armistice had the intensive efforts of wartime become most effective and the curve of efficiency made its most startling climb.

That was the period when Taylor's scientific management had spread from confined beginnings into many industries. The immense gain in productivity during that decade had had no precedent; it had amounted to about one-third. I repeated this fact. American workers in 1930 produced, on the average, one-third more in each working hour than they had ten years before. In one decade men had increased their power to produce more than it had been increased in any century of their history, or, for that matter, in any millennium except the last. The reliance on power and machines had come so suddenly that the adjustment to it had been a strain on everyone. It had affected directly the manufacture of shoes, shirts, automobiles, bread—everything made in factories. And this was as true—almost as true, at least—of agriculture. Nearly half the crop-land of the country had been used to feed horses and mules a few years ago. The tractor had released those acres—and no one knew what to do with the product.

The single most disturbing adjustment made necessary by the harnessing of nature was the new requirement that everyone share in the product. If all did not share, see what happened. When we were still "prosperous"—that is, before the crash—we had some four or five million men who were unemployed because the work they had once done had been eliminated. They had no jobs and no income for their families. They were eliminated as consumers much as the horses and mules had been eliminated.

Since they were fellow human beings, this was an intolerable injustice. Not only that, it was a downright economic necessity that they should continue to be consumers. The system had, in fact, broken down because goods made so incredibly quickly—and so cheaply—could not be bought by men who were out of work or by farmers who could not sell their crops. Since fewer and fewer were employed, and since they had no other source of income, demand was bound to fail. Factories do not operate when there are no buyers for their products.

Then too the situation had been made worse by the enormously enlarged profits of a few enterprises in favorable positions. Those profits did not come from increased prices. Roosevelt nodded when I mentioned the "profitless prosperity" which had been talked about in the speculative centers in 1928 because prices refused to go up. But, I pointed out, prosperity had not been profitless until demand had decreased. True, prices had not gone up; but prices not only ought not to have gone up, they ought to have fallen—by about one-third (the increase in per-man-hour efficiency). If they had, manufacturers would have been roughly as well off as they had been in 1920. There would have been profits —not excessive, but substantial enough. *Stable* prices and rapidly *falling* costs—this was the crux of the trouble.

Still another complication was that the gains from increased productivity had gone to security-holders as dividends, not to workers as wages. Those gains, being largely invested instead of spent, had led to the expansion of industry at a time when customers were disappearing, and thus had made matters much worse.

There was a strange and rather horrible accompaniment of this process: not only had profits from lowered costs been diverted from workers' wages to investments in our own industries; they had also been loaned abroad and were actually financing all sorts of bizarre projects—railways and superhighways, sports arenas, concert halls, and other immense public works. Some of this income should have gone to our wage-earners and some to displaced workers for retraining. The rest should have been invested in industries that were really needed. If it had, the expenditures would have kept the economy going. The depression simply would not have occurred.

Depriving workers of purchasing power, I said, had resulted in fading markets for goods of all kinds as early as 1926 and 1927. But installment selling, enormously expanded about that time, had put off the reckoning—only to make it worse when it came. What had happened in 1929 was not only the collapse of a stock-market boom but also the sudden uncovering of an appalling miscalculation. Many more goods had been made and bought than could ever be paid for by consumers with disappearing incomes.

So, since the debts could never be collected, they were frozen. Commodities were returned to sellers, and houses and farms were foreclosed and fell empty or idle. Those swollen debts had to be liquidated somehow, that was true; in other depressions they had simply been written off. The process was terribly slow and involved much hardship. But it would have to go on if nothing was done to re-establish the productivity that gave value to assets.

What had been lacking in recent years was fairness in exchange. To keep the modern economy going, everyone must be able to buy and sell to everyone else. This was the real reform we needed. Doubtful practices by bankers, gambling in securities, and frauds upon consumers ought to be eliminated; but all that could be done of this sort would not start one factory going again or move one railway car. Reform was not recovery.

That much of my story, with plenty of adjectives and embellishments, I had a chance to tell. It was midnight when Mrs. Roosevelt came in to call a halt. Ray told me, as we parted for bed, that he would say one thing for me: Roosevelt had never listened to anyone so long as he had to me.

I asked if he didn't usually listen.

No, Ray said, he usually did most of the talking. As soon as he grasped a theme, he enlarged on it himself. Once in a while he asked a question, but he had an enormous fund of miscellaneous information, and he was apt to trot it out and dominate the discussion. Visitors were deferential. They hesitated to interrupt a governor. So usually they went away with half of what they had on their minds unsaid. Ray warned me, however, that I needn't expect to have the same thing happen again. I'd caught his interest this time. Then Ray said thoughtfully that he guessed the Governor had actually been looking for something of the sort I was weaving together.

In bed I lay awake for a long time, thinking back over the two hours of talk. It was true. I had had a chance to say my piece. I hadn't said it all, by any means, but for a first time I had laid out a lot of it.

Roosevelt had sat, somewhat uncomfortably, I thought, in the corner of a sofa that let him down almost to the floor. His shrunken legs, ending in the curiously unworn shoes, stretched out. He had occasionally eased them by pulling at his knees with his hands. When he did this, enormous shoulder muscles bunched under his jacket and relaxed smoothly. It occurred to me that, during the now eleven years of his struggle to get back the use of his legs, the rest of his body had really become overdeveloped. I wondered what his jacket size must be. I imagined that if Roosevelt had not worn custom-made clothes, he probably could not have found his size in most stores.

His head, though, had the weight and carriage to go with the massive shoulders. The pillar of his neck curved down into the broad expanse below, not as though he had been born without much of any length there, but as though it had been developed into what it was now. What I later learned was that this was exactly so.

He had been so stringy and bony in earlier years that he never could make a decent showing in football or rowing. Even when he was Assistant Secretary of the Navy, his pictures taken beside the fat and benevolent Secretary, Josephus Daniels, showed him tall, thin, and patrician-looking. His neck and torso had taken their present shape from those agonizing exercises he had undertaken and kept up day after tedious day for years. This, of course, had been after his seven and more years in Washington. He was, in appearance, a different man now, immobile, but still athletic.

The face that went with the head had a jutting chin, a high fore-head, and wide-set eyes; it was a mobile and expressive face. It might have been an actor's. When I spoke of this to Ray, he said it *was* an actor's, and a professional actor's at that; how did I sup-pose he'd created and maintained the image of authority?

Wasn't what I saw the real Roosevelt, then? I asked.

He temporized. Yes, he said, in the sense that all this parapher-nalia of the governorship had become part of him. It was a real talent; it was a lifetime part that he was playing. But I needn't think he hadn't perfected it. He'd figured out what he ought to be like in order to get where he wanted to get and do what he wanted to do, and that was what was on display. Ray added, thoughtfully, that no one would ever see anything else.

We talked about this on other occasions, but it all came to the same thing. There was another Roosevelt behind the one we saw and talked with. For a long time I was baffled, unable to make out what he was like, that other man. I was gradually to discover what I believed him to be, but for now this was where we left it.

Next morning I had the experience of something that would be-come fairly familiar in the future. Roosevelt shouted to us across the hall, and we went to his room. He was sitting up in bed with newspapers scattered around. He had already gone through several cigarettes, judging by the ashtray on the bedside table, and as we came in he was inserting a new one into a holder about six inches long, with a quill stem and a yellow parchment funnel. He had used ones like this all the previous evening; he must have had an endless supply. He used a match to light the cigarette and, it seemed to me, was unusually careful about putting it out. I learned about that later, as I would learn about so many small habits of his. They were the kind a helpless man acquires, and most of them had been developed much against the grain.

The careful match-and-cigarette management had to do with his fear of fire. Being trapped is something no one likes to contemplate. For a man without legs, it becomes something to guard against as a special risk. The rest of us can make some quick and easy adjustment to circumstances, but a cripple who is otherwise vigorous has not only to see that his escape way is open but also to do so furtively. He knows there is a constant danger that those around him will think he is becoming obsessed. It is something he suspects they are watching for. The strained relation this sets up often makes it difficult for an attendant to get along well with a cripple. I never thought Roosevelt was kind to McDuffie, his valet, or to McDuffie's successors. He tried to pretend, rather, that they were not there, not needed except as his chair was needed.

I was to learn much more about this, and it explained behavior otherwise hard to understand. Why, for instance, did he take to some people and not to others? Those around him were, some of them, curious choices whose efficiency as helpers or assistants was minimal. There seemed to be certain qualifications; they must, for instance, be casual in a physical sense. That is to say, they must not be watchful and always trying to do something for him. This he translated into pity or even into suspicion of his competence. But he had succeeded in finding associates who were casual and intelligently helpful at the same time. I often thought Doc O'Connor and Sam Rosenman were perfect examples of devoted but undemanding friendship. It was not only that both had been around for many years, but that both ignored—or, shall I say, accepted—his condition. It was no stranger than another man's arthritic hands, or deafness, or nearsightedness.

Missy Le Hand, whom I had first seen at dinner the night before, had this special ability too. To begin with, of course, she had a quiet acceptance of the world with all its complexities, and Roosevelt's peculiarity was to her nothing to strain about. It was just something to go on with. She was an unobtrusive shield; she saw to it that a good part of his environment was shut out or adapted to his use. Her intensely sweet nature was a sort of gift. I often thought later that he took her, as he did faithful servants, far too much for granted. But her service was given without the least self-consciousness. It was simply the way she was.

It was the way he was too, although I cannot pretend to have more than begun to sense such things during that visit. I did begin, though, because I was so sensitized by the strangeness of the occurrence and by the consciousness I felt of what I can only call—and hope I will be understood—consequence. All this, every word and sign, was enormously significant; I knew it and felt it every instant. And I took in more, sensed more, than I should have done if I had not been so penetrated by the possibility of having influence in important circumstances.

So the man stretched out on his narrow bed, in an old sweater, surrounded by crumpled papers, represented something special. I knew it. I had no disposition to minimize it. But I tried not to let it get in the way. I am sure that it did. I was sure I had been too preachy, too professorial, too heavy, the night before. I should not have been surprised never to have had another call from him. But here I was by his bedside.

Was he being kind? In time I would learn about that too. This man was never just kind. He may have been in the past, but he was no longer. Whatever of that quality may have been in his nature had by now disappeared. If there was any kindness it was transmuted. I would see a good many unkindnesses, a good many cruelties, in fact, that were explained by recalling that he was dedicated to a larger concern. But about this, I had noticed that most politicians were *too* kind—kind to *some* people, not to *the* people. It is a deduction to be made from the virtues of democracy that all of us are attracted by personal sympathy. It is a betraying trait. It diminishes a statesman. Roosevelt had left it behind.

I did not know that in this first bedside conversation I was talking with a man thus purified for his future, but I did already sense something of the strangeness. Of all those who might serve him, and serve him well, there would be very few who would ever *love* him. They would give him the unreserved loyalty that good democrats know they must give the leader of their choice, but this was not fondness. The loyalty is given because there must be an object, not because they can expect from it a return in loyalty.

I would watch the unfolding of this characteristic through many years. I would watch too the variation of understanding in his associates. To some it was no problem—to Doc and Sam, for instance. Some others would never grasp it—people like Jesse Jones and Bernard Baruch. Others would break under the strain, as Jim Farley did—and even, to my sorrow, Ray Moley.

Loyalty was actually dedication to a cause for some of us. A soldier does not explain why he accepts discipline to the extremity of risking life. There is some end, some fulfillment he reaches for and knows to be compelling. There is an analogy with people like ourselves. The way to the service demanded of us was through this leader. He need not be someone we admired for himself and came to be fond of. He did need to promise the consummation of good for the country. For that we yielded him the right to decide, to plot the course, to exact service.

I had a strange feeling about the relationship right from the start. Being summoned to his bedside was being admitted to his confidence. Yet I did not altogether like it, I discovered. The uneasiness I felt was huffily spoken of a long time afterward by Dean Acheson, whose experiences with him were later than my own. Perhaps I may quote him:

> Then too came summonses to appear and report at the President's bedside while he breakfasted. . . . Gay and informal as these meetings were, they nevertheless carried something of the relationship implied in a seventeenth-century *levée* at Versailles. . . . He condescended. Many reveled in apparent admission to an inner circle. I did not; and General Marshall did not. He objected, as he said, because it gave a false impression of his intimacy with the President. . . . It is not gratifying to receive the easy greeting which milord might give to a promising stable boy. . . .

I must confess that when I read this passage in Acheson's *Morning and Noon,** I felt for the first time that my uneasiness had been adequately defined. I was not made to feel, as Acheson was, like a stable boy. But certainly I was not made, either, to feel that I was an equal.

On these occasions—and there would be many of them in the future—I always tried hard to remember that it was the President of the United States whose summons I was responding to; even if on this first occasion, it was a potential president. I usually succeeded—better, evidently, than Acheson did.

At the time I felt mostly gratification at having had a hearing on something I felt was important for my country. In fact, the next day in New York, a panhandler on upper Broadway caught my sleeve. I turned to him and said, "My friend, I did you a good turn last night." He was so surprised that he forgot the rest of his plea, and I escaped with a tribute of silver.

* Boston: Houghton Mifflin, 1965, pp. 164–165.

CHAPTER IV

Terms of Reference

❦ ❦ ❦

If I was excited, it was understandable. Not only Moley but others of my Columbia colleagues, mostly somewhat older, had been given assignments in Albany since Roosevelt had become Governor in 1928; James Bonbright, on power, and Robert Murray Haig, on taxes, were two I knew of. For me, however, it was something new and special. It seemed miraculous that suddenly my frustrations about public policy in those hard times could have such a release and that I could really expect attention for my ideas. I concluded at once that Roosevelt was actually going to be President. For this the attitude of Doc and Sam was partly responsible; they had no doubts. I trusted them about this more than I did Ray; they were so obviously confident old-timers. But behind their conclusion, as well as mine, was the evident assumption by Roosevelt himself that events were unfolding in an expected sequence. Only one outcome was possible. It would take some managing, but this was what he was trained for, and one could see that he considered it well within his competence.

We were part of the necessary preparations. He needed more information than ordinarily came to him about the peculiar events taking place in the economic world. No one had to tell him about their impact; he knew how destructive they had been. What he

32

wanted to know was why they happened and what could be done about them. The cataclysm was so much more massive than those he had read about—1873, 1893, 1907, 1921—that extraordinary conditions must have arisen. As a candidate, he would be called on to speak of them. He must be able to do so with assurance.

Classes over, I walked across to the old Barnard building where Ray's office was. That room would become familiar during the next few months. Celeste Jedel and Annette Gettinger, his assistants, were there. They were decorative and, at the center of a rising confusion, composed and efficient. Ray was in class. I asked if he had said anything about our Albany visit. Celeste reported that he thought it had gone well. I waited, and presently he came in, got out his pipe, settled behind his desk, and smiled in a self-satisfied way. He thought we had made a good beginning, he said, but there was a lot more to come. I said that if *anything* was to come it *would* be much more. If Roosevelt really meant to get into the depression issue, he would find complexities no politician had ever been able to do anything about. Look at Hoover, considered to be the ablest administrator in all our public life; the depression had been far too much for him.

I expressed misgivings generated overnight concerning my own usefulness to Roosevelt. Everything I had outlined in our talk was true enough, I said, but it was out of a background that was so different from his that I was afraid it might sound outlandish. I was worried too, thinking it over, for fear I might have seemed too teacherish. I had meant to present and argue, not to instruct, but I was afraid I had not succeeded.

Also, I realized that what I had had to say would be about as unpleasant for an old-fashioned progressive to hear as for a Hooverite, and I guessed that Roosevelt's progressivisim was orthodox. My view of our affairs assumed that if a real effort was made the economy could be managed, or at least brought to a balance that would ensure continuity. But management was something believed in by very few.

That our industrialism already had something of an organic character I fully believed. The trouble was that we did not accept this and so, of course, did not act on it. But there was evidence that part was so related to part that what touched the system anywhere affected the whole. Even if there had been no other evidence, it was only necessary to consider the present breakdown and its prolongation. It had started in some particular place—I thought in agriculture—but it had spread to other places until the sickness had become general, just as a sickness might spread through a living organism and finally reach the center.

This was the kind of thing institutional economists often said to each other but had learned not to insist on publicly; it was not acceptable doctrine. Our American premise did not conceive that we were a whole, an interdependent, operating organism. As far as there existed a coherent view of things, it was that the economy was bound together only by the fact that individuals and organizations tried to get the best of each other in a web of competition. No authority was responsible for the organism, and no individual had a duty to it—only to himself or his particular organization. When general sickness spread, nothing could be done about it. Either the source of the sickness could not be traced, or, if it was, no remedies could be applied. That would be to assume a connected system whose parts operated in concert, and, in terms of conventional economic doctrine, this was inadmissible.

When I said to Roosevelt that farmers had been unable to buy the products of industry and that this had caused shutdowns in the factories that made them, I was repeating something so elementary that it hardly needed saying. When, however, I suggested that agriculture and industry should be maintained in such a relation that each could buy the products of the other, I was really asking for a kind of management that everyone drew back from. Did Roosevelt really understand this? It was not, I said, in the progressive book he was supposed to follow.

Ray was soothing. I had not transgressed, he told me, and I had no need to be concerned. Nevertheless I sat for a long time afterward in my own office, recalling what I had said and wondering if I could have said it more persuasively.

I had insisted that the need for unity within diversity was no more urgent between the grand categories of agriculture and industry than it was among the lesser categories of industries themselves. Agriculture, we had grown used to thinking, was unique. Actually, it was just another series of industries. It was quite as important that railway rates or the price of steel should be brought into continuing relationship with textile prices or chemicals as that the growing of agricultural products, taken as wholes, should mesh and run together. People in all these occupations must work for each other, and unless they worked on a fair trading basis, there would be recurrent stoppages of production or, less spectacularly, reductions; there would be a lack of consumers. In a normally operating economy, each group would go along working for and with the others. But when disturbances of relationship occurred, what happened was like a natural disaster—a storm or an earthquake. In a forest such a disaster would be followed by nature's processes of healing and readjustment. But nature takes much time, and the suffering incident to adjustment is not counted. In human society such waiting and suffering were intolerable.

The war had been a sort of vast storm. It had destroyed some old institutions and crippled others. It had grossly expanded some industries—notably agriculture, but some others too—and left them after the war with a speeded-up rhythm that needed readjustment if they were to mesh smoothly with other industries. There were even some industries that had been pinched and must now enlarge while the ones that had had a forced growth were slowing down. Contraction was usually achieved by allowing prices to fall. Agriculture and other overexpanded industries went bankrupt, ultimately, when this process had run its unimpeded course. The problem was to establish a fair relationship. Similarly, those industries that ought to expand were encouraged only by high prices for their goods and, consequently, by new investment in productive facilities. This too was a process much delayed in a laissez-faire economy. It was not operating at all in the present state of paralysis.

The chance that these rising and falling prices for thousands of commodities, involving hundreds of industries, would come into workable relation through the free-price mechanism was slight—

unless, like the forests after storms, we could afford to wait for the slow and cruel re-establishment arranged by nature.

They had let me talk too much, I thought irritably. Everyone was letting me talk and no one was giving me an argument. What I had to say was practiced enough to come out smoothly, but what was new to me was the possibility of its translation into some sort of action. No professor ever really expects that. His students listen; they even dispute him on occasion; but when he has passed on to them his reasoning and conclusions, that ends it. He has contributed to their education. He does not expect them to go out and do anything as a consequence. It was different when there was a possibility that a student might conclude from what he was taught that something ought to be done. I found the weight a heavy one. I was not sure I was prepared for such a responsibility. Still I was right. I knew I was right.

Later, I forgot restraint again and insisted that there were agonies we need not undergo. We could always plan and manage. This we resisted. Unwillingness to admit the necessity of planning was almost universal, but there was no other way. Provision for continuing readjustments as they became imperative—these could only be reached by public, by governmental, means.

I was not discussing this theory with a beginner. Roosevelt had studied economics and public law at Harvard, but that had been in 1902–1904, some thirty years earlier, and the economics of 1902 was as obsolete as the farms and factories of 1902. He was, however, like most people: what he had learned as a student had stayed with him. I concluded that he did not recall anything specific, but his attitudes were those he had worked out at that time. I guessed that even if he was as extraordinarily well informed as he seemed, it was hardly possible that his Harvard teachers could have prepared him for the crisis he was now having to meet. The whole system was in chaos, every part of it warring with every other part, and no means existed for relating each to the other, even in the way of conciliation, to say nothing of regulation. What would he do, I found myself asking, when and if he realized this?

I said something of the sort to Ray, and his comment was that he didn't know. He fondled his pipe and suggested that I ask Roosevelt himself. He went on smiling like a Buddha. He knew very well, I thought, that I would never be so presumptuous.

It was at such a time that I wondered about Ray. He had been introduced rather violently to Berle's hard facts about the business world and to my gropings for explanations that really explained. It had not really been necessary for him to accept any of this. What he had meant to do was to bring Roosevelt something coherent and plausible. What was made of it he could wait and see. He was used to ghostwriting (though not so used to it as Sam, who went back to the gubernatorial campaign of 1928 and had been at it ever since, but still he was a practiced helper).

Still, I knew that Ray had written several books and many articles of his own. All of them had had to do with the administration of justice, but they were much respected as reformist documents. The reformist impulse had been nurtured in the Cleveland school of Tom Johnson, Newton D. Baker, Frederick C. Howe, and others like them. These heroes had given the rascals of their city a bad time. They had not hesitated to attempt the public ownership of utilities when necessary, and this, if extrapolated, might extend to national programs for disciplining unruly businesses. Besides, Ray was something of a practitioner himself, if in a small way. As a young man he had captured the mayoralty of the small Ohio town of Olmstead Falls, a success he looked back on and liked to talk about affectionately.

I had every reason to respect him. Besides, he was older in years as well as experience. I wanted something more of him than interest, and that I hoped I might get through his agreement with the Van Hise ideas. This was unusual to find in a lawyer. The profession, so far as I knew it, was entirely committed to the industrial philosophy implied in the antitrust acts. The progressive formula for reform since the 1880s had been the breaking up of big businesses and the protection of small ones. Otherwise government was not to interfere; competition would take care of everything. But Ray was not a professing lawyer; he was a political scientist.

So far as we had gone, I had every reason for satisfaction. But he was Roosevelt's man, and he had to remember it all the time. Would he want me to be more calculating, more tactful, more cautious? I had been anything but reserved; I had, I was now afraid, declaimed.

Ray and I talked briefly about the Republican position—that is, Hoover's. We recalled how recently he had been the "Great Engineer" of the editorialists and with what enthusiasm he had been supported in 1928. He had been one of those candidates the inner-circle politicians accept only with reluctance. He was not a recognized professional Republican. The regulars, however, had been afraid to put forward one of their own. The last time they had nominated an insider had been in 1920. The circumstances then had encouraged them to risk it, and their choice had been Harding. They had elected him, and even if voters' memories are short, the dismal results of that venture must still be recalled by a good many of them six or seven years later. If Hoover was distasteful to the professionals, his reputation as an administrator and a man of compassion was an asset they could take advantage of. He would erase the recollections of Teapot Dome and other Harding scandals. The insiders would get no favors. They had made the choice with reluctance and unhappy forebodings.

In 1928 the economy had been booming, and the Republicans had taken full credit for it. Hoover had inherited the boom. When the crash came, only a few months after his inauguration, he had been unpleasantly surprised. I raised a question I had begun to worry about. We were doing something more than offering an explanation of depression; we were hopeful that a public policy would result. We wanted it to be one that would lead to recovery and, beyond that, to such changes as would prevent future disasters. It was not enough to satisfy Roosevelt's intelligence; we had to do more. We had, in fact, to suggest politically attractive alternatives to the theory Hoover was relying on.

This theory was, I reminded Ray, that the depression was the delayed result of war. There was a good deal to be said for it. Farm production, for instance, had been enlarged to feed the armies and a Europe whose farmers were fighting; then that market had been shut off by returning productivity. Our troublesome surpluses were a direct result. Where Hoover was weak was in his attempted remedies. He had nothing real to offer the farmers, and he was also vulnerable, I said to Ray, about other phases of the depression. Aside from creating the Reconstruction Finance Corporation to hold off bankruptcy for banks, railroads, insurance companies, and similar large enterprises, the Hoover administration had done little. Loans to states for relief purposes were limited in amount compared with the need, and many states had exhausted their borrowing capacities. There was a bill now being fought over in Washington, but it was not likely to result in relief that would be ample enough or quick enough to restore purchasing power.

What we suggested to Roosevelt ought to be something that would promise genuine hope in the midst of Hoover's failure. The progressives, led by Bob La Follette, had opened the way. They wanted to *give* the states funds for relief, and they wanted a really sizable federal public-works program. We should take advantage of their proposal because Hoover was rejecting it.

What we should worry about was that the only possible means by which to straighten out agriculture was to limit the production of staple crops, and this seemed impossible politically. Furthermore, what had to be done to revive industry was to make large public expenditures for relief and public works, and this ran directly counter to the businessmen's demand for economy, a balanced budget, and consequent restoration of "confidence." All this, I was afraid, quickly got to be political rather than economic. Hadn't I already gone beyond my warrant?

Ray interrupted. No one had any warrant, he said. If the old explanations hadn't appeared empty, we wouldn't have been called on at all.

I pressed further. I must remind him again that my theories about lack of balance and about its restoration through controls on the one hand and supports on the other—controls of production

and prices, and supports for the unemployed and the farmers—
were not accepted ones; in fact, they were dreaded and would be
opposed. Was there really any use in putting them forward?

Ray understood my concern and respected it, but he also felt
and said that if we had any responsibility, it was first to be clear
about what was going on, and then—but only later—to be inventive about what should be done. Accepting political limits was
something he was used to, he said, and it was not always fatal. In
the present instance, why might I not discover some palatable way
of limiting agricultural production? And, for industry, perhaps the
time had come when the progressive group now calling for massive
relief could be supported. It was true that Roosevelt had heard a
lot from the businessmen about the need for confidence, but he
had seen Hoover try to supply that and fail. Maybe the source of
confidence lay in the purchasing power I wanted to restore.

Things might come together in some such way when Roosevelt
thought over our suggestions. Anyway, this was what we were supposed to do, and he did not propose to hold back. Ray bit on his
pipe, and the muscles worked in his jaws. I was reassured.

CHAPTER V

The Concert of Interests

❀ ❀ ❀

In evening talks with Roosevelt, we soon began to explore the sick economy. We got far enough so that I could ask one evening what would happen when what *had* to be done economically *couldn't* be done politically? That, he answered readily, was *his* problem. We'd lay it out together, he said, and he'd decide whether it could be done, and if it couldn't, and if it was important, we'd have to find modifications or next-best alternatives.

One thing he'd learned in give-and-take with a Republican legislature was that what was wanted could hardly ever be had; what he got was usually something second best, but still something. Sometimes the legislators gave more than they realized they were giving. An executive—a governor or a president—had the advantage of initiative and of being only one instead of many, and he could maneuver more readily. But legislators could always hold things up, and usually they did. Sometimes they settled for a compromise, and that was the thing to be prepared for. He looked a little smug about this. I had heard that he was a masterly manipulator, and evidently he was proud of his talent for overcoming opposition.

He went on. There seemed to be some rule about it. The lawmakers were simply not able to accept what a governor asked, especially if he belonged to the other party. They squirmed and twisted. They listened hard to everyone who might be affected even remotely. When they were afraid to block things completely and when delays were used up, they fell back on amendment. They amended and amended. They were often in agony because they tried so hard to please the interests that were always pushing for changes they "could live with."

But, I said, we could *talk* logically, couldn't we? We were getting ready for a campaign, not a legislative session. Wasn't the problem different? He would be asking for people's votes, not for those of partisan politicians, and he wouldn't be trying to get legislation that the lobbyists opposed.

Much the same thing applied, he said. It was amazing how many party people thought they ought to be consulted about what he said. They would even expect to edit speeches, and sometimes they'd have to be listened to. Just the same, he went on, we could work out what we wanted. It must end up, after all the talk, in a Moley draft. What happened after that he'd have to decide.

I had forgotten, for the moment, that we were supposed to be discussing substance, not method; so, apparently, had he. But mostly we kept to substance. Tactics were, as he said, his affair, and so was timing. We went back to the depression: causes and remedies. I still hadn't said all I meant to say, but he led off.

He wanted to talk more about my thesis that there had been resistance to adjustments when costs had gone down during the postwar years when efficiency was taking hold. He knew by now that I had been worrying about this theme for some years, making myself familiar with scientific management and its economic effects. I showed him my book, and he leafed through it, reading a few passages and commenting on them. He seemed to accept my principal generalization as realistic and as important in explaining the onset of depression and its persistence. The efficiency theme fascinated him, as it had me. It was such a clear instance of an advance in man's struggle with nature; yet it had been so mismanaged that it had precipitated disaster. It was tragedy in the Aristotelian sense—virtue resulting in punishment.

I explained that what I had said about costs affecting prices—

or rather *not* affecting them, since they had not fallen—was only an extended version of what economists knew as the "oversavings theory." He must have been introduced to that back in his Harvard days.

If he had, he said, he'd forgotten it.

I explained that it was usually attributed to the English economist J. A. Hobson, but that there had been hints of it in earlier works, and it had been elaborated by several others, among them some Americans. The reasoning ran that if what was produced was sold and thus turned into income, and this income went to wage-earners, they became consumers, so that whatever was produced would be taken off the market—all of it. Efficiency tended to increase of itself, one improvement leading to others, and being applied on a larger and larger scale. There would be an increase in goods and services. When an excessive amount of the gain from this efficiency was segregated by profit-takers, and used by those who were not customers (that is, for purposes other than consumption), the trouble began. It was a trouble that tended to get worse and ultimately could become—did become—what we were now experiencing.

Then where were we? Where did the cure begin? A paralysis could not just be stopped. That implied more paralysis, a ridiculous sort of reasoning. The answer was that activity had to be started by making potential demand real demand. Consumers must be supplied with purchasing power. If they had income, they would buy goods, and factories would supply them. There would be employment. There would be wages. Wages would be spent for goods that factories made. The producing machine would run and go on running.

But stimulation by the distribution of relief funds would not make a permanent change. It did not go to the causes—the disparities, the imbalance, the uneven distribution. Nothing would do but an arrangement to ensure fair prices and fair exchange. Each must buy from the other, in a closely tied system, at such prices that the exchange could go on and on. If costs were lowered, consumers must be kept as consumers by lowering prices. If this was not done, surpluses would begin to pile up and presently they would choke off further production, cause unemployment, and create the same situation all over again. There had to be not only emergency income but also a change in the system.

The truth was that we had to come to a time when people could not exploit each other and get away with it; they had to work together, in concert, with an equitable mutual arrangement. This was not for the sake of justice, or welfare, or humanity; it was for the continuation of productivity.

This is a simplified version of what was a long conversation, or several of them, joined in by Adolf. Ray listened, but he had heard it all before, and when he had had a hard day, he wandered off to take a nap. The others—Doc and Sam were usually there, and often Bobby Straus—were wide awake, but usually silent. It was a two-sided conversation unless Adolf was present; if he was, he often took the lead and I could watch Roosevelt. I suspected that he was making policy pictures in his mind, arranging and rearranging. We sometimes had glimpses of the pictures when he talked, but they were mostly beyond our sight. What we were suggesting had radical implications, and I thought he was fitting our notions to political possibilities. That, it became clear in time, was exactly what was taking place. I continued to worry, though, about his unwillingness to make the logical conclusions from the reasoning he accepted.

This worry gradually turned into a sort of admiration for the agility of his mind. I became more realistic about political influences on logical solutions as I gradually learned that he had to persuade rather than dictate, to approach rather than conclude. I even found myself working with Ray to adapt harsh reasoning to the sensitivities of people who probably hated its conclusions.

I had some advantage over the others in coming closer to Roosevelt. We had a common interest in agriculture and conservation, and in our being upstate New Yorkers, but neither of these really accounted for the confidence he seemed to feel in me. Besides, there were others he might have relied on—if by now he needed to rely on anyone in such matters. There was, for instance, the Cornell crowd that had helped develop his New York agricultural program. Henry Morgenthau, his conservation commissioner, was their liaison man. Henry did push too far, and if he was reliable, he was not very bright. The Cornellians' thesis that agricultural prices could be raised by monetary means—cheapening the dollar—had a deceptive simplicity. But even though Roosevelt looked longingly in that direction, and I was stubbornly opposed to it, he asked me again and again to re-examine the whole agricultural problem.

The activities of the congressional farm bloc, mostly Westerners or Southerners, during the past ten years had had no support from the Cornellians, who were belligerent supporters of free enterprise. Any talk of governmental interference seemed to them outrageous. Farmers should be let alone. Just raise their prices by manipulating the gold content of the dollar, the Cornellians said; then their debts would be paid and the old prosperity would come back. What would be done with all the wheat, cotton, and corn-hogs they would continue to raise? This difficulty they ignored.

This last, however, was the consideration I would not consent to slight in our conversations, and Roosevelt acknowledged the potential trouble. The successive farm-relief bills of recent years (the so-called McNary-Haugen Acts) had relied on the common illusion that the European markets of wartime could be recovered and even expanded. It was not so. Farmers in other countries would not consent to compete with subsidized exports from the United States; they would not allow dumped products to be sold in their countries if they could help it. And because they were listened to by politicians, they *could* help it. There were farm blocs in European countries as well as in our own.

There was really no way of escaping the need for adjusting production to the domestic demand. Eleanor rebelled at this, and we had some argument. How could I suggest such a thing, she asked indignantly, when there were so many hungry people? But Roosevelt knew the answer to that. They couldn't eat all that wheat and use all that cotton, he said, even if they got these free. They were hungry, all right, but not for wheat. They were short of clothes, but not those made of cotton. What they needed was a lot more milk and meat—proteins—and in the recognition of this there was the suggestion of a policy, faint yet, but actual. Retire some land and resettle the farmers; reduce staple crops—wheat and cotton—and persuade the farmers to increase production of milk and meat.

There were, of course, other things to be done, disadvantages to be corrected. Farmers had heavy taxes; they could do with public improvements (farm-to-market roads); they might be given easier and cheaper credit. The federal government could do what Roosevelt had begun to do in New York and do it on a far larger scale. There remained, however, the bitter business of reducing production, almost impossible for a politician to countenance. We discussed it again and again.

In our early conversations, these agricultural questions kept intruding. Roosevelt was fascinated with them, and even when we escaped into more general problems he kept coming back to more talk about the farmers. They were much on his mind. This interest was reflected in the first public address I really paid attention to. It was a ten-minute speech delivered early in April on the Lucky Strike Hour, and it is usually called the "forgotten man" speech, because of a phrase that had lingered in Ray's memory from reading an essay by William Graham Sumner. The speech was a sort of test for much that would come later. Ray was pleased with its success, and it was not surprising to find his pleasure reflected long afterward in *After Seven Years*. In that account, he included a letter written at this time to his sister, who feared that Roosevelt was only very doubtfully a progressive. Ray was writing to himself as well as to her:

As I look back at what I have scribbled here, I see I haven't conveyed any sense of his gallantry, his political sophistication. When I was working with him on [the speech] I was trying to suggest the ideas, words, and phrases that would make that picture of him over the radio and would fix the image in the public consciousness. He was trying to reach the underdog and I scraped from my memory an old phrase, "The Forgotten Man," which has haunted me for years.

But that speech, without Ray's really willing it, developed into a discussion of the farmers' woes. They were the forgotten men whose buying power had been lost; because of this, Roosevelt said, "many other millions of people engaged in industry in the cities cannot sell industrial products to the farming half of the nation. No nation can endure half bankrupt. Main Street, Broadway, the mills, the mines, will close if half the buyers are broke."

This was a first test in political adaptation for Ray. For me it was a novel and exciting experience, there is no doubt of that; but I was not so happy with it as Ray seems to have been. There was a vague reference to a tariff revision that would enable others to sell their goods in our markets so that we could sell in theirs. Nothing at all was said, beyond this, about the adjustment of supply to demand. This went no further than the farm bloc had gone. It was not good enough.

Later I tackled Ray and Roosevelt about it, but at the moment I got nowhere. I insisted again on the hard fact that neither American nor foreign consumers wanted—at any price—all the wheat and cotton we were producing. Although Roosevelt himself had made this comment in private, he was evidently not willing to make it in public. I began to suspect, from this experience, that the measure of success for these addresses usually would be: what will be acceptable? And this meant, to be crude about it: what would gain, or at least not lose, votes? What really *ought* to be done could not compete with what the voters would like to think ought to be done.

Still, it was something to have had it suggested that mutuality in the economy must be maintained. This was an important principle. The applications might come later; they were clearly demanded.

Roosevelt's next speech, made later in April, was an improvement from my point of view. A Jefferson Day dinner in St. Paul, although we did not know it then, was the occasion for the most important of all the preconvention statements. By now the whole nation was attentive, and it was a satisfaction to have the speech generally spoken of as the "concert of interests" speech. This was my phrase, and I was as complacent about its adoption as Ray was about his success in identifying the unhappy millions in the concise allusion to the forgotten men. I crowed that he had only borrowed his (and had ignored the original meaning) and that mine was original.

This was one time that I could identify with certainty a paragraph as one I had drafted; usually my drafts were cut, or extended, or elaborated, or softened. This one came out fairly whole:

> I am not speaking of an economic life completely planned and regimented. I am speaking of the necessity that there be a real community of interests, not only among the sections of this great country, but among its economic units, and various groups in these units; that there be common participation . . . planned on the basis of a shared common life, the low as well as the high. In much of our present plans there is too much disposition to mistake the part for the whole, the head for the body, the captain for the company, the general for the army. I plead not for class control, but for a true concert of interests.

The effect of the speech was enormously enhanced by the furor that followed the "forgotten man" address. It tumbled Al Smith in a heap when he was quite certain he had a cause to exploit. Here is the story. The Jefferson dinners that spring were, as usual, held in many cities but on different days; the birthday of democracy's founder was as flexible, almost, as that of royalty in Britain.* Roosevelt was engaged to speak at the dinner in St. Paul on the 18th. But the dinner in Washington was held on the 14th, and since the "forgotten man" speech had been on the 7th, there had been a week for those who would speak in Washington to consider whether Roosevelt had to be answered. The names of those present read like a roll of the faithful. Besides senators, congressmen, governors, and bosses there were many others, among them Newton D. Baker, from Wilson days, who was, as everyone said, most likely to be the nominee if the stop-Roosevelt movement should succeed; also there was Al Smith, who was thought to have given up for himself, but whose fierce resentment at Roosevelt's mounting roll of pledged delegates was quite apparent. These two were

* Actually, Jefferson was born on April 13.

the main speakers. When the dinner was over, hardly anyone recalled what Baker had said; Smith had captured the headlines.

What Smith had to say was surprising to those who had not followed his recent maneuvers. He evidently had more reasons for attacking Roosevelt than simple jealousy or resentment; at least he said so. He regarded the successor he himself had chosen to be governor of New York as having turned into a dangerous radical. The high point of his speech was reached in the line declaring that he would take off his coat and fight "any presidential candidate" who persisted in a demagogic appeal to the working classes. This was generally understood, as *The New York Times* said, to be a warning that Smith would prevent Roosevelt's nomination if he could. And he had rich and powerful allies.

Throughout the press the reverberations of this intemperate attack by Smith, on a strictly party occasion and so short a time before the convention, centered attention on Roosevelt's forthcoming speech in St. Paul. Everyone wondered whether he would lose his temper too and respond in kind.

His speech about the concert of interests was a complete surprise. It took the play away from Smith. It was statesmanlike when recklessness and anger had been expected. *The New York Times* did say that "by reiterating an insistence on help for the workingman, the small homeowner and the farmer, Mr. Roosevelt made it clear that he would stand emphatically by the philosophy he set forth in his radio ["forgotten man"] speech." It could hardly say less since it had devoted a whole editorial column to praise of Smith's forthrightness in contrast with Roosevelt's evasive liberalism. But other papers, having predicted something more sensational, were inclined to agree with the *Omaha World-Herald* that it had been "no demagogue's unscrupulous plea," and even with the *Hartford Times* that "such sound philosophy and safe principle" did not deserve the heated denunciation of Roosevelt's critics.

Cordell Hull, that ancient of the Senate, who had already committed himself to Roosevelt, was delighted. He was even excessive, we thought, when we were shown his letter. "Words could not express," he said, expressing in words, "how much it inspired us."

He went on: "The party may well be proud to know that a man of your type and calibre is certain to be its standard bearer."

The old boy wanted to be Secretary of State, was Ray's comment. He added thoughtfully that very likely Hull would be.

My gratification, although considerable, was yet moderate, since I had expected more, or perhaps something else; but there were two comments I particularly relished and put aside for Ray. The *New York Post* said scornfully that the speech was a "bundle of clichés," just what might have been expected from Roosevelt. *The Herald Tribune,* somewhat more elegantly but to the same effect, said that Roosevelt was "reclining upon platitudes."

I said that, to be honest, the production taken as a whole was terrible, and it had looked so good when he went off with it. Ray had been visiting in Ohio and had been summoned unexpectedly to the train going west. He had joined it in Detroit to make, as the dispatches said, "last-minute changes." He had changed it all right, I said sardonically. He laughed and said this training to be a ghost-writer wasn't easy on the artistic sensibilities.

I comforted myself. Anyway, I mused, I'd gotten one phrase set up to be shot at, and it was a good one. Its implications would gradually dawn on people in spite of all the fuzzy trimmings—and, with luck, would dawn on Roosevelt as well.

I could not know that the implications would be enlarged in an-other speech, a really satisfying one that would carry the name "Oglethorpe." But the speech at Oglethorpe University, in Atlanta, was still more than a month in the future.

CHAPTER VI

The Roosevelt Drawing Room

🏵 🏵 🏵

An expert could not have arranged a physical situation more discouraging to a group of discussants than the drawing room of the Executive Mansion in Albany. What Roosevelt called "Smith plush" was everywhere, in yellowish-brown curtains and furniture coverings, in polished oak flooring with heavy rugs, and in enormous lighting fixtures. Every place to sit was overstuffed, so that even the lightest sitter tended to sink nearly out of sight. The pieces were too heavy to move, so theses or criticisms were fired across deadening expanses at listeners who were struggling to find room for their legs and who returned fire as they heaved around in the cushions. It was hot, too. The generous fire would have been welcome for a drowsy after-dinner hour, but if alertness was desired for probing delicate and difficult issues, this was a very poor place.

I recall particularly several of those Rooseveltian dinners that would become notorious in time. Food was one of Roosevelt's grievances, but "the Missus" was supposed to run the house, and it was not in their tradition to have the gentlemen interfere. This particular Missus was a kind and gentle lady with many good qualities, but she had always had a houseful of servants, and they were

51

evidently not as competent as they might once have been. What was provided under her direction uniformly discouraged any discriminating guest. The Governor disliked most of it intensely and, without being directly critical, wistfully spoke of dishes he wished he might have. It was obvious that Eleanor, being unable to boil water herself, and interested in nobler matters, would never remedy the situation.

One of those dinners, then, was no way to approach a serious discussion, even if the drawing room had been a proper place to have it. This, however, is leaving out of account the gaiety, the interested comment, and the free exchanges about the most diverse matters both weighty and trivial. It was assumed at that table that everyone had a right to give his opinion and to have it respected. This included the boys when they were home—which was not often, although two of them were there that evening—and Anna, who was occasionally at home. It also included a miscellany of visitors with all sorts of interests. It was the Roosevelt habit to treat all visitors as trustworthy. The most explosive gossip I ever heard was exchanged during those long meals. But I never knew, as I presume visitors generally did not, whether what was said was to be taken seriously.

One of the characteristics of the Roosevelt social life, and one that made visitors go away with a sense of participation, was that Roosevelt himself really did appear to abandon all discretion. He often related incidents and made comments that seemed to be most unwise revelations. Then there were his stories. As I was to learn, he knew very well the uses of parable. Those who knew him best became familiar with many of these tales and were amused by their improvement as they heard them repeated. Other disquisitions did, however, have to do with his current problems. For a lady on his left, or even for one across the table, he could make a dull economic issue into a romantic thriller, and an official lapse into a suppressed scandal.

Eleanor was equally voluble. She had a simple air that invited instruction, and she appeared to appreciate it. Those who knew her, however, recognized this as one of the courtesies she had been taught in boarding schools for young ladies. When she began to write, in later years, she spoke very frankly about having been, as she described herself, the ugly duckling of the Roosevelt clan. It may have been this that made her so eager to please and so tolerant of others' opinions. Her own convictions were very firm, if sometimes not well based. They were, however, anchored in such a wonderful good will that she was forgiven them even by those whose own views differed radically from hers.

Most of the after-dinner discussions at which I was present that spring started at the table and continued as we got settled in the drawing room. They would not become what Doc O'Connor called "deep" until the move had been completed. Most likely, up to then they would have been controlled by Eleanor, who always had some good cause to further—one of those suggested to her by Frances Perkins, Rose Schneiderman, or some other of that remarkable group of social and welfare workers who found her so sympathetic. She was deeply concerned about the worsening effects of depression and was earnest about finding ways of easing the situation of its victims. She watched closely the efforts of the state relief organization headed by Jesse I. Straus, with Harry Hopkins as his assistant. She knew how inadequate its funds were proving to be. Her travels were not yet as wide as they would soon become, but she knew that farm as well as city families were desperate, and she was apt to chide her husband when he claimed more than he should for his efforts during the past four years. Tax relief, better roads, and easier credits seemed to her inadequate. He—and we —were trying to keep to cause and cure rather than discussing temporary relief, and she got less satisfaction from us than she would have liked.

Really serious talk at table was avoided if Roosevelt could manage it. Eleanor, so humorless and so weighed down with responsibility, made this difficult. Surprisingly often, nevertheless, there was gaiety. Sam and Doc were so disillusioned with the cuisine and so prone to be annoyed with Eleanor's well-meant probing that they often turned up after dinner rather than before. This had the added advantage, they said, of enabling them to avoid Roosevelt's cocktails, and I sometimes joined them at one of Albany's excellent restaurants. But this was not always possible. Sam was present at the table oftener than Doc; he could stand it as long as Missy LeHand was there. Her presence was like a quiet blessing on any company she graced. She never said much, but when she did speak, it was softly, and always sensibly, about something immediate. Everyone felt her friendliness. Like others, I often went to her for comfort.

During one before-dinner talk, when Ray and I were planning the evening's discussion, Doc, speaking from his corner, said he hoped we knew that one of the first jobs we had to accomplish was "to get the pants off Eleanor and onto Frank." I recall this remark with a certain starkness because it was completely unexpected. I was relatively new and just in process of sizing up the relations of everyone to everyone else. To have this appraisal voiced without the least reticence had two effects. One was to give me a new view of Doc and Sam: they evidently regarded themselves as in process of strengthening a character about to assume responsibilities he had never had to carry before and might not be able to carry now. The other was to make me wary of Eleanor, not so wary as Sam and Doc, perhaps, but still cautious until I could make a better appraisal of that overwhelming goodness. It might indicate softness, and this was no time to be fuzzy. The remark, at any rate, crashed into my mind like a brick through a window.

Several things occurred to me in sequence. One was that Doc must really judge that Eleanor had become too influential in Roosevelt's affairs. If this was so, she must think our conferences with her husband something she ought to participate in. When Sam agreed with Doc's remark and they began to describe her repeated interferences, I was further set back. Was it possible that Eleanor *did* do her husband's thinking for him? Was his progressivism not his own but only that upper-class decency toward the lower orders that Doc and Sam attributed to Eleanor? They contended sturdily that this was the case. When I tried to reduce it to mere interference and, on Roosevelt's part, tolerance, they would not have it so.

It was not very happily that I joined the family at table just after that. I found myself trying to judge whether the worries of Sam and Doc were justified. I had to admit that I could see what they meant. Eleanor was always in touch with Louis Howe, or he with her, and was fully up to date on political matters. Whether she was only being informed or was being consulted I had no way of knowing. The latest accessions of delegates were making the nomination probable. Roosevelt pledges had become a majority by late April, but it took two-thirds to nominate, and this seemed an unattainable number. Eleanor was urging that still more aggressive tactics were called for. The first time this happened, I noticed that Roosevelt let her carry the conversation only a short way. He then turned to banter with me about being an upstate Democrat. It seemed to me deliberate, and I thought my friends were perhaps too concerned.

The diversion was in itself interesting to me. Roosevelt demanded to know how it was that the Tugwells were Democrats. No Democratic candidate had carried Niagara County since the Civil War. I didn't know offhand whether this was so, but I knew that the party had been almost nonexistent for many years. I tried a diversion. The Tugwells had originated in Chautauqua County, I told him, and had moved to Niagara later. My grandfather had hardly arrived in time for the Civil War; he may have been a Democrat because he disapproved, but if so, I had never heard of it. More likely, everything was new to him; he may not yet have been a full citizen. Unfortunately, I recalled later, he must have been, because he had bought a substitute, something I held a secret shame. I did not know then that Cleveland had done the same thing.

Roosevelt pressed. Chautauqua was even more Republican than Niagara. How could my father, a businessman, be a Democrat even if *his* father, for some more reasonable cause, had become one? I admitted that it wasn't easy to explain. The Tugwells, if they had stubbornly remained Democrats, had said nothing about it that I could recall. If I looked it up, he said, I'd find some Copperheads back there. I was stung. I said that politics in

Chautauqua was not so different from politics in Dutchess. The Roosevelts' county, I ventured, had never been Democratic either. This was a mistake; I had forgotten for the moment that he had been elected to the State Senate in 1910 from a district comprising Dutchess, Putnam, and Columbia Counties; there once had been a Democratic majority. But I suspected that the proportions in a normal year would be about the same as in Chautauqua or Niagara—two to one.

My recovery was not graceful. I spoke of "Cleveland Democrats," and since we were beginning to discuss money and I already had a suspicion about his fidelity to soundness, I asked if he was certain his father had voted for Bryan rather than McKinley in 1896. When Bryan had been nominated by the Democrats and was rampaging through the West advocating free silver coinage, Cleveland, then retiring, had refused to support him and had been much relieved when the Republicans had won. Hadn't *his* father, like Cleveland, been a "gold Democrat"? That was, in a party sense, much like being a Southern sympathizer thirty years earlier—not that I was ready to concede that my grandfather had been a secessionist.

It was perhaps a stand-off, but it saw us through that meal, and it did shut off Eleanor. We were still exchanging such remarks when we moved. As he swung himself into the one firm chair in the drawing room, he came at me on much the same subject, but in modern context.

Speaking of cheap money, he said that Bryan was probably ahead of his time, but hadn't he been essentially right? He went on to express doubt that my alternative to inflation—the forcing down of selected prices so that a balance was achieved—was practical. How could it be done? It was very well to say that equalization had to take place; doubtless it did. Fair exchange was necessary to the kind of full activity we had been talking about. We did want everyone working for everyone else and getting the right pay for it, but a multiplicity of deals would be involved. How could prices be regulated? In our system, prices were fixed in bargains. And how could they be made to have any relation whatever to the costs I talked about? He just could not visualize any device or mechanism or rule that could do these things—not in our system.

I mentioned one such interference—the minimum wage, already quite generally accepted. Prices of commodities were more difficult. But we did regulate public utilities. That was a category susceptible of expansion. Food was even more important than electric power or railroad rates. Why was its marketing not a common calling too?

He admitted my examples. Wages, yes; but prices—the public utilities I spoke of furnished services, not goods. Regulation of their prices had never been attempted; it might even be rejected by the courts.

I went on further: consumers used to bargain for goods. Nowadays they paid what was asked or they went without. Where prices were fixed privately by agreement, public authority could legitimately be brought to bear. That was conspiracy in restraint of trade.

He let me talk for a bit. I reminded him of what I had said before—that any sharp general change in the price level had disruptive effects, mostly because prices of particular commodities and services had varying resistances. When some went down fast and others more slowly or not at all, exchange between them became sticky and might even stop. I was not surprised when he suggested that if all prices were raised, and raised quickly, by some general means, the old relations could be put back where they had been when there had been high activity and full employment. I objected, of course, that this did not cure disparities, and I had a good deal to say.

The discussion about these related matters went on through several sessions. I recall another evening when Adolf surprised me by supporting Roosevelt's position. Being a lawyer, he saw the startling implications of the pressures I was suggesting to force prices down. Take steel, he said; how would you *make* those fellows bring down their prices?

I had an answer, and this was the time to give it. It wouldn't be too hard, I said, if all such industries were able to bring pressures *on each other.* If they bargained, made mutual arrangements, and so really related themselves to a whole market complex, an equitable situation might be restored. I didn't think, I said, that the steelmakers really wanted to shut down and create unemployment. There were some, I supposed, who after generations of virtual civil war with labor might not care how the unemployed suffered, but there were wiser ones among them. There were, in every industry, managers who saw that the whole was more important than the parts, that actually the parts had to work within the whole. They even saw, some of them, that unemployment was bad for business—that is, for profits. After all, it was fairly obvious that workers were customers.

Roosevelt was interested. I had caught his attention, something that usually resulted when a device was suggested. He liked to elaborate possibilities, play with alternatives, and suggest operating improvements. I knew in this instance that I had really reached his imagination. He had at one time been the promoter of something called the Construction Council, one of those trade associations that had sprung up in predepression days—fostered, incidentally, by Hoover and the Department of Commerce. These organizations had fallen apart in the grind of competition as hard times came, but many of their members had got to the point of considering the welfare of their industry rather than of their one firm. They understood, if only dimly, that working together had become desirable.

This, I guessed, was something even Adolf had not thought much about. His exceptional mind had been at work on quite another appraisal of the same body of facts I was alluding to here. He and Gardiner Means, as a matter of fact, had already completed—but had not yet published—*The Modern Corporation and Private Property,* a study that was to become a noted document in legal-industrial scholarship. But its implications went in another direction, that of showing how far concentration had gone. Adolf had been astonished to find into how few hands the control of industry had fallen, and what the consequences might be for the economy.

As I recall, however, he had not yet gone so far as to consider certain other implications. I was suggesting that there might be practical ways to take advantage of the concentration he deplored. I too had already written a book (it was ready to be published) called *The Industrial Discipline and the Governmental Arts*. Like Adolf, I was speaking from a decade of study. I believed that modern concentrations could be taken advantage of, that government could become a senior partner in industry-wide councils and maneuver their member elements into such arrangements that fair exchanges could go on continuously.

Each of us was trying for a statement that could be grasped and discussed, that would not be obscure or confused. It was only one issue, but contained in it, we believed, was not only an explanation of the extraordinary violence of the depression and its lingering resistance to the ordinary corrective of deflation—when all prices should have reached bottom and had no way to go but up—but also the suggestion of a way out.

This would not do for agriculture, I pointed out, which was so deeply in trouble and suffered from so long-fixed a disadvantage that special and drastic means must be taken to elevate its status, probably selective subsidies to bring about adjustment. But eventually argiculture too must come into a general scheme for relating the productive units of the economy to each other under a common rule.

Adolf outlined his discoveries for discussion in a series of memoranda, and they were fascinating. They could, however, be ammunition for the trust-busters as well as for believers in concentration and control. This was what I feared. I had developed a strong antipathy to the trust-busting tenet of the progressive creed. I thought it a diversion; Wilson's conversion to it, I was convinced, had been responsible for delaying the development of any positive policy. I had feared more than anything else that the next Democratic President would conceive it his duty to carry on—to complete—the old progressive agenda, and would consider this enough. I said so here, but Roosevelt made no answer.

After one such evening I said to Adolf that I suspected we had exposed a nerve. I did believe that a renewal of trust-busting was in the back of Roosevelt's mind, though I also had the impression that he couldn't see how it related to recovery from the economic sickness we were having now. Either that or it was politically unacceptable; I didn't know which. Busting the trusts and instituting drastic so-called reforms might be good political doctrine still, but—I repeated whenever I could—such actions would simply not start things going or keep them going.

Prosecutions for conspiracy might be a means of reducing prices, and I wanted that, Adolf said. I shuddered. That was going at it with a bludgeon. When I discussed the matter with Ray, he said this course was exactly what Frankfurter was recommending to the Governor, and Frankfurter came from Brandeis. Ray reminded me that it was Brandeis who had started Wilson on the New Freedom. I did recall. It had been Brandeis, at Wilson's bedside on a winter's day when the President-elect had been suffering from influenza; all students of progressivism had read about the incident.

Yes, Ray said, and Brandeis had been Wilson's dark angel for years after—until the war began. And he was hovering again in our neighborhood, only he was a Justice now, and he had to have deputies. Hadn't I noticed that Frankfurter came to Albany pretty often? I hadn't, but I understood at once what he meant.

CHAPTER VII

Conservation, at Least

🎖 🎖 🎖

As my involvement in Roosevelt's affairs seemed likely to go on, even if only as a second to Ray, what had been a casual interest in his career became a more serious one. How did it happen that he had become by now the most likely Democratic nominee for the presidency? And if he should be chosen, did he have the resources of character to support the responsibility?

Although the answer would have seemed doubtful to me before I met him, I had learned almost at once to respect his alertness, his fund of knowledge, and his ready acceptance of suggestions. In my few contacts with politicians, I had been used to two sorts. One was dull and unresponsive, actually, although he might have a highly developed talent for intrigue. The other sort, illustrated by the progressives I had consorted with, was intelligent, critical, and talented, but not often studious or careful in learning lessons. Most of the progressives reached conclusions intuitively rather than by research and analysis, and with few exceptions—Bob La Follette was one—none had any sense of the way the economy really worked. Roosevelt seemed quite different. He was a progressive, as Ernest Lindley had insisted in his recent book,* but this description left a good many questions.

* *Franklin D. Roosevelt: A Career in Progressive Democracy* (New York, 1931).

Lindley seemed to think that anyone was a progressive if he had the same sort of welfare interests as Al Smith, Roosevelt's predecessor in the governorship. I had concluded that this sort of thing would not help much. True, the congressional progressives had seen that the first need of the nation in its present crisis was action to relieve the distress of workers and farmers. Their proposals had been a harassment to Hoover since 1930. A few of them, notably La Follette, had spoken for planning and social management. Those aims distinguished them sharply from an older group of progressives who believed in enforced competition and regarded planning as an invention of the devil. They saw, all too clearly, that it led straight to collectivism, and also that it was part of the "bigness" they abhorred as resulting in monopoly and the ruin of small business.

About Roosevelt's affiliation in this ideological confrontation, I should only gradually become certain. I was already watching for signs, but the truth was I could have argued either way from our discussions during this early period. It had to be accepted, for one thing, that he meant to see what was necessary, but he also had an overriding interest in what would be acceptable. I was unhappy about this, but I was certain from our first meeting that he had a dedicated concern for people's welfare. Also, that proprietary interest in the nation's estate that I had so quickly discovered was, for me, a strong attraction.

As I learned from talks with Sam and Doc, who were entirely frank, an almost impenetrable concealment of intention, acquired from the experiences of public life, was by now a habit with him. No one in his position, Doc explained, could let anyone know what he even thought about anything until he had estimated what the consequences of a decision would be. When I said, "What consequences?" Doc found it incredible that I should ask such a question. He would go into it further, he said, when he got around to it, but I should not need telling that there was one thing to be thought of—the election.

I said impatiently that I could understand that—although everyone seemed to think I'd never heard of politics—but after all, elections didn't cure depressions, and *that* was what I was here to talk about. Besides, since I was here, offering a cure must have something to do with getting elected. Doc laughed and said, not as much as I might think; Roosevelt shouldn't make any mistakes about what needed to be done, of course, but Hoover had made so many that all Roosevelt needed to do was to point them out. I said that just doing that would show where he stood on a good many issues, and Doc said that was right; that was what I would be useful for. But I mustn't expect him to follow my line; couldn't I see that he was working one out for himself?

I had been reluctant to admit that this was what was happening, but now I acknowledged that it was so; when he seemed to accept my reasoning and spent hours, perhaps, in following along to devices for carrying it out, he was feeling his way, doing exercises, not making commitments. With this in mind, and being properly subdued, I found a new interest in guessing what sort of system he was working out for himself and, indeed—although this was next to impossible—how he was doing it. This would be a summer-long pursuit. In the end, the answers would be found, and they would be simpler than I then thought, but they would be the result of more experience with him and more study than I yet anticipated.

The most satisfactory thing about the early explorations was not Roosevelt's quick understanding of my proposals for meeting the challenge of the depression, but my discovery of his real commitments up to this time, the ones he had no reserve about. These had to do with welfare, as Lindley had insisted, and also with conservation. This pleased me well enough, but they were unexceptionable interests, developed in his general recognition that no one in public life could deny them if he expected to get ahead. They might or might not be pursued to the point of embarrassing powerful interests; being in favor of them was merely a sort of classification.

As a result of my curiosity and Doc's tutoring, I gradually deduced that the candidate of 1932 was a construct, not necessarily the individual that a younger Roosevelt might have wanted him to become. At some point ambition had taken charge and he had decided that he would become President of the United States, no less. He was well along toward that end now, and I suspected that he had made up his mind what he wanted to do about a good many things when he became President. These were the commitments he no longer had doubts about. Some of what he had in mind came out as we talked, and a lot of it was very clearly seen.

Walter Lippmann (and others like him, including his Hudson Valley neighbor, Ogden Mills, then Hoover's Secretary of the Treasury) did not grasp what had happened to the dilettante they had known. They had been acquainted with him casually since boyhood, or at any rate since college days, and thought they knew him. They just could not believe that a charming but second-rate young man had any possibility of becoming a formidable leader. I had the advantage of not having known the younger Roosevelt, and this made it easier to assess the one I saw and talked with.

At the time in his career when he had decided that he could and would make his way to the top, he had realized that to be a success in politics he must make himself over. In the course of twenty years, more or less, he had transformed himself into the highly visible public servant now on display as Governor of New York. I got hints of this when I opened the subject with, for instance, Frances Perkins. She ventured the guess that Roosevelt's illness had sobered him and that the ordeal of regaining the use of his body had hardened his resolution. It remained unexplained, however, why he had not become a self-centered hypochondriac, as many such stricken individuals did. As I looked at his career it seemed to me that there had been a foundation of resolution since his student days, not always visible but always there, underneath, and that not even the trauma of polio and crippling had been able to kill it. I concluded that there had been no sudden conversion and no change of character. He had sloughed off overlays and cultivated a talent for politics, setting his intention very early and pursuing it without remission. Because he was persistently underestimated, there was incredulity among his acquaintances when he emerged as a serious presidential contender. Besides, there were confusing traces of the young man remaining—in his quick smile, in his readiness to use first names, in the many other ways he seemed to admit people to his confidence. This was not all false or meant to deceive, although some of it was (since politics required it). When I tentatively opened the subject with Eleanor, she said seriously that he *did* give people false impressions sometimes, but that this was a deliberate use of an early training in manners that had become "second nature." Even she, as she admitted a little ruefully, was not quite certain about the "first nature."

Many years later, when I had written a biography of her husband and ventured some explanations of the seemingly unexplainable, she read the manuscript and, looking at me strangely, said that I might be right . . . she had always wondered. . . .

Some of the influences were obvious enough when they were looked for. One was the example of his cousin Theodore—Uncle Ted, as he was always called in the family. This had excited him as he watched the campaign of 1904, and participated a little in it, organizing student committees, meetings, and parades. He had been twenty-two then and emerging from his undergraduate years. If one Roosevelt could do it, he must have said to himself, another could.

The second Roosevelt presently conceived a way to move up: by joining Woodrow Wilson, the coming political figure who was Governor of New Jersey. An inner seriousness was now taking charge. He made a hard decision for the Democratic Party and progressivism. They were not only the wave of the future but congenial to his developing sense of responsibility. After he got to Washington, where he was to stay for more than seven years as Assistant Secretary of the Navy, he made a number of mistakes. He pushed too hard; he had difficulty in learning discipline; and when in 1920 he was chosen to run for the vice-presidency and lost, it might have been assumed that he was finished. That conclusion would have become final, if anyone were considering it at all, when he was prostrated by polio in 1921. Anyway, the Republicans, with Hoover succeeding Coolidge, had everything their own way in national affairs. They would doubtless keep control of the presidency for a long time to come.

Still, the way he had corrected his mistakes and fought the crippled immobility that followed polio was evidence that tough metal was being hammered into the mature character of the Governor. This was the man we were acquainted with. All that earlier development—the successes, the disappointments—we only heard about. I could believe that, in a curious sense, he was a self-made success. It was no advantage in American politics to be wellborn and well off. He had to prove that he was tough, practical, and disciplined.

Beginning to understand him in this way, I was not surprised to have him turn a number of times to something he could be quite open about. He was a devoted conservationist and meant no one to have any doubt about his devotion. In one of the conversations about this he referred to his long-time interest. If I wondered why he bore down so hard on conservation, he said, it went back to his first service in the legislature, when Boss Murphy thought to punish him with membership on what was considered the Senate's dullest committee, the one that dealt with forests, waters, and wild life. He did some hard work there, he said, and learned some lessons he'd never forgotten. One of his contributions was a top-lopping law. This saved many acres from being burned over and everyone accepted it now, but at first the timber interests had fought it in the usual way. It made them get the tops of felled trees together for burning. When these were left in a litter, they were an invitation to fire during the first dry spell. It was a small regulation, but it established an important principle—that operators must behave themselves, even if it cost them something.*

---

* I was to discover years later that Roosevelt's contemporaries in Albany at that time did not recall these experiences as he told them to me, at least not exactly. And careful work done at the Hyde Park library on this phase of his career was even more disillusioning. But when we were discussing it the events seemed vivid enough, and certainly he felt that they confirmed his claim to be a conservationist of the T. R.-Pinchot class.

He'd worked for the expansion of forests and parks, too, and a lot that had been done since, some of it during Smith's administration, but more during his own, had been started at that time. Even the retirement of submarginal land—a feature of the Tompkins County project, then under way—had grown out of this early work. And such retirement would certainly spread everywhere in the next few years.

Partly because I had always known Chautauqua so well, I responded warmly. Our county was west of Tompkins, but not far, and it had the same hills and valleys. But it wasn't for reforestation and for prevention of erosion that I had so much interest in land retirement. The people who stayed on those hills in their decent small houses, finding year after year that competition from the newly settled western lands was harder, and that seven-month winters made a worse and worse handicap in dairying, were some of them my own relatives. They were only a few among many of the same sort, but they gave me an intimate interest. I wished they could succeed right there where their grandparents had started, but that had become impossible. I said I would rather see them moved out than starved out.

Roosevelt contended that those hills could profitably be reforested. He always had, he said. But there were difficulties. He had tried commercial tree-growing on his own place at Hyde Park. He always had the best advice, and he could afford to wait all those years for trees to grow because he didn't need the money to live on. A farmer couldn't do that. Oh, he could do it on his own wood lot, where he cut firewood in winter and other trees for a local sawmill—

I interrupted: the sugar bushes shouldn't be forgotten.

Yes, he said, the sugar bushes! We were speaking of something that moved him, started his imagination, unloosed ideas. This was, let me admit, something I felt the same way about. As much as he, I wanted to do something toward making the countryside more orderly and more productive. The possibility released hopes, generated plans, made efforts seem rewards in themselves.

I learned something of his motivation. As a small boy, he had been instructed by his elderly father, who had explained to him in all seriousness a proprietor's responsibility for the land under his care. But also, he would inherit the estate. There was not one acre of that place on the Hudson that he did not know intimately and had not studied for its productive potentialities. He had had disagreements with his mother, who, after all, had life ownership and was a very opinionated lady; but he had had his way about a certain amount of tree-planting and the uses of certain fields. She had insisted on the continuance of many arrangements even at extravagant cost, and he fancied himself an economical manager. He especially deplored the expensive dairy herd, and often spoke of it.

I sometimes wondered if it was not partly frustrations on the home place that caused him to use it so often for illustrative purposes. It was much on his mind, but lessons he drew from it were doubtfully justified. Still, he drew lessons equally doubtful from experience with his Pine Mountain farm in Georgia. Newspapermen who covered his activities for long periods had a good deal of fun with the variations he allowed himself. His comparisons, like his dinner-table stories, tended to improve. Fred Storm, Ernest Lindley, Jim Kieran, and others of the Albany press corps had mental compendiums of such Roosevelt weaknesses, not always accurate, but always illuminating. I had picked up a good deal of background from them.* None of them had any particular enthusiasms except, I should say, Ernest Lindley, who did feel himself involved in Roosevelt's success. He was a progressive of the Kansas (or mild populist) variety. His journalistic detachment, despite his closeness to Roosevelt, and his real devotion taught me lessons in restraint.

I was well enough aware that these fellows were a long way ahead of me in political lore as well as Rooseveltiana. They had peculiar and close relations with the Governor. They knew many

---

* A compendium of Presidential weaknesses for useful but not necessarily truthful parable is Merriman Smith's *Thank You, Mr. President* (New York, 1946); Smith also wrote *A President Is Many Men* (New York, 1948). But he became a Roosevelt watcher at a later time. He was not one of the Albany correspondents.

things they were not telling. They were reticent because they were on some sort of honor not to betray his confidence. It was more practical than that, for some; if they began to tell, their sources would narrow. This was evidently acknowledged by their papers, whose policies were uniformly conservative.

I must say that with conservation they easily became bored. Perhaps they had heard too much about it from Roosevelt, and anyway it had very little news value. Their editors were interested in politics, politics, more politics, and, in those days, the incidents of the depression: failing businesses, closing banks, disheartening profit sheets, and the current drive for economy, balanced budgets, and restored confidence. These carried the sign of emphasis. Some subjects were frightening and therefore sensitive, in the sense that hopeful news was given precedence; but the remote plans of statesmen, if they had any at all, for the general benefit of future generations had no call whatever on the space available to newsmen.

Roosevelt was determined that somehow he would change this. His talks with me about the various possibilities—I think these were not shared in by Ray or Adolf, or shared only nominally— had this tag of immediacy. I understood that it was part of my job to enlarge such suggestions as he himself had to make and to contribute any I myself could think of.

That the Tompkins County project had an interest for me outweighing the retirement of submarginal land or the reforesting of those hills was something Roosevelt knew. Perhaps he shared the interest, but until then it had not kindled his imagination. The Cornell people had been trying to find better farms in the nearby valleys for the hill farmers whose land they wanted for reforestation, but this was only to get them off the land they wanted to assemble and protect. I tried to convince Roosevelt that rural resettlement was a workable variation of his subsistence-homestead scheme.

When I referred to the subject again—without Eleanor present —he laughed. He said he knew what I thought of moving the unemployed into the country. I could see that he did not agree with me that his scheme was impractical. But I said that to bring people who were already farmers down to lower locations and to see that they were outfitted with the means for farming—an art that had been developed over lifetimes—was something else again. That I was all for.

How many such people were there in the nation? I was ready with a rough guess. I thought there were at least four million families that were ready, because of their situation and prospects, for such help. Not all would want it, and, with exceptions, such programs ought to be voluntary; but, discounting everything, we could speak of two or three million families who were in hopeless circumstances and would undertake a new start, perhaps with hope. *There* was a program, if you like!

We talked about it at great length on different occasions, avoiding, I must admit, the matter of the unemployed. We canvassed the areas. There were not only the Appalachian uplands, running all the way from southern New York to northern Alabama, and taking in most of West Virginia as well as much of Pennsylvania and Tennessee; there were also the old cotton lands of the South, such as the ones he knew in western Georgia, and much of the Piedmont, exhausted by corn and tobacco after four hundred years of intensive cultivation. I showed him a picture taken in Ducktown, Tennessee—rolling land eroded to the yellow subsoil and cut by gullies that looked like shallow canyons. In the whole region there was no plant to cover the earth. He had heard of Ducktown, had seen places almost as bad elsewhere in the middle South. Then of course there were the unfortunate settlers in the short-grass country, a belt hundreds of miles wide just east of the Rockies, running from North Dakota to Texas. The plains had been broken further and further west during the early years of the century. I was able to tell him of church bazaars where collections were taken to bring Chautauqua County migrants "back from Kansas." They had struck a dry cycle, lost their whole investment, and become so destitute they could not even move.

Finally, there had been the fatal extension into the regions of buffalo grass during the war when wheat had been needed to feed

Europe and the armies. It had coincided with a wettish cycle and improvements in dry-farming methods. There was also new machinery for extensive cultivation, and farmers had borrowed to buy it, getting deeper and deeper into debt. The dry years had come; the broken soil had taken to blowing, and what had been wheat fields became desert. It would not get better. It ought to go back to grass, and the farmers ought to be helped in moving to other situations—west, east, or to irrigated valleys.

A little later I brought back from Washington the suggestion of an old immigrant forester, Raphael Zin, that a shelter belt of trees could be made to grow all the way down the short-grass plains. It was being done in Russia, and we ought to be able to do it better. Roosevelt responded to that. A shelter belt would stop the wind erosion, perhaps even change the climate a little—induce more rain—and it would certainly conserve what moisture there was. But, he said, we shouldn't mention the Russian precedent.

There really was no end to the possibilities. I could see him trying out in his mind the political reaction to them. Even in those early days we discussed two measures, one of which would appear in the acceptance speech delivered in Chicago. That was the joining of unemployment relief to conservation—one way, he said, to get agreement. We were moving toward the idea that emerged as the Civilian Conservation Corps, and I was already reading up on its possibilities, but an actual scheme was not made ready until after the election, when the foresters could be put to work on possible organization.*

What became the Tennessee Valley Authority he was already reaching for, too. This united conservation with public power, another of his enthusiasms. But it had a grandeur no earlier scheme had ever had—nothing less than the rehabilitation of a vast drainage system. Rivers were to be dammed for power and flood control; industries were to be rehabilitated; farmers would be relocated and assisted; employment was to be enlarged; reforestation

---

* At that time I discovered another precedent that he liked as little as the Russian one concerning the shelter belt. Mussolini had a well-developed army of youths working in Italian forests. That, too, would not be mentioned when the Civilian Conservation Corps was established.

would save the land; and the whole region would become a play-ground.

His comparatively long reference, in the acceptance speech, to this uniting of recovery and conservation I thought remarkable, considering the scrutiny undergone by every word of that document and the vicissitudes of its repeated rewriting and drastic shortening. I felt that our discussions had had something to do with the survival of these passages in an ultrapolitical document.

I knew that this was no new subject for him and that my own contribution had been, so far, one mostly of encouragement and some documentation. He had been developing these themes. He knew the work at Cornell, and Henry Morgenthau was also a pusher of the Cornell ideas. But Henry had a tendency to make subjects of the most intense interest seem suddenly dull. Roosevelt depended on him, but he did not expect either startling ideas or useful data. It was a relationship that would puzzle a good many people in future years, and some of those who were puzzled would suffer from Henry's jealousy, which was much like Louis Howe's. But Roosevelt chose to ignore it so far as I was concerned, and I followed his lead.

It was strange indeed that a Columbia professor, rather than one from an agricultural college, should be confided in about such matters and singled out for evening-long conversations—and in the exigent atmosphere of springtime in 1932! But if it was to be that way, I was willing. There was no cause I would rather encourage.

Think, he said, what could be done with all that land!

I was not one to discourage so good an idea. But the distance between the idea and the reality might be considerable. I ventured some such remark.

What he said was: exactly, but we might take some long steps.

And perhaps we had reached the time for action after generations of talk. Things that had been merely bad were getting worse. In an atmosphere of emergency much might be done—some of it not directly connected with the emergency.

CHAPTER VIII

Freshman Economics

🌿 🌿 🌿

E very college teacher of economics—and, I suppose, of other
subjects as well—develops a routine as he deals with one
generation of students after another. I had been teaching freshmen
and sophomores at Pennsylvania and Columbia for fifteen years,
and the texts were by now familiar. Since Roosevelt had had
courses at Harvard not only in economic theory but in such spe-
cialties as finance, transportation, taxation, and insurance, he was
far from a beginner in economic theory. Still, this had been more
than a quarter of a century before, and it was apparent that much
of his Harvard learning had been superseded in his mind by the
common-sense notions that seemed axiomatic to most businessmen.

He felt, and said, that he was fortunate not to have read much
New Era economics. He scanned newspapers. The financial news
and special articles about economic conditions were not the columns he turned to first, but, generally speaking, he was aware of
opinion about most of the matters we had to discuss. One of his
Harvard instructors, now become an authority, was often being
heard, as we met, on the dangers of public-utility holding companies and the need for a federal department of transportation. It
was not necessary to read William Z. Ripley's books to learn the

73

substance of his complaint. In this instance, the same thoughts were expressed equally well by James C. Bonbright, one of our colleagues at Columbia, who was a member of the state power authority. Roosevelt could well have instructed us on utility problems from what he had learned during his controversies with the power companies. Adolf and I were familiar with these issues as students and had wrestled with them for years; in the process, we had come to conclusions we thought were defensible, but these had not had the testing of trial. I felt that public ownership was necessary. I was surprised to find that Roosevelt thought it necessary only as a standard for the private utilities.

On such matters, Roosevelt was apt to be amazingly detailed. He could argue by the hour about valuation, a most involved theoretical question at the center of the rate-making controversy. His exposition of the prudent-investment principle as opposed to that of reproduction-cost-new (which the utilities were trying to establish) was worthy of a lifelong student. But a general policy for the nation, to be argued for in the campaign, was something different. Would he be converted to nationalization of all power facilities? The resentment generated by the Insull revelations of the past spring would create public support for such a step. As a "gas and water socialist," to use the British term, I saw no reason to hesitate because the United States was larger than New York. But it soon became apparent that Roosevelt was not prepared to go beyond the compromise conveniently offered by those who advocated enough public power to act as a "yardstick," a position he had often spoken for in public. It seemed to me an illogical withdrawal. If it happened in an area where he had a really heroic record, and where current scandals furnished campaign material, could we hope for anything more in other fields—transportation, finance, radio?

Quite soon we learned to expect from him the kinds of attitudes and arguments he would have acquired from those he came into contact with most often. His expertness on power was not duplicated in many other fields, but it also has to be said that he was better informed on others than most citizens would be, even if he had not given serious thought to solutions. It was disconcerting, however, to have theories persist even when we thought their supports had been demolished.

An illustration of this was his clinging to the notion that shorter hours would cause employment to be spread among more workers, and that labor-saving tools should be avoided on public jobs so that work could be spread among a greater number. Economists knew this as the "make-work fallacy" and had grown weary refuting its illogical reasoning. It depended on the assumption that there was a limited amount of work to be done. Economists pointed out that there was, on the contrary, an unlimited desire for goods and services. People's wants were never satisfied, and there was always a shortage of useful public improvements. To slow up work in order to spread it was also to limit production and reduce purchasing power.

Roosevelt seemed to accept our reasoning, and yet many of his plans continued to depend on the fallacy. Public work was to be of some use if at all possible, but it must be largely labor with hand tools, of the sort that was later called "boondoggling," with ample justification. This was typical of his latent ideas, those he allowed to control his decisions when he did not stop to reason. Such ideas were not improved by the fact that they were widely shared. Organized labor, for instance, was devoted to the make-work theory, and almost everyone else accepted it as an expedient—including most relief administrators. By subterfuge, we might prevent him from making a speech advocating the make-work theory, but we could not prevent him from using it as a rule of action.

So with other notions that were popular but fallacious. They came up regularly, and as regularly we worked out ways of demolishing the propositions they supported. It was exasperating to find that despite our efforts they still lurked in the background.

In some of our passages with him, shock tactics worked. It might be thought that he would have resented this, but I soon found that it seemed to bring back the lessons he had learned so long ago (and learned very well, as I came to believe). Often, as soon as our exposition began, he picked it up and carried it on. His teachers, he recalled, had used the same arguments. Our repeated reminders of elementary economic rules were useful to him in a way I did not at first understand. He expected us to help in preparing statements, speeches, and documents that must be safe from critics, but also to arm him for emergence into a public forum he had not yet had to contend in. This seems strange to say of a public man with so long a career behind him, but in fact he had always been able to shelter himself from controversy and keep to generalizations calculated to offend no one. Even during the last two years, state problems had been a protection from larger national ones.

It was true that at one time or another he had taken some positions that he now had to revise or defend. But these were limited in number, mostly belonged to the past, and had once been within the orthodoxy of the party. It had been this way with his advocacy of the League of Nations. During the campaign of 1920 he had made ardent speeches supporting the League, and he had continued his advocacy afterward. This last winter, more than a decade after 1920, the Hearst press, violently isolationist, had carried on a crusade against the League. To appease Hearst, now that his support was needed, Roosevelt had made an awkward retreat. What he had said, rather lamely, was that the League had changed and was no longer the sort of thing he had advocated at the time of its forming. This giving way to isolationist sentiment, now grown so strong, had dismayed the old Wilsonians of the party—Daniels, Hull, Colonel House, and Baker, for instance. He had difficulty in explaining to them that his present position did not preclude future international co-operation. His equivocation made them uneasy.

This fairly represents the position-taking that he had learned to be wary of. It was his avoidance of such commitments throughout a period when he was obviously a potential candidate that had given Walter Lippmann and others the opportunities for ridicule they had been glad to exploit. They used the words straddling, trimming, evading, and even worse ones implying ignorance and dishonesty. He had become sensitive on the subject, but he was still certain that it was the only practical course for a prospective candidate to follow. Lippmann might object again and again that any seeker for democratic preferment had a duty to let people know what views he held, but it was still true that in the present situation Roosevelt must first consider how to get, and how to keep, delegates to the convention. He had a substantial number now, but not all were firmly instructed, and positions taken on controversial matters might offend some of them. What, the politicians asked, was to be gained by taking risks?

Particularly to be avoided were certain economic issues, such as the tariff, international debts, the veterans' bonus, monetary questions. But there were only a few of these. More numerous were sensitive matters of social policy. Prohibition, so prominent in the 1928 campaign and still being pushed to the front by the Smith-Raskob-Shouse faction, was the most embarrassing issue. The time was coming when, as a nominated candidate, he would have to make speeches not only on the affairs he preferred to emphasize but also on many questions of public policy he had hitherto been able to ignore.

The most urgent issues he would have to meet were entirely new ones related to the depression. It was true that Republican and Democratic positions were rapidly being adopted on unemployment relief and even on recovery. Robert Wagner, together with several others in the Congress, was fixing the Democratic position. Roosevelt would have to accept it or repudiate the progressive group. It would not be easy to come into such a concordance because, for several years, he had emphatically agreed with Hoover that relief was, and should remain, a state and local matter. The Wagnerites had outrun him, no doubt of that, but actually he had discovered on his own that local resources were hopelessly inadequate. Though it would be embarrassing, he would have to end by agreeing to federal assistance, perhaps to a complete federal takeover.

He had also believed in a pay-as-you-go policy and had attempted to meet New York's greatly enlarged expenditures with a fifty-per-cent increase in income taxes. This had not been enough, and he had had to resort to a bond issue as the only means of maintaining relief for the unemployed. On local responsibility and on pay-as-you-go, then, he had to manage reversals. Even Garner was now advocating a federal program for relief to be financed by borrowing rather than by taxing. Roosevelt had been particularly critical of schemes that would "make future generations pay for present emergencies," but there seemed to be no alternative. So he finally spoke in favor of Wagner's unemployment-relief bill, and this did not even specify what sums were to be borrowed, much less provide for payment from current revenues. Roosevelt could only hope that no one would recall his former views.

It was over this ground that an early skirmish developed. There was a touch of acrimony in it. Roosevelt had simply leaned back, flourished his cigarette, and, looking at the ceiling, told me (or us—I have forgotten whether others were present) that he had always known that states could not meet the problem without federal help and that this was one of his differences with Hoover. This was so patently a fiction that I protested. Moreover, I said, he need not hope to make anyone else accept it as true. Someone would look up the record, and he would be embarrassed. Claiming independence and self-sufficiency for a state came natural to a governor. He had done it emphatically in an excess of pride, and he had been overwhelmed by the number of unemployed. He was right to endorse Wagner's bill, but not to pretend that he had always been for the policy it represented.

It was an unpleasant moment. Roosevelt gave way, after hesitating, and said that anyway the unemployed came first and balanced budgets only afterward. On this we agreed, and the incident passed. I found, when I rather cautiously inquired of others, that he often did this sort of thing. He had learned what I did not yet know, that the record is seldom cited and that claiming to have been right was a political habit. The habit annoyed people like Frances Perkins, with her passion for veracity; often, in her old-maidish way, she refused to countenance his looseness with facts when he needed to rearrange them.

I wondered whether the recollection of our skirmish might make me unwelcome afterward. It seemed to have the opposite effect.

When he did the same thing again, he smiled his confidential smile. He was trying on me what he would try on others, but he did not expect me to believe it, only to judge whether those others would.

I still do not know just where I came out on this. Did I reprove him because he prevaricated, or because the prevarication was blatant and inexpedient? Probably the latter. I was learning that if politicians were to be liked, they had to be liked as a whole.

His endorsement of Wagner's bill might please the progressives, but it frightened the conservative Easterners. Bernard Baruch, advising the Smith-Raskob-Shouse people, bitterly assailed the acceptance of an obligation without provision for its financing. This was no way to keep businessmen's confidence. It would drive out of the party all those who believed in honest fiscal policies and in paying legal debts. This included the whole financial community and most of the businessmen as well. The Democrats might not have many supporters among them, but there were some, and they ought to be reassured. Fiscal irresponsibility could become an issue.

Roosevelt could, of course, say that if he had reversed himself, or nearly so, it had been done on humanitarian grounds. This would be the honest thing to do, and I could see no harm in it. He had not yet given way publicly on "asking future generations to pay." But he would have to; if no one else did, Smith would force him to admit that there was no other way to meet the bills for relief and public works. He might better do it voluntarily with the excuse of needs beyond anyone's forecast. Obviously involved were the consequences of an unbalanced budget so frightening to conservatives. Economists were not entirely unprepared on this; it does seem incredible now, but Roosevelt simply had not thought of the simple reasoning that economists, of my school at least, had been putting before college classes for years. It was the sort of thing I had learned from Patten, Mitchell, and other of my teachers. We did state it in a slightly different way; we said that the federal government, because it could enlarge demand (by giving relief), could increase production and also the income of businessmen. Their taxes would then, with the same rates, yield increased receipts. The way to fiscal soundness was not to retract and pare and save; it was to stimulate enterprise and so to enlarge the sources of revenue. Unemployment, I argued with Roosevelt, was an opportunity to marry concern for distress to improved public facilities. He liked this last. He was always concerned with the public domain.

But this was not the only sort of well-practiced lesson I could remind him of. Others had to do with familiar matters, but the general reasoning about them was as naïve as that about the "make-work" fallacy. He would have to argue about them in the months ahead, and he had better be ready.

One of these familiar fallacies was that increases in the use of machines and power resulted in the permanent loss of jobs for workers. It had begun in the English textile mills a century ago and had never ended. There were still Luddites around. Practically all union members were convinced that machines and power were their enemies. Perhaps in the short run they were, but for the long run it had always seemed obvious enough to economists that increases in the use of capital multiplied jobs, because output was increased, and when the output was sold it became income; income was purchasing power, and purchasing power was demand. The bothersome problem was that of protecting those individuals who were displaced when machines came in, but to keep the machines out in order to preserve obsolete jobs would be to prevent the rises in the levels of living so characteristic of our expanding economy. The displaced ought to have their incomes ensured, but not their jobs.

Perhaps I may use one more illustration of academic reasoning that ran contrary to popular conviction. One faction of organized agriculture, whose spokesman was John Simpson of the Farmers Educational and Cooperative Union, was agitating for the fixing of prices by legislation. This evidently seemed practical because millions of farmers thought it ought to be done. They wanted a law that established a price of ten cents a pound for cotton, seventy-five cents a bushel for wheat, and so on through the list of staple products. Buyers would have to pay what the law said, and justice to the producers would be simply ensured.

A solution of this sort would certainly be a relief from the complications involved in planning to give producers who sold abroad the difference between the foreign price and that on the domestic market—or, for that matter, in devising arrangements for reducing production. Both these formulas had had endless attention in the Congress as successive McNary-Haugen Acts were formulated. Price-fixing was so loudly and confidently argued for by Simpson and his numerous followers that Roosevelt was considering what the situation would be if they should turn out to be a majority of the producers.

It was easy to forget, we told him, that the price system actually was a system. Prices measured relationships among producers. If one price was fixed, all the others must be fixed too, or the gyrations around the inflexible one would grow more and more erratic. Prices that were set too low could result in reduced production and increased unemployment; those that were set too high might yield abnormal profits. One cause of the depression was that this very thing had occurred, not by governmental action—that is, by public law—but by monopoly—that is, by private law. Some interests—the big steelmakers, for example—had gained such power that they could fix their own prices and refuse to revise them. This placed a burden on interests with less power that depended on products they had to buy from the quasi-monopolies. If the price was too high, they reduced their buying. Then the monopolies themselves felt the pinch and had to curtail or even halt their operations. In the steel industry, the result of protected prices had been reduced output, reduced wages, closed plants, and widespread unemployment—not to mention the loss of customers.

Fixed prices for farm products would create a series of economic problems. In the end they might actually have the effect of reducing farm income, and from the very beginning they would increase the surpluses that were already hanging over the market. What needed to be done for farmers was not to freeze their prices but to unfreeze other prices and to approach the problem by equating supplies with demands. Prices could be raised either by boosting the general level of values or by so reducing output that demand for products would intensify. But unless a whole system of fixed prices was contemplated, no individual or group could successfully exploit other interests in the economy.

These are fair enough illustrations of the economic reasoning we supplied and illustrated with considerable care. Roosevelt was always willing to follow through and to see how practical policies were affected. But we did find soft spots. These were usually in matters he had been forced to do something about. When he had accepted the relief obligation it had sounded good to declaim about independence from federal interference and about the ability of the state to go it alone. He had found out the hard way that New York industries belonged to the American economy; and a Governor who expected to be President could only be embarrassed by having put the state ahead of the nation.

He was recovering from this appeasement of local sentiment when we came on the scene, but we had a chance to see how he would arrange his retreat. After our argument, I was particularly interested. It was amazing; he made no explanation at all. He simply ignored the inconsistency and was soon agreeing with Wagner and the others that the federal government would have to come to the aid of the states. If this betrayed an ambivalence, he would never resolve it, at least not very clearly. On the other hand, he did not claim publicly that he had always been right.

CHAPTER IX

At April's End

🌿 🌿 🌿

By this time Adolf and I were fairly deep in Roosevelt's affairs
without having planned it or having consented; it had just
seemed to happen, a little more every day. When I thought about it
after a few weeks, however, I could see that a mutual concern for
farmers and for the land had had a good deal to do with my own
involvement.

I had been born in the westernmost county of New York State's
southern tier. That hill country—and my village—had had two or
three generations of promising growth when settlers were moving
west in the early nineteenth century. Some of them, coming across
the state by water-level route, had turned down valleys running
south and pushed up the slopes on either side. To get to Sinclairville, deep in a pocket of the hills, they had come all the way to
Lake Erie and then taken the road that ran west along the lake. At
what is now Dunkirk, they found another road—or track; it could
have been usable only in spells of fine weather—and, with two or
four spans of oxen, got their heavy wagons over some formidable
passes.

My own grandparents, being late-comers (1852), had had a
canal passage from New York to Black Rock, near Buffalo, and
had been met there by relatives with suitable transport. They had

found an already settled community of English settlers who had preceded them. One of the most magnificent white-pine forests in the world had covered the Chautauqua hills. Almost none of it was left after fifty years of slashing attack to clear fields and pastures. What had not been foreseen was that this would open the slopes to erosion, which had quickly reduced their productivity. Then farm lands farther west had begun to produce grain and cattle so cheaply that New York hill farmers were gradually reduced to grubbing a poor living from wasted upland acres.

As a boy, I had seen the last chapter of this story, and my own people had moved in 1904 to better country a hundred miles north on the shore of Lake Ontario. They had been not farmers but villagers; still, they had felt the decline evident everywhere in the countryside.*

Roosevelt was the first Governor who had really understood the hill farmers' troubles. Smith had been sympathetic about recreational needs and had moved to set aside park and forest reserves, but this was not the same thing. Roosevelt had not invented the Tompkins County resettlement scheme, but he had supported it. His special interest in farmers had been shown again in his sponsorship of tax relief, better roads, and other helpful measures. As in the case of everyone who had learned about his governorship only from what could be read in the metropolitan press, my knowledge of his administration was colored by his apparent compromises with Tammany, which annoyed all good-government people; besides this, we read about his continual bickering with the majority in the legislature—for New Yorkers, as they had so often done before, had elected a Republican legislature even when they chose a Democratic executive. And the Governor was not always thought to be in the right.

The truth is that I, at least, had had occasion to think well of Roosevelt only when I heard from my colleague James Bonbright about his fight for public power or from Robert Murray Haig about his efforts for tax reform. About Moley's work to improve the administration of justice I had heard only casually.

* A tale told in *The Light of Other Days* (New York, 1958).

Adolf was in the same situation about this; when Ray asked him to go to Albany the first time, he agreed to go, but said frankly that he "had another candidate for president." This was probably Newton D. Baker, but I was never told directly, nor, I think, was Ray. Like myself, Adolf gradually became so involved that all his energies were given to assisting in Roosevelt's preparation for national responsibilities. When we got closer to the political goings-on, it was at once apparent that only something unusual would prevent him from becoming President, and Americans—at least ones of our sort—simply do not refuse any service asked of them by their President. Also, we should probably have to admit that we were somewhat brash; we thought we had some answers, and we thought Roosevelt ought to know about them. We were considerably humbled, I may say, and were becoming much more useful after a month of discussions as penetrating as any we had ever taken part in. We had to defend our proposals, and, again and again, we had to ask for pauses while we refreshed ourselves from books, from colleagues who were experts of some sort, or from quickly undertaken researches.

Respect for Roosevelt's mind, for his energy and persistence, and for his political skill—something we had been in no position until now to have any informed knowledge about—led to a curiosity about him that we satisfied whenever we could. Most of what I learned in those first weeks came from Sam and Doc, who almost at once accepted me as a confidant. I made no pretense of being a political sophisticate and they took some pains to instruct me.

They were surprised to be asked many of my questions. They assumed that everyone knew not only Roosevelt's past, his family, his interests, but also his strengths and weaknesses. About these they were entirely frank. Some of the conversations between them in my presence, after they had admitted me to the intimate circle, amazed me. I tried to conceal this for fear they might feel they were going too far. Either I succeeded or they were unable to imagine anyone's retaining such innocence at my age. It was not long, naturally, before I had heard enough and seen enough to understand the attitude they proceeded from. It was much longer, though, before I reached it myself, for theirs was the curious view that Roosevelt, the presidential candidate, was something they were creating. He might not be a perfect subject, or in some respects even a very good one, but he was the one they had adopted as theirs. They knew what they wanted him to be and do, and when he disappointed them, as he often did, they regarded it as willfulness that must somehow be checked. They not only had to deal with Roosevelt's insouciance about matters they thought serious; they also had two active nuisances in Eleanor and Louis.

Eleanor, about this time, began to be more communicative with me, probably because she had begun to travel on a kind of summer circuit and, since she was making speeches, doubtless felt that she ought to keep some correspondence with the conclusions of the group her husband was consulting.

Her pronouncements infuriated Doc and Sam, and I am sure she realized it. I took them less seriously; besides, even if not profound, and somewhat platitudinous, they went cautiously in the right direction. Several times she made occasion for talks with me, asking about our explanation of the crisis. She was as unlearned in economics as a child and was puzzled that Christian good will should not have more force in economic affairs. It did not come easy to think of businessmen as indecently wrong—that is, responsible for the general paralysis. The people involved must lack understanding; yet why should they have done so badly? She listened patiently when I spoke of technology and the lack of adjustment to it, of price differentials and the recovery of balance, but she did not really take these in. She always reverted to the simple solution of better behavior, one to another, among all peoples.

What she had to say in her speeches still did not exactly anticipate the ideas her husband was working out, but she was talking about them at a time when he was not yet ready for commitment. The only actual and direct comment I heard Roosevelt make was to ask once whether someone he was talking to—perhaps Ray— had seen "what the Missus had said at Chautauqua." We had seen, and we had no particular objection. We did not say that it had seemed naïve. This, however, was later—in July—but already I was wondering how, with so little consultation, she was managing to hint at some conclusions that Adolf and I had been arguing for but that Roosevelt had not spoken about. It might have been because, although she was never present during our long and detailed discussions, she often came in just before they ended. Toward midnight, Roosevelt was calling for the bedtime beverage cart, and we were ending on a summary note. She sat down and listened, offering a comment or two. By then Roosevelt was busy with the little ceremony of mixing drinks, and the evening was breaking up. She seldom got an adequate answer to her questions.

Sam and Doc did genuinely appreciate our efforts. For one thing they had a certain pride in having got us together; for another, however, they felt that we were persuading Roosevelt to focus on problems that would prove a most terrible embarrassment if he should not know what to do about them later on. The weight of the depression with all its confusions, together with such other problems as that of agriculture, whose complexities completely baffled these two city-dwellers, might simply overwhelm a man who had been a successful Governor of New York but now would have to meet a serious national crisis without having had to deal with its issues. He might even look foolish during the campaign.

Their way of showing confidence in Ray and me was the convincing one of assuming that we regarded the situation exactly as they did. They often plotted to circumvent some action or some pronouncement that they regarded as unwise, and I could at least formulate alternatives.

It was amusing to hear them plot the machinations that constituted their relations with Eleanor and Louis. Sam and Doc were no closer to political affairs than we were. Louis regarded both of them with disdain, but especially Doc, whose place in the scheme of things was, in fact, not easily defined. Sam, of course, was Governor's Counsel, so he had work to do. When he kept to it, Louis tolerated him, but when he impinged on politics, the blast from New York City would have blown a less dedicated man out of Albany altogether. I became convinced, as time passed, that Roose-

velt knew about these jealousies and was amused by them. It was
the sort of thing that did amuse him, and there were times when I
suspected him of fomenting suspicion just to see the reaction.

Eleanor, even then, regarded it as one of her duties to bring
back information from her frequent journeys, such as that to
Chautauqua. That was Republican and very conservative country, but the Chautauqua gathering was accurately representative of
small-town Sunday-school opinion; she found the people there
deeply disturbed but unshakenly Republican. She thought, however, that they were likely to vote against Hoover if Franklin
offered something they could accept as a Christian approach to national ills.

As Louis was sure to do, he found out about our activities at
once from Eleanor, with whom he nowadays was in close communication. He regarded her as his agent in Albany, and it was hard to
say, often, whether she was amused by his possessiveness or disposed to carry out the orders he barked wheezily at her over the
phone. About us I think he had little concern at first, especially as
Ray took pains to conciliate him. Still, we were consorting with
Sam and Doc, and about them he was alertly suspicious.

For Adolf and myself, all these relationships were something we
had to pick up as we went along. At first we were pretty well hidden behind Ray, who was our front. Until now, we had never
caught sight of some characters we were involved with, but the
critical weeks were closer and there was more talk about politics
than economics even in our gatherings.

I had never visited the Hyde Park home we heard so much
about, much less the Warm Springs retreat far down in western
Georgia. I had no difficulty with the Hyde Park syndrome; I heard
so much about it from Roosevelt himself that I felt I knew all
about it. His efforts to make a dairy pay were unhappy ones, but
he did not seem certain whether this was because dairying was a
losing business or because his mother would not let him run it as
he wanted. She had told him firmly that a sizable herd of milkers
had been favored by his father for family reasons, not for profit; if
money was lost, she would gladly make up the deficits. She still

shipped cream and butter, as well as eggs and many garden products, to members of the family wherever they were. James, his son, now in business in Boston, got a weekly shipment and spoke of it as the most costly milk route in existence. The Albany table was similarly supplied.

This was a half-humorous grievance. The ventures into apples and Christmas trees, and his own reforestation project, were no more profitable. The deductions he made as a result of his own experiences were of doubtful usefulness, and I used to wonder how the rural audience that listened to his weekly broadcasts regarded him. There was no doubt about his sympathy, but his assumption that the experiences at Hyde Park meant anything to an average farmer must have caused skeptical smiles.

We heard—or rather I heard, for this was an interest none of the others shared—a good deal about the Pine Mountain farm in Georgia. His operations there had been losing ones too, but he represented them to me as having been undertaken as demonstrations rather than with any hope of profit. This was something I later learned more about; there was no doubt that he had thought he could at least break even. But the help of devoted county agents who practically ran the place for him was not enough; the losses were so considerable that before long he was to let them taper off, and gradually the effort would come to an end.

At this time, though, I heard a good deal about improving the breed of cattle that ran in the brush of old, abandoned cotton fields. He bought pure-bred sires and loaned their services to his neighbors. He also tried to find crops that would pay. Cotton had fallen to almost nothing per pound, and anyway was being eaten by boll weevils before it could mature. As a substitute, he had tried scuppernong grapes and apples, and he had looked for the best and quickest-growing long-leaf pine to substitute for the weedy and worthless second-growth jack-pine on much of his acreage. But his farm was high, rocky, and dry; nothing prospered.

I was so constituted that I could enjoy endless conversations on this theme. Doc said to me in wonder, after one day's talk when he had simply picked up and left, that I must know most of that stuff about the Georgia farm was fairy tales, didn't I? I said yes, but it was the kind of fairy tales I liked.

I did not get the full story of the Pine Mountain venture until much later, when I found it very different from the version Roosevelt used as illustrative material in his speeches. Evidently people liked to hear it the way he told it, and he would keep on with it for years. At this time, however, he was still hoping to make something of the place. He was being advised and helped by Cason Callaway, that curious and attractive survival from an earlier day, who had enormous land holdings of his own. Callaway's farms, and the lovely, large gardens he had created in honor of his mother, made some of the most beautiful landscapes to be seen anywhere. Roosevelt told me about them, and later, when I saw them, I fully agreed. But whether the Callaway family considered these operations to be purely in the public interest, as Roosevelt believed, or whether they really turned in a profit, I never knew.

When he mentioned Callaway, in telling me about his own farm before he left for the South, he did it with a certain respect that told me how much he would like to have had such holdings himself. I inquired of Doc, who laughed and said that I ought to hear the two of them together. Callaway carried on like an old-fashioned squire. He built Baptist churches with kitchen facilities; he gave pensions and annual picnics. He might have paid fair wages, but he ran union organizers clear out of his county. And there was Roosevelt, the perpetrator of more labor legislation, much of it just to please the unions, than anyone in the country, and he'd do more of the same when he was President. Callaway knew all about it, of course, but whenever Roosevelt was down there, they were thick as thieves. Callaway entertained Roosevelt at his place and invited his whole crowd. He hired the Governor's favorite local music-makers, and both of them sang for hours at the top of their voices. Those were wonderful picnics.

It was hard to picture the two of them, Doc said. They certainly must keep off the subject of labor legislation—and a good many other subjects too. People interested in farming could go on forever about that, he supposed. Besides, Callaway was one of the angels for the polio center at Warm Springs; that came in the category of doing something for the folks, and it was another thing they had to talk about. But Doc still thought it was a weird friendship.

Doc told me a little about the financial involvement in the ramshackle old hotel Roosevelt was turning into a rehabilitation center. The project had already cost a small fortune, and somehow, if he was going on in public life, a way would have to be found to relieve him of a debt he could hardly carry on his income. One of Doc's immense services in later years would be the assumption of this burden.

My curiosity was still not appeased, but I could see I would not get much more from these friends. I tried Eleanor. I should have been warned. She had been against her husband's venturing so much of the family fortune in such a doubtful enterprise, and moreover she detested western Georgia and the western Georgians. She was gentle about it, and I learned more later on from the local people there, who disliked her as much as she disliked them, and a good deal more viciously. Their dislike was due partly to her outspoken racial views and partly to her suspicion of the Callaways and all the upper class of the vicinity. Unlike her husband, who could find things to talk about with anyone, especially if he knew anything about the countryside, she had no common ground whatever with any of them. She seldom went there any more, and she was not going this spring. It was not worth the abrading of her principles.

She did tell me one thing, though, that gave me some light. How, I asked her, if the Governor spent so much time down there at his rehabilitation exercises and in the management of the institution, did he manage to get around so much? He seemed to know dozens of local people, politicians and farmers; moreover, he knew the countryside with an intimacy that must have been gained by close and repeated investigation. It had certainly been quite strange to him, a New Yorker, when he had first gone.

Then I heard for the first time of his important victory over the immobility that overtakes most crippled people and keeps them closely confined. Years before, an ingenious mechanic had rigged a small car so that it could be controlled completely by hand, and there had been successive improved versions of the original. In these Roosevelt had spent part of nearly every day, sometimes whole days, exploring the back roads, visiting with farmers—simply driving into yards, pulling up under the inevitable chinaberry tree, and hailing whomever he could see. In these casual conversations, he had learned more about farmers' grievances than he would ever have discovered in New York, where they were filtered to him through professionals, or could have learned in Hyde Park on what was not a farm but an estate.

In Georgia, until recently, he had been a visitor from the North, a kindly one, crippled and therefore commanding sympathy, retired from active life. There were no barriers, or anyway none such as existed wherever else he went. He learned something real about life down the dirt roads and in the farmyards of Meriwether County, and he learned it for good.

I spoke to Doc about it, and he said it was true. He also told me belatedly about Eleanor's dislike of her husband's favorite resort. It got him away from her, anyway, he said, and it did him a lot of good physically.

He must have had many talks, as Doc told me he always did, with the local political crowd. They probably swarmed around now that they saw his nomination as practically ensured. He had been cultivating them for years, and now was the payoff. A good deal of fun had been made, by his Northern critics, of that "Southern home." It was not so funny any more. And if the politicians told him anything, it must be what the farmers he saw had been telling him too. Conditions in the old cotton country were about as bad as they could get. What he heard from these sources may have helped to bring on the bold indiscretion of the speech he was soon to make at Oglethorpe University.

"Bold, Persistent Experimentation"

🏵   🏵   🏵

There was really an additional member of our group after the first meetings. It was inevitable that the Albany newspapermen should discover us, and, although there was little enough drama in our doings, they mentioned our presence occasionally. James Kieran made hard weather of it for *The New York Times;* his line was that we were "preparing data," or "gathering material." But Ernest Lindley went a good deal beyond his correspondent's warrant; he wanted Roosevelt to become the leader he felt the country needed. And his talk with us—and with the Governor—was often about issues beyond his newspaper's demands.

I soon learned that no one knew Roosevelt better than Ernest. This was not only because he had looked up his history with sufficient care to write a biography, but because he had watched the Roosevelt governorship and had drawn conclusions about his skill as a politician and his intentions as a leader. Lindley was no soft-minded admirer. He thought highly of Roosevelt's skill and of his intentions, but obviously he was continually being disappointed. What was lacking, in his opinon, was the same apparent lack that had begun to bother me. He was quite certain he was reporting on a future President who ought to have all the help he could get, but also on a man who needed to escape from his political halter. Roosevelt ought to say more than he had been saying about what had to be done, whether or not the politicians approved.

When we went to Albany and stayed overnight, there were hours when Roosevelt was busy with other affairs, and then we would talk among ourselves, perhaps somewhere away from the Mansion. Ernest sometimes joined us, and we came to trust him. For one thing, he reported no more than that we were "discussing various matters with the Governor," and so we could speak freely, even about doubts and disappointments. His own remarks were those of a well-informed partisan. Substantially he agreed with us, but more seriously than any of us he deplored Roosevelt's caution. He thought we were not pushing hard enough. The situation called for harsher judgments, more decisive forecasts of action, and it was his contention that a harder line would turn out to be better political policy. When it became obvious that Roosevelt was satisfied with the accumulation of delegates and had concluded that only the usual deals with favorite sons would be necessary for a two-thirds majority, Ernest acidly remarked that nominations were made by politicians, but that elections were decided by the people, who were now in a mood for change. Democrats should not compete with Republicans to see who could be more conservative. If they had something to offer—and they had better have—they ought to say so. He said most of this in exchanges with Roosevelt himself.

This difference about the value of a mandate came up again and again. One school held that a new President was best off if he made no promises; the other held that only public commitments by the party's candidates would hold the party's legislators, once in office, to the agreed policies. With us, Roosevelt could cut these arguments short by reminding us that this was *his* business. I recall with sharp clarity his saying to us on one occasion, "You fellows have a lot of things you want to see done. Don't you realize that none of them *will* get done unless I am elected?" He went on to say that he was supposed to be the expert at that.

It may be that we held more closely thereafter to our limited terms of reference. Lindley felt no such compulsion. He never sat in on our evening sessions, but he saw even more of Roosevelt than we did during the course of most weeks, and his needling never stopped. Since he had chosen the champion of a cause he believed in, he felt justified in pushing for fulfillment.

After going about as far as we could with the causes and cure of depression, and after arguing at length the part of agriculture—admitted by all to have a causal relationship to the crisis—we came to a number of other issues that had to be got straight. Some of these were Adolf's areas more than mine. The banks were failing, and insurance companies were certain to be insolvent if they should be called on to liquidate. Home-owners with mortgages were defaulting, along with farmers, on their obligations, and fore-closures were becoming as frequent in cities and suburbs as in the country. Businesses were going under in alarming numbers; rail-roads were failing even to meet operating expenses and were sus-pending payments on their debts; heavy industries were producing at slower and slower rates; and day by day more workers were losing their jobs.

The depression had been going on since 1929, but its most frightening happenings were now reaching something of a climax. The strange, lost feeling nearly everyone had was becoming chronic; actually, distress was just reaching the centers of the economy. It was no longer something merely reported to financiers and upper executives; it had invaded their own safe enclaves.

Since the worth of capital was determined by what was produced, property values fell when production stopped. There seemed to be no bottom to the market for the stocks and bonds that represented businesses. Since holdings could not be disposed of except at a sac-rifice, most of their obligations could not be met. This was repeated over and over in business circles (with overtones of despair) that "values must be restored." All this could possibly mean, however, was that securities must be given higher value by the earnings of the enterprises they represented. This was, of course, the theme I kept repeating, that earnings would only resume when there were customers for goods and services. The millions of unemployed and their families were not buyers. It was a tight round of logic; I insisted that it could only be broken into by the one agency with the power to create and distribute income—the federal government.

Gradually I became discouraged because I could see that Roosevelt was trying to find another way out of the dilemma, and I knew what it was. Adolf detailed it for him, and it was, of course, something I could see well enough as being possible. This was an induced rise in prices to liquidate the heavy burden of debt, unfreeze assets, and thus allow a new start. We differed in that I thought the best way to do this was by creating employment. This did mean temporarily unbalanced budgets, but there was nothing sacred about an annual budget that I could see. If a balance was reached within a few years, that was satisfactory.

In this argument I used a simile I had found effective in a recent address at Teachers College of Columbia University. I had said that Hoover's activities (I had in mind mostly the Reconstruction Finance Corporation) were like putting fertilizer up in the branches of a tree. Government loans to financial institutions and industrial concerns were treetop operations; what was needed was to feed the roots. The workers, including the unemployed, were the ones to be cared for. And, Adolf added, the small enterprisers, who felt the worst of the squeeze because they were closest to the consumer who could not buy.

I believed there had to be unemployment relief on an enormous scale. Also the government would need to be what amounted to a residual employer, giving jobs as well as cash for living expenses. It could only be done federally, partly because states would not tackle it in a uniform way, but mostly because they had used up their funds, just as New York had. If loans were made to businesses, most of the yield would go to the liquidation of debts; after that the resumption of activity would depend on the initiative of enterprisers. This, I contended, was an indirect, slow, and uncertain process.

This led to an argument about financing. It was agreed that in the long run—I admitted that it might be quite a long run—tax yields from increased productivity would more than pay for the relief expenditures, but there was no escaping the first, the beginning cost. There was another objection I had to meet. If the government printed money and distributed it as relief or in payment for public works, that would result in inflation, which meant higher prices and discouraged consumers. This was a true dilemma, and one for which I had no very satisfactory answer. I simply said that workers would rather pay higher prices than have no incomes at all. It could be explained to them that the one was the condition of having the other. I could see that a political candidate wouldn't like to make such a complex explanation, but there was this: he could promise incomes at once, and the inflation would be delayed. If productivity increased fast enough, the rise of prices might not be so important.

Besides, I argued, there could be a revision of taxes, with higher rates for large incomes. The yield, of course, could not possibly be enough to pay for the needed relief. There was no escaping the conclusion that if anything really remedial was to be done, it must start with a massive enlargement of buying power furnished by federal funds, and with immediate price rises. This would have to be endured; it was another kind of taxation. Such a program might have the same eventual result as the devaluation of the dollar being advocated by Irving Fisher, who wanted a commodity dollar instead of a gold one, or the Cornellians, who (mistakenly, I thought) believed that the dollar could be given higher value by the manipulation of its gold content.

There was no reason why institutions guarding people's savings could not be protected by moratoria, or why mortgage foreclosures could not be checked until production was resumed. Easier bankruptcy proceedings would allow small enterprises to write off old debts and make a new start. Still, everything depended on that initial injection of purchasing power, and it had to be a massive one.

Roosevelt annoyed us—or at least Ray and myself, not Adolf so much—by persistently coming back to monetary devices taken by themselves. We were at heart believers in sound money. Greenbackism was part of the populist tradition that we hoped had been left behind. We knew well enough that it hadn't; its advocates were loud and growing louder; all the old schemes for cheapening money were apparently still alive, and there were many new ones. The Governor wanted to know about all of them. We shuddered and got him the information.

Actually, I had long since been converted to Fisher's commodity dollar—that is, one having the general backing of many other commodities besides gold. This would give it a more stable value from one time to another, since the value of gold fluctuated wildly. But a time of crisis such as the present was not the time to make such a drastic change.

Roosevelt had us in a difficult spot when we argued for increased purchasing power and at the same time opposed what we chose to call greenbacks. Where was the government to get the dollars it paid out for public employment or relief? Either it must have increased income or it must simply print the currency it distributed. It was all very well to argue that increased productivity would in time yield the income. But that would not be until the funds had been provided that would eventually increase the national product. Temporarily, we were advocating an issue of greenbacks—weren't we?

Of course we were. When I spoke of higher income taxes, especially on the large incomes, I knew how small the increased revenue would be. No, there was no way out of it. There must simply be a distribution of printed money. But, we insisted, it would be temporary.

We were not monetary theorists, and we said so repeatedly. Ray did round up and escort to Albany some of those whose field it was; they were not brought so often during the spring as later when we got down to the issues judged best to be met in speeches; still, we could not really avoid the issue. It became more acute after Irving Fisher, who now had begun to talk about "reflation," made his way uninvited to Albany and spent some time with Roosevelt. Fisher had become something of a fanatic, and Roosevelt always enjoyed talking to fanatics. The impression this visit made was one we knew would have consequences. In fact, we had to deal with it at once, since Roosevelt would not let it alone.

It was more and more obvious, he insisted, that a total effort of some sort to lift values would have to be undertaken. There was no other way to liquefy assets, to get rid of debts, and generally to activate enterprise. I came back to asking whether he did not realize that this meant raised prices for potential consumers before they had been made actual consumers by having incomes to spend. My fear was that dependence on a program of this sort could postpone any extensive effort to provide public works or relief benefits. Recovery would at least be delayed, and this could no longer be afforded. As long as relief was regarded as a philanthrophy—a dole, as the Republicans preferred to call it—it would never be the boost needed for recovery.

Roosevelt was inclined to argue that raising prices would draw wages up to their new levels, and that the same rule would hold about relief: there would be an irresistible demand for increases. I objected that any such wage increases would be gained only by costly strikes and industrial disturbances. As for relief, the unemployed had no leverage. Besides, I reminded him, any gross general changes would have different results in particular industries that could not be foreseen. This was economists' language for saying that prices would respond to pressure in different degrees. Some would not respond at all; others would be too responsive. But the resulting situation might be no better than it was now. Exchange among economic groups would be constantly disrupted. Those with more advantages would tend to stifle those with fewer or none.

This brought us, on several occasions, to further discussions of planning for fair and stable exchange, a topic much on the minds of some thoughtful industrialists and bankers—among them Gerard Swope of General Electric, Henry I. Harriman, president of the United States Chamber of Commerce, and Fred I. Kent, the banker. There was, in fact, such an array of respectable support that the possibilities could be discussed with some feeling of approval in high places. The detractors of that sort of planning called it price-fixing, and they had a point; but it was price-fixing in the public interest. At the same time it was thoroughly inconsistent with orthodox progressivism, which held that fixing prices should be forbidden as conspiratorial. Prices were supposed to be fixed in the competition among sellers and buyers. If the planning was approached by way of Swope's ideas or, as I reminded Roosevelt, those he himself had put forward when he was arguing for a Construction Council, it was a serious departure from the principles of Brandeis and his supporters. They could be expected to object and to rally the old Wilsonian forces.

Roosevelt was at least willing to talk about an integrated system even if it did involve accepting a holistic conception of the economy. Its devices would be a complete reversal of antitrust policies. I had no desire to apologize for this, since the gain I could point to would be that we should have an organism rather than chaos. In such a scheme, progress based on increases in productivity might be encouraged, and the ups and downs of the business cycle might be smoothed out. The scheme had attractions, and I enlarged on them whenever I got the chance. Roosevelt joined in the argument readily. It was evident, however, that he would make up his mind about the feasibility of an integrated system after considering many other views than ours.

"Brandeis again!" Ray said when we talked about the political implications.

When Roosevelt left to go to Warm Springs on his annual visit, we had quite recently been discussing this matter, and we hoped he would be giving it consideration in his Southern retreat. This journey of his was represented as routine, an annual spring event, but it happened to be convenient as well. He had gathered as many delegates as could be harvested, and nothing was to be gained by further public appearances. The "forgotten man" and the "concert of interests" speeches had gone some way toward presenting the picture of an ardent progressive who, when he got around to it, would offer genuine alternatives to Republicanism. And especially his consorting with Floyd Olson, the Farmer-Labor Governor, when he visited Minnesota, had seemed to show the sort of friends he preferred.

It remained now to re-emphasize his affiliations. Although the Northern newspapers made fun of his "Southern home," the picture of himself as a resident rather than just a visitor was fairly credible. It was an old political idea, that of marrying the South to the West when the East could not be relied on, but in practice it had not often proved to be feasible. Bryan had not quite succeeded, Wilson hardly at all, and Smith had failed miserably. But Roosevelt meant to make the marriage; his courtship had begun long ago.

The entourage of newsmen who went with him was large, since he was now the probable candidate and, it appeared more and more likely, the probable President. Nomination was the immediate object of his strategy, and of course this was well understood by all politicians. He had done very well in the West, although there was worry about California and Texas. He could not count on Hearst, and so not on McAdoo or Garner. But McAdoo was not a likely nominee, and neither was Garner, really, although Hearst and Rayburn might think so. None of them would accept Smith. They might take Baker, however, and more and more he seemed the most probable candidate if the stop-Roosevelt movement should succeed.

The South had done well by Roosevelt; most of the states—except Texas and Virginia—had instructed for him or were going his way. It was a time to stop talking and trust to the weight of his already gained majority. He would supplement this by making news. The reporters would help. They would have picturesque material in the South, and when that was exhausted they would speculate. It should suffice. Of course what had attracted the West would have to be modified for conservative Southern tastes; that, however, should not be difficult. His daily activities would make an unexceptionable picture.

Take, for example, what we read of his activities in *The New York Times* of May 15, when a Kieran dispatch was published. It appeared far back in *The New York Times,* because Hoover was getting headlines with his economy drive, and much attention was being paid to Wagner's Senate proposals for relief. Roosevelt could not yet command the front page; he was given considerable space, but not in prominent places. Kieran's account was of a typical day.

His current visitor of news-note was Ike B. Dunlap of Kansas City, who had to report a whispering campaign running across the prairies to the effect that the Governor had made the trip to Warm Springs so that, in seclusion, he could "recover from a serious sickness." He had been taken there on a stretcher, it was said, and his situation was desperate. Dunlap advised him, Kieran said, to "enter into some activity to combat these stories."

Kieran reported, however, that Roosevelt laughed this off. (The disability stories, so frequent in one form or another, might have been serious if he had not developed a tested way to counter them. When they threatened to become a problem, he set out on new and strenuous travels and showed himself conspicuously, or he saw to it that some physical activity was reported.)

Certainly if Dunlap stayed with him through that particular day, not to mention those before or after, he must have been able to testify that the Roosevelt vigor was unimpaired. The day had begun with several morning hours spent in the pool, where he played such games as water polo with the patients and therapists. His team was as often beaten as victorious, but he urged it on to more competitive efforts. The hilarity and good-natured recrimination drew a crowd of cheering visitors. There were photographs, plenty of them, to show the action.

After such a start, he conferred with politicians coming from all parts of the South (and the West too, evidently), and while they were with him he managed to keep two secretaries busy taking his rapidly dictated answers to the mail. Later he

> . . . drove to the new airport where he was greeted by several thousand admirers who had gathered from miles around. . . . Former Judge J. Kendall Terrell and Col. Nathan Culpeper of Greenville paid tribute . . . and hailed him as the next President. The Executive, seated in his little car while the farm folk pressed close, spoke informally and reviewed local history to emphasize the change in modern life as illustrated by the airport. . . .

That was far from all. During the afternoon he tooled about the countryside he knew so well. Perhaps he visited his farm and had a talk with the man who ran it for him. Otis, the farmer, was quite conscious of his expected role and played up to the reporters. He discoursed about crops and livestock as long as they would listen. Very often Roosevelt drove into farmers' yards and called them out, with their wives and children, for a visit with reporters gathered round. On occasion he drove across the wide valley to "the cove," famous locally for its illicit peach brandy, the western Georgian brand of moonshine. He had been known for years to the folks there. With his introduction, his newspaper friends could return with a jar of the local product—something precious in bone-dry Meriwether County.

All this was colorful copy, but there was more. He got back to the Springs in time for tea, and after that he had more talks with a new accumulation of visitors. So it went into the evening, when there was a picnic supper—he was fond of these—with Brunswick stew and barbecued pork. Those outdoor gatherings might be at the home of Frank Allcorn, the mayor of Warm Springs, or at the Callaway place. Occasionally he had his barbecue with a gathering of church people from the country around Pine Mountain, or perhaps with a group of local politicians. For most of every day he was thus accessible; the reporters and picture-takers were always about, and every day he made stories they could use. But the stories had nothing to do with political issues.

Ernest Lindley wrote as voluminously about the ordinary Warm Springs activities as did the rest of the correspondents, but he was annoyed by what he regarded as shrinking from principle, and in several talks with Roosevelt he came close to implying that it was dishonest. He finally said so much about it that Roosevelt, exasperated, and perhaps ashamed of his own caution, asked what kind of speech Lindley would make if he had the same problem. There was an occasion coming up on May 22, when an address was scheduled at Oglethorpe University in Atlanta. If Lindley thought the speeches could be so much better than those that had been made, he might prove the point by writing one.

So it was Lindley who drafted the Oglethorpe script. He had some help from other newsmen, but that was only criticism; he was the real author. Roosevelt read the draft, and his shame overcame his political judgment. To show that he did have the courage of those convictions Lindley knew he had been concealing—and also perhaps for another reason connected with Hoover—he made up his mind to use the speech as written. For him it was the deliberate trial of the educational effort he knew to be needed. He faced forward.

The pronouncement did indeed come through clear and strong. It was almost a manifesto. It said that present policies had failed and must be replaced by wholly new ones. It went further, and here there was a hint of indignation:

> Such controlling and directive forces as have been developed in recent years reside to a dangerous degree in groups having interests which do not coincide with the interests of the nation as a whole. . . . Many of those whose primary solicitude is confined to the welfare of what they call capital have failed to read the lessons of the past few years and have been moved . . . by a blind determination to preserve their special stakes. . . .

The objective, Roosevelt said, was simple enough; it was well within the inventive capacity of man to ensure that all who were able and willing to work should receive at least the necessities of life. "In such a system," he said, "the reward of a day's work will have to be greater; and the reward to capital, especially capital which is speculative, will have to be less." Attaining this objective would not be easy, largely because "too many so-called leaders . . . fail to recognize the vital necessity of planning." If the nation could be united in this planning, then true leadership could "unite thought behind definite methods."

These sentences seemed startling enough, but it was the following ones that frightened Louis Howe almost to death, caused the professionals to rear back and look more closely at this front-

runner, and brought messages of support from those progressives
who were laboring hardest to make things better:

> The country needs, and, unless I mistake its temper, the country
> demands, bold, persistent experimentation. It is common sense
> to take a method and try it: if it fails, admit it frankly and try
> another. But, above all, try something. The millions who are in
> want will not stand by silently forever while the things to satisfy
> their needs are within easy reach. . . .

What the devil was he trying to do? Louis demanded over the
phone. Didn't he know that such talk would scare away all those
voters already suspicious of his radical tendencies? And didn't he
realize that it would not get him a single vote he did not already
have?

Roosevelt received the messages of support with apparent pleasure. It has to be recorded, however, that until the convention was
safely past and he was the chosen candidate, he said nothing more
of this sort. It may be that he had not intended to do so in any
case. Perhaps it was not Louis' warning that closed his mouth. *The
New York Times,* leading the press, ignored the passage Louis
found so politically objectionable and centered on something quite
different. Roosevelt may have known that this would happen.

CHAPTER XI

Roosevelt and Hoover

🏵 🏵 🏵

Although Eleanor did not go to Warm Springs, she had accompanied her husband on part of the southward journey. One feature of it was an encounter, the first in many years, between Roosevelt and Hoover. Eleanor told me about it after her return, in what for her was an unusual blaze of indignation.

The meeting between the rivals was a sequel to the annual governors' conference, which had opened in Richmond on April 25. Roosevelt spent several days at the conference, and he made a speech there. It was not an occasion for political pronouncements, yet anything he might say would be listened to intently. The speech, when it was ready, seemed unnecessarily innocuous, another sign that somewhere beyond our competence there had been a muffling influence. This might be attributed to Louis' growing assurance; it was about this time that he said of the Democrats that they could win this one with a Chinaman. If so, it remained only to make no mistakes, and the way to make no mistakes was to say nothing that would *lose* a vote. The Richmond speech was to be kept strictly within the bounds of a pious paean to Washington, the first president.

The tone of the Oglethorpe address a month later may have owed something to an incident following the meetings in Richmond. The Governors were invited to a White House dinner. What happened there may have been the result, or partly the result, in turn, of a passage in Roosevelt's carefully defused eulogy of Washington. He was saying how Washington had met his problems by patient and informed planning, and, after remarking that the first President had been "liberal for the time and circumstances," he went on to a comment that could well have meaning for a business community anxiously waiting for clearer signs than had yet been given of what he had in mind to do if he became President himself.

> Speculation, for example, was prevalent during his career. Some of this was unavoidable in a period of expansion in a virgin and immature country, but its effect . . . he deeply deplored. Writing to Jefferson, in 1788, he said, "I perfectly agree with you that an extensive speculation, a spirit of gambling, or the introduction of anything which will divert our attention from agriculture must be extremely prejudicial, if not ruinous to us." Some of my fellow governors have given voice to this same thought during these past three days.

This was not quite all. Washington, he said, had repeatedly emphasized the responsibility of government for the encouragement of agriculture, and he quoted a passage from a message in 1796 in praise of farming as a vocation:

> In proportion as nations advance in population and other circumstances of maturity, this truth becomes more apparent, and renders the cultivation of the soil more and more an object of public patronage.*

Then came the comment that might have given Hoover a preview of Roosevelt's intention to make an issue of something that Hoover must by now have known was a serious liability to himself. As President he had been hostile to all suggestions for farm relief; he had vetoed favorite farm-bloc bills; and even further back, he was known to have advised Coolidge's vetoes of similar legislation. What Roosevelt said, with a grin, was: "What a pity that recent national leadership . . . has so little heeded that precept."

* *Public Papers of Franklin D. Roosevelt,* edited by Samuel Rosenman, 1932, Vol. I, p. 592.

When the Governors were received at the White House, Hoover and Roosevelt, the protagonists who had now for two years been measuring each other, met for the first time since the Wilson administration. They had been friendly then, and the younger man had greatly admired the famous administrator of international relief. Much had changed with the years; still, how could they come easily to the level of equal political competition? It was hard for the older man to believe that the junior official of war days had become so formidable, and hard for the younger to feel comfortable in challenging a statesman so experienced and successful. The meeting was thus charged with emotions that neither could have defined, though they were powerfully present.

The gentlemen and their wives descended from the procession of limousines, were lined up, standing, in the East Room by rather officious aides in glittering uniforms, and then were told that the President would arrive shortly. They stood there silently—some accounts said for a full hour, none said for less than half an hour. It did not much matter; any time beyond a few minutes was difficult enough for a matronly woman in full regalia or for a man of a Governor's usual years, and it would have caused comment even if Roosevelt had not been one of the company. But he was, and for a big man who was kept erect on wasted pipestem legs only by the stiffening furnished by steel braces from hip to ankle, it was agonizing.

He was given no concession, and under the monitory eye of the aides he kept himself erect. Eleanor, beside him, knew what he was enduring and was so enraged she could hardly be decent through the dinner. When Hoover finally appeared, he shook hands down the line and led the way to the state dining room, where he presided gloomily and withdrew after a hardly decent interval. He had work to do, he said, leaving the aides to attend his departing guests.

Later Eleanor was to speak of the incident in her *Autobiography.* It is my own deduction—perhaps unwarranted—that Hoover was showing his rising rival that he was still President and meant to remain President. It is also my guess that the startling passages in the Oglethorpe speech may have been retained and even, as Lindley said, made more emphatic as they were spoken because of Roosevelt's resentment—and, I would add, because he was able at last to forget his antagonist's prestige. Those are only conjectures, but no one has argued me out of them.

All we knew of Roosevelt's activities in Warm Springs was what we read in the papers, and that was not very revealing. We had been left with certain assignments, but since the journeys to Albany were suspended, we had time to review the past weeks. True, we were coming to the end of the college year and our students had to have extra attention, but still there was a lessening of excitement and a little leisure.

Roosevelt's going away was a sign in itself. He evidently judged that as much had been done as was useful, and that more exposure might have an adverse effect. Ray pointed out that the indication was one of confidence. I had thought Roosevelt certain enough before, but I continued to be instructed in the problems still remaining. The half-dozen other contenders for the nomination, having belatedly become convinced that a Democratic victory was in the making, were now in full pursuit. Roosevelt's majority was still not invulnerable to attrition, and the pundits let us know that several conspiracies were being hatched. The Smithites especially were full of threats and thunder. Governor Ely of Massachusetts, Mayor Hague of Jersey City, Boss Kelly of Chicago, and other stalwarts were sounding off, and Smith himself seemed to peer out of the tiger's lair with sinister intentions.

Hoover was still comatose. It was apparent that he considered himself safe as chief of the Republicans. Their permanent majority and the enormous bureaucracy built up during years in office were sufficient safeguards. Democrats in the federal executive establishment were as scarce as Republicans in New York City. The bureaucrats would all work frantically to keep themselves in office. Besides, Hoover was busy and heavily burdened; the Congress was still in session and still harassing him with proposals he could not accept. Most of these were devised by the troublesome progressives, but the Democrats were active too; even Speaker Garner was emerging occasionally with statements or suggestions slyly devised for him by Charles Michelson, the publicity man for the holdover Democratic National Committee. There were so many proposals, and many of them were so plausible, that elaborate briefs in rebuttal had to be drafted.

The role Hoover found himself cast in was that of defender of the faith. He had by now erected a bulwark of Americanism, and he rose from behind it periodically to let off a volley at the threatening radicals. There was an American way, rooted in tradition, firm in moral understanding, and absolutely necessary to the continuance of the social as well as the economic system. Independence, liberty, initiative, individualism: these were the words of faith. He used them often.

He spoke not as one in panic but as one who would remind Americans of their faith. He knew well enough that there was disorder abroad and that the daily news was all bad; his intelligence was excellent and he had capable assistants; but he was certain also that weakening the system by concessions to clamor would only make matters worse. The fort had to be defended until the results of foreign failures could be liquidated and businessmen's courage rallied to undertake the ventures that would start recovery.

I had been studying Hoover closely for some two years now, and his stubborn refusal to compromise did not really surprise me. It was easy to see from New York what was hidden from him in Washington—that a trap was inexorably closing. The Quaker moralist was failing to bend what was about to be broken.

So valiant a defense might have commanded sympathy if the issues had not been so vital. Not within my recollection, and not within that of anyone I knew, had a President of the United States been vilified so often and so unrestrainedly. The stories going around, invented by detractors, were incredibly libelous. No one seemed to think anything of the infusion into them of obscenities and scatological allusions. When a certain sort of loud laughter was heard in any small gathering of men, it was almost surely caused by a new invention at Hoover's expense.

Obviously he did not know how isolated he had become. The White House was fenced off from the people. There were no news conferences and so no personal reports of the President's appearance or reactions. No one saw him but his confidants, and evidently he talked to them, not they to him. He knew a great deal about the depression, but he knew it from studying statistics, not from communication with those who were suffering its effects.

The occasional pictures of Hoover were those of a man exhausted by struggle, maddened by the recalcitrance of events, and embittered by the ingratitude of those he sought to protect. He had fattened; he never smiled; his double-breasted blue serge suits seemed to encase him in a sort of armor, and since he had never given up his high, starched collars, the armor went up to his chin.

He seemed to us less and less a formidable opponent. He had lost touch; he was full of explanations; and even when he offered reasonable proposals, people hardly listened or listened only in order to jeer. It was a terrible thing to see the presidency brought so low, and obviously the sooner the present situation ended the better. The politicians—those not engaged in trying to stop his nomination—were beginning to tell Roosevelt with the utmost confidence that it was clearly a Democratic year. The inference was that he had better be a good Democrat if he wanted to profit from the turn of events.

Those of us left in the North heard more and more of this sort of thing. Hoover was going; Roosevelt was coming. We guessed that this was why Roosevelt had gone off to Warm Springs and why the reports from there were chiefly the folksy build-up that resulted from his daily contacts with his newspaper entourage. To say that we were surprised when he broke out of this silence with the Oglethorpe speech is to understate the situation. We were, in fact, amazed. My own feelings verged on elation—that is, until I studied the speech carefully.

"Planning" and "experimentation" were words I had been

conditioned to suppose no candidate would mention in public. We had used them in private, but if Roosevelt had decided they were fit to include in a speech, he must think we had been too cautious about the rabid vigilance of the conservatives. Was that the explanation? Or had he decided to break out into new territory, to lead instead of being led?

When he used the words in conjunction with paragraphs about the redistribution of incomes—labor to get more and capital to get less—he did appear to be advancing into new country. He used the words so loosely, however, that it was hard to determine exactly what he meant; he seemed to be saying that we were to plan by laying out objectives and that we were to experiment with methods. In reality there was no need to *plan* objectives; we needed only to decide what they were. Where the planning was needed was where it seemed to be ruled out—in the methods. So, on reflection, I was less happy with the Oglethorpe speech than I had been at first. It was not much of an advance after all.

If Roosevelt had expected attention for the paragraphs with the forbidden words, he was mistaken. The headlines were taken by the suggestion that the national income would have to be redistributed; only subheads mentioned the advocacy of experimentation and planning. The whole speech was taken to be an attack on "selfish and opportunist" groups, and these were the bankers. It was regarded as a radical pronouncement, but the radicalism played up in the newspapers was really nothing but a good old-fashioned populist attack on Wall Street. Our surprise was a double one: that Roosevelt should thus have broken out and that, when he did, no one should notice what was most significant.

After the personal confrontation between Roosevelt and Hoover that followed the Governors' conference, there was a confrontation in the newspapers that resulted from the Oglethorpe speech. It was reported on a Monday, and that same day the papers carried a carefully prepared statement by Hoover in which he offered a program for ending the depression. Their way of handling the two pronouncements reminded me of the contrast they had drawn a month earlier between Smith and Roosevelt. Smith had spoken, it was said, like a forthright leader. His warning to Roosevelt was thoroughly justified, and his offer to take off his coat and fight the party's divisive demagogues was an act of courage. In the new confrontation, Hoover was deemed to be victorious; there would be editorial comment to that effect. Meanwhile Hoover's statement was awarded the right-hand column in *The New York Times,* while Roosevelt's speech received the less advantageous column to the left.

Hoover said roundly that we could not "surrender ourselves into prosperity; the budget must balance"; and, he went on, "only self-liquidating projects can be justified." He then proceeded to enumerate, very precisely, twelve elements of a program for recovery.

It was very late for him to offer such a statement; this was 1932, and the crisis had begun in 1929. Perhaps it was too late. Certainly the statement came after long delay in acknowledging the seriousness of the situation, after his trying ineffectual palliative measures, and, when these had failed, after another long wait for deflation to work its magic. This history was what had caused the loss of confidence in Hoover that was now so general. As far back as 1930, it had been evidenced by the loss of so many congressional seats that Democrats had come into control of the House and lacked only one vote of overtaking the Republicans in the Senate. The progressives, nominally members of both parties, who actually held the initiative in the Congress and were making Hoover's life so miserable, had continued to make proposals, all of them well publicized. Again and again they denounced the administration's inaction.

In 1932 Hoover's standing with the public seemed much worse by contrast with the former refulgence of his reputation. He had the misfortune to embody all that was meant when the "New Era" was spoken of with such harsh irony. He had been the strong and honest man of the Harding and Coolidge administrations. He had represented the thrust of American business toward new levels of productivity. And he had been swept impressively into office in his contest with Smith; his majority had been one of the largest in electoral history. The nation was going ahead; profits were enormous; speculation in the securities representing progress was a universal pastime. Everyone believed Hoover when he said the time was not far off when poverty would be banished and there would be "a chicken in every pot."

If so short a time later he was the target for every sort of imprecation, he had only himself to blame. His downfall seemed especially appropriate to those of us in the academic profession. During his time as Secretary of Commerce he had sponsored the most extensive explorations ever made of the business cycle, and the reports of his commission had made specific recommendations for action to be taken in such emergencies as had now occurred; but he had failed to follow the recommendations, except for a very few that he had followed in a timid and ineffective fashion. He had trifled and temporized, and his remedial efforts had been hopelessly out of scale with the emergency.

This reluctance obviously resulted from an unjustified confidence in the business system. He should have known, we felt, that enterprisers would behave as suited their own interests and not those of the economy. He had urged them to expand, to take risks, when doing so was unprofitable and might be disastrous. He had begged them to hire more workers when the markets for their goods were failing. And finally, with the wreckage already complete, he had set up committees to gather funds and dispense charity. He was still trying to reduce expenditures and balance the federal budget. It was a deflationary policy, and there was no excuse for it except the plea for "confidence"—the same plea that Roosevelt was hearing from all his businessman friends. Hoover was too sophisticated to be taken in by it; his compliance added to an annoyance with him that sometimes rose to anger in the intellectual community.

Still, we too continued to hear arguments of the same sort, sometimes coming from the same individuals. They were bound to impress the politicians, who always listen to moneyed men, and we sometimes wondered whether the campaign might not become a contest to see which side could most successfully reassure the wealthy. It would be such a contest if Roosevelt followed the advice he was getting from many of the people he talked to. We talked to them too, and the assurance they displayed was appalling. They hadn't the slightest doubt that they were right or the slightest reason for believing so.

Now, in 1932, as Hoover faced a re-election campaign, economic activity was diminishing, and because of this, unemployment was growing. Or, to put it the other way around, the increasing number of unemployed was dragging industry to a stop; the products of the factories were not finding consumers. Obviously it now required a massive effort to stop the downward spiral. It was not enough to help businesses in trouble by offering them loans; they would have no means of repayment since they were not really doing much business. The same was true of banks with frozen assets. The assets needed to be given value by earnings, not further congealed by the RFC when it accepted them as collateral for loans.

With professional interest we examined Hoover's new offering, set next to a report of the Oglethorpe speech on the front page of *The New York Times*. The occasion for Hoover's statement was a curious one. He was replying to the president of the Society of Civil Engineers, who had urged his support for a bond issue to pay for extensive public works. This was salt in an already open wound; the progressives in the Congress were offering bills providing for just such a remedy, and a Democratic group had made a similar proposal. Its sponsors were Senators Robinson, Bulkley, Wagner, Pittman, and Walsh, and they were party insiders.

The vice of bond issues, in Hoover's view, was that they really meant an "extraordinary budget" when he was trying his best to reduce the ordinary one. He was willing to make loans (through the Reconstruction Finance Corporation) because they were supposed to be returned. His proposals for public works had a similar bias. He would make loans to the states for this purpose, but he opposed grants. Grants would encourage the giving of relief, and he felt that men should work for their incomes. Also, the work they were given should be on projects that produced income, so that the loans could be paid back to the Treasury. Similarly with relief: he would not allow the federal government to accept responsibility for individuals. The declaration about this was made without equivocation. He wanted business, not government, to expand; he wanted employment to be in legitimately productive enterprises. There must be no "made" work.

So Roosevelt's expression of willingness to experiment found itself on the same front pages as Hoover's statement of fixed principle. We knew it was not quite the confrontation assumed by *The New York Times,* but the contrast seemed clear enough. Next day, a column-long editorial made the moral explicit:

> By a coincidence, not too fortunate for Governor Roosevelt, his speech at Atlanta was published yesterday in the same newspapers which carried President Hoover's letter . . . outlining his plans for . . . recovery. The contrast between the two leaps to the eye of every reader. Mr. Hoover is precise, concrete, positive. Governor Roosevelt is indefinite, abstract, irresolute. . . .
>
> He simply referred to the fact that many men . . . have suggested various remedies. Whether they are wise or not, whether they will be effective or not, he did not undertake to decide. His one firm conclusion was "above all try something." But something unspecified is not better than nothing. There are plenty of bustling and impatient men in our public life who agree with the Governor that "something must be done," but they will tell you exactly what it is. We must print a lot of fiat money. We must give up the hopeless gold standard. We must borrow all the money we need without regard to the effect on government credit. It is not to be supposed that Governor Roosevelt would agree to any of the proposals. But when he merely falls back and begs people to "try something," he encourages every man with a pet nostrum or private panacea. . . . As a matter of experience, the man most to be avoided in a time of crisis is one who goes about wringing his hands and demanding that something be done without explaining or knowing what can or ought to be done. . . .

The editorialist was not prepared to accept the Governor as a presidential candidate. This aligned him with the Tammany chiefs, who were not prepared to accept the Governor either, but the editorialist would rather stand with Tammany than support a hazy politician who would not know his own mind until it was made up for him by the demands of politicians.

CHAPTER XII

Echoes of Oglethorpe

❦ ❦ ❦

Even if we were not participants in the important proceedings of the moment—that is, the political ones—we could learn from them. To tell the truth, my skepticism as I watched them in April and May was not much quieted. Ray seemed to be less worried, but I was still wondering whether the critics were justified in the opinion that Roosevelt was apt to agree with those who happened to impress him momentarily, but was actually quite without hard convictions on pressing issues. Variations of this opinion were numerous, and they showed a tendency to spread rather than dissipate.

The other possibility was that he had inner convictions but was waiting for the assignment to speak out; after all, he was not yet even a nominee. If we were to believe that this was more than a possibility, we should have to rely on evidence nobody else seemed to see. Roosevelt had shown no concern about the economy except to furnish such relief as he could because he felt sorry for people who were in trouble. His governmental reforms did not go beyond those already begun by Smith. He had made no comments about national policy of any account, and he had withdrawn from support of the League of Nations. Most of our acquaintances had concluded that there really was nothing much to indicate resolution.

In our judgment, his critics had missed what we saw in our discussions with him. If the policies we had been thinking about were ones he approved, if they were ones he meant to see through, we could help to strengthen them. At least we could gather and organize the supports available in the academic world. If he was intending to find out what was necessary to recovery and t, a better future, why should we hold back?

What our friends said was that he was merely intending to complete his career and would allow himself to be turned in whatever direction would further it. If that was so, we ought to know it by now; actually, we did not believe it. Ray, who had been working with him for some time, was quite far along in accepting Roosevelt. I was having more difficulty and so, I believe, was Adolf, but both of us were at least doing what we could on the chance that our judgment would be justified.

If I cite Walter Lippmann in this connection, it is because of his extraordinary prestige with those of us who were a few years behind him. He was still insisting, as he had done for some time, that Roosevelt had no real concern for the country. He was a dabbler; he had been so at Harvard where Lippmann recalled him; he had been so as a lawyer and as a politician. His eagerness to please ought not to be taken as evidence of real concern about anything, because he had none. He had a deceiving trait of seeming to agree with those he talked with, and that led to much confusion. It was dangerous, and Lippmann—along with others, many others—was warning the country against accepting his bid for preferment. Roosevelt was weak; he would be managed by others, and not even consistently managed, because he would always look for the means to stay in power and would always sacrifice ends to those means.

Lippmann had seen as early as anyone the possibility that Roosevelt would be the Democratic nominee. He simply could not believe that the frivolous young man of Cambridge and the agent of the admirals in Wilson's Washington could have sufficient weight to be a major party's presidential candidate. Back in January, he had written the first of a series of articles showing alarm about the probable choice of the Democrats. In view of the less favorable opinions to be expressed by *The New York Times* in the course of that spring, it is interesting that he was then able to cite that respectable paper as a Roosevelt supporter—but, he believed, a confused and mistaken one.

It was plain, he said, that some of the Governor's partisans—along with *The Times*—were going to feel let down. Trying to be different things to different men could not possibly be kept up on such a scale as Roosevelt attempted. The band wagon was now moving in two precisely opposite directions. *The Times* was assuring its readers that "no upsetting plans, no Socialist proposals, however mild and winning in form," could appeal to Roosevelt. But Roosevelt was, at the same time, the highly preferred candidate of Senator Wheeler of Montana and other descendants of the populists who would like to cure the depression by debasing the currency. Roosevelt was, "without any doubt whatever," making a studied attempt to straddle the whole country. This was a strategy familiar enough in American politics. The question was whether his left-wing or his right-wing supporters were the more deceived. About this, no one could say; the Governor was

> . . . an impressionable person without a firm grasp of public affairs and without any very strong convictions . . . an amiable man with many philanthropic impulses, but not the dangerous enemy of anything. . . . The notion, which seems to prevail in the West and the South, that Wall Street fears him, is preposterous. . . . Wall Street does not like his vagueness and the uncertainty as to what he does think, but if any Western Progressive thinks that the Governor has challenged directly or indirectly the wealth concentrated in New York City, he is mightily mistaken.

It seemed to us that this Lippmann appraisal had already been shown to be superficial. The "forgotten man" speech had gone some way to persuade people of our sort that there were intentions he had as yet had no occasion to reveal. Conservatives suspected that Roosevelt was becoming or would become radical. They had not exactly taken fright, but they were alerted, sniffing the political air. In late spring, the hope that Roosevelt might declare for policies that would reassure businessmen was certainly evaporating. It was no longer certain that he was "sound."

Lippmann continued to feel that he knew the man he was writing about. He had said of him at the end of that column in January:

> Franklin D. Roosevelt is no crusader. He is no tribune of the people. He is no enemy of entrenched privilege. He is a pleasant man who, without any important qualifications for the office, would very much like to be President.*

In May, Lippmann continued to write in this strain. Still, he was a professional political observer, and he spoke with some admiration of the strategic maneuver that seemed about to succeed. What Roosevelt had done, he said, was to assume that he could count on Smith's following in the Northern cities and so feel free to concentrate on developing his own strength in the areas where Smith had been rejected in 1928. This latter part of his plan, at least, had worked. He had against him none of the prejudices that Smith had had to contend with, and he had benefited from a supposed opposition originating among the international bankers and the power trust. Also, he had managed, in spite of having a working alliance with Tammany, to dissociate himself from Tammany's operations.

But if this seemed to be praise for political acumen, the words Lippmann used betrayed continuing repugnance for a man who would resort to such means for political success:

> Finally, he has adopted enough of the key phrases of the Progressives, without committing himself to their programs, to achieve the reputation of being a great reformer. He has adopted a sufficiently vague and woolly attitude on the tariff to sound like an advocate of freer trade without giving any protectionist cause for concern. He has talked about the debts in an obviously popular way, and, in his anxiety to dissociate himself from the League, he has landed himself in a position of such

* Reprinted in *Interpretations,* 1931–32, edited by Allan Nevins (New York, 1932).

complete isolation that his position is quite indistinguishable
from that of W. R. Hearst.

Could it be that the man with whom we discussed contemporary
issues throughout long evenings really changed his mind every time
he heard a new opinion? Was it true that he had reached no conclusions about any issue of importance? I looked up some of his
speeches on public power in the 1930 campaign. This had been the
main issue then. What he had said was tough and clear. He believed in public ownership—as much of it, at least, as would be an
adequate yardstick. About his stand on that issue, no one could
have the slightest doubt. Why then did critics go on saying that he
was indecisive? Ambivalence would be bad enough, but Lippmann
was now claiming more. He was saying that there was deceit in the
Roosevelt scheme and that he was fooling people, deliberately misleading them.

After thinking it over, we could see a possible explanation, and
it might well be sufficient. The problems we had been discussing
were new to Roosevelt, as in fact they were to everyone, and not
only new but of an overwhelming magnitude. There had been hard
times before, but the present paralysis was so nearly total as to indicate systemic failure, something never seriously considered to
be a governmental responsibility. Politicians knew nothing about
such occurrences. But it was only too plain that this time depression was not going to cure itself, as it always had before. Nor were
those individuals and organizations most deeply involved going to
cure it. Volcanic pressures had disclosed weaknesses that, in boom
times, had been concealed. There were also hints of malpractice,
and punishment was due, but neither reform nor punishment could
conceivably reactivate an economy so far gone in sickness. What,
after all, would the restoration of competition accomplish? It was
not only not enough; it was even irrelevant. And certainly we had
discussed, and were still discussing, alternatives.

Lippmann was mistaken when he said that the financial manipu-
lators need not fear Roosevelt. Those of us who had argued with
him were more afraid that he would turn to drastic reform and
punishment than that he would be soft on speculators and finan-

ciers. We were afraid that recovery might not come first in his mind. Reform was a political mirage, tempting but deceptive. Politicians, we noted, had need of enemies to attack, preferably those with few votes and few defenders. The depression had exposed whole nests of these in the financial centers. Going after them would yield a rich dividend in votes. The trouble with such an attack was its irrelevance to the central problem of recovery. That would require a reorganization of established relationships; it would require government leadership and discipline; and it would require the earnest co-operation of active producers throughout the economy. We needed a new price structure; we needed new monetary mechanisms; we needed new incentives for producers and new protections for consumers. Above all, we needed to define fairness and balance and to devise means for their maintenance. Those were perhaps reforms, but they were not the sort politicians with progressive leanings responded to with enthusiasm—or were expecting from Roosevelt.

We had hoped that he would begin the education of the electorate in these matters as soon as possible, but we had not expected the Oglethorpe speech. Nor had either his supporters or his enemies. It was a shocker. To judge from the comments, no one could imagine what he had in mind. But we thought we knew.

Those we regarded as like-minded—not the conservative editorialists and not the personal acquaintances who had firmly set him down as an incompetent but ambitious politician, but serious commentators in *The New Republic* and *The Nation*—agreed with the Lippmann analysis. As a *New Republic* associate I tried to say something of what I felt to my colleagues there, but they were skeptical. As late as June 1, and after I had had many conversations with them, Bruce Bliven wrote a piece called "A Patron of Politics," picturing Roosevelt as a dilettante:

> He would probably agree with the editor of the *Yale News*, who wrote the other day that politics is a dirty business, but he would probably add that when men of his background go in for it, it is by that much purified and transmuted. He is a patron of

politics; despite the effectiveness with which he plays the game at its realistic worst, he, like Woodrow Wilson, condescends toward the people he would help and the problems he seeks to solve. . . .

I might as well have kept quiet. Some minds do not change. I was beginning to believe liberal ones did not. There was more of Bliven's nonsense. Roosevelt makes excellent speeches, he said, about the forgotten man; but he is no spokesman for that man; he has just read about him in books. "In this world of desperate problems, crying for desperate remedies," Bliven said, "I question the effectiveness of the scholar-gentleman even when he means as well as anyone can."

Some, but not all, of our Columbia colleagues had accepted this sort of appraisal or had made it for themselves. Ray asked some of them for contributions to our work, and there were a few responses; but none seemed to answer the need for sharp definition and concrete proposals, and we settled for occasional visits to the circle of those whom we knew well and who were willing to contribute. Those who would have been of most use to us began very early to be disaffected. They were the economists, and they were hearing from Wall Street or from Washington. The financial district was apt to think of the debtor regions as enemy territory. Columbia was inescapably, as the official letterhead said, *in the City of New York,* and its School of Business faculty had close connections with banks and other institutions in the canyons of lower Manhattan. The unwillingness of Roosevelt to make blanket declarations satisfactory to the financiers, and his allusion at Oglethorpe to "special interests" whose expert knowledge could be used, but who should not be allowed to control economic life, had been a danger signal. And it had indeed been forthright; these men constituted, Roosevelt said, a small group

. . . whose chief outlook upon social welfare is tinctured by the fact that they can make huge profits from the lending of money and the marketing of securities—an outlook which deserves the adjectives "selfish" and "opportunistic."

This was hard for the financiers to take, and it went far to explain the turnabout of *The Times*. It also explained the unmistakable coolness of some of our colleagues on the campus. If we were writing speeches for Roosevelt, we were in this with him. If we had ghosted this and other paragraphs in the "forgotten man" and "concert of interests" speeches, we were even more unreliable than we had heretofore been considered. It was suggested that none of us was anywhere near the head of the academic list and that with such views as these it could be seen why. Oglethorpe, after all the rest, was too much.

The most offended of all was H. Parker Willis, who *was* at the top of the university heap. He was famous, a pundit. He had been chief adviser to Carter Glass in the devising of the Federal Reserve System, an important achievement of the Wilson administration and still the containing frame for the banking system. He had become the expositor and defender of that institution. He would grant that by now it could have some amendment, but not in the direction that Roosevelt evidently wanted to go. It needed tightening, not loosening. And the implications of the Oglethorpe speech —mere hints, perhaps, but still, to a suspicious mind, obvious— were outrageous. *The Times* may have fallen back on a comparison of Roosevelt's indecisiveness with Hoover's clear and honest presentation; but it seemed to us that the editorialist could not really have read the speech and kept the opinion that it was evasive. And Willis did not consider it evasive. Quite the contrary; he knew exactly what it meant, and he supposed that Adolf and I had written it. We heard, not too indirectly, that he was furious. In effect he had sent word that we were risking serious disapproval.

Roosevelt had by now examined and rejected the stoic attitude toward depression; those who held it, he said, had "greater faith in immutable economic law, and less faith in the ability of man to control what he has created, than I." And his Oglethorpe speech had continued with these unsettling words:

> It is self-evident that we must either restore commodities to a level approximating their dollar value of several years ago or else that we must continue the destructive process of reducing,

through defaults or deliberate writing down, obligations assumed at a higher level.

It is true that he did not say how this was to be done, but the financial community shuddered when it contemplated the means their imaginations conjured up. He had gone even beyond this to make more dangerous suggestions. He said that the use of capital in purely speculative ventures must be stopped. Many of these turned out to be unsuccessful and were therefore a waste. The use of capital had to be planned and gauged to the rate of production the nation needed and could absorb. As for the present trouble, however, it was more than this sort of malfunctioning. It was

. . . an insufficient distribution of buying power coupled with an oversufficient speculation in production. While wages rose in many of our industries, they did not as a whole rise proportionately to the reward to capital, and at the same time the purchasing power of the other great groups of our population was permitted to shrink. We accumulated a superabundance of capital that our great bankers were vying with each other, some of them employing questionable methods, in efforts to lend at home and abroad.

This speech was certainly not indefinite or evasive if the background and the assumptions it rested on were understood. We soon heard that in the close precincts of the financial district it was regarded with something like horror. It looked to the national welfare, not that of bankers or even industrialists. I might not have written the words, but I had no objection to their implications.

I thought Walter Lippmann should have known better than to intimate that progressives would be disappointed in their expectation that Roosevelt would challenge Wall Street. But there were my other friends—John Dewey, for instance, and Paul Douglas Why did the Oglethorpe words not seem to them what they, as liberals, had been waiting many dull and some desperate years to hear? Why did they refuse to recognize in Roosevelt the leader they had been hoping for?

The Oglethorpe speech, for all my reservations about it, seemed to me a remarkably suitable beginning for the campaign to come.

We could ask nothing better than that it should be a principal campaign theme. When I said so to Roosevelt, however, it seemed that the signs then were not so good as I had been imagining. The speech had been pulled apart and attacked. Hoover had been lucky to have had his letter to the president of the Society of Civil Engineers juxtaposed with Roosevelt's more philosophical speech to the Southern students. There was very little praise for Roosevelt and much for Hoover. Then too, there was in party circles all that wringing of hands that Louis reported. Altogether, the bold new doctrine was a political failure.

CHAPTER XIII

Special Assignment

❧ ❧ ❧

Ray has explained, in *After Seven Years* (pages 21–22), how just before Roosevelt left for the South he made our assignment more definite. It was in the little sitting-room-office in his house on Sixty-fifth Street in New York. McDuffie, his valet, was fussing about with packing, and Roosevelt himself was arranging some papers on a small table and talking to Ray at the same time. He spoke of the need for a rest and said that this would be his only chance for one before the campaign. He also said, as Ray remembers:

> "Why don't you fellows go ahead, just as though I were here, seeing people and getting stuff together? Then you might send down a memorandum for me to study"—he laughed—"so I don't get too far behind on my homework."

> "Good. But who, specifically, are 'you fellows'?" I cautiously asked.

> "Well, Sam, of course, and 'Doc,' I suppose. You know, 'Doc's' got a pretty level head on his shoulders. And Rex, and Berle. Rex could go on with his farm thing, though he'd be good on other things too."

I can expand somewhat that casual "other things too." Apart from our group meetings, Roosevelt and I had found one subject that was serious, that we seemed to see alike on—and that it was essential we should have a clear conclusion about. It had not reached proposal form in his mind and certainly was not politically ready. It might not appear at all in the coming campaign; I had begun to understand that. It ran too deep and required too much argument to be material for speeches. Roosevelt had said to me—I cannot recall whether Ray was present when we spoke of this— that we must make it come clear and forecast how it might work. I thought he had begun to see—or perhaps he had seen for a long time but had no recent occasion to consider until I had brought the question up—that a way might be found to bring competitive businesses into some sort of organized relationship that went further than the familiar trade association.

The effect of the antitrust laws was to prevent any sort of social management. They kept competition at a destructive level. We were talking about an orderly mechanism that might enable industries to practice a co-operation now considered illegitimate—but why should it be so if government made and enforced the rules for the industries' behavior? This ran counter to the old progressivism, but I still didn't know how strong the Brandeis influence was. Anyway, it was certain that Roosevelt was interested, and he did tell me to go ahead and work out our ideas more definitely, perhaps even suggesting an agency for the purpose.

This was not quite Adolf's business, although his brilliant analytical mind had penetrated many of the problems involved. What was most important at the moment was that Adolf should keep on at immediate solutions, those that would alleviate pressure and gain time for reform and reconstruction. This he was doing in notes and memoranda that had the sharp lucidity so characteristic of his mind and made our Albany discussions practical.

What Roosevelt said to Ray before the trip to Warm Springs showed his appreciation of Adolf's special talent for quick, comprehensive analysis. "Berle," he said, "could work up something on debt and finance—you know, RFC, and mortgage foreclosures, and the stock market. . . . "

It will be seen that there was in these few words the suggestion of many tremendous happenings. Studies of public and private debts were the material for several of our discussions. Adolf even then saw the implications, and we talked of them. It now seemed settled that some price-lifting device would have to be found, and even I had come around to that. The liquidity of debts and obligations would have to be restored in order to clear the way for the resumption of investment. RFC, spoken of rather casually then, might be enlarged and given other responsibilities than the rescuing of banks and utilities. That Hoover had suggested RFC was not necessarily an obstacle; it had a legitimate ancestor in the War Finance Corporation of Wilson days and had been approved by a Democratic House.

"Mortgage foreclosures" referred to the dispossessions then going on all over the country. The collateral for debts that could not be met when due was very often farms, homes, and business premises, and creditors could legally foreclose. They would rather not, as a rule; they had no use for the property and could not readily dispose of it as things were, but when payment was due, usually to banks, there existed an obligation to depositors. That the staving off of wholesale bankruptcy was a stupendous undertaking was obvious; just how stupendous—and how feasible— it might be vitally necessary to know. There were signs of urgency. Farmers in the debtor country, for instance, were already in a mood to resist court orders dispossessing them, even if they had to use force. These were the country's conservatives!

When Roosevelt mentioned "the stock market," he referred to an institution that was necessary to the kind of private-share financing characteristic of American enterprise. It was no less necessary because the performance of the past two years had highlighted certain practices that needed reform. The stock market had become what a critic (William O. Douglas) would presently call "a casino." Since brokers could carry customers on low margins, very large transactions were financed with very little capital. And that little capital—this was another abuse to be looked into—could be had in the ready-money market, which had drawn funds from most unlikely places. It was known, for instance, that many large corporations having funds not immediately needed had loaned them to stock speculators at the exorbitant interest rates prevailing when markets were booming. This had been more profitable at the moment than using the cash in their producing operations, but it was not something they should have been doing. To have General Motors, for instance, in the money-lending rather than the motor-making business was to pervert both functions.

Many customs and devices of the stock market obviously needed correction, but one of the worst, already becoming a scandal, was the use of investors' funds for the benefit of insiders. This was made possible by the double function of many banks. They were investment institutions, supposed to gather up capital funds and allocate them to the productive uses of the corporations whose shares they sold to investors, but they were also commercial banks and could use the shares as collateral for loans to favored speculators or, sometimes, to themselves. Then too, they could profit from commissions for selling securities, and many of those they had unloaded on the public by means of high-powered sales campaigns had been practically worthless. As the depression deepened, these bonds and shares were not only not paying interest or dividends but were in default on payments of principal. The worst of the ventures were large investments abroad in enterprises of the most risky sort—and in places, moreover, where the repayment problem was growing worse because of restrictions on the export of funds.

Where all this was leading was not clear in its ramifications, but it was certain that there must be a drastic overhaul of the whole system. It had not been possible so long as the boom was on and even the smallest investors were joining in the speculative craze. They had wanted to get in on the profits, legitimate or otherwise, being raked in by the big fellows. But now that the squeeze had come, they realized—millions of them—that they had been hoaxed. They were losing the paper gains of gambling and their accumulated stakes as well. Ordinary folk who had risked their savings faced complete loss, and the elderly among them found themselves indigent.

The prospect of easy gain had turned to a perhaps unreasonable disappointment, but, reasonable or not, the indignation was sufficient to support a thorough reform such as had not been possible for a generation. Adolf had the job of finding his way through all this to separate what would be useful for the campaign from what would better be saved for the legal convulsion that was certain to come.

I am unable to distinguish what Adolf contributed to this discussion from the part I had in it; he was a lawyer especially experienced in corporate behavior, and I was an economist, but we had come to similar conclusions if by different routes. He was always good at exposition, lucid and forceful. Frequently he held the floor for long periods when I only expressed agreement. But I talked a good deal too; I had something of my own to urge, which was a more orderly and balanced scheme of enterprise than had been created by competitors each following his own preference.

As I have suggested, Roosevelt already had an interest in an alternative, together with a rather ambivalent view of businessmen and their activities. About the financiers and their operations he was disillusioned, especially about the betrayal of their trust by the New York bankers. But this was not business as we meant it, and not what we were discussing.

It did seem unlikely that a man of wealth, brought up as Roosevelt had been, whose experience was mostly law and then politics, would have any very comprehensive knowledge of industrial and commercial operations. But this man did. And I, who had grown up in a business family, had known my father's friends and shared their interests, found that I could begin without preliminaries to discuss with him what could or could not be expected from new approaches and disciplines. It may have been the creation and running of the Warm Springs institution. Anyway, we agreed that business was not monolithic and that businessmen were as varied and complex as the rest of us. There were all sorts of differences among them about the questions that would matter in any plans for recovery and reform. There were some who were indifferent to the interests of others, but there were those too who were sensitive and genuinely regretful when others were hurt. Some would be willing to take advantage of any situation regardless of its costs to the public; others would sacrifice a good deal to establish a record for decency.

Roosevelt asked me to bring him more information about scientfic management and about its extension from shop practices to industrial direction. The Taylor Society had been a sort of missionary enterprise for a generation, but its principles were now beginning to be used as a matter of course in ordinary operations. This was partly because many businessmen had been trained in such institutions as the Wharton School, where management was an important study. That was where my own interest had begun.

Curiously, Taylorism was largely ignored by economists, an omission that I had been at pains to point out. But it had changed the whole climate of management and made it more likely, I thought, that rationalization of production would be found acceptable. Roosevelt had missed most of this. He had many contacts with lawyers and with experts in the matters he had to deal with as Governor; he was knowledgeable about banking; he had at least a curiosity about money; but scientific management had escaped him entirely. He found it fascinating. I brought him my book about it, *Industry's Coming of Age* (1927), and he looked it through. The effect of efficiency in lowering costs had been important in my theory of the depression. It had a bearing, too, on my desire to have the government acknowledge responsibility for planning. He said that it was, of course, one thing for a businessman to have a personal sort of unwillingness to exploit others, and a pride in being co-operative, but quite another to see that only in subordinating individual rights to a general code of behavior could whole industries be kept to a level of fairness that many individuals supported. But there were many who did see that where competition was unlimited, standards would inevitably be lowered. There were those who would chisel and cheat to gain competitive advantage, and they could be restrained only by policing. Even a small minority could wreck a whole system. This was a sticking point. To begin restraining and disciplining was to start something that might end in embarrassing rigidity.

There was something else about this that we also agreed on. When even the most decent businessmen shied away from restraints, it was because they feared government regulators. This was a good reason for giving them the responsibility for self-regulation. If something like this should be planned, leadership must be developed and the conscience of the best be made the rule for all. What then would be the role of government? So far that role had been altogether one of restraint. There had been no positive kinds of business regulation, no suggestion that anyone should do anything or behave in any particular way, only the pronouncement that many things should *not* be done and that behavior should *not* be of certain kinds. How different it would be if better management were at a premium rather than better chiseling! There must be a way to encourage as well as to suppress.

Another thing: small businessmen were free of any rules of this sort. There might be restraints under police power relating to health or even welfare, but these varied from effectiveness in New York and Massachusetts to nonexistence in Mississippi and Alabama. It was true that business lobbies had always worked against all such advances, but there were many scrupulous businessmen who saw that the strengthening of regulation would be advantageous for them; their competitors would be deprived of sanctuaries for their sweatshops.

What was wanted was something more than standards of competition to define fair and unfair practices. That something more had clear enough objectives. One of these was the encouraging of efficiency and the enlargement of production; another was the better use of capital resources. When there were no projected general aims or plans, and when each concern shaped its program to its own projection with its own limited knowledge and interests, there were bound to be immense errors and so colossal wastes. But here again it would certainly be more acceptable if industries worked out their own projections and put them together for common guidance. That is to say, there would be less complaint of interference and governmental restraint.

But there was reason to think this would not work. I knew about the experience in the Department of Agriculture with the "intentions to plant" program and spoke of it. Roosevelt had some similar experiences from working with a trade association. There were always those who would take advantage of others' compliance to enlarge their own shares. A minority of farmers, finding out that the wheat crop was to be reduced by agreement, proceeded to plant so much more that the reduction became an increase. And the same was true of the businesses in a trade association. If there were no restraints from outside, the co-operative effort merely gave chiselers a chance to profit at the expense of those who did co-operate. There must, therefore, be penalties for noncompliance after an agreed plan had been made. As for the protection of consumers and workers, this should emerge from the enforcement of fairness.

Sam, Doc, and Ray sometimes listened to exchanges on this subject, but they did not often participate. It must be recalled that all were practicing lawyers except Ray, who was devoting his life to improving the administration of the law; none of them really had much interest in the administration of industry. Even Adolf had not concerned himself with the possibilities of economic self-government. Besides, this did not seem very likely to have immediate importance, either as a subject for a compaign speech or as a contribution to recovery.

As I recall, I was not even supposed to make any further report to go with the others when Sam took the whole bundle to Warm Springs. I was given other jobs of a more immediate sort. But this was one I was to develop against the possibility of its emergence into a workable scheme.

Before and after Warm Springs, Roosevelt was seeing many people every day. He was talking to businessmen and bankers as well as politicians, discussing the progress of the depression and getting such ideas as anyone had about recovery. He said that actually all he got was exhortations to reassure the business community. This idea was the familiar one we had all been hearing; if confidence was restored, activity would start up and all would presently be as it had been before 1929.

He had a question he asked his visitors now, he said, when reassurance was so extolled: how is it to be created? The answer was surprisingly unanimous: reduce public spending, lower taxes, and balance the budget. But, he had learned to answer, that was what Hoover was doing, and the situation was growing worse. Ah! Roosevelt was told, that was because businessmen feared *him*. He must give assurances that he too, if he became President, would economize and balance the budget, secure the integrity of the dollar, and give investors some hope of profits that would not be taken in taxes.

CHAPTER XIV

What Manner of Man?

🏵 🏵 🏵

Sam Rosenman's view of Warm Springs was unfavorable. He had been a city boy, and he had a limited appreciation of nature as seen in the pine country of western Georgia. Besides, he was depressed by the crippled patients. Going through their courses in therapy, wheeling themselves about in chairs, responding to the forced cheerfulness of attendants, they were still interested in nothing but themselves. So many of them were young, and they faced an alien world, a life lived apart from their contemporaries. It might be a long life, too, in which they would always be at the mercy of relatives or attendants who, with the best intentions, would have other interests. Yes, anyone could see that the cheerfulness in Warm Springs was forced.

Roosevelt himself had faced down the prospect of such a future. He had pretty well stifled the cripple's upwelling melancholy; his mind was turned outward, with what a wrench it could only be guessed. His visits to Warm Springs, however, seemed to have none of the depressing effects felt by Sam. He exercised in the pools with the patients, the exercise in his case being mostly lively water games. The sun was warm, the rain gentle (the Warm Springs weather was influenced by massive billows of Gulf air sweeping up from the south), and he could travel about the country roads in his manually operated car.

After his speech at Oglethorpe, he had journeyed north on May 25, and all along the way there had been amazing turnouts. He made as many rear-platform appearances as a campaigner might; indeed, those who crowded around regarded him as already chosen. This was their future President, and they looked to him for better times. In Greenville, South Carolina, for instance, the crowd was estimated to be four thousand, and he was cheered again and again as the hope of the South. "Yes," he cried as he gripped the railing of the rear platform, "every state in the South is for me but Virginia and Texas." Everyone understood the reference. Virginia was the domain of Harry F. Byrd, who still hoped some miracle might turn the coming Chicago convention to him, and Texas' favorite son was John Nance Garner, the Speaker of the House.

That those who cheered him as their likely President had something more on their minds than the future of one individual, Roosevelt knew better than anyone else. He had not been talking for years to those farmers along the red dirt roads without understanding their desperation. If he had looked at the papers that morning, as was his habit, he must have seen that cotton was less than six cents a pound and hogs three and a third. Out in the Midwest beef was bringing less than six dollars a hundredweight, wheat was running downward from sixty cents a bushel, and corn was below thirty cents. Low prices were a continuing and, it might be, a fatal fact for farmers. Many of them were already separated from their home places; they had had to move into town or were in process of being foreclosed. At worst they were existing in Hoovervilles, indigent and nearly hopeless; at best they were left on their farms, deep in debt, their land only partially worked, their machinery rusted, and most of their last crop still unsold. Townspeople were not much better off at the whistle stops along the route of Roosevelt's train. Their stores were empty of customers, their service stations closed, and all the loafing places were patronized by idle men.

Roosevelt's remarks to the crowds were mostly not recorded by the reporters; they were short and informal, but Lindley told us Roosevelt always promised to "do something." He did not say how it would be done; nevertheless, the reporters were enormously impressed. They were unanimous in saying that no one could see those meetings or hear what was said among the listeners without understanding that a promise was being made and that hopes were being raised. "He'd better have something," they said.

When we saw Roosevelt after his return to Albany, it was obvious that he felt renewed. He always did after a trip like this, Sam said with a mixture of wonder and tolerance. He was brown and had a kind of head-tossing vigor. He laughed loudly when there was something to laugh at, and he found a good many amusing incidents in the usual day. Also, he was full of ideas; they positively sprouted, and in our meetings with him he was more than ever the talker and we the listeners.

In such a session, I found myself looking hard to see whether I could understand something that was very like a miracle. I concluded that it was both physical and spiritual. The physical part came from rest and recreation, perhaps, but the spiritual lift may well have come from a sizing-up of the situation from a place other than Albany.

What I saw was a man with overdeveloped muscles that rippled under his well-cut coat and swelled the soft collar of his shirt. Close up he really was not a handsome fellow. His teeth were irregular, his hair was receding, there were discolorations under his eyes, and he had a chin that jutted but somehow failed to express determination. Besides, he was developing a noticeable paunch that made his wheelchair travels awkward. No man at the beginning of his fifties is what he was at thirty, but Roosevelt, despite his exercises, showed more deterioration than was normal for his age.

All this was true, but it mattered very little. He displayed determination if not youth; he spread optimism rather than gloom; he handled his cigarette holder as a mandarin might have used a fan; he smiled often, and his smile broke into boisterousness at the slightest excuse; he moved a good deal when he was behind a desk or a table, and it was easy to forget his legs. The cheerfulness and the optimism were his adopted image.

It is very difficult, now that his record has long since been completed and his image fixed, to recall that then he was merely the Governor of New York, not the President of the United States, and that he was not known to be a consummate politician or to have the magical radio voice that brought new courage to a country in crisis. In the late spring of 1932, all this was in the future. I wondered at the time why I still had reservations about him. Did it mean that we—Moley, Berle, and myself—were mistaken in thinking we had found a political leader for whom and with whom we could work for the things we believed must be done?

By now I had learned something of the Roosevelt history from those who had been with him in years past. It was definite that he had long intended to become President if he could and that he had shaped his career to furthering this intention. The governorship had been unwanted. He had been compelled to try for it against his judgment and had unexpectedly won. But once he had it, he had made full use of the opportunity it offered to advance his candidacy. Many people felt at the time that, so far as Roosevelt was concerned, this was its only use. Even Doc seemed to imply something of the sort.

About this I had a different conclusion even from short acquaintance. The office, I thought, had given him an outlet for his builder's instinct, something shown much earlier in such extensive projects as the rehabilitation of the Warm Springs institution for polio victims. The drive was strong; even if he had not wanted to be Governor, the state had been a worthy object for cultivation, and he had at once set about to improve everything: the institutions, the forests, even the government. It was more—a good deal more—than a demonstration intended to show what he might do as President; it showed the concern of one who was deeply involved. Sam and Doc might be right in saying that the governorship was only a way station; but if they meant that he had no real interest in what he had been able to do as Governor, they were quite wrong. No one could speak with such feeling about the land and its people, the highways, the rivers, the parks and forests, the public power systems, and the like, without meaning it. And no one could have used every method he could contrive to relieve the distress of New Yorkers in the ordeal of depression without having genuinely accepted responsibility for their welfare.

His earlier life, it was true, had been that of an only son in an old and fairly wealthy family settled in the Hudson Valley on an ample estate. He had been taught by an elderly father to live within a moral and religious pattern, and by a haughty mother to respect the family name. Since she considered the Delanos to be rather more aristocratic than the Roosevelts, this was a heavy obligation. To reinforce such parental lessons, he had been sent— rather late, and after being taught by governesses and tutors—to the safest school his parents knew of. Groton was not only exclusive but also doctrinaire. The headmaster—Peabody—and the others there intended to make their charges into worthy Christian men, and the boys were taught to think of themselves as the elite of their generation, destined to leadership as well as to privilege. Also it was insisted that leadership implied duty and that privilege imposed obligation. A dozen reasons could be thought of for his becoming a dilettante at his present age, indulging his hobbies and enjoying his inheritance. This was how his older half-brother James, who lived close by his Hyde Park home, had turned out. Franklin himself had so much interest in perfecting his collections of naval prints and stamps, in working out interesting puzzles in local history, and in growing Christmas trees that these avocations might understandably have absorbed his entire life.

For some reason—or a number of reasons—he lived as differently from James as could be imagined. The same ambition that activated still another Roosevelt, the older and distant cousin Theodore, worked in him. It was quite as strong in the younger man and, because of the example, more sophisticated. The intention of becoming at least as famous as Uncle Ted, and in the same ways, was too obvious to miss. Emulation at some point had turned into rivalry, but both fed on the same impulses. He would not only become famous; he would improve things, and improve them more than Uncle Ted had been able to do.

At the right time, the Groton graduate had gone on to Harvard, and there he had associated with his own sort, living in a Gold Coast suite and consorting with old Grotonians at table. Until pretty late in this progress, he had dutifully tried to be an athlete, although his long and thinnish physique condemned him to be always a second-stringer. His family connections, and the Groton-St. Marks society centered in Boston, had made extensive demands on his time and had kept him from developing any deep interest in scholarship.

He had always been concerned to make a good impression, and he had acquired an English wardrobe. He had been content with "a gentleman's C's," and, having been forced to recognize his mediocrity in athletics, he had fought his way up to the editorship of *The Crimson* as a substitute way of gaining status. Although the post had given him a certain standing, he was not regarded as a big man in his college class. He had, however, learned some lessons in politics. He had tried for several student offices before he had got the hang of campaigning. He had finally learned the necessary techniques, but not before suffering some defeats. One of the lessons, well learned, was that he must develop a bonhomie to replace the standoffishness of the Grotonians.

Was there a change after this phase? He had lost his father during his freshman year, and his mother had moved to Cambridge, prepared to take over the direction of his activities. He had evaded her. Although he was outwardly dutiful enough, she had never been able to manage him. Her worst failure, and the one she most deplored, was his insistence on marrying Eleanor. She was the cousin he had met again, a visitor in the Bostonian circle, greatly changed from the young girl he recalled from earlier family gatherings; despite his mother's opposition, he had engaged himself to her. It was symbolic. He appeared to be dutiful, but he went his own way, and he would persist in this independence.

One of the most attractive things about him, I thought, considering all I heard, was his loyalty to Eleanor. She had been a Roosevelt of the other—the Oyster Bay—branch, but she had been an orphan whose father had fallen into alcoholism and was one member the family would rather not mention. She was also large and awkward, and this had made her unduly retiring and twittery. It turned out that she had the Roosevelt energy and will, but they had been suppressed until the time had come to battle for her husband's future with the *grande dame* who had so far dominated her married life. This had not been until all her children had been born and until the polio attack; then her Roosevelt qualities had come out.

They had been married while Roosevelt was a student at the Columbia University School of Law. The law was a concession to his family; he himself would have preferred a career in the navy. After he had clerked in the office of a big firm (Carter, Ledyard and Milburn) for a few years, the opportunity had come to enter politics in Dutchess County. It was no more than an outside chance that a Democrat could succeed in that Republican district, but he had accepted; he had to start somewhere if his ambitions were to be satisfied. That being a year of Republican troubles, he had been elected to the state senate.

Why was he a Democrat? We had bantered about this, but the question of conviction had been avoided. It was Lindley who pointed out to me that the example of Uncle Ted had lighted the path in this direction as in others. Uncle Ted had been less a Republican than a progressive, and also there had been the example of his father, a follower of Cleveland. Putting the two together made him, reasonably enough, a progressive Democrat.

Lindley knew him for a progressive, but he also knew him for a Roosevelt who was going the way of his rather distant cousin and intended if he could, and if it was possible, to go even further. There is nothing wrong with ambition; if men were not driven by it, there would be no leaders. The question is whether a man's ambition is to be a leader of causes or only to arrive at positions of prestige. It was the question I was asking about this Roosevelt, and so were others.

It might not be important at this late time. He was likely to be the Democratic candidate, and the Democratic candidate might well be elected. He would do a better job than Hoover. Or would he? My fear that he might use the presidency for Wilsonian purposes—going back to the New Freedom—was not relieved, and if this happened, his accession would be a doubtful gain. If he had reform in mind—he was very critical of the bankers who had risked and lost their depositors' funds, and he shared Louis' phobias about "middlemen"—that would not advance recovery, and might even retard it. A clean-out would be a good thing if it was not regarded as all that needed to be done, but sometimes the completion of the Wilson agenda did seem to be what Roosevelt had in mind; was it *all* he had in mind?

Ray too was concerned about this. It might indicate a weakness for the trust-busting that we thought obsolete. A rousing campaign of harassment for big business might just finish the American economy, sick as it was. Orthodox progressivism might still be good for political advancement; we were afraid it was, but it so easily became sheer demagoguery. No answers to contemporary problems were to be found in the Bryan-Brandeis-Wilson book. The tradition was meritorious; it called on good impulses; it put the public interest above all else. But its purpose had got lost in the tangles of free enterprise. Progressives no longer advocated public ownership of utilities, for instance; they talked about the glories of freedom to do business, and no banker was more caustic than they about "government interference." Their determination to break all big businesses into small components and keep them that way by compulsion had become an orthodoxy.

We had one reason for being hopeful that Roosevelt's adherence to this view was not so final as we sometimes feared. When he had confronted the power interests in New York, he had really come to understand that monopoly was inevitable and that the competition of many small units was impractical. Perhaps this would carry over to other issues. If power production could not be fractionalized, neither could other similar industries.

But the trust-busting impulse was not dead. It had gathered strength since the eighties and burst out when Wilson, desperate for an economic program, had accepted the atomistic theory. The central principle of the New Freedom had been enforced competition. With vigorous regulation, it was believed, there would be no need for other governmental efforts. It was, of course, pure Adam Smith. As each competing unit sought to make a profit for itself, it would be led by a hidden hand to further the public interest.

We were wasting our time when we argued with an ardent breaker-up of the orthodox school by telling him that the costs of large-scale industries were lower because they were more efficient, and that the prices of their products could be controlled in ways other than fractionalization and competition. The problem, it seemed to us, was to get the benefit of integration and avoid its disadvantages. The Oglethorpe speech had seemed to accord with this conception. But we knew it would infuriate the old Justice, and Ray prophesied that Frankfurter would be in Albany before the dust had settled. As a matter of fact, he was. We had no communication with him, but we knew he had been there; we always heard, one way or another.

As to the Roosevelt progressivism, everything we learned indicated that the record was a spotted one. He had joined in a battle with Tammany during his first year in the state legislature, when Charles F. Murphy, the grand sachem, had tried to make a United States senator of Blue-Eyed Billy Sheehan, who had brought into the campaign coffers large public-utility contributions. A little later he had enlisted in Wilson's progress to the presidency and had made such a rumpus in supporting him at the Baltimore convention that Josephus Daniels, Wilson's supporter in North Carolina, had noticed. But when Daniels had made him his Assistant Secretary, Roosevelt had become a big-navy and pro-war agitator, markedly disloyal to the Wilson-Daniels neutrality policy. He had carried his advocacy to such an extreme that he had barely missed being disciplined. He had tried to escape from his civilian job and put on a naval uniform, but at the end of the war he had still been a bureaucrat. When the party nominated Cox in 1920, underlining its repudiation of Wilson by turning to a candidate as far removed from the administration as possible, it had made Roosevelt his running mate. Ostensibly this had softened the offense; actually, no member of his official family was less pleasing to the retiring President. It was interesting, however, that Tammany's Murphy had made this nomination possible, perhaps even arranged it. If Roosevelt was no favorite of Wilson, Wilson by now was no favorite of the party.

Cox and Roosevelt had lost, but they had accepted the League of Nations, so obviously shunned by the party professionals, as their main issue. This was a good mark for Roosevelt among the considerable number of Wilson's admirers, and the vigor of his campaigning had brought him favor from all the party notables. He had behaved as though it were he, not Cox, who was the presidential candidate, crossing the country on campaigning trips, making numerous speeches, conferring with local leaders, and making himself familiar with the needs and desires of every region, especially the West. He began then the long wooing of the party regulars that was bringing returns in 1932.

It had not ended there. After that campaign Louis Howe, having enlisted in Roosevelt's service, began a long and systematic cultivation of leaders with whom acquaintance had been set up during the campaign. They were encouraged to correspond about party matters and were sent long and considered answers. Roosevelt was the leading young Democrat from 1920 on. Cox made no effort, after his defeat, to hold the position of leader.

The disaster of polio in the next year had not kept Louis from going on in Roosevelt's name, and it had caused the emergence of Eleanor from the obscurity her modesty had dictated. She had had to do battle, finally, with the mother-in-law she had never before challenged, and, being victorious in winning her husband back to public interests, she had submitted to the tutelage of Louis, for whom she had had little liking in the past. He taught her to make political speeches, she learned to control her high and quavering voice, and she joined the women who were doing so much during Smith's governorship to advance welfare in New York.

It was thought to have been courageous for Roosevelt to undertake the management of Smith's preconvention campaign in 1924, and he was even more approved for making the stirring "happy warrior" speech at the convention. It had not convinced the anti-Catholics that Smith ought to be nominated, and a compromise had had to be reached on Davis, who was then badly beaten by Coolidge. At Houston four years later, Roosevelt had again nominated Smith in a speech characterized by *The Times* as "statesman-like"—quite unlike the usual blowsy spouting on such occasions. This time Smith had won the nomination, after Roosevelt had spoken bitingly of "bigotry" to shame his fellow Democrats. It was a year when it was hard to believe ill of anyone in authority. The boom was in full sweep; the country was bursting with prosperity; and the Republicans had nominated Hoover, the man who embodied the philosophy of efficiency.

Having put Smith in nomination, Roosevelt had gone as far back into the shadows as his party position would permit, allowing Smith to monopolize attention. It had been quite clear to him from the first that there was no chance whatever of Smith's winning. Presently it became apparent that Smith even stood in danger of losing the state where he had four times won the governorship.

In September of 1928, with Roosevelt sheltering in the obscurity of Warm Springs, the Democratic state convention had met in Syracuse. He had heard the suggestion that he be the candidate for Governor, and it was an idea he hoped would die. He was already a national figure, available for the presidency when there might be a chance of Democratic victory—possibly in 1936, when Hoover would have finished the two terms that seemed inevitable. To run for the governorship and lose would be to surrender his present position of prestige. But he was not allowed to escape. He evaded as long as he could, and even managed to be out of telephone reach for some time. But Smith was adamant, and the others with him; it was a time to use every resource, and Roosevelt was an up-state Democrat. They let him know that this was a party call; if it was refused, they intimated, there would never be another. Eleanor was a delegate to that convention—showing how far she had come in politics—and she told him it was inevitable. Louis, protesting from New York City, asked if his long efforts were now to be wasted on a hopeless campaign. But there was nothing he could do; he had to accept.

Roosevelt had returned to New York and campaigned as vigorously as he had done for the vice-presidency in 1920, appearing everywhere and speaking, when on tour, many times daily, on all sorts of subjects. He presented himself as a Smith follower, willing to carry further the welfare program—and to stand for public power, something particularly at issue in New York. He said so much in praise of Smith that his campaign manager reminded him that his first duty was to the governorship.

If it was to be a sacrifice, Roosevelt meant to demonstrate to the party professionals that he had done his best; he meant, moreover, to make a better showing than they thought he might, just as he had done before in Dutchess County. It turned out better than he had imagined it could, and he pulled through with a majority— slight but, considering that Smith himself had lost the state, creditable. His sacrifice had turned out to be a triumph; it gave him good marks with the Democratic politicians. But Smith was a power in Tammany, and he might be humiliated beyond toleration. Roosevelt was presented, even in victory, with a very trying decision.

He did the unexpected thing. After his inauguration, he allowed Smith no privileges because of having sponsored him; he behaved as though the victory was his and his alone. When Smith lingered in Albany to advise him about the matters under way, Roosevelt ignored him. Presently the former Governor disappeared from his hotel suite; he had got a business job in New York, and Roosevelt continued conspicuously on his own. He must have feared that Tammany, led by Smith, would try to refuse him the nomination for re-election in 1930. But Smith had made up his mind to leave the competition. Roosevelt was not only renominated but re-elected, this time by the largest majority that any Governor had received to that time.

It was a long record. It had been one of many trials and hard decisions. It was far from certainly a progressive one as we understood the word, but then his opportunities had been only such as were open to the Governor of a single state. There was no indication, in the welfare measures he sponsored or in his efforts to improve administration, that his progressivism had any economic connotations beyond those of Wilson's New Freedom. From anything he had said or done, it could not be inferred that he planned to do more than complete the Wilsonian program. On the other hand, his mind was open. He was not a traditionalist. And there was that passage in his recent career when he had worked for the Construction Council. At that time, he had been in touch with Hoover and had known about the sponsorship of trade associations by the Department of Commerce. He might have concluded that bigness was permanent and that public direction of the economic system was possible.

We just did not know. We had only the Oglethorpe speech for encouragement.

CHAPTER XV

Portents of the New Deal

🎖 🎖 🎖

Sam Rosenman would contend in later years that no one should have been surprised by what happened when Roosevelt became President. It was all foreshadowed, he maintained, by what had happened in Albany between 1928 and 1932.*

When we were called in for discussions, the governorship was passing into history; for the sake of consistency, and so that we could find out more about the Governor's intentions, we made some inquiries. Moley knew a good deal; so did Doc; but, because Sam had actually lived through it at Roosevelt's side, he knew more.

What we learned, with Sam as tutor, was that the program had been generally liberal, but that, as far as doing anything about the depression was concerned, not much more could really be claimed than a few starts in the right direction. What had been done showed an intention to use government and to use it more for the benefit of people who were in deep trouble than for those who, even if they had lost a good deal, were still able to look after themselves. If it had demonstrated beyond any doubt that there were narrow limits to what could be done within a state's resources, still

---

* Samuel Rosenman, *Working with Roosevelt* (New York; Harper, 1952), Vol. III; "The Genesis of the New Deal."

the attempt had marked out a sharp difference of view from the Republican legislators that Roosevelt had had to contend with. In general these lawmakers had opposed doing anything at all, but even more indignantly they had opposed any specific efforts to re-balance economic forces in favor of those who were unemployed and facing hunger and cold. In this way they reflected conservative opinion, as did most Republicans everywhere, while Roosevelt had taken the progressive side.

There were always those who were exploited and always those who offered themselves as their champions. From the time of Bryan on, most of the protesters had been Democrats. Spectacular attempts by progressives to capture the Republican party had never been successful. Sometimes they had been formidable, as when Theodore Roosevelt made his assault in 1912, but the con-servatives had always smothered the rebels. T. R. in that year had taken with him out of the party more Republicans than had stayed, but after his defeat by Wilson he had refused to run again in 1916. The next attempt, that of La Follette in 1924, had been buried in the Coolidge landslide. Even now, in 1932, there were progressives among the Republicans—a few—to match any the Democrats could display. There were Senators George Norris and Hiram Johnson and Representative La Guardia, besides the La Follette brothers. They made a team with Senators Wagner, Costigan, Cut-ting, and Wheeler, Democrats who had little in common with their conservative colleagues.

Few as the progressives were, they were men of political potency not only in their own states but also as a bloc in the Congress. It was obvious that when Roosevelt had journeyed to Trenton in 1911 and pledged himself to Wilson, he had meant to join this company and had thenceforth felt himself ideologically identified with its Democratic branch. His whole state program had been con-sistent with this interpretation. He had sought to better the situation of the farmers; he had fought aggressive battles with the power monopoly; he had strained the state's resources to provide relief for the unemployed; he had asked for stricter regulation of financial situations; he had tried in all the areas of welfare to improve the lot of the indigent and handicapped, especially that of handicapped children. He had sought protective legislation for workers and had, in fact, gone ahead with the whole welfare program so well begun in Smith's governorship. All this had followed the well-marked progressive line. In addition to being a notable conservationist, Roosevelt had made important improvements in the administration of justice. Taken altogether, it was a record I was ashamed not to have known more about.

It was quite apparent, from his long history as a Democrat, that he meant to stay within the party. He obviously felt that it could be used, as Wilson had used it, for progressive purposes. The Republicans still treated their progressive members as mavericks; the Democrats were more welcoming. For this there were several reasons, one being the Democratic link with the populist movement of the 1880's. The revolt of those years in the farm states, directed against Wall Street and "the money power," had been climaxed by Bryan's capture of the Democratic nomination in 1896.

There were signs now that the Democrats longed for the contributions of the moneyed and were willing to compromise their principles to get them. The Straus organization had really wealthy members, and Roosevelt treated them with a tenderness that I found a little repugnant. Still, I thought much could be done with those among them who thought of the system as a whole. The ones I distrusted were those who were evidently the most generous and also the most demanding—the speculators, Baruch and Kennedy. If they were statesmen, my definition of the public interest was all wrong. Roosevelt, however, furnished them with the public impression of intimacy, whatever his private reservations.

By reviewing the incidents of the past four years, we were able to relate what we were asked to study and discuss to what had gone before and to what we understood that Roosevelt meant to do in and with the party. It would seem that Sam afterward exaggerated the similarities between the state program in 1928–1932 and the later federal New Deal, but there was indeed a common willingness to experiment and a common determination to make use of governmental powers. It might also be possible—I came to think it was—for a man like Roosevelt to make use of the Baruchs and Kennedys without really conceding more than fitted his own scheme.

He had a difficult problem in moving from what a *state* could do to relieve distress and injustices to what the *nation* could do to abolish their causes. The one was an effort at alleviation when pressure bore hard enough on individuals to cause distress; the other involved the establishment of a system that might eliminate such effects. The one was superficial, in a sense; the other was a deep and radical readjustment of relationships. It was because of this difference, indeed, that the discussions with us were felt to be necessary. Something more drastic and far-reaching was needed than had been possible in the State of New York, and this was what we were being called upon to suggest.

As time passed we began to have a clearer picture of Roosevelt's estimate of possibilities for action, although he was chary of admissions in this field. He obviously preferred to let conclusions develop and mature in his mind. Since we were normally sensitive, we soon uncovered reticences, and they were hard to maintain when he wanted to argue, as he often did. When he gradually opened up, we were freed to advocate and evaluate in a more lively way than we would have done if we had felt any responsibility beyond that of trying to amplify and clarify the issues he needed to explore. Some of the issues were gone through very quickly; some were lingered over and returned to again and again with new information or new suggestions. There were problems we explored at such length that we detected the emergence of a potential policy. Some others we barely touched. We went on, when we could, to more general implications, but about this we felt the need for a good deal more direction and hoped it would be forthcoming. Sometimes it was, but often discussions seemed to end before any sort of conclusion was reached.

Ray had an eagerness of his own, an ambition I felt I understood but did not share. I concluded that he had a cause in mind. It was not because he wanted to hold office; it was because he had a sense of development and wanted to see policies take an orderly and consistent shape. He was much more devoted to means and had much less interest in ends than either Adolph or myself. Perhaps, also, he had in mind writing about his experiences. His gift for exposition was so remarkable and so carefully cultivated that it may have amounted to a motivation.

Adolf and I were more insistent reformists, in the sense that we wanted to see changes made of a kind we had concluded were necessary. Ray developed some such feelings later, and he already had them about the administration of justice—the court system. It was this, of course, that had brought him into Roosevelt's household. It was something he had become expert in, and he wanted to improve operations. I should say that his expertness was more specialized than ours and that, paradoxically, it made him more useful as a drafter of speeches on quite other subjects.

At any rate, he had no trouble in helping Roosevelt say well whatever he might decide to say. He was much less inclined to put words in his mouth than we were. This may have been partly because he had fewer he wanted said, but it was probably more because he understood better the necessities of the political mode.

He was constantly worried about Roosevelt's insouciance, irritated by loose ends and half-materialized ideas. But indeterminate exchanges were about all we had to show for some weeks of fairly earnest endeavor and long evenings of discussion. There may have been more progress than Ray, in pessimistic moments, judged there had been. Still, he would have liked more control of the approaches to the man we were trying to help. In his own way, and for a different purpose, Ray was as jealous as Louis Howe or Henry Morgenthau. He was annoyed, sometimes to the point of fury, when he discovered that an important study we had been assigned to make had been let out to someone else as well. When Roosevelt, getting back one of the memoranda he had asked for from some visitor who took him more seriously than he meant, turned it over to us, Ray could hardly control his temper until we were alone.

I learned that these turbulent spells would pass. It was like the wind that comes with summer storms; the calm could be expected soon. Besides his two patient secretaries, I was the only one with whom Ray had no reserve. I valued the association and mostly wanted nothing more than I had. His tempers were never directed at me.

For Louis' special place in Roosevelt's regard, there was good reason. It had been he who, as an Albany newspaperman, had undertaken to make the green young senator from Dutchess County a public figure during his very first term, back in 1911. When Roosevelt had joined the conspiracy of some older anti-Tammany Democratic legislators to defy Boss Murphy and hold up the election of Blue-Eyed Billy Sheehan as United States senator (senators were still elected by legislatures), Louis had written up Roosevelt as the central character of that incident. He could, because he was *The Tribune's* reporter. Close study would have shown that Roosevelt's contribution was a good deal less heroic than Louis made it appear; it would also have shown that the settlement with Murphy was not so triumphant as Louis pictured it; but the benefit to Roosevelt in the way Louis intended was very important indeed. The publicity made him a character Woodrow Wilson paid attention to as a young party worker of progressive strain, and Wilson was about to become President.

When Roosevelt went to Washington, Louis went along and served all through the Navy Department years as Franklin's political handy man. Early in that service, he engineered a *rapprochement* with Tammany; he also smoothed over Franklin's offenses as an administration executive who was less loyal than he should have been to Wilson's neutrality policy. Both these were matters that might have ended disastrously. Then, in 1920, he had managed the Roosevelt vice-presidential campaign. When that adventure ended, however, and the long Republican years were beginning, Louis had had to look for work; he could no longer be kept on the government's payroll, and Roosevelt's expensive family was using all his income. A suitable job had just turned up when the polio attack came in 1921. Yet he had dropped everything, gone to Campobello, hovered over the stricken man until he had recovered enough to be moved, then had conceived and carried out a most elaborate deception so that no one knew that Roosevelt was a stretcher case.

Then had begun the struggle not only for Roosevelt's recovery but also for the reactivation of his ambition. This was complicated by the determination of Sara, the matriarch, to repossess her son. He ought to retire, she felt, to genteel life at Hyde Park, as his father had done. Now that he was crippled he ought to take himself out of the constant struggle for yet another advantage in the political game; it was an unseemly competition anyway. In his old home and among people of his own sort, he could devote himself to the pursuits she knew were agreeable to him—casual researches in local history, travel, collecting stamps, and, along with cultivating the estate, taking his position as the local squire. Louis had enlisted Eleanor, and together they had encouraged the old ambition to re-establish itself in the invalid's mind. In the process Louis had conquered Eleanor's dislike and had become almost as proud of what had been done to make a public figure of her as of Roosevelt's own rejuvenation.

In the course of time Louis became increasingly enfeebled by many debilitating ills, centering in the asthma that tormented him continually and that nothing ever seemed to ameliorate. He was more and more a wizened gnome. He had a family, but they seldom saw him. He held the secretaryship of a crime commission and had an office on Madison Avenue, but this was little more than a cover for his real occupation while Franklin was Governor. Actually, he was at the center of a communications web that reached into every district of the country and had as its sole end the forwarding of Franklin's presidential drive. The gubernatorial victory of 1930, coinciding as it did with the beginning of the depression, set Louis off in hot chase of the delegates necessary for the culmination of his mission in life—getting Roosevelt into the presidential race as a Democratic candidate. He had Jim Farley to do what he could not do—travel around the country slapping backs, radiating optimism, and hinting that rewards would be forthcoming when Roosevelt succeeded to the Republican empire. Jim was a big man in the Elks, and this gave him an excuse for travel; then too, his position as chairman of the New York State Democratic Committee provided an introduction to the party organizations in other states.

When, between them, they had accumulated a majority of the convention delegates, Louis relaxed a little, and Ray found him almost genial on occasion. Ray even reported that he himself was, in a lesser way, being recognized as a helper in the cause, more or less as Farley was. But he knew, and he warned me, that Louis' tolerance was thin; there might be outbreaks of jealousy at any moment, and we should be eternally discreet. Roosevelt himself took Louis' crotchets lightly and often laughed about them, but no one had better presume that if a showdown should be precipitated on any issue, Louis would come off worst.

I never saw this spiderish character during the spring, nor, I think, did Adolf. Both Louis and Farley would first be revealed to my curious eyes at convention time, but then we would lose sight of them again for the duration of the campaign. Ray attended to liaison.

Ray did not tell us, and may not have realized, what the inner strategy was. Louis was secretive about it, and so, for that matter, was Roosevelt. The two of them, with Farley as an innocent, if professional, missionary, were out not only to capture delegates; they were out to capture the party as well. Before long I should begin to suspect that Roosevelt meant to own it. To be sure, this was not merely to serve his ambition. His intention was to use it for purposes that lay deep in his mind. I define these now, with the benefit of hindsight, as a better life for all Americans, and a better America to live it in. I think it was that general. There were items in it, but only a few he saw as fixed. One of these was security; if Europeans could have that, so could Americans. Another was a new framework for industrialism, and still another was a physically improved country. But those, as I see it, were about all.

This, however, is a conclusion from afterthoughts. We were not introduced to any such intentions then; we were held, in fact, by fairly tenuous threads until later. If materializations of his purpose began to appear, they were still without substance.

It was becoming clear that my proposal for organizing opposing interests under governmental supervision was not acceptable, at least as a sufficient device, and certainly not for campaign purposes. Alternate proposals were discussed over and over, these mostly relying on financial or monetary manipulation. The possibility of raising prices in one convulsive effort was always, it seemed to me, in the air, never quite respectable, but not dismissed. It was hardly consistent with the repeated pledge of sound money, and still it would not take itself out of the list of possibilities.

Roosevelt said I was repeating myself when I came back yet again to the need for bringing prices into relationship with each other, and of course I was. The cigarette holder seemed a foot long as it waved in the air. I replied that it was a necessary step. The only suggestion I was offered as an alternative was inflation. I knew it was fashionable to speak of it now as "reflation"; that might not sound so dangerous to some people, but we ought not to fool ourselves: it meant cheap money—no better than greenbacks or freely coined silver. I repeated what there was against it. Our real trouble was lack of correspondence, of fair relationship, among prices, and a *general* lifting would not cure that. It might even make it worse, because for two years now an adjustment had been going on at a lower level, and the process would have to begin all over if the level should be raised.

Ah, Roosevelt said, I was neglecting the debt problem again. Unless we got values back to where they had been when the debts had been contracted, the load could never be lifted. The insurance companies' investments were impaired; the collateral for bank loans really could not be liquidated for enough to meet depositors' demands—if they made them; and farmers and home-owners were being foreclosed every day. All this was fact. An equalizing mechanism (whatever it was called) couldn't meet this immediate need.

It was a good answer. There *were* the debts. And the creditors in the financial district might like to see them paid off in dollars of much higher purchasing power than had been loaned, but such a demand was in no sense fair. It was, in fact, not possible.

It was now too late to talk about dollars of stable purchasing power—that is, too late to be useful in the present crisis. It was something for the future if support for such a scheme could be found. What was needed was to restore purchasing power, and at once. Also, I reminded myself, I was asking for temporary inflation when I maintained that purchasing power had to be restored by massive spending for relief and public works. I insisted on the "temporary," but not with much conviction.

This argument might have come to nothing, any of it, if the situation had not presently become so much worse—that is, had not reached so many more centers. Businesses in thousands had already found themselves bankrupt, and the number was increasing; the bread and soup lines for the unemployed were lengthening, and many of the applicants were new to charity and shamed by the need for it. What had been a cause for worry and public discussion a few months ago was now becoming a crisis. It was difficult to keep in mind anything but emergency measures.

Roosevelt was not always clear about this. But when he spoke of the need for a general price increase that would enable debts to be paid, he did seem not to be thinking altogether of the institutions—the banks and insurance companies—now going into bankruptcy. He seemed also to be concerned with the individuals who would be hurt, the depositors, the policy-holders, and the borrowers. To hear him speak of the necessity for action that would relieve the strains so many people were undergoing, and to understand the seriousness of his search for what was right and effective to do, made the criticisms of Lippmann, Bliven, and others seem

irresponsible. The Westerners, I was certain, were justified in believing him sincere. The editorialist of *The Times* and, probably,
his clientele were mistaken in their estimate.

To one of our sessions I brought along a new book by Paul H.
Douglas, *The Coming of a New Party* (1932). Roosevelt read
the newspapers and certain magazines, and he spoke occasionally
of Lippmann, to whose criticisms he was especially sensitive. But
he had not seen the Douglas book. Paul, I told him, was a professor at the University of Chicago, a man of my age, and very
concerned about public affairs. He had become convinced that
nothing could be done with the old parties, and he thought the
time right for a new one. When Roosevelt asked who his friends
were, I told him the book was dedicated to Norman Thomas
and the introduction had been written by John Dewey. Roosevelt
would, I said, be interested in one passage about himself:

> Governor Roosevelt, although he wants to be a good man,
> knows that the fate of political heroes inside the old party orga-
> nization is hard. . . . Farmers, workers, and liberals should be-
> ware of placing excessive reliance upon a well-meaning though
> ambitious man to effect a deep sea-change in the Democratic
> party. It would require a whole army of Herculeses and St.
> Georges to transform the Democrats.

I asked if I might read some more. What came next he might
resent; I myself considered it unfair.

He said to go ahead; he had learned not to take the so-called
intellectuals too seriously. They were free with suggestions, but
most of them were of a kind that would make him lose the nomination, probably, and certainly the campaign.

I thought he overstated the intellectuals' offering of advice; actually, there was very little but criticism, and that could not be
called helpful counsel. I read the paragraph:

> It is a sobering thought that twenty years ago many Progressives
> were pinning similar hopes on Woodrow Wilson, who, with all
> respect to Governor Roosevelt, was a far keener thinker and a
> more determined fighter. . . . Yet, after eight years, Wilson re-

tired with the Democratic party as cancerous as ever in its composition and as conservative in its policies. If such was the fate of Wilson, how can we hope for better things from Franklin Roosevelt?

I cannot recall just how this evening's conversation ended, but I recall well enough the embarrassing question I was asked. He wanted to know if Douglas, or any other of his group, could expect to be elected on a platform such as was suggested. It implied a third party. Would Douglas, for instance, egged on by John Dewey, try that? Or would he try to wangle a nomination from a major party? He thought the question answered itself. If either way was tried, it would not succeed. But, he went on, suppose someone with similar ideas, but with more political foresight, did get a major party's nomination and was elected; wasn't that better? In a practical sense—that is, in the sense of making headway toward such objectives—was there any other way in a democracy?

It would be possible, he said, to stir things up, to cause discussion, and to get issues into circulation in Douglas's way. Bryan had been the best of that sort. But even Bryan, who was a gifted demagogue, had never gotten himself elected. What he himself was doing, Roosevelt continued, was trying for election and for operative advance, not for mere agitation and argument. The Democratic offering would be less than the radicals would like, but it would be something voters would accept. The Republicans were committed to an ideology that cramped their actions, and this, accepted by Hoover, was hurting him. The Democrats, being more flexible, had a chance to become the majority party. A leader with this support might continue to advance, perhaps for a generation. In the end he would have got further than he would if he took early risks with public opinion and jeopardized his majority.

I was not happy with this statement. The depression had to be overcome, and in ways that might not be generally approved unless they were campaigned for. There was much more to be said, but there would be other times to say it; for now, further argument was postponed.

The steward came in with the bedtime tray. Roosevelt as usual mixed for himself what he called a horse's neck; it seemed to be ginger ale with lemon peel dangling over its edge. But there was something else for the rest of us if we wanted it. I wondered—but did not ask—who his bootlegger was. But of course I knew that Democrats, like all politicians, have many connections. Some kind friend left a bottle with him once in a while, and no questions were asked. Like the others, I had learned to avoid what was in those bottles. Anyway, Roosevelt seemed to enjoy the misbehavior of having them more than the stuff they contained. Refusal was not regarded as an offense to his hospitality.

CHAPTER XVI

Privy Counseling

🎖 🎖 🎖

It was a long time before we had any recognition, if it can be called that; but newsmen did begin to be curious about us. Sometime in June, Roosevelt answered a question by saying lightly that "Moley's crowd" was his "privy council." * This might be regarded as putting us in our places, but it was not so much that, I think, as a way of eliminating all formality from our frequent gatherings. He meant to indicate to us and others that he was finding us useful as volunteers—momentarily, but no more—and that the relationship was personal, not official.

We were to learn that this was characteristic. Roosevelt would organize endeavors only if he could close them out simply by not mentioning them again. His custom of consulting many and diverse people was already known to us. The issues we were discussing so seriously he had often asked others to "think about" or even, sometimes, to "work on." Naturally we suspected that there were more such assignments than there actually were. We frequently wondered, in our conferences, whether he was speaking from material furnished by others, and sometimes we were certain that we recognized the source.

* He had first used the term in a late-April private conversation with Moley, who was distressed by it. See *After Seven Years*, p. 23.

It was when he was approaching problems about which he would have to do or say something that he most disliked any regularity, any suggestion likely to be interpreted by outsiders as indicating that he had taken a position. He wanted information, analysis, even views if he respected their author, but in matters that were unsettled, especially when they were controversial or might become so, he was careful to keep his associations casual. He did not explain this, and even when Ray was worried and asked for more definition of his assignments, he usually got no satisfaction. This habit of Roosevelt's may have been instinctive and not acknowledged even to himself, or it may have been part of his politician's apparatus. There were potentially useful people who were so frustrated by the hazy assignments he gave them that they simply went back to their own concerns. He seldom asked us what had become of them.

We understood that his saying we were a privy council was a way of denying that we were really privy to anything. The scatological implication tickled him, and he laughed at Ray's obvious dismay. He seemed to be certain that newsmen would not drop their protective habit and make fun of us, or of him for having us around. They told us he had always kept his contacts with them light in tone. That was an advantage to him and to them; more formalization would have made many of his approaches to them, and theirs to him, much more difficult. Also, when they got hold of anything he wanted to keep to himself they were cautious with it for fear of an annoyance that would cloud the atmosphere. More was off the record than the remarks he specified as such.

In a long experience of public life, I have never seen anything quite like this. There were several—Lindley, Kieran, Storm, Stevenson—who were as much in his confidence as we were. They had freedom of the premises much of the time, they affected not to see what they were not supposed to see. Everyone, including their editors, knew that this almost family relationship had become a settled custom, and it worked very well. Lindley, for instance, wrote voluminously almost every day for *The Herald Tribune,* a Republican paper as hostile to Roosevelt's ambitions as it was possible to be. His dispatches were informative, but they were not colored.

When we began our work, the newsmen of this group were already established intimates. At the moment they were being pressed by their editors about numerous subjects, some of them with immense potential. Were we discussing the money problem? Many a speculator would have given much to know exactly what Roosevelt threw out in his talks with us, or even what we were suggesting to him. And this was only one of the subjects of interest to many who could make profitable use of such knowledge. We had to be very discreet indeed. But so far as the reporters were concerned, it was understood, without Roosevelt's ever saying so, that we were to be anonymous.

None of us, fortunately, was known to favor or oppose policies of consequence to large interests. If one of us had been an Irving Fisher, for instance, the conclusion would have been reached at once that ways to raise the price level and perhaps to reform the monetary system were being considered. If we had so much as hinted abroad that Roosevelt had such an intention, he would have stopped all further exploration of the subject. Too many financiers were trying their best to bring him around to their view. He was being watched with the sharpest eyes in the speculative community for sympathy with schemes for cheapening the currency and thus relieving the burden of debtors. There was suspicion but no evidence.

Since I had told him frankly that my own knowledge of monetary theories came only from dealing with them as a part of the courses I taught, and since the others were no more expert, I wondered why he discussed them with us. I knew something about the devices most often proposed. They were fully described in my texts, and I even made an outline of their supposed virtues, attaching to each a name—or perhaps several names, those of their advocates. Such an elementary review was useless to him. He had read at least one of the popular Foster and Catchings books, which had supplemented his Harvard recollections.

His difficulty, it seemed to me, was that he did not distinguish clearly between monetary and fiscal policies—that is, the expansion or contraction of money and credit as distinguished from the use of taxation, public expenditures, and governmental loans. Both could affect business activity, but monetary manipulation seemed to be more frankly inflationary than public expenditures. Also it was easier and would be enthusiastically accepted by the populist West.

It was while this was going on that I began to guess why his Cornell connections—of several years' standing, with Henry Morgenthau as the liaison man—were not being used: the Cornellians were identified with a proposal. When I let him know that I had guessed the reason for exploration with me instead of real experts, he laughed and said I was guessing at things a professor ought not to get into. If I didn't watch out, he said, I might turn into another Paul Douglas.

There was some embarrassment when, one after another, Ray brought around experts we had searched out and then found that Roosevelt had no desire to see them another time. Ray had to do some explaining about this, but it did have the advantage of eliminating some we would have found it disagreeable to associate with for any length of time. Among these were several monetary theorists, and also those with widely known "plans" and those who had been associated with some such "movement" as technocracy, just then being much publicized. It also made a whole class of others ineligible—the financiers and businessmen who would have given anything to have had it known that they were being consulted.

Later, after his nomination, this particular prohibition was relaxed, and old acquaintances from his own Wall Street days with the Fidelity and Deposit Company, or even from Groton and Harvard, were allowed to come and sometimes were even sent for. This was true of some of the wiser and more moderate ones, including Russell Leffingwell, Averell Harriman, Walter Wheeler Stewart, and a few others. It was one of these—a banker, René Leon—who made the important suggestion in a later crisis that a forgotten law would legitimize the sequestering of gold.

I too had some acquaintances in the Street. After all, I had had years of association with the Wharton School as student and teacher, and friends from those days had found occupations in the financial district. I was, however, not encouraged to renew my acquaintances; Roosevelt preferred to keep our present discussions among those of us who had no contacts there. We were merely university people; we might not be practical, might not even be expert in procedures, but we had the virtue in his eyes of being free, and also of being bright enough, he thought, to bring him the stuff policies could be made from. Adolf was questionable, from this point of view; he had an office in the financial district, but it was a *law* office, and this evidently cleared him.

Immediately after Roosevelt's return from Warm Springs, Ray was commandeered for further work on the Walker case. We were, of course, going on with other assignments, but nothing else seemed to Ray so exciting or immediate. As a matter of fact, he had been involved in the case since January, but by now Judge Seabury had exposed such financial carelessness on the part of "the little mayor," as Roosevelt called him, that the scandal could no longer be ignored. Jimmy Walker's pleasure funds had been so extensive and acquired in such dubious ways that removal might have to be undertaken before the convention. At any rate, the proceedings had to be carefully developed. If the nomination went off as hoped and the case was still pending, it would be an unwelcome diversion during the campaign.

In addition, however, Ray had to get the acceptance speech into shape, an entirely new sort of job and one to be approached very seriously. It would, we hoped, forecast new departures, but in deference to the elders it had to acknowledge some traditional policies as well—lower tariffs, for instance. It had to say everything, be a preview of the whole appeal, make the workers enthusiastic, and establish Roosevelt's position.

One evening when I happened to be alone with Roosevelt, I said to him that from what we read in the papers, he must have done that homework he had said he was doing in Georgia after he went to bed. He seemed to have been busy about sixteen hours every day—at other things. Had he really managed to get through any of the material Sam had brought?

He had been pushed some, he said, and when he was down there he liked to get in some exercise. It was hard to get any either in Albany or in Hyde Park in these days. Without really answering my question, he set off on a description of the depression in western Georgia. He had not only seen its effect on the farmers as he drove about the countryside but had got from Calloway and others moving accounts of trouble in the textile industry. These were lessons he could learn only in such circumstances, among people who thought of him less as an official than as an influential friend.

He spoke, also, about the speech at Oglethorpe; he supposed we must have approved it. Not everyone did. He smiled around his cigarette holder.

Seeing an opening, I said it was the "continuing balance" passage that had excited me. If, however, he really was thinking of some sort of organization for fair exchange, we could hardly stop where he had ended in the speech. I reminded him that we had already talked about this and said that it seemed to me he might have said more than he had.

He hesitated; then he said that, thinking it over, he was more bothered about the antitrust laws than I seemed to be. This surprised me. I had thought we were past that obstacle, but as he went on I soon understood that his reference was not to the laws themselves, but to the assumptions about free enterprise they represented. We were back to orthodox progressivism. I said I had hoped this matter of industrial planning and co-ordination could be made one of the important themes for the campaign. The prospect of stabilizing machinery that would avoid future depressions ought to be good news for an exhausted country. It was not what was needed for the lift that would bring recovery; that would have to come first, as an emergency action; but looking beyond to the prevention of future depressions could at least be suggested. Or couldn't it?

I'd probably heard from Ray or Ernest, he said, that Louis had

had a fit and had claimed that the politicians were all scared. But anyway we'd talk about it—maybe next week.

So it was postponed. Meanwhile, our difficulty as privy councilors was that the material we had gotten together was in no shape, really, to be depended on—especially if, as we assumed, some form was meant to be imposed on the whole for a consistent series of presentations during the campaign. That remained to be done. We had started late, and the weeks were crowded. Ray had not really found a way to get many usable contributions from others. He asked for them, but what came in was not often what we needed.

We were learning that memoranda presenting the result of research or giving an outline of ideas were not to be thought of as more than preparations for sessions of talk. Now that the Southern interlude was over and we were getting on toward summer, Roosevelt was up against it, and we went on with a sense of some urgency. After our longish talks he could feel that what he concluded made sense, was defensible. This was especially true if we had fought over it with him until all of us were satisfied that everything had been said, but this required repeated sessions, and even then things were often left to be considered further when we had more material. Too often this further discussion never took place and we had to leave things disturbingly inconclusive. I must say that this state of affairs worried us more than it did him.

We did get help from two members of the public law faculty at Columbia—Howard Lee McBain and Joseph D. McGoldrick, one an old and experienced professor and the other a much younger instructor. We were suggesting ventures into territory forbidden to government by custom and perhaps by law as well—although there was no certainty about this, since "law" consisted so largely of changing court interpretations. Regulation, of course, had long been part of the American complex of relationships, but all controls had been contested so long and so bitterly that what was forbidden, and what was only objected to, were often hard to distinguish.

In practice Roosevelt looked at our memoranda rather hastily —more hastily as time passed—and as something to go on rather than something finished. Everything was put off until we could get down to critical appraisals in Albany evenings. We still had these, and they were still serious and sometimes long. They tended now to practicality. My long-term concerns were usually shelved.

Commentators were complaining more and more sharply about Roosevelt's continuing evasiveness. They asked why he did not "speak out." After Smith made his play for attention, there was an evident desire to give Roosevelt more space, but this was hard to do interestingly with nothing more than a daily recording of visitors, travels, and neighborly events. There were echoes of the rising demand, too, from the Western politicians and especially from the progressives. Those in the Congress thought he ought to support actively their program for planning, relief, and public works, but the editorialists who wanted him to be more explicit had no clear suggestions to make. Neither did Louis Howe, among his intimates, but Louis suspected that anything definite might be frightening to someone. He had the fixed opinion that not a single delegate was to be won now by anything that could be said; the only possibility was a loss. Since the Howe-Farley team had been put more or less in charge until the convention was over, Roosevelt deferred to their judgment; either that or, as I myself concluded, he concurred in it. At any rate, he continued to evade all questions of substance, and the progressives grumbled.

Those of us who had been putting together material while he was away now had several memoranda to be discussed when he got around again to problems of recovery, reform, and institutional changes. I had been in touch with Bob La Follette and Wagner, who had already taken the lead—usefully, as I thought—and they continued to get attention. As their proposals developed there was fairly complete coverage of their activities. They had agreed on, and were pressuring for, sizable bond issues to pay for relief and public works. There were differences about cost, but estimates tended to increase as the situation grew more critical. Only Bob La

Follette, however, was demanding the billions I now thought needed. Wagner was asking for no more than what would be adequate; even that seemed beyond any imagining to conservatives, of course, and the politicians were impressed by the pained outcries from Democrats as well as Republicans at the thought that Roosevelt might agree.

Hoover was still holding out for loans to the states instead of the grants urged by the progressives. Bob rested his argument on the exhaustion of the states' borrowing capacity; only grants, he insisted, would be of any use. Roosevelt's friends naturally urged that at least the Wagner bill ought to be endorsed, but he held off for a long time. What had been done in New York, as well as what he had previously said, committed him to some such action, and he had admitted that efforts by the states were inadequate because, however their resources were strained, they could not by themselves meet the need. This was enough, he told us, until he could speak as the nominee. I soon discovered that he was no less shocked by the figures than were many of the conservatives. They were far higher than he had imagined. We assembled them. Take thirteen million—the number of the unemployed—we told him, or reduce it to ten million, to be far inside reality; then multiply by four, the size of the average family; that made forty million men, women, and children without any source of support. At a dollar a day, much less than a defensible minimum, that added up to more than a billion dollars a month. His eyes narrowed and he swallowed hard when we spoke of twelve billion dollars added to the annual budget.

Nevertheless we went on. Suppose half the unemployed got jobs at work that was self-liquidating, and suppose the rest still had to have that dollar a day or starve (and he was certainly not going to let anyone starve); the cost was still staggering. Where could six billion dollars come from, when the national income was down to about forty billion?

So much for relief. Obviously, the cause and cure of depression had to be looked at harder than he had been looking. There had to be the sort of realism that we had been outlining for relief but that only the congressional progressives had dared suggest. We began new discussions in the hope that he was now ready to accept reality. If we took the Oglethorpe statement literally, we had only to work out implications. The trouble was that his venturesomeness seemed suddenly to have evaporated. He began to be evasive even with us.

About reform, he had already said something. He had spoken harshly of bankers and speculators and had assured his audiences that there must be stricter regulation of their activities. What form the regulation would take and how far it would go was worrying not only those engaged in such businesses but the politicians as well. They were all trying to find out what he had in mind, and they were very free with advice. But we now had some hope that he was contemplating something further. At Oglethorpe, the theory had been outlined; the deep trouble, he had said, after reviewing other explanations, was

> . . . an insufficient distribution of buying power coupled with an oversufficient speculation in production. While wages rose in many of our industries, they did not as a whole rise proportionately to the reward to capital, and at the same time, the purchasing power of other great groups of our population was allowed to shrink.

This was a clear reference to the oversavings theory we had discussed so thoroughly, and we were prepared to expand on it at any length. I was still afraid that the conclusion to be drawn was a change more radical than Roosevelt yet realized. He had spoken of a time when "the reward for a day's work will have to be greater . . . and the reward to capital . . . will have to be less." But it was one thing to say so much and quite another to suggest the forcing up of wages and the forcing down of profits and interest; besides, this would have to be done continuously, not just once as an emergency measure, if a balanced relationship was to be maintained.

What came of these talks at the beginning of June was that I was encouraged to go into the subject further. Actually several of our conversations were very free and fairly detailed. I cannot recall exactly what he said and what part I contributed, but I do recall that I had been mistaken to suppose he had not realized many of the implications. During the weeks in Georgia he had done a lot of thinking, and obviously this was only an extension of ideas developed in the past.

The theory was simple enough. What the productive system existed for was to produce and produce efficiently, making its services and products available to consumers. What it did, in fact, was to pursue profits whether goods and services resulted or not. Often more return could be got by withholding than by providing. This was an anomaly that could only be corrected by a device for resolving the contradiction. I was able to cite not only Veblen's sardonic theorizing but Wesley Mitchell's *Making Goods and Making Money,* the final verdict on free enterprise.

The public interest demanded that goods and services flow to consumers at prices they could pay—that the total income available in the community absorb the total product with no shortages and no surpluses. This meant that there was not only a welfare interest in wages and other forms of income—interest rates, profits, dividends, pensions, and benefits of other sorts—but also a strictly economic one.

This was important. Interest rates had to do with attracting capital and so with increasing production; profits were necessary for incentive; dividends encouraged investment; wages and benefits were used by the ultimate consumer to energize the whole process. It had become an inescapably interrelated complex, and its delicate adjustment must be continuously maintained.

When the complex was not recognized as being interrelated, and when its various segments operated as if they had no connection with others or with the whole, it was inevitable that the system should fail here or there, a factory slowing down, an industry going into decline or having a boom, capital failing to go where it could do the most good, people unemployed and unable to consume. This was the problem.

Through the intricate web of credit and finance, these over- or under-emphases would be multiplied until the financial complex itself reflected the irregularity and began to wobble. A bank here, an investment house there, would find its debtors unable to pay up because customers for their goods had vanished and they could no longer do business. Such a trouble was a disease. It could spread like an infectious fever. That was what had happened.

It was not only necessary, therefore, to do what could be done to repair a wreck here and there, to bolster up one or another damaged institution; it was necessary to make a system out of what was no system at all: to stabilize, and to *prevent* wobbling, not just correct it once and then let business alone to go through another similar cycle.

We had discussed all this several times before, and when Roosevelt said at Oglethorpe that *planning* was necessary, we knew that this was what he meant. Industry must plan for itself in these ways, and government must plan for its role in the economy— limiting, by its rule, the power to exploit. It must set the goals for production and, if necessary, direct investments and establish fair standards for all concerned.

I was prepared to go on arguing with Roosevelt that he would fail all those hopeful people who had come out to cheer his progress toward the presidency unless he found ways to set the economy running again and then to stabilize it. That was his first duty. Failure to grasp this had ruined Hoover. It would ruin any statesman from now on who did not obey the present imperative of industrialism—to manage it as a whole.

I was more afraid of the old progressives than of the big businessmen. In conversations with La Follette, Wagner, Costigan, Cutting, and La Guardia, agreement had been reached among us on the general shape of the needed reorganization. Bob La Follette had even been ahead of me; he usually would be, I was to learn, and I could say to Roosevelt that there was at least this source of support. I knew that he respected it, but I was beginning to be aware, if I had not known it before, that there was a powerful hidden influence. There were not only the conservatives to take account of—the reactionary, extremely individualistic farmers and small-town people, who might not stand for any more talk of "bold, persistent experiment"—but also the Brandeis progressives, and they included such elders as Wheeler, Norris, Hiram Johnson, and Walsh. The platform would be shaped during the next weeks; what they would put into it would be orthodox—that is to say, the "bold experimentation" mentioned at Oglethorpe would find no echo. Its place would be taken by platitudinous and general remarks about free enterprise.

We hung there for the moment, I for one hoping that some miracle was materializing, but not actually believing that it would appear.

CHAPTER XVII

I Lose One Argument

🏵 🏵 🏵

On May 27, in an address to Westchester County Democrats at Tuckahoe, Roosevelt made an announcement. He said that on his return from Warm Springs a plan worked out after careful consideration of existing conditions had been presented to him by the Temporary Emergency Relief Administration. He had discussed it with Harry L. Hopkins, and every public-welfare commissioner in the state was being authorized to place such families as they were able to on "subsistence farms."

The rent of the small farms would be paid by the state, and the tenants would be furnished with tools, seed for planting, and household necessities. Already 244 families had been so established, and this was only a beginning.

Directions for this scheme and its presentation must have been given before he left for the South, and it must have been in process all the time I had been marshaling arguments against it. In the course of several long and some short discussions of the idea, I had been given no intimation, either by him or by Eleanor, of its preparation—an illustration of that separation I have spoken of before.

It would now almost certainly be argued for as a national policy. There might be a speech about it. It would be put forward as an escape from unemployment and the hard conditions of urban life; hardy gardeners would produce their own food, and their wives would preserve it; they would have a secure home on their own acres—and they would no longer need public relief.

The publicity man who wrote the accompanying release was suitably eloquent, but the sentiments, I was sure, mirrored quite faithfully the Roosevelts' enthusiasm:

> The name of New York has become associated with sky-scrapers, machines, and a great industrial complex. . . . A living from the land is still in the heritage of the New Yorker. . . . The plan . . . seems to me a profoundly significant one, because it is a bold step toward alleviating the critical situation of those who have suffered so devastatingly in the depression. . . .
>
> Both from the point of view of the unemployed families and the taxpayer, the plan for subsistence farms is a constructive measure. It reduces the huge cost of relief, while it places dependent families in a position to at least partially support themselves in healthy surroundings. . . . They may secure through the good earth the permanent jobs they have lost in overcrowded industrial cities. . . .*

When I opposed subsistence homesteads, it had been careless of me not to have inquired more closely into the background. I had thought it must be merely the kind of fancy to be expected of goodhearted but impractical upper-class folk with an idealized view of going back to the soil. The hearty-peasant syndrome was quite prevalent; it could almost be said to have become a movement. It was supported by such formidable publicists as Bernarr MacFadden, the health cultist and publisher, and Ralph Borsodi, who had written glowingly in a widely sold book about bread made from home-ground cereals and fresh vegetables grown by "natural" methods. Borsodi had a good many sympathizers. I had reviewed his book rather caustically, I am afraid, saying that before joining the nature cult I would like to hear from Mrs. Borsodi, who must be the one who did all that grain-grinding and bread-making, and perhaps the hoeing too. I had been amused to have a

* *The New York Times,* May 28, 1932.

long letter from that lady telling me how right I was. If time—or women's labor—was worth anything, the food so highly praised by her husband was far more expensive than any that could be bought. Not only that, the whole business was a literary romp, got up by sentimentalists who hadn't any idea what they were talking about.

Silas Strawn, the Chicago banker, was another who had been eloquent on the subject and was presumably prepared to make some financial contribution. I found later that a long list of enthusiasts were in touch with Eleanor; moreover, one of her fellow cultists was Louis Howe, who wouldn't have known a tomato plant from a pole bean.

The picture could be made an attractive one if the difficulties were minimized and the benefits exaggerated. Somehow the Roosevelts had managed to persuade themselves to do both. The first time I had a chance to comment on the proposal, I pointed out that agriculture was already burdened with surpluses, and that if anything was *not* needed, it was more producers. On the contrary, what was needed was more consumers and fewer homesteads.

Roosevelt replied that the proposal had nothing to do with the farm problem; it was intended only to help reduce the cost of relief by making the unemployed, or some of them, self-sustaining. They would not produce crops to sell, only crops to consume. What about clothing and fuel? I asked. There were many goods and services a family must have besides food.

Eleanor had convinced herself that manufacturers would establish factories to give employment and thus offer the homesteaders an income. As a Wharton School graduate, I was outraged by this idea. People go to employment, I told her, not employment to people. She said she had reason to believe manufacturers would cooperate. If they did, I said, they would have to charge some added costs to charity, and this did not exactly fit the pattern of a profit system.

Roosevelt thought and said that on at least two points of our difference I was not up-to-date. Both the family farm and the relocated farmer on a subsistence homestead would be favored by progress that I seemed to ignore. The adaptation of machinery to small operations was going forward rapidly; the use of electric power was sure to favor the decentralization of industry; and automobiles, together with good roads, made it possible to go many miles to work every day.

The family farm, he argued, would be more efficient and secure in the future than it had been in the past. And industries, not having to think of big power plants using coal, would be glad to move to places where there was a better environment. He looked forward, he said—and he had been saying this publicly, I learned—to nothing less than a transformation. Workers would be living on their small places, raising subsistence crops, and traveling to work five days a week in their own cars.

I should have abandoned the argument at this point. What would be done of this sort would not and could not be extensive, because of the immense work involved in planning communities, finding suitable locations, acquiring land, and so forth. When Eleanor persisted in reviving the argument, I did continue to object, in a muted way. It was a matter that was quite beyond the reach of reason, and it was not important enough to jeopardize our relations. What bothered me most, then and later, was the implication it conveyed of impracticality, of a man who wanted to be President of the United States but who was actually a dilettante given to joining in the follies of the well-to-do who wanted to improve the lot of the poor. This was laudable enough, but he wanted to do it by removing them from the main stream of economic events— thus forming a kind of self-sustaining pool of labor held in reserve during hard times. If they had no work they could still sustain themselves. The word "subsistence" attached to "homesteads" somehow annoyed me. Besides, an approach like this to the problem of a disorderly economy might confirm the opinion, already too prevalent, that Roosevelt was hardly tough-minded enough for the job he was seeking.

The proposal, I was also afraid, would be confused with the very different one of resettling such farmers as those in the hill counties of New York—the ones we had often discussed—where erosion, and competition from more fertile areas, had made the farms unprofitable. This I hoped could be made a national policy. But the unemployed in the cities—how could anyone suppose them capable of cultivating the land successfully? Or, for that matter, of settling happily in the country?

There was a stream of tradition here coming down from T.R. and such others as Gifford Pinchot. It was stretching matters beyond reason to bring homesteads into this category, but the Roosevelts seemed to have no difficulty about it. No President had done more than T.R. for the cause of conservation, and mixed with his concern for the preservation of natural resources had been a notion that rural life possessed qualities that city life sadly lacked. This, I should have known, reinforced the predilections of his Hyde Park relatives.

Pinchot, who had been through many battles with the exploiters of the public domain, had been an admired senior. Now he was Governor of Pennsylvania, a progressive, and as such at least a potential rival. This rivalry might be for prestige with the liberals and not for immediate political advantage, but Roosevelt felt Pinchot's presence just the same. The "back-to-the-land" project might possibly be a sort of challenge to him. It might be a friendly one, but challenges in politics are only nominally friendly; they do not go to the length of conceding much to a rival.

But there was something else involved in the homestead project. Eleanor might be moved merely by the prospect of families settled in rose-covered cottages in the midst of a few garden acres, but Roosevelt himself had in mind some other considerations. In 1931 he had taken steps to halt, if he could, the terrible inroads of misery before the winter should add cold to the prevalent hunger. Pinchot just then had proposed to call a conference of Governors on unemployment. Roosevelt could hardly refuse to attend; yet he had objected that something must be devised at once; there was no time for long-range planning. He tried to get Pinchot to accept this limitation in his call, and when he addressed the assembled executives, he had asked insistently how the actual emergency of the approaching winter was to be met.

Actually, nothing came of the suggestions for co-ordination made at the conference. They had little relevance to the emergency of the moment. Roosevelt had done what he could with no help from others. He had recommended to a special session of the legislature that a Temporary Emergency Relief Administration be established. He had used the words "temporary" and "emergency" to stress his intention of using the agency only to get through the crisis; it was not to become a permanent organization. There were two reasons for this, and, whether or not Pinchot was a spur, they did have some relationship to Roosevelt's genuine emotion about a homestead movement. There was, at the time, a campaign of criticism in the press directed at the British system of social insurance. Its benefits were called a "dole," and if there was one word more fancied by the conservatives than any other during those years, it was this; they rolled it over and over on their tongues. They succeeded fairly well in attaching to it all the connotations of willingness to be supported in idleness, saying that it was ruinous to character and a direct affront to individualism; red-blooded Americans rejected help in caring for their dependents; that was a father's duty.

Roosevelt had accepted this view. He often claimed that his TERA "avoided the dole." It was at this time that he proposed the fifty-per-cent increase in the income tax to meet the expense.

Those who called this a "grandstanding gesture," as many did, were mistaken. He felt that bond issues to finance such a program would represent a transfer of its costs to the future and would excuse those who had got themselves into it from having to get themselves out of it. Looked at later, this seemed a curious and, in many ways, an inconsistent policy. To carry on what he had undertaken, he would later have to ask for authorization to borrow, but at the moment he was being critical of Hoover for a seeming willingness to allow the present generation to escape from paying for its own mistakes. Hoover, who wanted even more earnestly to escape borrowing, was being forced into it by the insistence of progressive legislators. The demand that the Congress accept his recommendations was being treated with growing ridicule by La Follette and others, and they were getting wider and wider attention.

Roosevelt's TERA had been well started in 1931 by Jesse I. Straus with Harry L. Hopkins to help him; it was the first such state organization to be set up, and it gave Roosevelt a claim to practical concern for the unemployed not matched by others. Hopkins recruited his staff from the social workers he knew so well (he had been one of them), and they did what they could. But it was not long before most of their funds were being used for the "dole" Roosevelt had been saying he would avoid. Jobs were hard to invent and hard to supervise; money went much further when used for relief. When the Brains Trust meetings began, TERA had been functioning for a year. Jesse Straus had resigned in March to organize the Business and Professional Men's League for Roosevelt, and Hopkins had succeeded him as director. Hopkins was practical. It was his job to reach as many families as possible. For this, relief was much more effective than works.

We began in May to hear rumors of another conference to canvass the unemployment situation, this one to be called by Roosevelt. It seemed that already he had had invitations prepared, saying in part that all the conventional remedies had been tried and had proved to be insufficient; more effort was urgently called for. But Frances Perkins, Henry Bruère, and Hopkins among them persuaded him to call off the meeting. A preliminary survey had convinced them that nothing new would come of it; moreover, he would inevitably be pictured as challenging the United States senators who had actual bills in the legislative mill.

What he could do as a Governor really had been done, and done as well as could have been expected. He was dissatisfied with the results because they made so poor a showing after his rather inflated promises. His strong affirmation—still of record—that relief was not a federal responsibility was by now so absurd that the sooner he abandoned it the better. He had to abandon it without saying so, hoping that no one would notice. He endorsed Wagner's proposed measure, and thus joined in the larger effort. He still insisted that relief ought not to be a permanent obligation of the federal government, but hunger and cold were crisis matters and could not be allowed to go on even if things had to be done that would not ordinarily be approved.

When, presently, I became more familiar with Roosevelt history, I began to realize that in the homestead matter a conviction was involved. This was one way of doing something on his own, something not thought of by others. I could reconstruct afterward what had happened. At the time Harry Hopkins had taken over from Jesse Straus, he had for the first time really come into contact with Roosevelt, who realized that several of his firmest notions, including pay-as-you-go and avoidance of doles, had been undermined by circumstance and had to be abandoned.

Hopkins was an opportunist; policy was not one of his interests. When he discovered, in a dinner conversation, that the Roosevelts had one remaining thing they would like to try in this baffling field, he simply proceeded to organize it. If they wanted subsistence homesteads, he would give them some. I imagine he never asked himself whether the scheme would succeed or what its effect would be on other programs, such as farm relief. When it was ready, he had a speech written for Roosevelt, proudly proclaiming one contribution to the self-help list that was the Governor's very own. It was no dole; it was not even a public work; it was an opportunity for the unemployed to re-establish themselves.

Perhaps Hopkins had read, as I had not, what Roosevelt had said at a Country Life Conference in 1931. He had spoken glowingly of the benefits of "contact with earth and with nature" and of the privilege of "getting away from pavements and noise." In the country, he said, there was an opportunity for permanence of abode, a chance to establish "a real home in the traditional American sense."

I was a little profane, I suppose, in complaining to Ray about my nasty surprise. He laughed and said that I had not had the advantage of acquaintance with Louis Howe.

I asked how Louis came into it. He wanted, Ray said, to put all
the unemployed on little farms and kill off all the middlemen; that
was his brand of radicalism.

I asked if Eleanor and Louis had got this up between them. Ray
said that Roosevelt was in it too. It seemed to him no more than a
trivial side interest. He thought I took it too seriously, and perhaps
I did.

I was somewhat gratified (in a malicious way, I suppose) that
presently Roosevelt had to back-track, and for the reason I had
predicted. In June he announced that his homesteads were not to
be interpreted as a back-to-the-land movement, but only as a relief
measure. He later on suggested the project again to some Ohio
farm editors, and what they said to him about surpluses and about
city people on farms stopped any further development of the
theme.

In those early days almost the only real sympathy I got about
this minor disappointment came from Doc. That salty Irishman reminded me that he had said we had to stop Eleanor from wearing
the pants in the family; she would ruin this whole shebang if we
didn't. Frank, he said, was corny enough with his fables about
Hyde Park and Pine Mountain; but what would the Iowa farmers
think? They couldn't get tractors to plow with, couldn't pay off
their mortgages, and here these worthless city bums were to be
given a free home with everything else thrown in. How did I like
that for a picture?

We discussed it further. One of my troubles was that I could
not reconcile this aberration with Roosevelt's infinitely detailed
and practical approach to some other problems: power, insurance,
railroads, the credit structure. He had assembled in his mind not
only operational knowledge, but arguments pro and con about
what to do. In this matter he was certain that people wanted the
amenities of country life with such ardor that they would take to
the land by the millions. This led him, I thought, to exaggerate
everything favorable about the country and to foresee a pattern of
civilization that was pure fantasy. I thought that cities were destined to grow, that when factories were established in the country-

side it would be only to exploit labor, and that the workers would soon learn that this was so. I also thought that some would have a facility with gardens, but not many, and that their allotments, for the most part, would simply be neglected. Subsistence homesteads would soon become rural slums.

But this was the controversy that taught me lessons I ought not to have had to learn about the operations of our political system. When I thought over my arguments with the Roosevelts, I had to say that the homestead impulse, even if mistaken, was a good one. They meant to find ways to improve the lives of people for whom they had responsibility. Those who most urgently needed drastic change in their circumstances were certainly the urban unemployed living in the squalor of death-trap tenements. To take them away from that, to give them a new chance, and particularly in an entirely different and—as the Roosevelts felt—a better environment, was an important objective. It also offered some other advantages, such as promising to take them off relief and make them self-supporting.

I was certain that none of this was so. But I had to make up my mind whether, in such situations, I would accept the judgment of the man who had a right to make it or whether I would sulk because I disagreed. This, and other disappointments—and I could already see others coming, much more important than this—would be a test of loyalty. It was something every individual in such a situation had to make up his mind about: would he or would he not value his own judgment above that of the individual who had been awarded the right to decide?

I considered seriously that right to decide, and the conclusion I came to affected not only my future relationship with Roosevelt but the whole of my future public work. I concluded that I could not take the alternative of refusing to work further with him. I had already seen some of my colleagues do just that. When they were asked for opinions and these were not accepted, they "took a walk," as Al Smith would later put it—and very likely they justified it as a matter of conscience. I was tempted to this sort of refusal. I had come to some conclusions about public policy. If they were not accepted, I could refuse to go on. My insisting, of course, would come to nothing more than making a record; it would not influence the conclusions of the person who was offering himself for public approval—in this case, Roosevelt. I had done what I could about that when I had arranged my arguments and presented them as persuasively as I could. To take the line that, if he did not agree, I would quit was to make myself the arbiter of his judgment.

As to his judgment, I was beginning to realize that it was of necessity far more complicated than I had conceived. We had been talking about public policies, mostly economic, and it had been obvious that in his mind they were being fitted to the requirements of his bid for the presidency. Doc, Sam, and even Ray were teaching me this lesson without having any such intention. They assumed that I already knew as well as they what was going on; as they discussed it, they brought me into their circle. My lack of sophistication made me more humble than they knew.

They were enlisted in the Roosevelt cause. They were utterly loyal. They would persuade him, if they could, to do what they believed best. I hesitated over this word; did it mean best for Roosevelt or best for the country? This was a question they had settled for themselves a good way back; for them the two were identical. When I thought it over, I realized that I was in process of accepting the means to agreed ends. Roosevelt wanted to better the lot of the impoverished; he wanted to conserve resources; and he meant to use government for these purposes. How he would manage to accomplish these things was another matter. That depended not on how he *would like* to do it but on how he *could* do it.

When it came to that, how could I set my judgment against his? I saw quite suddenly—it was like a revelation—why Sam and Doc saw things so simply, why they were not tense, as I was. They had long ago made up their minds that what they wanted to see done was most likely to be done by helping Roosevelt to reach a position of power. This may not have been conscious, for neither man was self-examining, as I was apt to be. It was wonderfully satisfactory, I could see, to have reached that state of certainty. I had been surprised to discover what I should have known, that it was neither a servile nor an uncritical state. The things I heard them say about Roosevelt and his actions would have been outrageous if they had not been said in the framework of this placid and settled loyalty.

Louis was sometimes called Roosevelt's "no man." I understood that Doc and Sam were "no men" too, and so, I thought, was Ray, although I was less certain about him. Could I be one of them? What was involved—supposing Roosevelt accepted me in the same way—was either to submit myself to the discipline of service or else to return to the academic independence I had always considered so important.

This amounted to something more than distinguishing between ends and means. I did not have to admit that good ends could be reached by bad means, although, in a digression, I thought seriously about this. I had already seen some means approved that I thought likely to affect adversely the ends they were intended to achieve. I foresaw that there would be more of these, and that I should have to go along in spite of strong feelings about them. Doc and Sam did this all the time, protesting bitterly within the Roosevelt circle, but of course never in public. I could do that too if my loyalty was as settled and unshakable as theirs.

I struggled with this in some lonely hours, and I concluded that this was our political way. Roosevelt had a claim to such service. If I felt abused, I must not complain. If decisions did not go my way, I had done what I could if I had tried my best to be convincing. I could complain and even feel sorry for myself, but I must stay in the circle of the dedicated.

There was something else; the power Roosevelt was achieving would be shared with others of many sorts. He would design its strategy as he saw best, accepting from others what he thought useful, expecting them to give this support unreservedly and without conditions, especially the condition that it *must* be accepted. Something more than one man's direction had to be recognized; a sort of group loyalty was involved.

I was to wonder sometimes in the future—and I did foresee some of it this early—how I found this simple acceptance possible.

It would prove to be one of the clear channels of my whole life. After thinking it over, I believe I know. I shall not explore it at length here, but I shall make an acknowledgment to the group I worked with at Columbia. I had learned there to make my contribution in the setting of a co-operative plan requiring such a sacrifice of independence. My elders there had accepted my earnest contributions. They had expected me to argue for what I wanted and to take what I could get. They had allowed me what liberty could be allowed—perhaps even somewhat more—but they had trusted me to do no damage to our common endeavor out of spite because I had not determined the design by myself and for myself. This had not made me either subservient or defiant, as happened to so many academics.

I think now that my disciplining by Roosevelt was undergone with quite good grace. He obviously thought so too. He seldom said anything that showed the least appreciation, but in my future work with him he would on three different occasions reward me by saying, in no particularly warm way but as though he had expected it, that I had "taken it very well." That was all; there was no discussion of what he meant; there was no further reference to the issue; just that. In the course of time I did take a good deal from him, as Sam and Doc did, and an acknowledgment was clearly owed. To my mind he paid the debt in full.

By the middle of June my conditioning was well under way; I considered, a little wryly, that if I could accept subsistence homesteads I would have no difficulty with other such ordeals in future.

CHAPTER XVIII

Almost Too Late

🟊 🟊 🟊

There were times when we felt ourselves to be of very little use. We had come late to the progress of a candidate who, after all, was a politician with twenty years' experience in the public service.

For Roosevelt's purpose now—winning the nomination—one tactic would be to hold fast and refuse further comment on any issue, to stand on his known commitments. Still, if he stood on what he had already said and done, there would have to be explanations, perhaps even some retractions. He did seem to have been unusually discreet about taking sides on most national issues, and yet some reconciliations with present circumstances would have to be attempted. In this we could help. But whether hopes for the new policies we were interested in had any chance of materializing was another question. He was bound both by his past pronouncements and by the tradition he was identified with, and where he was thus confined was where we most hoped for a change.

Older men of influence in the party had joined to push the interests of this younger leader. Such senators as Hull, Byrnes, Pittman, and Walsh; other Wilsonians, such as Daniels of North Carolina and Colonel House, Wilson's close associate, felt that an unspoken pact existed. They respected it, and they expected Roosevelt to

honor it too. It implied a faithfulness to Wilsonian policies that
Roosevelt might find he could not always honor; for instance,
he had already deviated seriously from the elders' position on
the League of Nations.

Such departures were dangerous, and Louis was anguished by
them, more so than Roosevelt himself, perhaps because it was he
who had to assuage the growing doubts of the elders. Then, all during the spring, the gathering-in of the machines—in New York,
Massachusetts, New Jersey, and Illinois—had to be considered. It
was obvious now that the bosses would go for Smith at Chicago.
Louis was guided by the political rule that friends can be sacrificed
to placate enemies, but a nice calculation had to be made concerning tolerance among the elders. How far could Roosevelt go? As it
turned out, they absorbed their punishment without defection.
They were pained, but as old politicians they understood Roosevelt's necessities. Still, their unhappiness was a constant worry for
Louis, and Ray often spoke of it to me. I am afraid that I was impatient and lacking in understanding. To me nothing counted but
those millions of unemployed and that paralyzed economy.

About agriculture, I discovered, Roosevelt had talked more
freely than I had known when I had conversations with him. For
instance, he did not tell me that he had been corresponding with
George Peek, the farm-machinery manufacturer whose advice
Smith had taken during the campaign of 1928. Peek had been active in promoting legislation of the sort the processors rather than
the farmers wanted, but with their influence behind him, he was a
formidable figure, and he was more formidable for having an alliance with Baruch. It was his view that exports might be subsidized
but that the real salvation for agriculture would be in making
marketing agreements with middlemen—packers, millers, and textile manufacturers—providing for higher prices to farmers. In return, the processors would be exempted from the antitrust acts,
and this would allow them to combine and raise their prices. Consumers would be forced to pay the costs of farmers' gains.

Roosevelt had also corresponded with John Simpson, who was a
shouter for "price-fixing, pure and simple," and had gained a large

following in the wheat and corn-hog areas, though he had done it by strident and irresponsible demagoguery. Peek and the processors regarded him as a fanatic and would not be seen in his company, but since he had a following, Roosevelt had listened to his exhortations with apparent sympathy. Like me, neither Peek nor Simpson knew that he had consulted the other.

The two men could hardly have been further apart; yet both had been led to believe that their views were shared. What was almost as bad, Roosevelt had endorsed the resolutions of the newly formed National Farm Conference early in 1932. Those findings called for the dumping of surpluses abroad, for "tariff equality," and for an "honest dollar" that would be "fair" to farmers. This was obviously a holdover from populist days, a revival of the cheap-money campaigns of Ignatius Donnelly and, of course, Bryan.

I discovered also—but only when I read some reference to it—that Earl Looker had written an article that had been published under Roosevelt's name, endorsing the dumping of surpluses abroad. This, of course, was the principle of the McNary-Haugen bills. At the end of July, unknown to me, at least, this would be incorporated in a whole ghosted book called *Government, Not Politics*. Looker, it seemed, was a free-lance writer who had approached Roosevelt a year earlier with a scheme for getting an authoritative answer to doubts about Roosevelt's physical condition. By arrangement, he had publicly challenged Roosevelt to allow an examination by a committee of physicians to be appointed by the director of the New York Academy of Medicine. The findings had been published in *Liberty*.

These were wholly favorable, and the article seemed so important to Louis that he had ordered thousands of reprints and sent them to every county organization in the country. So Looker, who was a shadowy presence so far as I was concerned, had a certain standing. Roosevelt obviously gave him a good deal of freedom—too much, as it turned out, in the case of the farm problem and some other issues. And for a while I wondered whether or not Looker really did speak with authority.

Roosevelt's way of escaping responsibility when he was taxed with former commitments was to say that the farm organizations must find some agreement among themselves. He did not say outright—not yet—that whatever they agreed on he would support, but he came close to it. When everything was considered, he had certainly been evasive, if not contradictory, and this made things so difficult that I later wondered why I had attempted anything further.

I told him again that he could not go on evading the necessity for crop reduction, and I explained, again and again and at length, why this was so. After our discussion I could be certain that he understood the necessity of restriction, however much the farmers might object; still, I said, we might find a more acceptable way to reduce surpluses than had so far been suggested.

I knew as well as he did that the farm vote was likely to be crucial in the coming campaign, and that the Midwest was for once, and largely on this issue, ready to abandon its Republican allegiance, but I argued that the farm proposals of the campaign would have to be convincing or the farmers could not be won over. Years of frustration had made them skeptical of all political promises. He finally agreed, but he emphasized the acceptability I had spoken of. Some better device would be a tremendous contribution.

This was a considerable responsibility, and I would not have undertaken it if I had not already seen the possibility of a new approach. At this stage, I had not much more than a hope to offer. The organization politicians who called themselves farm leaders were as afraid of crop restriction as was Roosevelt, and he had been arguing that they ought to take the lead. This delicate stand-off had to find some resolution. It was the negotiations in and about this question that governed the discussions about agricultural policy all the rest of the summer and became so complicated that no one was satisfied with the result.

Agriculture, however, was not the only difficult subject we had to deal with, and not the only one weighted with an unfortunate history. The complicated issues of international economics offered challenges to the most ingenious talents. It was possible that the campaign could be got through without anything more being said about tariffs, for instance, than that they ought to be somewhat lower. In the same speech (on February 2, before the New York State Grange) that had offended the old Wilsonians by repudiating the 1920 stand on the League of Nations, Roosevelt had made an obvious effort to placate the elders by what he said about tariffs. He had attacked the Republican Smoot-Hawley Tariff Act, reminding the Grangers that they were having to buy commodities in a protected market and to sell their crops in a free one—at competitive world prices. This was true enough, but since farmers were perversely attached to protective tariffs, he had spoken for a "reciprocal trade program," implying negotiated trade treaties, a sort of *quid pro quo* arrangement.

After reading this I concluded that he had been discussing the subject with George Peek. It was clear that what the suggestion amounted to was trading our wheat and cotton for manufactured goods from abroad, but what these goods could be, in any amounts, except steel, textiles, and similarly sensitive commodities, it was not easy to see—and these were the very interests that for seventy-five years had dominated the writing of one protective tariff after another. In 1888, Cleveland had been defeated for re-election because he threatened to lower such duties, and even though he had been re-elected for a later term, he had never succeeded in reducing the most important schedules. We—Ray, Adolf, and I—knew this history, and we were very skeptical of any trading successes. Of course, trading might be something to talk about —if something had to be said.

Besides making this suggestion, Roosevelt had attacked European nations for their reluctance to pay the war debts. They were spending enormous sums on projects of doubtful value at home, he said, but were trying their best to escape from their just obligations to the United States. We knew this was the truth, because we had furnished his facts. In Europe the domestic public works were extensive and even magnificent, and it would not be hard to argue that they were built at American expense. But any economist would also have reminded him that the Europeans could pay their debts to us only by accumulating dollars, and to do this they must sell goods in the American market. It was not so simple, therefore, as he made it appear. If trade was to be reciprocal—that is, an equal exchange—foreign debtors could not accumulate dollars to cover their obligations. They would take as much as they sent, and no more. This might appeal to farmers who wanted to dump their surpluses, but the farmers, like most other Americans, were also determined to hold France and Britain to their debts, and speaking of the two policies together made no sense.

Roosevelt knew this well enough, as we found in discussing it. He also knew that sometime he would have to get out of the inconsistency. He simply hoped it would not be during the campaign. There was this to rely on: foreign affairs were traditionally avoided; many campaigns ran their whole course without any mention whatever of such issues, or, if a candidate did make a speech or two about them, it was of the usual meaningless, xenophobic variety.

This did not apply to tariffs, however. They were traditionally controversial. Protection, as the Republicans saw it, was responsible for prosperity and high wages; to Democrats, it was a way of shielding manufacturers from competition that might lower prices to consumers, increase international trade, and so provide a market for, among other goods, farm products. These were fixed positions for hard-core party traditionalists.

It was true that this argument had seemed to soften and become more reasonable as the economy matured. The Democrats had been embarrassed by opportunities, when they were in power, to make good on their free-trade protestations, and they had let the opportunities pass. They had lapsed into sullen sabotage when Cleveland had insisted on action. The Republicans, for their part, had moderated their protectionist propaganda and had put forward a cost-of-production formula which, they said, would exclude only goods produced by low-paid foreign labor. They avoided saying that it would also keep out goods produced more cheaply for other reasons.

In fact, the apparent moderation of the Republicans had proved to be only a political convenience. When they had won with Harding and then with Coolidge and Hoover, they had reverted to their earlier position. The outrageous Smoot-Hawley tariff of 1931 had been written by industrial lobbyists pretty much to suit themselves, just as the McKinley tariff had been written by earlier lobbyists and argued for by Benjamin Harrison.

How we could expect to sell farm products abroad without admitting imports it was impossible to imagine. Yet for years this had been the main reliance both of the bipartisan farm blocs and of the Republicans. This nonsensical contradiction made a convenient target; Hoover found it impossible to explain why he had signed the Smoot-Hawley bill. Roosevelt's attack on it pleased the old-time advocates of freer trade, but he had his own inconsistencies and he could only hope they would not be noticed. Since the reciprocal trade he advocated would do nothing to enable the Europeans to resume payment of the war debts (now suspended by moratorium), we thought we might have made a more rational approach to the problem if we had started earlier without the handicap of that speech to the Grangers. But when we spoke of this and other international matters, Roosevelt obviously wanted to put them aside for more pressing domestic issues. So we simply noted them for future consideration—if it should be necessary, and if we could think of something to say.

We asked him about the probability that statements about the debt payments and tariffs would appear in the platform, but he thought that whatever they were they "could be lived with." In fact, this was his attitude toward the whole platform. It is my belief that he made no effort to influence it or even to find out in detail what it might contain. It seemed that there must be an understanding about this with the elders, although no more than a tacit one; in politics no contracts were needed when interests coincided. In this case they did, and there was an amazing lightheartedness about anything that might be *said;* the agreement ran deeper than words.

The possible consequences of this seemed appalling to an amateur. As a candidate, Roosevelt might have to expound whatever

policies Senator Hull and his colleagues felt were traditionally
Democratic, and this might be fatal to the attack we hoped to
make on the problems of depression. The platform might even include statements that Roosevelt could not possibly advocate with
any credibility—for instance, that relief was a matter for the
states and not for the federal government. Also, there might be an
unacceptable plank about the war debts, something that would be
totally inconsistent with what would be said about the tariff.

These were examples. For my part I feared that the platform
might have a paragraph reiterating the 1928 advocacy of dumping
as a solution for agriculture. Worst of all, it might have a stirring
boost for free enterprise in the old progressive tradition. It probably would; that very likely was one reason for Louis Howe's anguish about the Oglethorpe speech. But even Ray, in touch with
Louis, did not penetrate his reserve about promises to the elders.
It was quite possible, of course, that there were none—none, that
is, of a formal sort. Louis might merely have allowed them to assume that Roosevelt would accept whatever they agreed on
among themselves.

I did not know, nor, I think, did Ray, that in the winter of 1931
Louis had gone to a group of senators and asked them to begin
studies looking to a platform that would forestall what Raskob was
likely to insist on at the meeting of the Democratic National Committee in March of 1931. The meeting would be called by Raskob
since he was still the holdover chairman, and he would offer resolutions supporting the policies advocated by Smith in the 1928
campaign. A declaration for the repeal of prohibition would come
first, but other declarations might be equally embarrassing.

Senators Hull, Walsh, Byrnes, and Pat Harrison were, however,
expected to sound out their colleagues in both Senate and House
on the subjects to be mentioned in the platform and the attitudes
to be formulated; they would then engage a draftsman to formulate
their conclusions, and these, no matter what Raskob wanted,
would become the party policies. To be aligned with the elders and
to edge out Raskob were important aims.

Louis' mission was the more difficult because he had to imply

that it was Roosevelt's wish. It assumed that these senators were
supporting his candidacy. He had proceeded with the usual cautious feeling-out. It seems, however, that he had an old understanding with Hull and knew that Hull would consult only likely
supporters. Louis had not ventured to interfere in the deliberations;
he had merely said that Roosevelt favored a short and readable
document with broad appeal. This I heard, and I read that he had
gone so far as to ask the senators to indicate what they thought the
platform should say about a number of topics: recovery, unemployment relief, agricultural policy, the tariff, and prohibition. To
these, the conferees added currency reform and foreign relations,
but if Louis offered suggestions of his own about treatment, I
never heard of them.

Roosevelt, somewhat later, spoke of the platform to Senators
Lewis of Illinois and Byrd of Virginia, but without any mention
of policy. By the spring of 1932 a draft had been prepared at the
behest of the senators by A. Mitchell Palmer of Pennsylvania, who
had been attorney general during the last Wilson years. We were
not aware of this—at least I was not aware—and perhaps it was
just as well. Among liberals of all sorts, Palmer was the most discredited of all the old Democrats. He had directed the Red hunts
of the postwar years when Wilson was incapacitated, and he had
carried them on with a vindictiveness that had not been equaled
since the Alien and Sedition laws of the John Adams administration. Nothing he could have said or done would have been acceptable to me.

Roosevelt, however, did get the effect he wanted. The elders,
that is, the most powerful faction of the party, were lined up
against Raskob's group in the National Committee, and Roosevelt
was their candidate. Whether he had ignored Palmer or warned the
senators about him, I do not know. The important thing was that
Roosevelt's enemies had been blocked. They had been forced to
abandon Smith as their candidate and to fall back on an entirely
different strategy. They had begun to encourage favorite sons,
wherever one could be found, in the hope that the convention
could be stalled by competition among these until it became appar-

ent that Roosevelt could not get a two-thirds majority. They would then agree on the most likely of the contenders (it was rumored that they had in mind either Baker, who had been Wilson's secretary of war, or Melvin Traylor, the Chicago banker); they would again be able to place their own people on the committee, run a campaign to suit themselves, and, so they hoped, capture the White House.

Our discovery that the party had already made declarations, or was about to do so, on the most important issues likely to be discussed during the campaign, and that Roosevelt had made a politician's kind of agreement about those declarations, was a shock to me, but the situation had to be accepted if we were to go on. I did not learn about it until convention time, and neither did Sam Rosenman or Doc O'Connor. It might seem that our discussing subjects Roosevelt knew quite well had already been agreed on by the party was entirely futile. As it turned out, he would march with the elders only so far as it suited his purpose, but this intention was still not fully understood by those of us who were only partly in his confidence.

It was Louis' idea—Roosevelt's really—that Roosevelt should become the symbolic head of the party apparatus; it would deliver delegates and then set out to deliver votes. In return he would behave as the inner circle expected him to behave. Only bit by bit did we come to understand all that was involved in this bargain.

To anticipate, I may say that except in a few matters the platform declarations were easy enough to endure; as Roosevelt had no doubt foreseen, most were so general that they offered no limitation that could not be evaded. There were, however, a few exceptions and these were potentially embarrassing. The strong endorsement of drastic reduction in government expenditures, for instance, would soon appear ridiculous. It should be said about this particular matter, however, that Roosevelt himself was more to be blamed than the platform.

It seems almost incredible that Ray's drafting work on the acceptance speech could have been carried out without his knowing what the platform was to contain or even having been told that

Roosevelt had promised strict adherence to its pronouncements, whatever they might be. And I may be mistaken in supposing that Ray's ignorance of the platform was as complete as I recall it to have been. Roosevelt did, of course, give instructions as to subject matter and offer indications of attitude. Whether these corresponded to the draft of the party solons, Ray did not need to know. If there were contradictions, they would be eliminated in Roosevelt's final revisions of the speech, or modified as he felt necessary.

Ray proceeded, as he was learning to do, by making drafts, discussing them, or parts of them, with us, getting Roosevelt's amendments, and then doing them over—again and again. In the present case he was worried by his awareness that he was not getting full attention. For the first time in his work with Roosevelt, a state paper was being prepared, but there was so much going on and Roosevelt had so many distractions that the needed time was hard to find, and when it could be found, concentrating came hard. It was wearing and unsatisfactory. Still, the job had to be done, and there was, by convention time, a draft. It was one Ray was uneasy about. Last-minute revisions would be made; they might be extensive; and he might not be present when they were made. He had cause for uneasiness.

Domestic Allotment

❀ ❀ ❀

Adolf had accepted his assignment to business and finance and I to the depression—with special attention to agriculture—hoping they would somehow interlink. That ought to happen as we compared conclusions and made revisions. Ray's special responsibility as co-ordinator was to bring everything together. Ultimately he must expect to have emphases established and a set of policies outlined. Otherwise his work and ours could not really give Roosevelt what he would need when the time came.

This hope of reaching a consensus was never realized in any comprehensive way. We each had separate talks with Roosevelt in addition to those all of us had together; we each seemed to have our own interpretation of the general discussions; and we never had time to reach agreement. Differences grew more marked as time passed and as our relations became more intimate. Roosevelt had a way of assuming that we agreed about conclusions and that they need not be discussed. The fact is that only a very few times was general policy referred to; the most notable instances I recall were when Roosevelt and I happened to be alone. Although joint discussions ranged very widely, they were nearly always about specific subjects and perhaps the relation to each other of banking and insurance or taxes and business; seldom were they concerned with the ends we might be working toward.

For my part I had all the agricultural material to review. There was a good deal of it, from many sources, and besides, my own ideas had to be put in some sort of presentable order. The same was true of Adolf. His assignments to corporate finance, the debt structure, and banking were technical and demanding, and he carried them out brilliantly.

One participant in the discussions who seemed somewhat alien in our group was Charles W. Taussig. Charles, a businessman, had sent his card to the Governor on the train coming north from Warm Springs and had been asked in for a talk. He was familiar with the Caribbean, and he had ideas about tariffs and international trade. When he found out about our group, he became attached simply by asking Roosevelt if he could join us. Without status, he wandered in and out of our company. Ray rather resented him, but Taussig was often around, persistent even when Ray's glances were coolest.

We also were given the services of Robert K. Straus, whose father, Jesse Straus, had resigned the New York State relief job to Harry Hopkins and was now organizing the Business and Professional League for Roosevelt. Bobby became one of our most faithful researchers and most willing workers. No duty was too difficult, no task too disagreeable for him to undertake, and his good humor was indestructible. Perhaps because he made no pretense of being a senior at our level, he became one of our most useful colleagues. He had no interest in the family business—that is, as an active participant—and so could devote himself to public service. This was his first chance, and he made the most of his training at Harvard's Graduate School of Business. He was fresh from contacts with a set of professors interested in the same problems we were meeting.

He brought with him an associate, John Dalton, an instructor in the School of Business. Between them they gave us both cheer and assistance. Looking back, I think Bobby has had small recognition, as a result, I suppose, of his modesty. For the scion of a wealthy merchant family, whose father was making a large financial contribution to the Roosevelt cause, his happy subordination was remarkable. He never put himself forward, and I am afraid we presumed on his willingness.

Luckily for all of us, our university was shutting down for the summer, and there were no more classes to interrupt the work that was becoming formidable. There was, especially, the acceptance speech, now an immediate problem. Even if it was Ray's sole responsibility, he would look mostly to us for the materials he would need.

What would it include? There would be the amenities, of course, but then words would have to be said that would serve as intimations of policy and a forecast of the campaign. Should this be a preview of the major speeches we already foresaw—about the depression, first of all, but then about such other issues as the farm problem, banking and finance, transportation, government reorganization, public power, and conservation? Or should the whole speech be devoted to the statement in modern terms of a progressive political philosophy?

I learned almost at once that the farmers' troubles would be touched on and that it would be my responsibility to bring all our discussion into the focus of a few paragraphs. These would need to be something different from what had been offered before if they were to attract attention. When I mentioned a meeting to be held at the University of Chicago during the week before the convention, both Ray and Roosevelt urged me to go. I told them of hints I had heard of an ingenious scheme that might even quiet the quarrels of the past decade and be acceptable to the beleaguered farmers. Too good to be true, Roosevelt said, but still we ought not to overlook anything. So I made my arrangements.

Agricultural economists are likely to be conservative, but I knew a few lively-minded ones—in the Department of Agriculture, at Cornell, at Wisconsin, and at other universities. I had some claim to travel with them because of writing I had done, and there would be no difficulty about my welcome; but I did arrange for an invitation just to make my visit regular.

The history of the past decade had come in for exhaustive review at our meetings in Albany. Farmers' demands had been hard to meet because they wanted relief without making any contributions or sacrifices themselves. Consequently, new ideas got a hearing in agricultural circles only if they promised to make two blades of grass grow where only one had grown before. The worthiest achievements of the Department of Agriculture, of the experiment stations, and of the colleges of agriculture had been exactly that. More scientists of higher quality worked in the Department of Agriculture than in any dozen of the largest universities. Their discoveries of ways to enlarge yields and to raise better animals made an amazing record. And now their efforts had resulted in surpluses—more to eat and wear than Americans could absorb or foreign countries could afford to buy.

Middlemen had always been a problem. Farmers were interested in prices, naturally, and it might be expected that the department's economists would indicate how to get more money for farm products. The trouble was that middlemen and processors wanted to buy them for the lowest prices they could manage; since their influence was formidable, advice on raising prices was to be avoided.

The economists pointed out, somewhat timidly at first, that the recent rapid increase of production first had prevented prices from rising and then had caused their rapid fall. This effect was not the same in all cases. For wheat and cotton, low prices had followed declining demand. Wheat prices had fallen because people at home had taken to avoiding starches and because foreign farmers had gone back to work; cotton prices had fallen because Europeans preferred to use materials from their colonies or dependencies.

Our tariff policy had been protectionist, and, so long as we refused entry to European goods in payment for our exports, debtors could pay us only in gold, of which they had dwindling stocks. The double effect of exclusion from Europe and protection for manufactures in America had been devastating. The product of millions of acres was simply not wanted. Farmers had found themselves with increasing holdovers from year to year, and the twenties, prosperous for the rest of the country, had been years of almost continuous depression for them. The government economists were in a trying position; what they knew to be fact they dared not say. In Republican times, businessmen were in control; processors were businessmen, and bureaucrats were necessarily discreet. They gave no advice about ways to increase prices.

They had another handicap; they were incorrigibly orthodox. It was their thesis that farmers would have to combat falling prices by cutting their costs. Otherwise, how could vast and costly researches to improve efficiency be justified? There were those here and there who doubted that this was enough, since it also increased production and so enlarged surpluses, but they were not very vocal. The so-called farm leaders—officials of the national farm organizations—had grown impatient about this pussyfooting; they were politicians and their constituents were getting out of control. They saw that they had to speak for higher prices, but they were fearful of saying to their farmer members that obtaining them would involve any serious changes in farm practice—such as, for instance, deliberately decreasing production.

There were various proposals for raising prices, but none was in an accepted pattern, and this made things difficult for agricultural economists, who had to accommodate themselves to conflicting views. Most of them were intimidated by the farm politicians, who held that exports should be subsidized in one way or another. The economists knew that dumping always caused a backlash of restriction and so never succeeded in the long run, but a politician who wanted an immediate solution tended to ignore this fact. The most talked-of dumping scheme had got itself into successive congressional acts. It went under the generic name McNary-Haugen, after the sponsors of the bills embodying it. One difficulty with the bills had been that they always involved a two-price system, one for the domestic and another for the foreign part of each year's crop. This, added to the fierce opposition of foreign farming interests, had given Coolidge and Hoover an excuse for vetoes in spite of farm-bloc pressure.

To arrange one payment for each farmer's domestic sales and

another for whatever foreign sales were made was an administrative problem with formidable complications. Something better was needed, something that did not involve dumping. This was an old problem for me. I had, in fact, devised a proposal for the Smith campaign in 1928, only to have Smith reject it on the advice of Peek, who spoke for his processor friends. I had argued that averaged farmers' prices would be "fair" (in accord with the concert-of-interests principle) if they could be given the same relation to an index of other prices as they had had in periods agreed to have been prosperous all around. If the ratio between agricultural and nonagricultural prices, once established, was maintained, farmers would have all the return they could rightly expect. To reach this situation, however, it was essential to control production, and this was something the processors disliked. Dumping schemes seemed to hold out the promise that farmers could sell, and processors handle, all that could be produced.

One of the arguments against limitation was that production ought not to be reduced when there were people who were starving and freezing. Just stating the proposal in those words made it seem heartless. Surely, it was said, the better way would be to arrange for the people who were hungry and cold to get the food and fibers they needed. The argument, however, was largely sophistical. What was called restriction and pictured as heartless would merely be a rearrangement of what was done on certain acres—grass grown instead of wheat, soybeans instead of corn, alfalfa instead of cotton—and so not really be restriction at all. I had gone even further in an article published in 1930. I had argued that an agricultural policy must not only be concerned with the control of production and prices, but must also take account of the national interest in conservation. This could begin by better use of the land not needed for producing the staple crops. Products more needed than wheat and cotton could be grown on surplus acres, or this land could be used for forests or parks. This would not only help to adjust supply to demand but would improve the soil for the future. The most destructive crops, so far as the land was concerned, were corn, cotton, and wheat, the American staples.

There was little hope of combining the two objectives—that of making farmers immediately better off and that of establishing a land-use program. No politician, no farm leader, no editor of a farm paper, even, had shown a genuine interest in conservation, though most of them subscribed to innocuous sentiments. Farmers were in business for profit. I had insisted that European markets were closed, probably for good; tractors did not eat grain as mules and horses once had, and also people's eating habits had changed. Politicians, however, could not admit these plain facts that everyone knew to be true.

Roosevelt laughed when I stated the dilemma thus plainly still another time. If I could find a way out of that, I was pretty good, he said, giving me again the chance to recite the obvious answer, that the farmers and the farm leaders knew it as well as we did, but that there was a general conspiracy of avoidance.

What was needed, I said, was a reduction program that was proof against chiselers; there would have to be some sort of penalties or rewards to enforce compliance. The new suggestion was that adjustment to national estimates might be enforced by farmers themselves. The Department of Agriculture would work out county quotas, and each grower would have an equitable fraction fixed by local committees. This was about all I knew so far, but I hoped to find out more. Roosevelt remarked that in principle it seemed much like the scheme I had already outlined to him—a national quota, divided among individual farmers on the basis of their usual production. So it was, I said, but I had not thought of self-enforcement; that was new. Also, I understood, the program included a device for raising prices at once so that farmers who complied would have an immediate income. That, he said, would be a real miracle. We ought to find out if it was really feasible.

There were to be two people at Chicago, I answered, who would know. These were M. L. Wilson and Henry A. Wallace. I told him something about both. Wilson was a Montana Agricultural College professor who had the affection and trust of an extraordinary assortment of people. This wide acceptance was unusual in caustic intellectual circles. Lately he had been traveling most of the time, seeing important people, making homely talk, visiting numerous scattered colleges, attending conferences, sitting on committees, never urging, but continually arguing and explaining.

Wallace was an Iowan, the son of Henry C. Wallace, who had been Harding's secretary of agriculture. He edited the family journal in Des Moines, *Wallace's Farmer,* and he was something of an expert in biology as well as in farm economics. It was natural that he should be a member of the study group that had come up with the new device. I had never met Wallace, but I knew a good deal about him, and I thought that he, like others in the Midwest, had had enough of Republican obstructionism. In fact, he had a special grievance: his father had been a victim of Hoover's overbearing influence in two administrations.

I anticipated one difficulty. There had been a formidable conspiracy, one I had never been willing to join, to preserve the family farm at any cost. I believed that both Wilson and Wallace were among the enthusiasts. I had no objection to family farms where they were suitable, I told Roosevelt, but I saw no reason why farming should be exempt from the general evolution of productive processes. Struggling against this blind defense of the family farm, and looking for ways to make progress in spite of it, I had wondered whether co-operatives might not be the solution. They might get some of the benefits industry got from large-scale operations— lower overhead costs, expert management, better financing, scientific soil exploitation, and the most efficient use of power and machines. At the same time they seemed to be a logical development of such homely American customs as corn-husking bees, roof-raisings, sugaring-offs, and work-trading at harvest time.

Clearly some new approach must be found. In no year since 1921 had farm income equaled the full costs of production, and no group, no industry, could live indefinitely on its capital. We had been mining our soil for a long time, but we were now doing something even worse—we were exploiting our people, using up their savings and their capital goods and reducing their levels of life. It had become a desperate situation, but its very desperation, I said to Roosevelt, was his opportunity.

I knew I was talking to a man who believed in the family farm, but I hoped I had moved him toward a more realistic view. He might think that this had to do with a longer-run policy than we now had to devise; but if it was true, as I believed, that the situation had really become calamitous, and if a new approach could be made, it was terribly important to explore it.

Roosevelt accepted this, tentatively at least, and I went to Chicago at his urging. I conveyed to Wilson and Wallace the suggestion that Roosevelt was aware of the agricultural crisis and disposed to grasp the advantage it offered. I reminded them that he was "farm-minded" and told them that his knowledge of conditions was astonishingly realistic. People interested in a solution, I said, had never had such an opportunity.

Strangely enough, I had some difficulty in getting them to concentrate on the immediate problem. Wilson wanted most to discuss philosophy; he flattered me by knowing about things I had written and also about our course in social studies at Columbia. Wallace wanted to talk about money, international trade, relative prices, and the like. He warmed to me after I had been goaded into making an extemporary talk on planning, thus breaking my resolve to sit and listen. His was a fine clear mind. We were deep into economics before we had been together five minutes.

Presently, however, I was able to tell them that Moley, calling on others for help and assuming that Roosevelt would be nominated, had already drafted most of an acceptance speech. The section to be devoted to agriculture was, however, incomplete; as yet it was too vague to be of any use. I spoke about conversations I had had that spring with Beardsley Ruml in Washington and of the memorandum he had shown me at the time, which they—or anyway, M. L.—had helped to draft. What did they think now, I asked, of this device called "domestic allotment"?

Wilson was delighted to explain it at length. The gist of the scheme was that national quotas for the great staple crops were to be determined by past experience, and that they were to be broken down and allocated to states and then to counties. Individual farmers would then have quotas allocated by county committees elected by themselves. It was nothing so new after all.

The effect of the plan would be to raise the price to the consumer and to give the farmer not only the price he received for what he sold, but an additional amount for what he did *not* grow. I asked where the funds for this would come from. Then Wilson did produce a novelty. It was proposed to tax the first processing of the crop at an amount fixed at the difference between the existing price and what the price would have been if farm products had kept the same relationship with other prices as had existed in a chosen period when it was agreed that exchange had been fair.*

Fair exchange was already a sufficiently familiar concept to me, but I listened to M.L.'s exposition. The farmer ought to be satisfied, he said, to get as much as he had had in good times, and consumers could not object if prices, plus benefit payments, rose to such an equitable level—that is, one at which everyone had been well off. Both farmers and consumers ought to be glad for a return of such conditions. It was a concept I was glad to see spreading.

The meetings went on for several days. We were housed in the University of Chicago dormitories, always a kind of living that American college men go back to as a familiar home. We ate in the cafeteria, strolled from building to building, met and talked endlessly. Apart from Wilson and Wallace, most economists, whether from the Department of Agriculture or from the colleges, were completely at a loss for a program—not only at a loss, but instinctively hostile to every novel suggestion. I was impressed again, as I had been before, with their dullness. They had only facts: facts about prices, crops, market movements, exports, and so on, running back over many years, the stuff that economic life is made of, but lacking all the life. There was all the knowledge, I thought, to support what needed to be done, but there was no will to do anything.

* The tax idea originated with Henry I. Harriman, then president of the United States Chamber of Commerce. It proved to be an Achilles heel, since it was this that the Supreme Court seized on to declare the Agricultural Adjustment Act, passed in 1933, unconstitutional. But at the time it seemed a clever way to produce an immediate income for farmers.

At the end, I was satisfied that the domestic-allotment scheme was, after all, only a variation of the sort of thing I had been familiar with for some years—an improvement, but not strange. My problem was to make it clear and simple for Roosevelt, if it was to find its way into the speech next week. It need only be suggested, not described in detail. He needed to promise distressed farmers a new effort at relief and to be credible about having a device for providing it. The device, as at present outlined, was dependent on farmers' acceptance; they would, in fact, have to operate it themselves. This would require preparation. It was a job of political leadership, really, more than of invention. It did have the drawback that it required reducing production, but talk of "adjustment" instead of "reduction" might soften the fears and prejudices of the past. Wilson thought so, and if anyone knew farmers, he did. I was not so sure that he knew the farm leaders. These were the politicians Wallace feared. Getting them to undertake a joint effort was asking a sacrifice they were not likely to make. They survived by *not* joining with others. Could Roosevelt persuade them to agree?

Wallace was doubtful. So was I, but the possibility would have to be explored. The acceptance speech was the place to begin. Pressure on the leaders would have to come from the farmers themselves. If Roosevelt could stir hopes and hint at a solution, he might force them to co-operate.

CHAPTER XX

The Month of the Politicians

❀ ❀ ❀

June was the month of the politicians: Howe, Farley, and their helpers. It was the climax of their work, and they were not so certain, even at the last, that things would go their way. They had amassed an impressive number of delegates, but it had to rise to a two-thirds majority, and that had become impossible before the opening of the convention. They were disappointed and disorganized.

True, the stop-Roosevelt movement could hardly be said any more to have real momentum; yet it had prevented further adherences to Roosevelt after April. New York would be split. In spite of Farley's efforts, Tammany had not come round. To organization Democrats in New York City, the immolation of Mayor Walker was unforgivable. The findings of the investigation, well publicized by the righteous judge who conducted it, made it inevitable that the Mayor would be called on to explain the sources of his swollen income. His responses were obviously going to be feeble, but he had been front man for the organization and the leaders blamed Roosevelt for letting Seabury get started, or for not shutting him off somehow at an early stage. It is quite possible that Roosevelt would have been pleased to find a way to do so. By now, however, the disclosures were too glaring and too public.

Except for the Tammany spokesmen, almost every public voice was condemning Roosevelt for not removing Walker condignly, although Seabury's charges had not been presented formally and with the detailed allegations necessary before gubernatorial action could be taken. Jimmy Walker had been so gay a figure and so absent-minded about his public duties that serious citizens regarded him as obviously unfit for his job. Without waiting for evidence, they were impatient to see him punished. Very likely Roosevelt was delaying out of discretion, but there was real danger that he would lose more by temporizing than by acting without formal and specific indictment.

He could not hope to have Tammany support in any case. He had counsel; Ray had enlisted Martin Conboy, himself a Catholic and an old Tammanyite, an inspired choice. But Conboy was against moving—as was Roosevelt—until all was in order. It might not be soon enough to suit the critics, but the case would be carefully prepared. What Roosevelt wanted was overwhelming evidence, not mere adverse opinion. If he had to remove Walker, it must be because he had no alternative; that might at least soften the effect on others of Tammany's wrath.

After New Jersey and Connecticut went the way of Massachusetts into the Smith camp, it was clear that very few delegates from the boss-dominated Eastern parties would go to Roosevelt. The additional number needed for nomination would have to come from those instructed for favorite sons. Following the usual custom, their delegations would hold out only for a ballot or two and then go to one of the front runners for some promised favor.

It was certain now that they would not go to Smith, although he was behaving with the assurance of a confident contender. The full-dress speech presenting his program not only for recovery but for the rehabilitation of the country's morale was evidence of his seriousness. It had been, however, a Shouse-Raskob as much as a Smith speech—that is to say, one coming from the national committee held over from the campaign of 1928. It relied on the formulas popular among businessmen: governmental economy, reduced taxes, a balanced budget, and something for the unemployed. It might have been written by Baruch's ghost-writers—or Raskob's—but Smith had produced it as his own.

Doc guessed that Farley was not worried now about Raskob's being the holdover national chairman. His term would be over at the beginning of the convention. Jouett Shouse was more of a threat, being a clever politician with many connections among the elders. The stop-Roosevelt bosses, taking advantage of this approval and counting on Shouse's loyalty, meant to make him permanent chairman of the convention. If they succeeded, the rulings he made might be very helpful to them; opportunities of the sort did arise in almost all conventions.

Farley and Howe had made up their minds, Doc said, that this threat must not be left in their path. To remove it they were putting forward Senator Walsh of Montana, whose prestige was immense. There was certain to be a fight, but it would be a preliminary skirmish in the bigger battle, and there was nothing to lose by undertaking it. If they failed, they were destined to lose much more. In *Behind the Ballots* (page 108), Farley later told of an agreement on strategy reached at a Hyde Park meeting on June 5. The meeting, organized by himself and Howe, was attended by seventeen of the politicians they would depend on most at Chicago, and it resulted in a fairly complete plan, with parts allocated to each individual. Since they were all experienced operators, they felt themselves well prepared to contend for the uncommitted delegates on the floor in Chicago. Walsh was an honored hero of the Teapot Dome battles back in the twenties. They should be able to substitute him for Shouse.

We could hardly be blamed if we too found it hard to think of anything beyond the coming melee. Ray did have the Walker case to worry about, and the acceptance speech lay heavy on his mind, but he was obviously distracted by the uncertainties and complicated maneuvers that lay ahead. Sam had now become a New York Supreme Court Justice, having been appointed and confirmed just as the legislature was adjourning, so we had lost him from our councils. He made a brave effort to sit on the bench in

New York during the day and come to Albany for the evenings, but it was difficult. Doc was often around and helpful, but he no longer took much interest in our academic labors; he regarded them as over until there were speeches to be written for a candidate. So the privy council was now a compact one of three—but three in a state of suspense.

Roosevelt himself was lifted to new levels of vigor and euphoria as the time drew nearer and the circumstances grew more critical. His blithe liveliness did, however, begin to seem somewhat strained—either that or we imagined so because we could not conceive how he could feel otherwise than terribly concerned. For one thing, he could not tell what the effect of the Walker matter would be. Because of Tammany's efforts, enough delegates for the nomination would be hard to get. And if he saw with whom a deal was possible, we did not guess it. Knowing that he had all this on his mind, we looked at him with an awe we had not felt before. He was so close to great possibilities and the decision was so imminent that the suspense was hardly to be borne.

My own recollections include occasions when I inadvertently found myself sitting on the periphery of a circle intently considering matters quite outside my competence. I could not get up and leave; for one thing, I was interested, but for another, Roosevelt seemed not to mind my listening. I even heard his end of telephone conversations—a few—with Louis Howe or Jim Farley; at their conclusion he would sometimes make a comment, sometimes merely smile and go on with something else. I did not hear enough for reassurance or enough to form the basis for a guess as to his strategy for getting another hundred or so delegates. He did keep in his pocket or on his desk a list of figures that located the uncommitted ones. Once in a while he pulled it out or took it up and looked at it. Something was forming or had formed in his mind, but it was evidently not something he was sure of. This gesture of his worried me. But whenever he was on view he hid any concern he may have felt.

He seemed never to let down, he was alert and tireless; besides holding endless conferences, he dealt with piles of documents and commented casually about information that came to him from dozens of sources, many of them unasked and some unwanted. What amazed me most was his aplomb. He was as ready and charming as ever. No one unfamiliar with what was occurring would have guessed that the determining days of his career were passing and that the outlook was worse rather than better as day followed day.

Ray continued, for a while, to bring such experts to Albany or Hyde Park as might be of further use, but it was late for that now. The emphasis had clearly turned from the exploration of long-run policies to the search for expedient ones. Even that gave way, by the middle of June, to concentrated consideration of what ought to go into the acceptance speech, now being written and rewritten many times over.

The drafting of this first real state paper was Ray's job, and I at least was not asked for any direct contribution. This did not preclude the offering of suggestions or even of paragraph-by-paragraph criticism as the text developed and was recast. There was a good deal of this, but there were other distractions as well. We were more than ever harassed by people who had to be given some attention. Dozens of those who belonged to the middle level of public affairs were passed on to us for interviews. Most of the visitors were guessing that Roosevelt might be chosen and were crowding closer to the center of power. This was nothing to the rush that would begin after the nomination, but there would be more recognition then for our situation and we would have somewhat better defenses.

At this time we were operating mostly out of Ray's office at Barnard College. Mine, on the seventh floor of Hamilton Hall, was quieter, and most of my real work was done there. But we were in Albany a good deal, too. When we were there, the confusion prevented us from settling down to real consideration of anything. The four-hour trips on the New York Central's trains were protected and productive interludes. We grew to be fond of those trains.

The sort of thing we had started out to do was needed as much as ever, and we had not completed anything, but we had less and less chance to go on with it. We were constantly aware that if a campaign was to be undertaken, what Roosevelt would say would have to be produced in preliminary form by us. It would be revised out of all recognition, but to be revised it had first to be written. There would have to be a lot of it, and it would have to be relevant, foolproof, and politically acceptable. Mistakes in a candidate's speeches or statements would be inadmissible, and the opportunity to make them in such circumstances would be constant.

It was exciting enough, but we gradually lost our elasticity. When Ray was most needed, I remember feeling very sorry for him because he was working against so many difficulties and had the added one of being deathly tired.

It is not strange that all of us were tired. During those few months we had worked more earnestly, I am sure, than during any similar period of our lives. What we produced were memoranda, summations, arguments, and suggestions, each requiring research and earnest concentration. This was the stuff used for endless discussions, first among ourselves, to get matters clearly in mind, and then with Roosevelt to see whether they could be made clear in *his* mind. It was not finished work and was not meant to be. Not many of those memoranda ever got into files to be saved, but each was the very best we were capable of producing.

Generally speaking, the depression was overwhelmingly the issue we concentrated on. There was no escaping any longer the responsibility of government—for recovery from it, for relief while it went on, and for taking measures to prevent recurrences. This last we felt to be most important. We were insisting that since the Republicans had taken credit for good times, they must accept the blame for hard times; there was no intention of letting them escape. The corollary of this, however, was some intelligible program to offer as a substitute for neglect.

It struck us as frivolous beyond belief that, in such circumstances, the Smith-Raskob-Shouse crowd, including Hague of New Jersey and Ely of Massachusetts, should have continued to insist that prohibition must be the issue most emphasized. Aside from comparative triviality, we felt that the argument about it was practically over. Repeal was inevitable, and Roosevelt had said so in Buffalo earlier in the year. He had added that prohibition was a matter that ought to be returned to the states for determination in accordance with local preferences. He considered that this was enough; it would be foolish indeed to allow such a peripheral issue to bulk large in the Democratic appeal for votes. Prohibition was one of the items referred to by those who said that Roosevelt was a trimmer, but when he commented on it to us, we were quite agreed that he was right not to speak further about it, thus deflecting attention from the economic situation.

When Roosevelt first came back from the South, and again had meetings in the evening at Albany after the day had quieted down, he usually began by discussing one of the memoranda we had prepared; but the discussions quickly became so fragmented that they had little value as probes. It was difficult to concentrate. We could not compete with the impending Walker proceedings and the maneuvers now made necessary by the shortage of committed Roosevelt delegates. We heard the disturbing echoes. Our business was secondary. Yet Ray had to produce an acceptance.

Walker's situation, coming to some sort of resolution, would have enormous impact on the convention. Conboy was often closeted with Roosevelt, and Ray was often there too. They had challenged Seabury to present official charges rather than the "findings" he had publicized freely. This seemed to them a distinction of importance, showing that Seabury, if not now a hopeful candidate himself, as he had certainly been at one time, was quite willing to embarrass another candidate. Finally he did formulate and present charges, and Roosevelt, as Governor, had no alternative to demanding that Walker make a public defense. This, coming shortly before the convention, and making Tammany's defection even more certain, was one of the developments that had begun to make failure suddenly seem quite possible. Roosevelt himself gave no sign of acknowledging this, but we understood well enough the fright that was demoralizing the political brethren.

Ray concluded, and we concurred, that a comprehensive document, rounding up most of the clear conclusions we had reached, would best bring Roosevelt to concentration on the speech. Otherwise it might be put together in a last-minute rush. It was inevitable that revisions would be made in this way—they always were —but the body ought to be ready for the operation. So it was undertaken. Ray's first bulky draft gradually took slimmer shape. He worried it, I worried it, and both of us speculated about Roosevelt's decisions.

Acceptances, in the American party tradition, were important statements. Until late in the nineteenth century, when Garfield, who was a compulsive orator, made a few speeches, and when Bryan, somewhat later, enlarged the precedent and took to the road, the nominated candidates retired from public view, making no other appeal than was contained in a letter replying to the notification committee of the convention. This statement acknowledged the honor, endorsed the party's platform, and enlarged on traditional principles. There might be special emphasis on some issues the candidates thought important, but there was no further pursuit of the subject. The notification ceremonies were customarily delayed for a month after the convention, and during this time the candidate pretended not to know that he had been designated; afterward, when he had made his acceptance, he went into retreat and behaved with the dignity suitable for a potential President.

This procedure had gradually given way as communications improved. McKinley's front-porch performance in 1896 had been the last complete abstention from active canvassing. But notifications were still delayed, and an acceptance speech was customarily regarded as an important formulation of the candidate's views. This and the platform were party commitments; the candidate from then on confined himself to expounding the announced doctrine. He was not privileged to inject anything really new or to reject any of the platform's planks. Smith's violation of this rule in 1928, when he had reversed the party position on prohibition and had, moreover, made it a central issue, had not been encouraging. It had offended many workers and had put the party faithful in an awkward position. His defeat, many of them thought, had been deserved.

There was the complication mentioned in a previous chapter: we would have no part in preparing the platform. We knew by now about the party elders and were aware that they would decide what it would say, but we could only guess what that would be. Ray was now conferring as often as he could manage it with Louis, who ought to know what would be said. Louis seemed to agree that Ray must be allowed to draft Roosevelt's speeches, but he was not communicative about what the party powers were likely to lay down as policies. All Ray knew, really, was that the platform "would be the regular stuff." When he pressed, Louis flared up and told him that if he didn't know by now what the Democratic Party stood for, he ought not to be writing its candidate's speeches. This is about as I recall Ray's relaying it to me. It was evident that we would have to work without further directives until Roosevelt sat down across the table from Ray in a drafting session and ended the period of waiting.

When we began to make guesses, we thought as before that the speech must refer to recovery measures, agricultural relief, power and other utility regulation, lowered tariffs, banking reform, and perhaps prohibition, somewhat in that order. We thought Roosevelt would want to restate the theory of the depression now generally accepted among us. This in itself, we felt, indicated certain measures to be taken for recovery. But beyond that, there was only uncertainty. Perhaps the concert-of-interests concept would also be restated as a goal to be reached and a condition to be maintained. I hoped so. Everyone wanted better times; everyone should help to bring them back. This seemed to offer a contrast with the Republican offering and might serve as the foundation for a program of recovery and reform.

The first draft was some nine thousand words long. Roosevelt finally found time to indicate some preliminary cuts and a few changes of emphasis, but the attention he could give to the speech was much less than was needed. Even after more revisions, Ray still had little confidence in the text he had prepared. He shortened it drastically, on the basis of the hints and suggestions he had been able to elicit, and the second draft came out at something like six thousand words. Since there are only four thousand words in the acceptance speech as printed in the Roosevelt *Papers,* and since they include some last-minute additions to Ray's text, it can be seen that many things were still to happen to the poor creature now on the operating table. Sam Rosenman and Roosevelt himself would each have a hand in the revisions, and some of the cutting was murderous.

About the third week in June, worry about Chicago began to exclude all other interests. The outlook was more and more ominous. As soon as the Republicans cleared out of the Chicago stadium, Farley and his men moved in. Most of the preliminary activities went on in Loop hotels—the Congress, the Blackstone, the Stevens, the Drake, and the Palmer House—but his command post had to be ready. Now the barrages of statements from all factions began. The Smith supporters were sharply and meanly aggressive. Hague of New Jersey was especially vicious in anti-Roosevelt manifestoes and agile in planning confusing maneuvers, but the Massachusetts, Connecticut, and Illinois bosses were also working and plotting energetically. For Farley, it was a strange experience to manage a party faction with its main strength in the West and South and to be under attack by leaders from his own territory in the East. Mistakes were made because of his unfamiliarity with Westerners, and some of them were serious. For a time before the convention actually began, it seemed that they might be fatal.

Some days before the opening, Arthur Krock in *The New York Times* listed the series of questions sure to be fought over:

Would it be Roosevelt or someone else?
Who for Vice-President?
What would be said about the repeal of prohibition that had split the
    Republicans?
What would be said about tariffs?

Being an amateur, I was amazed at this and other forecasts of the controversies likely to be most important. What had become of the depression? Where were the suggestions for relief? Didn't the politicians know that the nation was sinking further and further into a paralysis that threatened its existence? Were they really going to leave out all mention of unemployment and the disaster to agriculture?

Prohibition, it was true, had split the Republicans, and the Democrats were likely to have some trouble with it. But it seemed like fiddling while Rome burned to give it an important listing. That this holdover from 1928 still seemed so important to the cabal of Eastern bosses was a measure of their leadership. The platform would certainly call for repeal, and even if the drier territories were reluctant, Farley knew they would not really try to prevent such a declaration.

About tariffs, surely there could be no Democratic quarrel. Hull would want a stronger declaration for lowering duties than was likely to be granted, but it could not be imagined that the party of Cleveland and Wilson would quarrel seriously about reduction from the levels of the outrageous Smoot-Hawley Act.

No, the Chicago battle would be among contenders for the nomination, not about issues. The Smith forces had already lost. Having lost, they had the handicap of having no ready alternative. Every one of their possibilities was unlikely. Even the best of them, Newton D. Baker, had become, in recent years, a corporation lawyer no longer much interested in popular causes. As far as was known, he was also without ideas for combating the depression. He belonged to the progressives without quite being one any more. He was eminently respectable, a man of integrity and good reputation, a citizen of the highest repute. But he was not an appealing candidate for the Democratic Party to put forward, no better, really, than Davis had been in 1924. If Americans wanted a conservative President, it would be a Republican, not a Democrat.

Roosevelt, however, did not have enough votes; that was the

hard fact. And it was still not apparent what deal might produce enough to make a two-thirds majority.

Our own exchanges during those last days of confusion and anxiety were extremely truncated, though Ray did take time to tell me what he knew and what he deduced. I was fascinated and went to Doc for more sophisticated comment—we were now installed in Chicago—but I soon discovered he was no better informed than myself. He was complaining that nobody told him anything. Then, in an access of discouragement, he asked me why in hell was the Governor so confident? This admission appealed to me as so honest that, since he allowed it, I speculated with him about all the phases of the events going on behind screens we could not penetrate.

We developed an intimacy that was very satisfying. But it did not enlighten me about prospects, especially since I soon understood that Doc was always inclined to pessimism—or, really, to fear cloaked as cynical comment. It was when I saw that he thought the nomination almost certainly lost that I really despaired myself. For two weeks before the convention, and for its first days, I was convinced that I was watching—and participating in, a little— a failing attempt.

CHAPTER XXI

Jim Farley's Problem

❦ ❦ ❦

What happened in Chicago during the ten days after Farley's well-publicized arrival on June 20 has been told from his point of view in *Behind the Ballots* (1938), and others have written their accounts.* We who were observers did, however, have a somewhat different view of events from that of the political operators. The newspapermen saw things in a special way; they seem to have been commenting rather than reporting. To us, the commotion, the glitter, and the confusion were a new experience. We were mildly surprised to discover that what we had heard about such proceedings was indeed true; it was my first actual participation (or near-participation) in the disorderly and sometimes disgraceful proceedings that have gone on quadrennium after quadrennium in the name of democracy. I was at once amused, appalled, and astonished; at the same time, the excitement was fascinating.

Whether the electorate would have a Roosevelt to oppose Hoover, or one of the proposed alternates—Baker, perhaps—was still in doubt. There were no rules, no set place, no fixed time for

---

* See also Peel and Donnelly's excellent *Campaign of 1932* (New York, 1935). Sidelights also may be found in Moley's *After Seven Years* (New York, 1939) and in Rosenman's *Working With Roosevelt* (New York, 1956), and as part of the history of the times, in Schlesinger, Freidel, and others.

meetings among supporters. There were not even any formally appointed representatives to make deals. Yet bargaining was obviously active, even if Farley and Howe had entirely different notions of what ought to be done. Roosevelt himself did not always know what was going on in Chicago, and in any case he was carrying on his own conversations. We suspected from the swirl of rumor that this must be the situation.

Before Chicago, what I knew about such events I had learned from books. I had concluded from them that there were deals among the bosses, but I had not realized that conventions were a coming-together of delegates in blocs representing mostly state and city machines, some—not all—instructed by primaries that were binding in different degrees.

Most of the bosses themselves were there maneuvering and bargaining in a professional way, but the final meetings were yet to take place. Smoke-filled rooms, we learned, were not fictional, but who would prevail in them depended on bringing to bear, at the last minute, the needed power, the critical suggestion, the winning compromise. Two bosses would realize, perhaps quite suddenly, that a merger of their forces would produce something for each, and that no other arrangement would produce quite as much for either.

In a few days I learned more about political choosing than I had learned in all my previous life, although the lessons still had to be sorted out. The sequence of events ending in the Roosevelt nomination seems simple enough in retrospect, with the confusion cleared away and the significant incidents standing out; but while it was going on, and especially for those of us who knew only what we picked up from busy and uncommunicative participants, everything seemed always about to dissolve in chaos.

There were only a few on the immediate Farley-Howe staff. Arthur Mullen of Nebraska, the floor manager, and W.W. Howes, his second, a South Dakotan, were the most conspicuous; the others were lesser lieutenants and mostly anonymous. Sam Rayburn, Garner's sponsor, and W. G. McAdoo, who represented California (and Hearst), were the operators in what happened finally, but they came in only at the last. Until then they were watching to see how Farley or Howe progressed in the other efforts we constantly heard about as rumors.

Of course we did not know that Roosevelt himself was now cashing in on his appeasement of Hearst. Until McAdoo came to the platform and all became clear in a single moment, we had not been sure that the overheard calls and conversations, the mysterious visits, the whispers really meant anything at all substantial.

It seems hard to credit, now, that those of us who were watchers had been resigned from the beginning—that is, from Saturday or Sunday—to failure; but it is fact. We had remained convinced that the stop-Roosevelt movement was succeeding, since it seemed impossible that an opposition so substantial and determined could be beaten. Even when the second and third ballots were dragging out, there were no encouraging signs. None of the favorite sons was giving up. Roosevelt was not gaining, and some delegations were known to be in a mood to desert. The most imminent defection was said to be the Mississippi delegation. If even that small contingent should go, it would start an avalanche, and we knew of no means by which the Mississippians could be held. There were two days when we looked for a dark horse to appear. More and more the candidate seemed likely to be Baker—but perhaps that was because we read the newspapers; in retrospect it seems unlikely enough.

A simple majority in a Democratic convention would not make Roosevelt's victory certain any more than it had Champ Clark's in 1912. The difference from that convention in Baltimore was that here no formidable runner-up like Wilson had appeared. Smith was bitter and had strong support, but he could not win, and there was no other who had such a loyal following. If we had kept this difference in mind, we might not have been so concerned.

What we did not calculate, as very few others seem to have done either—because by now it was so unreasonable—was that Smith was still fixed on getting the nomination for himself. We thought he was working to stop Roosevelt, then to put forward another man. Incredibly, he was still hoping and still unwilling to help any candidate his fellow bosses were waiting to push. This lost the opposing coalition any cohesion it might otherwise have had. The several doubtful Roosevelt delegations—Illinois, Indiana, and especially Mississippi—looking to Smith for some suggestion, got no response from him other than the insistence that they back him. It was perfectly evident that his nomination was impossible, so they left him alone after some tentative conversations. He went on making belligerent statements, but no one was listening.

It was obvious, of course, that none of the other contenders had developed any attractiveness. Running over the list of them, we agreed on this point. If we had talked to the shrewd editor of the *Emporia Gazette,* William Allen White, we should have recognized the hopelessness of Smith's effort—and indeed of the whole stop-Roosevelt movement—much earlier than we did. While we were most discouraged, he was writing:

> Mr. Ritchie's managers hoped that Al Smith, in a speech from the floor—his swan song—withdrawing as a candidate, would blast the Roosevelt boom and make Roosevelt's nomination impossible. But with the Democratic party in the hands of Mr. Roosevelt's Western and Southern friends, it makes small difference whether Al Smith commits hara-kiri for the cause of his personal liberty or eats his heart out in oblivion. His chance to pass out in a blaze of glory, defying the Roosevelt set-up, is passing. In another day the sun will set on his opportunity.*

White's custom was somewhat like that of William Jennings Bryan, who went to Democratic conventions as a delegate, and sometimes even got nominated, and then immediately afterward went to the Republican meetings as a reporter. White did this in reverse. He was a Kansas Republican, but as a commentator he looked with an approving eye on Roosevelt for the Democrats.

* *The New York Times,* June 30, 1932.

Roosevelt noted this during a later campaign. "Bill White," he said, "is a friend of mine except for a few weeks every four years."

White sat in the press pen alongside the other old-timers, hunched over his typewriter, his rosy face and rotund body telling of Kansas corn and hogs. Politics was for him an entrancing business. He and H. L. Mencken near him looked a good deal alike, I thought, and the daily copy they produced, in spite of some differences, betrayed a common love of political shows in the American manner. I did talk with some reporters—including Mencken—but not with White. That was a mistake. In contrast with Mencken, he knew what was going on and reported it. Mencken had no such intention. He was a propagandist for any reactionary who might show strength. He wanted Ritchie, but he would have settled for Smith. The events he watched he had no intention of reporting. This confused me and made me more discouraged than ever.

The trouble with Smith, even if he could have been nominated, was that he could not have been elected, even in that obviously Democratic year. This gradually became clear to all but his own two hundred delegates. And if there was one prevailing sentiment in the corridors and on the floor, it was that twelve Republican years were enough; they must be brought to an end, because if they were not, the Democrats might simply disappear. They must sometimes win to stay in existence as a national party, and this year they could. Tammany might not care if this happened, but others did.

Looking at it that way, and sizing up the situation as an amateur, I thought that Baker was a possibility. True, he had almost no pledged delegates, but he was from Ohio, a populous state, and he did reach back to the stirring Democratic years before the advent of Harding. He had long ago withdrawn into corporate law practice and lost touch with politics, but he was deeply respected by the elders. His War Department had been run creditably and had stood the scrutiny of partisan postwar investigation. Except for Josephus Daniels, he had been closer to Wilson than anyone else in the wartime official family. He had once been a liberal; whether he was now, no one could really say. The Westerners did not think so. And anyway, most of them were not so saturated with Wilsonian memories as were such old-timers as Hull, or Glass. They would prefer a man of their own.

Ritchie of Maryland and Byrd of Virginia, despite their attempts to gain notice, were supported only by their own states, and a swing to either man of the released delegates from other favorite-son states would still not furnish any considerable strength to build on. Neither was a real contender.

Curiously enough, it seemed that the Smithites, when they considered whom to mass behind if they lost, had settled on a Chicago banker, Melvin Traylor. This was an interesting confirmation of Ray's theory that this group had learned nothing from their experience in 1928 and would completely misinterpret the sentiment of the delegates in 1932. A banker? And one, at that, who was unable to attend the convention because his bank was fending off a run by its depositors!

Presently we became aware that the newly arising possibility— discarding the lunatic fringe represented by Alfalfa Bill Murray of Oklahoma—was Garner of Texas, Speaker of the House. Garner was represented by Sam Rayburn, and Hearst, speaking through McAdoo, was said to favor him. Texas and California between them massed more than a hundred votes.

Although he could not be tagged as a Wall Streeter, he was known as a small-town banker and a land speculator. His propagandizing for, and his trying to get accepted, a proposal for a federal sales tax was the mark of his mind. Out his way it might be thought that such a man was a presidential possibility, but there were not many from other states who agreed. He was shrewd and domineering but, to tell the truth, provincial and ignorant. It would seem that the Democrats could do better than that. Still, this was the year when they could elect almost anyone (the "almost" in this refers to Smith). Even with Smith out, there were others besides Garner who *could* be elected, and this gave Rooseveltians their worst worries.

In the background of all the Democratic activities were some strategic agreements reached at the Hyde Park meeting of June 5. Neither Ray nor I had been there, of course, nor had Doc or Sam; we had merely heard about it. As has been related in an earlier chapter, one of several decisions made at the meeting was to support Senator Walsh of Montana for the permanent chairmanship of the convention. This soon became known and caused indignant denunciation of Roosevelt by the Smith supporters. It was claimed that at a meeting of the Arrangements Committee in April, Senator Barkley of Kentucky, who would make the keynote speech as temporary chairman, had been conceded to Roosevelt in return for a promise that Shouse would be given the permanent chairmanship. Roosevelt, asked by the committee if he agreed, had pointed out that the permanent chairman would be elected by the convention, not by the committee. However, he said, the committee could *commend* a candidate for the post. Evidently the word "commend" was interpreted to mean "promise"; at any rate, when Senator Walsh was indicated as the Rooseveltians' choice at a preconvention strategy meeting in Chicago, there were loud cries of bad faith. Even among many professionals on the Roosevelt side, it was felt that an agreement had been repudiated—a high crime in politics.

If the Shouse incident was deplored, the outrage was nothing compared to that aroused by an attempt to abrogate the two-thirds rule. It was a play that ought not to have started and that, if started, should have been stopped at once. It was attributed to Roosevelt, and he was condemned all the more because nearly everyone suspected that Farley was allowed to take the blame after resentment arose.

The two-thirds rule, like other arrangements, was a rule of the meeting. It had to be accepted anew by each convention, something that could not have been gathered from the accounts in the press. It was pictured as something so sacred that any attempt to question it, much less to abrogate it, might have been regarded as an attack on the Constitution itself. The fact was that every convention since 1832 had adopted it, but it did not follow that every Democratic candidate was in honor bound not to propose an alternative. It had begun with Jackson, who had needed it to assure Van Buren's selection as Vice-President. It had been kept because it gave the Southerners, who could not hope to nominate a candidate of their own, a strong bargaining voice in the selection of candidates put forward by others. They had profited from it immensely, and not only in the way of patronage; they had been able to insist on "doughface" candidates (Northern men with Southern views) right up to the Civil War. Even in later years they had often made a strong push for the vice-presidency in exchange for supporting and furnishing the votes needed for a two-thirds majority.

Roosevelt supporters had made casual suggestions that the rule was vulnerable, since refusal to adopt it needed only a simple majority. *That* they thought they had, and the prospect did look inviting when the convention was about to open and the two-thirds necessary for nomination was not yet in sight. At the first rally of the Roosevelt crowd on Thursday, June 23 (the convention would open on Monday the 27th), the suggestions became a proposal. There were sixty-five delegates present at this rally, and Farley was presiding. He said afterward that before he knew what was happening the meeting had been stampeded into enthusiastic agreement that the rule should be abrogated. The stampede followed a whooping speech by Huey P. Long of Louisiana, who thus established himself as a Roosevelt enthusiast. "He asked permission to second his own resolution," Farley says in *Behind the Ballots* (page 117), "and then with coat open and arms flying, he delivered a stem-winding, rousing stump speech that took his listeners by storm."

Huey was one of the characters at the convention about whom we were most curious. He had made big noises in Louisiana, creating so many enemies that a contesting delegation had come to Chicago. He stormed through hotel corridors, held forth in the bars, and invaded Louis' quarters with noisy demands. When he was barred from Louis' retreat, he made such a disturbance in the halls that Louis had to pacify him. He was allowed to talk with Roosevelt by telephone, and when his delegation was successfully seated, after a terrific row, he voluntarily went to work on the doubtful Mississippi delegates. He was accumulating credit.

Neither Farley nor Howe quite dared to suppress this perpetually erupting volcano, and he would hardly speak to any lesser captains. He glanced at us several times in passing, but having a shrewd instinct for power, he passed us by without notice. We saw a pudgy, overdressed loudmouth. He was one of the sights of the circus—one of its least dignified ones—but to us he was a curiosity, nothing more.

His noisy interference did, however, dominate Farley's preconvention meeting, and after he spoke, a resolution was passed to oppose the two-thirds rule. Farley seemed to be overwhelmed by Huey's display of energy, but when he recovered, he got Roosevelt on the phone and was told to wait and see how the Southern delegations reacted. Farley thought afterward that Huey might have been right; the proposal might have been accepted if it had not come so early that the reporters could make a cause of it. As things were, the opposition press—and that was most of it—at once went to work on this new evidence of Roosevelt's underhanded methods. The outcries were so fierce that Farley, frightened at that moment by his failure to win over more than a few of the Indiana and Illinois delegates—even though favorite son Jim Ham Lewis of Illinois had withdrawn from the race on Saturday—and knowing how the rule was valued by the Southerners, told Roosevelt that they were in too tight a hole to risk going on with the scheme. Roosevelt, from Albany, issued a statement saying that he thought the rule undemocratic, but that since the issue had been raised without previous discussion, he would ask his friends in Chicago not to insist.

Farley was still left with the seemingly insoluble problem of converting a simple majority into one of two-thirds, with the problem made worse by weakening in several places. How was he to do it? He considered it possible, when he counted up, that some of the delegations would respond better than most others thought. And he had very little choice anyway, so he would go to the first ballot claiming that it would nominate Roosevelt and hoping that, if he went on confidently making the claim, the uncertain ones would join the apparent winner to share in the profits of victory.

It was quite obvious even to us that persuasions and promises were being offered in all the doubtful delegations. Farley, rushing into Louis' room and talking into his ear—Louis crouching in a chair or, a good deal of the time, stretched out on the floor, a telephone to the other ear and with girl secretaries and several political characters hanging about—could be pictured as staving off a disaster that might happen at any moment. We believed it would take only the rumor of a defection to start a landslide for some dark horse. Everything could be lost in a deal made in a corner somewhere that Farley might know nothing about. How could he hope to hold a fluid majority while a way was found to accumulate another hundred votes?

On Monday, June 25, the Rules Committee had complied with Roosevelt's telephoned wish to abandon the attack on the two-thirds rule. By that time another resolution, also proposed by Huey Long, who was now quite out of control, had been adopted. It provided that if six ballots should pass without a two-thirds choice, the convention might proceed to nominate by simple majority. For this, Farley had to disclaim all responsibility. He knew there was no such easy way out of his problem, but it caused another night of hasty conferring and communicating with Roosevelt. The Rules Committee was convened again on Wednesday morning, and this time, after considerable argument, voted down Long's resolution and adopted the two-thirds rule for this convention, but recommended that it be omitted thenceforth. Farley now could concentrate on his other troubles—if he could find out where they were likely to arise.

One of them, at least, was highly visible. It was a plan, adopted late Tuesday night by the Rules Committee, to defer action on the platform until the nominees for President and Vice-President had been chosen. The committee was looking forward to an impending struggle over the plank calling for repeal of the prohibition amendment. Roosevelt wanted this to go over until he had been nominated and could soften the issue by a moderate statement. Farley, however, saw that the plan would be regarded as another reversal of traditional procedure and that it would provide still more ammunition for those who were claiming that the Rooseveltians were not playing fair. Shuddering at the prospect of a melee over this extraneous issue, he begged the Roosevelt followers not to support the plan, and it was voted down. By this time he must have felt that friends were more troublesome than enemies.

On Wednesday the platform was adopted. It included a provision for repeal. As it turned out, only seven states wanted a milder provision, and the plank, as worded, was enthusiastically applauded. That difficulty was disposed of, and there were no controversies about the other provisions. The nominating speeches could begin.

At last we were able to examine the platform. Thinking of future speeches, we hoped that some of the rumors we had heard were unfounded. Our immediate reaction was a discouraged one. My worst fears about the elders' devotion to free enterprise were confirmed, and as for the tariff plank, it was to be hoped that we would not have to explain its meaning. The rest was not so bad, but the rest was not likely to be at issue, either, so that was little consolation. Meanwhile the whole problem of writing speeches would be purely academic unless Jim Farley managed to corral those hundred additional delegates.

CHAPTER XXII

At the Congress Hotel

❀ ❀ ❀

The command post of Louis Howe, as field marshal, was in a corner suite of the Congress Hotel on Michigan Avenue. The hotel was already old and rather worn, but it had the solid quality of an establishment intended for the carriage trade. Several whole floors were occupied by aspirants' headquarters. Those of Smith, Garner, Ritchie, Byrd, and Murray were just below those assigned to the Roosevelt workers. Out of curiosity we inspected them all, but mostly we stayed higher up where Louis was. Doc O'Connor's suite, where I felt most at home and where I got much of my education, adjoined it. Professional helpers and hangers-on made it a stopping place. Most of them assumed I had some part in what was going on, and I was often asked questions that I evaded. Conversations thus started were apt to be one-sided, but by dissembling and seeming sophisticated I was usually able to escape exposure as an interloper, and sometimes to gather information myself.

A mountain of water in motion could be seen from Doc's windows to the north, a massive up-pouring formation worthy of Chicago's pretensions. By day it heaved into the air and fell back in a broken cascade; by night it was a lighted tumble of colors. Above it a geyser of glittering spray spread out on the wind. This moving water, with the pale lake behind it, empty and vast, a sweet-water sea, was the background for the confused proceedings around us.

By some good fortune, convention week was bright and cool. When Chicago has one of those spells, it is an incomparable summer resort. Winds coming off the prairies can be fiercely hot; when they come off the lake, they are clean and cool. Michigan Avenue is a miles-long cliff of clean façades with an occasional aspiring tower; Chicago on such days is a pleasant place to be.

Doc and I could think of such things. Everyone around us seemed very busy indeed, but we had nothing much to do. There were intent faces, restless pacing, and calculating whispers. All were related to a performance we could see and hear so exasperatingly little of that it had the quality of a Kafka novel dramatized; the actors crossed the stage, exchanged cryptic remarks, made despairing gestures, addressed us absently, threw their cigars or cigarettes into any convenient receptacle, and reached for others so that they could go on smoking furiously; they signaled to one another and then disappeared through doors as newcomers indistinguishable from themselves appeared. It would have been an insane performance even if the plot had been known and the script read; for me, a neophyte, it was incomprehensible even with Doc's coaching.

I gradually realized that I was looking for meaning that was not there; none of the activity had any relation to the outcome we were anxiously waiting for. I accused Doc, finally, of pretending to know more than he really did. He laughed and admitted his ignorance. Neither he nor Ray was privy to the continuing maneuvers. Ray was, besides, distracted by mounting worry over his draft of the acceptance speech. Doc did feel privileged to stop one of the insiders occasionally and demand information or pretend to give some, but this was not often productive, for none of them was told very much even about the errand he was running. Most of them felt compelled to make pronouncements, but these were apt to turn into anxious questioning. Doc enjoyed a certain prestige because he had a congressman brother, who of course belonged to the political fraternity and could mix with the minor characters. Following Doc, I frequently sat or stood in a group and, by keeping quiet and looking wise, could join some parts of the puzzle to other parts. Presently I began to achieve a little sophistication too. At least I learned the language and could venture to speculate.

Louis or Jim, or one of their recognized emissaries, occasionally crossed left to right, and a door was sometimes left open while their colloquies took place. Louis, we found, considered us harmless—either that or we were invisible to him. He never acknowledged our presence, but also he seemed not to be bothered by us. I discovered long afterward that he rather liked me, but the only sign of it then was that I was ignored when I might well have been told to remove myself.

So the days passed from Sunday to Wednesday. We made unprofitable excursions to the stadium, far out on West Madison Street. It hummed and crackled with private talk as the delegates conferred in aisles and corridors, and occasionally there was a shout of laughter or a burst of loud talk from a group. I discovered simply by listening that, like us, they were waiting for "the word," and meanwhile passing the time as best they could. When the proceedings really required notice or when the entertainment amused them, they watched and listened. The attention span was short for dull oratory, and after they gathered what was being offered they began to wander. The place always seemed full, but so did the corridors, and the bars and lobbies of the hotels were always crowded.

It was soon obvious that the galleries and even the floors of the huge hall were overrun by outsiders. These were mostly Ed Kelly's men, city and county employees, under instruction and with a system of communications. Political mobs of the sort were nothing new, but this was something outrageous. There were some complaints from the Roosevelt people, but they were not as stiff as I would have expected. Doc explained. The uproar was the result of consenting to Chicago as the meeting place. Actually, the nomination was being arranged somewhere else than on the convention floor. The possibility of a stampede for Smith had long since disappeared. The hoodlums were an annoyance, but nothing more.

We may not have understood the moves, but we did know what the excitement was all about, what the end was meant to be; everything centered on capturing blocs of delegates and holding those already pledged. Beyond that we could guess that inducements were being held out and that they must be substantial for those who rated as rulers of political domains. But we knew neither the currency being used nor the values put on various deliveries. No one was allowed to know any considerable part of these operations; subordinates were assigned to segments. We gathered that Farley and Howe were the responsible merchandisers, that they parceled out large inducements and allowed subordinates to dispense small ones, that they expected to be consulted when anything more than ordinary was involved. We knew that when the stake was substantial the open line to Albany was used, and heard some of what was said. Roosevelt sometimes agreed with the proposal relayed to him by Farley or Howe, but sometimes he spoke directly to the individual involved. This was the final word, the giving of *the* promise. It was good in the political market—as good, Doc told me, as the traditional bond.

Transactions of moment were thus begun and closed. Many a heavy-set man chewing on a dead cigar and spreading a rich aroma of bourbon left Louis to go on his errand of delivery; usually he was satisfied, or so it could be guessed from his look of satisfaction. It occurred to me that no historian would ever know what the transaction had been.

"Don't they ever get mixed up?" I asked Doc.

Oh, sure, he said, but they straighten it out; no one really refuses to deliver; it's just not done. I protested that there was no record and that several people were making deals. Even if they had good memories, there must be duplications and crossings. They weren't immune to mistakes, Doc said. And political promises not kept were very dangerous, because the rumor of them spread. So professionals trained themselves to remember, and they got to be remarkably good at it. Conventions, he said, were the only time those big guys got together; it happened only once in four years.

They slapped each other on the back, had drinks, and joked a lot —but actually they were putting their heft on the line to match it with others' accumulations. They knew the score long before any adding up was done. Outsiders only made deductions about the published results. Even old newsmen did a lot of guessing and made a good many miscalculations. Thus, Doc.

Right now, he reminded me, Jim knew he had about six hundred votes, but he was claiming 690 and was still saying that the rest would turn up on the first ballot; if not on the first, then on the second. He knew it wouldn't happen. That extra hundred must look like a million to him, and it was too late now to get them one by one in little deliveries; he had to have blocs—Indiana; the rest of Illinois, which Ham Lewis couldn't deliver; Ohio, where White, the Governor, was holding out; or the Virginia crowd Byrd was bargaining with. But Mississippi could slip away, for instance; so could others. Farley talked big, but he was a scared man.

Since we had no information about Farley's major deals, we watched the outward signs. The superficial tricks of the trade seemed ineffective even to us. For instance, Howe and Molly Dewson (women's division) had rigged up a public-address outlet in a large room where there were seats for a sizable delegation. There the Governor himself could talk to them for a moment or two from Albany. He was able, in this way, to show off that matchless knowledge of the country and of its political idiosyncracies that so amazed everyone around him. Even by long-distance telephone he was sure-footed among those sensitive hearers. It was the same talent he used in speaking from the back platforms of trains at whistle stops, or when people came to see him in Albany. I could see how this would be good for keeping the flock together, but only for reassuring those sheep that were already folded.

I still had to learn that Roosevelt's was a magic voice. I had listened to his radio talks and had thought that the voice was too cultivated, too mannered, and perhaps too high in the tenor range. I was wrong. But however effective it might be, using it seemed an unconscionable waste of time in the circumstances, now become desperate. There was still a lot of this sort of thing, and we knew that Louis and Jim were allowing many delegates to speak, even if only for a moment, to Roosevelt sitting beside his radio in Albany with a microphone on the table at his elbow. When did he find time to carry on the vital negotiations for the big deal he had to consummate?

The confidence exhibited by Farley, phony as any professional must have known it to be, and the time Roosevelt spent in casual talk with delegates of no special importance impressed even his enemies. Doc kept saying that although we might be discouraged the coalition had no real belief that they would in the end defeat him. After Tuesday, the reporters who had been most determined to play up obstacles were no longer predicting that he would be beaten. Even under editorial pressure they hesitated to risk being wholly wrong. The exception was the staff of *The Chicago Tribune,* whose matchless indifference to fact and holy dedication to reaction enabled it to pursue the anti-Roosevelt line long after others had abandoned it. Repeatedly *The Tribune*'s special editions, impossible for anyone in Chicago to ignore, screamed what was palpably fiction. Next day, so little was made of complete reversal that the paper might be thought to have been perceptive and truthful all the time. In itself this was an outstanding performance.

On Tuesday, Roosevelt talked with me. I had been picturing the Albany scene as I heard others speak to him, and I had several times wandered into the room where the loudspeaker magnified his voice for the delegates rounded up by Louis' emissaries. This sort of thing was still going on intermittently. But during the afternoon, when movement to the stadium was at its height and he had just been talking with Louis, the phone was suddenly held out to me.

The voice at the other end was clear, unhurried, and rich. He had been a little amused, I think, by something Doc had said to him earlier about me—that I was learning fast, or something of the sort. Roosevelt said, Well, Professor, how did I like politics? I said I found it hard to be detached enough to enjoy it. That had always been his trouble, he said; besides, it got so complicated, it was hard to follow. But there was not such a stalemate as it looked like right then. Something had to give somewhere.

He went on to say that he assumed I had got what I wanted out of my meeting with the farm people. I must think what ought to be put into the speech, and when the time came, we'd talk about it again. When the nomination was over, he'd have to work fast. Whatever was said would have to be got into a paragraph or two, not more.

That was about it. He asked for Louis again, and they went on talking about who was weak and who was solid. I had then, as I was to have often in the next years when I talked with him, a guilty feeling. I never had it when I had business with him. These reminders of conscience came at times when he had things on his mind I was in no way concerned with, and when I felt that his time must be budgeted in seconds. I would have many such recollections from later years, but this was the first, and therefore it stayed in my recollection. I might speculate about it, but it would be only that.

With Sam beside him and Missy LeHand hovering near, and with Eleanor out of it because matters had got beyond her competence, but probably knitting in a corner, we could imagine him spending the days and most of the nights at his desk in the old mansion. If there was ever a man sustained by the thing he was doing because it was what he was made for, it was this one; he was getting it right, continually making adjustments, using to the full a complicated art.

Was Roosevelt's apparent confidence real? I had a discouraging thought. It might be worse than a pretense; he might be mistaken. I brooded over it. Doc and I discussed it. We concluded that the more important preliminaries had been inefficiently arranged. It was true that the election of the permanent chairman had gone as planned, even if there had been outcries about the martyrdom of Shouse and an appeal to that political code I have mentioned. Opposition delegates would now be gaveled down and friendly ones recognized. Farley would be able to say whether recesses should be taken or sessions continued. If the band wagon began rolling, he could keep it in motion.

Whether this actually proved to be vital, I never knew. It seemed afterward that decisions about procedure had mostly been mistaken. Jim pressed for immediate balloting after the nominating speeches and the demonstrations, and he held the convention all night while a third ballot was taken. No landslide started, however, and it was obvious that he ought not to have risked voting until he had a combination put together. One ballot had shown exactly what three had confirmed—that no break was coming without a major deal. Jim had to allow a recess finally because it had become a physical necessity. He had already risked making himself absurd by insisting on continuation. Exhausted as he was from all-night pleading with delegates to abandon their instructions and go over to Roosevelt, he now had to make the supreme effort, and those with whom he had to make the effort were exhausted too; but if he failed in the next few hours, defeat would be inevitable.

It was true that no dark horse was anywhere within sight, but one might appear. Such things had happened at other conventions —for instance, the one that had nominated Polk, who was so little known that the Democrats that year had had to contend with the Whig slogan: "Who the hell's Polk?" This year it might be: "Who the hell's Baker?" Farley certainly risked it by his convention tactics.

Then there was the original mistake of agreeing to hold the convention in Chicago. It was enemy ground, and the hostility was as open, as crude, and as massive as that city's political reputation would have led anyone to expect. The hoodlums were mobilized in thousands under the foremanship of Kelly's henchmen. They loved trouble and they were at their ugliest during these days because they considered Smith one of their own, and because Roosevelt was making a martyr of Jimmy Walker, another of their own.

The galleries all week were monopolized by these characters. Their chanting often drowned out attempts of speakers to be heard; they roared and sang when their own speakers roused them,

and there were menacing growls and groans as the voting proceeded and Roosevelt's strength appeared. If this was meant to
demonstrate a popular demand for Smith, it was a failure.

I learned from it that an important process of democracy was
open to minority disruption. I must confess to having been appalled. I concluded that the convention was one device that had
better be reformed; but everyone else seemed to enter into the proceedings with gusto. Even Ray and I joined the parade, as it were,
having abandoned our usual habits for that week. We slept on
couches without taking off our clothes and ate sandwiches in the
headquarters of the Businessmen's League for Roosevelt. When
the votes were taken, we kept score and watched for breaks. The
frantic proselytizing that went on everywhere must be having an
effect, and we tried earnestly to guess what this might be.

On Thursday we happened to be sitting in a corner of Louis'
room, Doc and I, when Judge Mack finished his nominating speech
for Roosevelt. The organ boomed from the loudspeaker, and the
yells of the loyal delegates competed with the menacing roar from
the galleries. The band tried several melodies, among them "An-
chors Aweigh," suitable, someone evidently thought, for a former
Assistant Secretary of the Navy. Louis, squirming on the floor,
gasped into the phone to Mullen, the floor leader, "Tell 'em to go
back to that 'Happy Days.' " It became the campaign song. People
did long for happy days to be here again, and shouting the melody
seemed to suggest that good fortune might be on the way. Even the
hostile galleries soon joined in. What was most needed was to be
cheerful and confident, to assume that the candidate knew what to
do and that all would be well again when it was done. "Happy
Days" was a wonderfully suitable tune. We spoke of it, and Doc
said that he hoped more would be done to back up the promise
than seemed likely to him. "Happy Days" . . . Hoover, sour and
tired, had run out his string; Roosevelt was the rising sun. Doc said
he'd rise all right, but what would he do when he'd risen?

On Friday, after the long night session, Louis seemed at the last
extreme. He wheezed and moaned; he lay on the floor with a pil-
low under his head in what seemed a semicoma. Doc pointed out,

however, that this did not interrupt the stream of fixers who reported to him. They squatted beside him and talked into his ear, whereupon he indicated decisions by economical gestures. They understood, but I could not quite see how; it must have been the fraternal communication of professionals. Louis also had a telephone that seemed attached to him like an arm or a leg. It ran, we knew, to the convention floor when necessary, but elsewhere too. One of the precautions he had taken was to set up a switchboard of his own, operated by his own people brought from New York. His knowledge of the bosses was completely cynical. At least his communications would be secure.

Each day we moved back and forth through indifferent streets from the hotel to the stadium. A few thousand visitors obviously made no impression on Chicago, except in the immediate neighborhood of the stadium. There the taxis congealed in an immovable pool, and we had to get out to walk the remaining blocks. This was along West Madison Street. Derelicts from the whole Midwest loitered in doorways and at the corners. These were men who belonged to the fraternity of the lost; they were recognizable at a glance. West Madison was so crowded with them that we had to push our way through.

To come through this swarming indifference to the stadium where power was being bargained for, and to do so repeatedly, was to be reminded of elementals. There were salvage operations to be undertaken before the fancier reforms wanted by those who were merely in distress. Lesser troubles seemed trivial on West Madison. There were not many delegates who were moved by this evidence of our state as they elbowed their way through the outside swarms. The callousness of another excitement made them impervious.

We had special passes of some sort and could wander anywhere about the premises. We kept strictly away from Jim's hideout, but there were other vantage places. The first day was mostly given over to entertainment while the platform committee wrangled about prohibition. Eddie Dowling, the master of ceremonies, called one after another of his show-business Democrats to the platform, and they sang or played or clowned for the crowd. Will Rogers got top billing. He asked the delegates to be patient, saying that he was supposed to keep them in their seats until the prohibition plank was fixed up; he'd heard, though, that they were having trouble getting the committee sobered up, so he might be there for some time. Will was better received than the others, but they all did their best.

The suspense built up and up as Jim failed to enlarge the Roosevelt majority on the first or second ballot, his reason for going on through the night. I kept a special watch on Jim after it became clear to me that he, not Louis, had the ambassadorial powers. The other leaders acknowledged Louis' position, but, said Doc, they talked turkey to Jim.

He was formidable, but he soon began to show wear. He wore a painted grin. He was an outsize fellow anyway and had to bend when his ear was whispered into. His round, red face ran sweat, and his jaws were always working on gum, a large wad of it. He never used tobacco and had never in his life tasted liquor. When he listened to confidences, he looked elsewhere, perhaps signaling to someone or touching someone's shoulder. Three or four communications might be going on at once. I was told that he knew everyone's name, his home, and his connections. This store of knowledge was for present purposes a priceless asset acquired by long effort. Certainly there were hundreds in those crowds with whom he was on first-name terms. Since he was always carefully dressed, he seemed easy and competent even when he must have found the strain almost unendurable.

Toward noon on Thursday, when the nominating speeches were starting, Doc said to me after about our tenth cup of coffee that it looked bad; Jim hadn't made it. He talked big, said Doc, but that was only for effect. Ray agreed. I still thought he must have something up his sleeve. No one who *knew* he was beaten could *look* so confident. Oh, sure, Doc said, he'd been hoping that he could shake things loose somewhere. Even a small break might start the landslide. But it hadn't happened. Now his own troops were shaky. He had real trouble in Mississippi; if it hadn't been for Huey Long that outfit would have been lost already.

Doc trailed off, and we sat in gloomy ignorance as the afternoon began. Finally he said what I had in mind too. If there was anyone else. . . . He brightened. The fact was, he said, that there just wasn't; it was a momentary comfort.

But Ray was despondent. He had a kind of hesitant nasal drawl that was more marked in situations of this kind. He was baffled now and almost incoherent. I tried to lighten his load a little by suggesting that what he was afraid of was that his speech was never going to be used. He refused to banter about it. He said seriously that all the effort he had put into it these last three weeks was going to be wasted. Even if it was used at all, everybody and his cousin were cutting it up and putting some indescribable nonsense in. He could just see Sam hanging onto the radio with the Governor back in Albany and once in a while taking a swipe at the pages he had in front of him. That was no way to work.

Ray wandered out disconsolate.

Doc suddenly said, What *about* that speech? Had I read it? About a hundred times, I said. There were even words in it that I recognized—not sentences, by now, just words.

He laughed, the first laugh of the day. I'd talked to them back in Albany for an hour yesterday, he reminded me. Hadn't I got my farm stuff in? I explained that either I had made it too complicated or Sam and Roosevelt had had their minds on something else; they hadn't seemed to get it very clearly. And I had no idea what would finally go in.

This was true. I had had a second talk with Roosevelt. I had explained to him again the advantages of domestic allotment. We had talked about some such possibility so often that I could go at once into detail. I stressed its voluntary nature. Farmers would vote on its adoption. If a majority was for it, the minority would not share the benefits going to those who participated. This was a way of escaping from the chiseler trouble which was always experienced in voluntary schemes and which had made all former attempts at crop control useless.

I illustrated. The farmers with a history of wheat production would vote. If they voted favorably, county committees would be set up throughout the wheat regions. These committees would allocate acreages needed to meet the nation's usual demand. Farmers would be paid for keeping out of production the acres they usually planted but now left fallow. This would reduce the opposition to control, and the locally elected committees would avoid the charge of Washington dictatorship.

I suggested that he ought to say at once that the enormous existing surpluses made crop reduction absolutely necessary, but that a way would be found to make reduction possible without putting the whole burden on farmers. Roosevelt said he guessed I was right. He then shifted me to Sam and I went over it again. But Sam had no feeling for farmers' troubles, and I was not too sure he took it all in. Finally Roosevelt had come back on. Professor, he said, you put all that in a telegram—no, just say what you think should go into this speech; you know, a paragraph.

Next day, here we were, sitting and worrying. Doc said, come to think of it, *he* hadn't even *looked* at the speech. He knew Sam was used to working under pressure, but this was outlandish; Sam was in no condition to make a decent job of it. If that speech was needed at all, Doc said, it had better be a good one. If we got through the next day or two, and if this fellow was nominated, he'd sure get to be President.

He sat thinking about the possibility, and presently he asked if I had a copy.

I said that Ray had it in an inside pocket, next to his heart, but that I had a safe-keeping copy in my briefcase—only I knew that Sam was sitting there in Albany scratching out and writing in. There couldn't be much left of the original.

Why didn't I get it, he asked, so we could take another look at it?

I brought it. He took it and went into the bedroom. He said to come on and we'd pretend it was really going to be used. And if we pretended that, we could go on and pretend we'd been told to rewrite it.

So he started to read it, sentence by sentence, paragraph by paragraph—aloud and slowly. When he got to about the third page, he went right on, in a reading tone of voice, to say that it was the most damned awful stuff he'd ever known to be thrown together and called a speech.

I agreed, or so I said, but I imagined that he was thinking of a lawyer's brief, and I was thinking of the kind of exposition I was used to. What Ray had had to write was a political speech. And he'd had several sessions on it with Roosevelt. I reminded Doc that he was no speech-writer, and I'd found out that I wasn't one either.

He said he knew about political speeches, but this one was the limit. It was obvious that it had been cut down from a much longer one. When the cuts had been made, all the connecting stuff had been crossed out. There weren't any transitions; the ideas might be there—I interrupted to say that *some* were—but some had been deleted altogether, either by design or accident. Besides, Doc said, my farm stuff wasn't there at all. I said that it had been left out on purpose until I had come to my Chicago meeting, but the couple of paragraphs I had sent in yesterday presumably would be put in. They would fit in right after that passage (I pointed it out) about the farmers' troubles.

He thought some more. Then he said that no one else was going to do this, and maybe we wouldn't get anywhere doing it, but someone ought to write something that resembled a state paper. It ought to call the signals for the campaign; it ought to please the customers; and it ought to get the party workers steamed up. He proposed that we do it all over.

I wouldn't dare, I said. Ray would murder me.

Ask him.

So I did. Doc, I said, wanted to smooth out some of the transitions in the speech. Ray said to go ahead; there wouldn't be any speech anyway, the way it looked. He hesitated, then said to be careful; we weren't to let anyone else see it. Obviously he thought

Doc and I were merely exercising. It would take our minds off our worries. There was no relief for him. He was going to hover over Louis.

So Doc and I closed the door. We worked on that draft all the rest of Thursday and into Friday morning. Doc got a stenographer; we wore her out, and he got another. We kept at it, putting together materials we knew thoroughly enough but getting them into a strictly prescribed form and length. It was beautiful. We both said so. That, Doc said, *is* a state paper.

We were completely exhausted, but hardly more so than the delegates at the stadium, for we had been writing during the session that lasted all night. Inquiring around, Doc reported that things were no better at the convention; when we got through, the third vote was being taken. Jim had made no real progress, and it was no more obvious how he might force a break. Doc said he'd known all along that Jim was fumbling.

We knew we couldn't sleep, not yet. Ray had given up and gone out to the stadium. What we had done did seem very good, but what use would it be to show it to anyone? They were all counting delegates, wondering what was coming next, waiting for something to happen.

I said that we'd had a good time—our kind of a time—but we might as well forget it now.

Not on your life, Doc said. If there should be a break, couldn't I imagine the situation? Who'd have a clear enough head to straighten out that mess Ray was carrying around? Or the one Sam would bring with him?

So what? I asked.

What he did was to get Sam on the phone in Albany. Sam was as incoherent as everyone else, after that night-long vigil beside the Governor's radio. Sam was also, Doc said, too full of chocolate milkshakes, which he consumed serially in times of stress. Anyway Doc told Sam he had something for him and he wanted a stenographer to take it down.

After some argument, Sam found one not too far gone to listen and make marks on paper. Doc dictated the whole thing. It took the better part of an hour, although we estimated the reading time at thirty-five to forty minutes, not allowing for applause or interpolations.

"You type that and see that the Judge gets it right away," Doc told the girl. She promised, and he hung up. We tore up our notes for fear someone would get hold of them. At least I did. If Doc had a copy, he kept it in a secret file.

That production was never heard of again. Whether it was ever transcribed, or ever seen by Sam, let alone by Roosevelt, I never knew. Our compact, closely reasoned acceptance speech exists somewhere in limbo, perhaps, but not among the nation's papers. Afterward it seemed to me part of the nightmarish Chicago week, no more substantial than the rest of the experience. Indeed, we forgot almost immediately that we had written an acceptance. We took a short nap and went out to the stadium again. When things began to happen that evening, it all went so fast that we were gathered up in the general incoherence. The shift from no hope at all to the realization that there was actually a campaign ahead was overwhelming. Anyone could see that what mattered now was that Roosevelt should appear and just plainly and clearly accept.

CHAPTER XXIII

The Big Deal

🌿 🌿 🌿

Monday had been a day of tumult and irresponsible maneuvering. Tuesday had been Farley's testing day, with some successes mingled with the defeats. Roosevelt delegates from Minnesota and Louisiana were seated after Huey Long had again seized an opportunity to exhibit his eloquence in a crowded committee room. But the contests showed finally that the Roosevelt strength was something like 650 votes; two contested issues were won by 638 and 658 to 514 and 492. This was hardly more than the majority for Walsh as permanent chairman (626 to 528).

It seemed a distressingly long way from the 770 that would be two-thirds. That Louis and Jim thought so too could be read on their faces. Pallor and sagging flesh might be only signs of fatigue, but under it was obvious desperation. On Wednesday most of the newspapers concluded that Roosevelt could not win, and there was much speculation about who would benefit from the dispersal of his delegates. Our spirits fell lower than ever. Even Doc retreated into morose silence.

On Thursday the nominating speeches began. There were nine of them, each followed by the expected demonstration. A recess was declared in the late afternoon, and then a session began that went on and on into the night. After the first ballot, Farley came to Howe for a consultation. We overheard it decided that there should be no recess; another ballot should be taken at once. Farley was still hopeful of accessions. Doc commented that they must have lost their heads; it was a tenable comment.

On the first ballot Roosevelt had 666½ votes, more than a majority and 450 votes more than his nearest rival. On the second he had 677¾; it was a trifling gain, not the hoped-for break. Farley still refused a recess and called obstinately for a third ballot. This time Roosevelt won only 4¼ additional votes; his count stood at 682. It was 9:15 in the morning. Defeated, Farley consented to adjournment. The physical exhaustion of everyone concerned was so apparent that both sides were ready to quit until some further deals could be made.

Even we could see that things might finally go either way during that recess, and more probably against Roosevelt than for him, because his strength had already had its test. The instructed delegations might well begin to disintegrate; they were bound only for a limited time. Was there any way at all of gaining the votes needed to win? They could come from very few sources, because the necessary number was so large and because there were very few possible combinations that could supply them.

There was an apprehensive quiet in our quarters during the next few hours, but for Farley and Howe those were the hours they had lived for, the hours for testing their professional skill. For Roosevelt they were the time for finding out whether his compromises had produced the effect he had estimated. Fortunately one of them had done so: abandoning the League of Nations now paid off. Hearst gave in, as I think that Roosevelt learned, while keeping the knowledge to himself for the moment. Louis and Jim continued their search for delegates, with Louis concentrating on Byrd of Virginia. His effort to find votes in that quarter seemed absurd to the rest of us for a number of reasons, including the simple one that Byrd did not have enough votes to offer, but Louis insisted on continuing his negotiations. Not until he learned about the success of Roosevelt and Farley would he admit that he had been mis-

taken. He simply could not believe that Jim was a shrewder opera-
tor than himself.

Still in a daze after the all-night meeting (as he tells us in *Behind the Ballots*), Jim went to a rendezvous with Rayburn and
McAdoo, Garner's handlers. They had cleared with Hearst in California by then, and Garner himself, from Washington, had urged
compromise. What none of those involved ever revealed was
whether Roosevelt encouraged Farley to negotiate with the Garner
camp against Louis' judgment, or whether, as I now think probable, direct conversations of his own with Hearst in California produced the settlement. Roosevelt knew Byrd as an incorrigible reactionary who was ambitious in the way of all politicians. He also
knew Garner as a professional who meant to serve the party, not
make it an instrument for his own use. It was this difference that
Farley also understood. Hearst owed Roosevelt something, and the
debt was now collected.

It would be years before any outsider knew how long the winning deal had been in the making. Garner himself, being at least a
realist in politics, had never expected the nomination; his name
was being used for quite another purpose. Watching from Washington, he felt after the second ballot that the Hearst-Rayburn maneuver, with himself as the puppet, had gone quite far enough. The
convention in Chicago was threatening to carry the party into another of those fanatical disputes from which it had suffered so
many times. Democratic victory was in plain sight, but it might be
lost if the dissension—abetted as it was by the press—continued
for another day. Garner no more than others had understood that
Smith was really working for himself alone; and he watched for
some break in the opposition to Roosevelt. Smith would not release the eastern bosses from their commitment, and the Smith
delegates, impossible for Roosevelt to get, simply went on voting
as they had promised to do. Garner saw as soon as Roosevelt and
Farley that he held the balance of power—or, more accurately,
that it was held by his sponsor, Hearst.

What was necessary was for California and Texas to co-operate.
Together they would furnish the delegates to make the needed two-

thirds. The real problem was Hearst, who wanted a more amenable man than Roosevelt and had begun to see that none could be nominated. McAdoo was his man at the convention, but others of his personal staff were there, and they had, it seems, been warning him that if the impasse went on, the turn would be to Baker. This frightened Hearst. He was an almost pathological xenophobe, and Baker was an old Wilsonian who had gone on working for participation in the League all through the Republican years.

There was no danger that Hearst would turn to Smith. Between them was a deep antipathy going back to the years when they had opposed each other for control of the party in New York State. Hearst had finally given up and moved to California, but he was not one to forget.

After all, his men in Chicago reminded him, Roosevelt had repudiated the League under his prodding, and, too, Roosevelt's nomination would be a humiliation for Smith. They also told him none of the outright conservatives—Ritchie, Byrd, or Traylor—had any dark-horse possibilities. Hearst finally came round, acceding to the pleas of his own men, of Farley, of the Texans, and, I think, of Roosevelt himself.*

Garner had no wish to be Vice-President, a position he frankly despised. I can still hear Roosevelt's guffaw when he was told the Speaker's opinion of the office. "It was," the Texan said, "not worth a quart of warm spit." This remark, made when he was re-

* An abbreviated table of ballots shows how little Roosevelt gained from the first to the third ballots. It also shows the hard ballots for Smith, persistent even through the final one before adjournment. It shows furthermore how logical it was for Farley to approach the Garner forces and how illogical of Howe to approach those of Byrd.

	FIRST	SECOND	THIRD	FOURTH
Roosevelt	666	677	682	945
Smith	201	194	190	190
Garner	90	90	101	
Traylor	42	40	40	3
Ritchie	21	23	23	
Baker	8	8	8	

Votes for White, Byrd, Reed, Murray, and Cox (and 22 for Will Rogers!) are omitted. Fractions are also omitted. The total number of delegates was 1154; the number needed for nomination was 770.

quired to give up what was usually regarded as the second most important official position in the United States—the speakership—for the vice-presidency, characterized him. He was sharp, shrewd, narrow, vulgar, and philistine; John R. Lewis said of him that he was a whisky-drinking old reprobate. This was factual only as to the whisky; as for the rest, Garner was no better or worse than most of those who had become Speaker.

At this moment he was probably hearing from the other powerful party figures who were in a panic at the prospect of such another fatal split as had happened in 1924. All the old Democrats were afterward enormously grateful to those who worked out the deal that gave Roosevelt his two-thirds majority. They saw it as a professional party job. They happened to be on the sidelines except for that pressure on Garner, because they had nothing to trade with; but they lent their approval—which was important for all concerned—to an arrangement that gave the party a cohesion it might well have lost.

Before the fourth ballot was taken, Ray Moley tells us in *After Seven Years* (p. 30), he walked to the stadium with Harry Hopkins and me. "The tenseness of the scene we found there is almost indescribable," he continues. "The Chicago politicians had apparently been planting great numbers of leather-throated mugs in the galleries for the purpose of shouting down the Roosevelt defenders on the floor. . . . The delegates were red-eyed, haggard, taut, as McAdoo rose dramatically to announce that California was giving her forty-four votes to Roosevelt, and as Texas followed with her forty-six." Other delegations changed their votes, except for those pledged to Smith, which remained stalwart. The final count, omitting fractions, was Roosevelt 945 votes, Smith 190, Traylor 3. We heard the announcement—no news to us—that Roosevelt was flying to Chicago and would accept the nomination in person.

Sullen and disgruntled, Smith and his friends—Ely of Massachusetts, Hague of New Jersey, Curry of Tammany, *et al.*—abandoned the convention and took a train for New York. No one knew whether Smith would even support the ticket during the cam-

paign. Sam says, in *Working with Roosevelt,* that only the personal
appeal of Dorothy, Sam's wife, prevented Smith from exploding with
resentment when he met reporters at the station in New York.

On Saturday I was in the crush at the airport and looking on. I
saw how Louis elbowed in, gathering his feeble energies to push
others aside. Farley deferred; Roosevelt listened to the whispers in
his ear. It was the late afternoon of a summer day on Lake Michigan. Roosevelt emerged from the plane looking every bit the con-
queror in this political free-for-all. His grin was meant to show
confidence that, with the fighting now over, all good Democrats
were Roosevelt Democrats.

Dozens of politicians crowded in, shook his hand, and spoke a
few words. He looked across the crowd and sent a special word or
smile to a hundred individuals in the ten-minute pause, even
though the harassments of the milling reporters and photographers turned the proceedings into a mob scene. For me, standing
some distance away and below him, there was one word as he
looked directly at me: "Rex!" In all this celebration of a process
outside my experience, this was the climax of an endeavor I only
dimly understood. I had a small but recognized part. I belonged,
that word said.

There were a dozen waiting automobiles. Something of a political ranking was established by instant protocol. I had no business
there except as one of the helpers in what had been and what was
to come, so I was further back than Ray or Sam. Still, my car was
only fourth in line, and Doc was in another car in back of me. Our
attempt to keep together had been frustrated.

At the stadium, Ray and I listened together to Roosevelt's acceptance. The first page of it sounded completely strange. After
that I began to recognize familiar phrases, including another last-
minute addition that I was responsible for: the section on farm relief. The paragraphs dealing with agriculture in the earlier draft
gave way to one I had telephoned from Chicago. As for that
wholly unfamiliar first page, it had been written by Louis in a last-
minute attempt to monopolize the whole address. Ray tells the

story, or one side of it, in *After Seven Years.* Eloquent as he is in this account of his anguish, his state of mind during several Chicago days is actually played down. Between his alternate moods of optimism and pessimism about the nomination itself, and his awareness that the speech was being cut to pieces, he was in a dreadful state of disorganization.

In this matter again, there are differences in the accounts of Ray and Sam. And I must make an amendment to whichever account is accepted. Both agree that Ray made the first draft as well as the presumably finished one that remained in Albany when Ray followed me to Chicago. My amendment is that Ray had more help from Adolf and myself than his account seems to indicate. He perhaps forgot how preoccupied he was with the problem of Jimmy Walker. His attention, as well as Roosevelt's, was only reluctantly centered on the speech.

I say this both from recollection and from recognizing my own words in at least three places. For instance, the paragraphs including these sentences are not exactly as I wrote them; they were made more orotund; but the original statement was mine:

> In the years before 1929 we know that this country had completed a vast cycle of building and inflation. . . . Now it is worth remembering and the cold figures of finance prove it that during that time there was little or no drop in prices . . . although those same figures proved that the cost of production fell very greatly; corporate profit resulting from this period was enormous . . . the consumer was forgotten . . . the worker was forgotten . . . and the stockholder was forgotten . . . .
>
> What was the result? Enormous corporate surpluses piled up. . . . Where did those surpluses go? . . . Chiefly in two directions: first, into new and unnecessary plants which now stand stark and idle; and, second, into the call money market of Wall Street. . . .
>
> Then came the crash. You know the story. Surpluses invested in unnecessary plants became idle. Men lost their jobs; purchasing power dried up; banks became frightened and started calling loans. Credit contracted. Industry stopped. Commerce declined and unemployment mounted.*

* *Papers* (1928–1932), p. 650.

I also recognize other passages, shorter ones; but the important one was this. It restated for his audience of delegates, with typical verbal softening, the thesis we had gone over and over in our evening discussions. Something of Roosevelt's conception of his hearers' minds is to be understood by dwelling on his flourishes; such, for instance, as his "Now it is worth remembering and the cold figures of finance prove it." I could not have written in that tone, nor could Ray; it was purely his own. Then there was the rhetorical question: "What was the result?" And the orator's statement: "You know the story."

Roosevelt usually made a more orderly plan than was made for the acceptance. It is easy to deduce what had happened. As the flight to Chicago was more and more delayed, his uneasiness about the delegates' fatigue grew more acute. The excising became drastic and large hunks of exposition were simply penciled out. There was no time for a final look at the whole to see if it hung together. Of course it did not; as delivered, it was a badly mutilated composition.

Our agreed theory about the cause of the depression did, however, remain the principal theme. Originally the exposition of this had gone on to build up a plan of recovery on the premise of the explanatory paragraphs. This was lost in the slimming process. What remained was, for instance, the promise of a million jobs at forestry work without the more general preceding promise of relief and diverse public works as a way of furnishing the purchasing power that was missing. The excisions here left an argument so truncated as to be hardly intelligible.

After this promise of public work came the statement I had telephoned from Chicago about relief for farmers. Sam had put this into his own words, and it was used to introduce a "declaration of interdependence":

> . . . we are going to make the voters understand this year that this nation is not merely a Nation of Independence, but it is, if we are to survive, bound to be a nation of interdependence, town and city, North and South, East and West. That is our goal. . . .

This, it will be seen, was a restatement of the "concert of interests" theme used in the April speech in Minnesota. Inadequate as the phrasing was, it pleased me to see the idea recur.

Ray, worrying in Chicago, might have worried more if he had actually known what was happening in Albany to the draft he had left there; his fear would have become certainty. Even this would not have been the worst; he now had a more immediate threat to deal with. Louis was on the rampage, swearing that he would make a wholly new draft and see that Roosevelt used it. The one Ray showed him with hopeful pride had evoked the outburst of rage. The little man professed to see in it Sam Rosenman's influence; Ray, he declared, was too smart to have concocted such a mess. Ray, insisting, was left with his mouth open. Louis would not argue.

It was about what happened to the original draft in revision and the Howe draft in Chicago that Sam and Ray differed when in later years they wrote about it. According to Ray, it went this way:

> Pretty disconsolately . . . I went out to the airport to meet the plane. . . . There I found Louis with his draft, as evasive as ever. In the midst of the tumult that surrounded the plane after it landed, I got to Rosenman and told him what was up. He said that the Governor had a copy of the speech as finally revised, in very minor degree, on the plane, and that he would try to get word to him to make no changes. . . . Louis decided on one of the most desperate, and, it seems to me, one of the most foolish courses that I have ever known. He undertook to get Roosevelt to accept his speech sight-unseen at the very moment before addressing the convention.*

What Roosevelt did, at this moment, according to Ray's further recollection, was to take the pages handed to him by Louis and, while he was standing before the convention and responding to the cheers of the delegates after the introduction by the chairman, lay them on the lectern beside the original draft taken from his pocket. After no more than a glance through Louis' first page, he substituted it for the first page of the original. He read it to the delegates,

* *After Seven Years,* p. 33.

then laid the remaining pages aside and went on with the original draft.

One reason for thinking this may not be accurate is that Ray says he had meanwhile pushed his way through the mob to the back of the hall and anxiously followed Roosevelt's delivery. My recollection is somewhat different. He and I stood close below the platform looking up out of the crowd and commented to each other as the proceedings unfolded. This is a minor disagreement and is recorded only to indicate that most recollections are fallible. What Ray went on to say was true enough:

> The ideas were those of the Albany draft: the phrasing was unfamiliar. Louis, the little devil, had merely rephrased the introduction. . . . After a minute or two I began to hear the familiar sentences of the Albany text. . . .

Sam tells of the substitution in quite another way. According to him, Louis handed his draft to Roosevelt almost at once after he was transferred from the plane to the automobile. Sam, warned by Ray, overheard Louis say, "I tell you it's all right, Franklin. It's much better than the speech you've got now." Roosevelt said at once that it was silly to think he could make a speech he had not even seen; but when Louis persisted, he took it and said he would look at it on the way. Sam recalls "vividly" how Roosevelt, as his car sped through the streets and he waved and shouted hello to greeters, "from time to time glanced at Louis' manuscript in his lap." Furthermore:

> In later years I heard him many times describe the episode with great glee, and with many gestures showing how he waved his hat and read the speech at the same time. With each telling, the wave of the arm would be wider and the "hellos" more numerous.*

The final comment, made by Roosevelt himself, is attached to the reading copy in the library at Hyde Park. It confirms the substitution of Louis' first page for the original; but it does not say whether his reading and deciding were done in the car or whether,

---

* *Working with Roosevelt,* p. 76.

when standing at the lectern with the cheering crowd before him, he did read an introduction whose words he had never seen until that instant.

Both Sam and Ray were intimately involved in the incident they describe differently, but neither seems to have realized what Louis expected to accomplish in the substitution that certainly occurred. They regard it as having been irresponsible and motivated by jealous determination to share more fully in this climactic experience of long years in Roosevelt's service. This may have had something to do with what was after all, as Ray says, a desperate and foolish action. But there was, I am convinced, a much more important reason. Louis must have said something more to Roosevelt than was overheard, and it is not difficult to guess what it must have been.

He had to make good with all those Democratic statesmen he had been cosseting so long and had, for the last two years, been assuring over and over that Roosevelt was a regular and well-behaved Democrat, devoted to the party's interests and of a mind to accept the direction of its elders. Year in and year out since 1920, he had taken elaborate pains to picture his man as suited to his times, liberal but not radical, reasonable, rather, on all the touchy issues—money, tariffs, even international organization. He favored small business rather than large, relief for debtors, and an agricultural program that would meet farmers' demands for assistance and yet not require sacrifices. Furthermore, he was only moderately wet; it was understood that his compromise on this issue was the same one that others were having to make.

It had been the Wilsonian statesmen who had written the platform; they had made Roosevelt their choice, and Roosevelt must behave as their adopted candidate should. Here in Chicago, where he had been entrusted with the party's best opportunity for victory in many years, he must reiterate his loyalty—and reaffirm the pledges Louis had made in his behalf.

Moley's Albany draft said nothing about the platform; it made no reference to Wilson; it was short on deference to tradition and principle. For the candidate to be progressive, to offer leadership, and so on, was all very well, but the party was, after all, an old and going organization. Its faithful must be reassured that the future would be built on the past they had helped to make.

One of Louis' paragraphs in that disputed draft was an allusion to Wilson, the "indomitable leader." Another statement was, "That admirable document, the platform which you have adopted, is clear. I accept it 100 per cent."

It took me some time, and some help from Doc, to arrive at what must be the explanation. When Louis handed Roosevelt the draft he seemed to have fixed up overnight but could well have had in reserve all along, he may have said what either Sam or Ray reported; but he must also have protested that the Albany draft neglected the elders, failed to reaffirm the Wilsonian faith, and had no explicit acceptance of the platform. Roosevelt, spoken to sharply, must have recognized the obligation to conform.

Why had he himself overlooked the pious necessities? His failure in protocol can be explained by the excitements of the past month, as well as by the not-so-strange omission of Ray, who made drafts for him, and myself, who knew nothing about Louis' treaties. It could very well be that Roosevelt himself knew about them only in a general way. Louis was the man who had maintained the contacts, had made the assurances, and had kept his candidate in the exact center of the Democratic tradition or, if Roosevelt diverged from it—as on the League of Nations—had seen to it that the most adequate possible explanation was offered.

Roosevelt, I suspect, had not seen the platform either, regarding it as a formality he need not concern himself with after Louis' assurance that there was nothing in it to worry about. After all, these two had been in close communion since 1911. Even if he had read it, the sentiments and rhythms must have been familiar; there was nothing in it he could not confirm and then interpret.

Doc and I figured, as we worried about the matter, that the strategy was something like this: Roosevelt had to have this identity with the inner circle to approach the nomination confidently. He might be Governor of New York and a good vote-getter, and he might have a depression going for him, but he also needed an identity with the party ethos. The danger that he might be labeled a maverick—as Uncle Ted had been—was a real one, and it had been Louis' job to see that such a disaster was avoided. They both knew very well that Smith had never been accepted in this sense.

What Roosevelt may not have made explicit even to Louis, and what he had no intention of suggesting to the statesmen, was that after he had been nominated and elected—as a true Democrat— he would then be the party's leader and shaper. "Roosevelt" and "Democrat" would be words identified with each other in people's minds. When that happened, and Smith had been eliminated, neither House nor Hull nor Byrnes nor Pittman nor Daniels nor Glass nor Palmer—nor all of them together—would possess or could control the party apparatus. It would be Roosevelt. He would not have said this to Louis because he would not have needed to. Nor would he have breathed it to anyone else.

So now he accepted—100 per cent.

Even if Ray and I knew—or thought we knew—that he had his tongue in his cheek, we made no signal to anyone else. Anyway, it was all right with us. The nation just now needed nothing so much as a leader with freedom to act.

Later that evening I told Doc, who had sensibly stayed away, about the whole experience, so new to me, of following Roosevelt's progress to the stadium and listening to the speech. I had been in a car with Tom Lynch, who was an old retainer. He and his wife were indignant when hoodlums on the curbs shouted epithets at the passing parade. Their boss's defeat in the attempt to force Smith's nomination still rankled. Political communication is informal; it spreads by a sort of osmosis. Kelly's henchmen had been instructed to cheer for Smith and revile (an exact word) Roosevelt, and they were performing. They shouted obscenities, the women screamed, and altogether it was a good deal like Hoover's reception in Detroit toward the end of that year's campaign. Roosevelt, of course, had been warned. He knew what had been arranged and who had arranged it. He also knew that these were spear-bearers in a battle that was now over. He acted exactly as though the boos were cheers— as they would be tomorrow.

Anyway, this was a fringe of instructed hostility; beyond this crowd were the millions that bosses could not reach. He meant to reach them as the chosen candidate.

Lynch had been with Roosevelt on the campaign trips in 1920 when he was running for Vice-President. He had felt worse than Roosevelt himself about the defeat, he said. And Roosevelt had told him, "Never mind, Tom; 1932 will be our year."

Here it was 1932 and the prophecy had turned out to be miraculously true. He repeated over and over, "How could he have known?"

"How could he?" I asked Doc later. Lynch certainly recalled it accurately.

"Oh, Tom's a sentimental Irishman," said Doc, "He made it up."

I thought this Irish allusion peculiar coming from an O'Connor, but I did not say so. Nevertheless, I wondered if Lynch *had* made it up. It could be that Roosevelt had seen what was coming, but to have said that it would come in 1932 instead of 1936, when Hoover would have had his eight years, was to credit him with belief in a sort of miracle.

PART TWO

To the Election

CHAPTER XXIV

Heading into the Campaign

❦ ❦ ❦

W hen the speech was over and the stadium began to empty, Roosevelt established himself in Louis' quarters at the Congress Hotel and soon was meeting all comers, many of whom he greeted as though they were old friends. He seemed as fresh and elastic as after a long rest. Right there and then he was starting the campaign.

His departure from traditional procedure in coming to Chicago seemed to please everyone. It was obvious that he meant to center attention on himself and his activities at once. Those of us who were newcomers thought his crippled condition had something to do with this; but we were reminded by older associates that this sort of thing had always been characteristic. This was his fourth campaign, counting two for the governorship. Tom Lynch recalled the campaign for the vice-presidency in 1920; this one, he said, was starting out to be another of the same sort. Lynch rejected the suggestion that the flight to Chicago and the immediate acceptance might be calculated to demonstrate his physical capability; and Sam, who had been with him when he ran for the governorship, said he had covered the state with the same energy. To see Roosevelt now was to be persuaded that Tom Lynch and Sam were right. Besides, as they pointed out, he won elections.

The many callers who came and went were delighted. Professionals as all of them were, they were able to appreciate the performance. Calculated or not, it was just what was needed in a candidate. They could see, if they had not known it before, that he was a political person. If he was moving up to the place he had always wanted and always expected to occupy, that was what politics was for. They could not care less that he meant to use his talent in a cause only he could define. They had a winner. When he had power, they would share it. He was letting them know that he was their man and would still be their man when he was President. They would now go home and get things going at once.

While the coming and going continued, I turned occasionally to watch the lakeside fountain charging up and falling back in its bath of lights. Thinking of what was ahead, I discovered suddenly that I had no doubt at all that he would win. It hardly seemed possible now that only yesterday we had concluded that the nomination had escaped him. It was quite obvious that all he need do was live until November—and not make any mistakes of ruinous magnitude. The really anxious time was over.

But, Doc said, there would be enough excitement anyway. He added thoughtfully that we seemed to keep forgetting that this fellow had a good deal more in mind than winning.

I asked what Doc thought that was. He replied with no hesitation at all that, with the White House as this fellow's base, the *party* would be just a convenience, one that would be used in ways surprising to the pros. Some would like it and some would not, but they'd all have to go along.

Quite late that evening the door to the inner room was closed, the visitors drained away, and Ray was called in. Doc and I waited. The time stretched out—one hour; the better part of a second. Finally Ray came out. He had pages of notes. I had never seen him so elated. He said we might not believe it, but the whole thing was planned. He had it right there, the whole list of trips and speeches. Also, he said triumphantly, we were to do the policy chores just the way we had been doing them. Most immediately—in about a week—Roosevelt, with two of his boys, was going to sail up the New England coast and would be gone for some ten days. We were to have something ready on "half a dozen big issues" by the time he got back. That would be our first assignment.

Ray and I went back very late to the Drake Hotel and had the first real sleep of the week. On the way east next day, on the Wolverine, I could look at a moving landscape instead of an agitated fountain that never got anywhere. Since I had concluded that the presidency was virtually won, I found myself thinking how fortunate it was that Roosevelt moved and spoke as though constantly aware of what was expected from one with a part to play in events that stretched with conscious connections into the nation's future out of its past. It was not so much that he kept watch on word and action as that he had the spirit of our institutions in the background of his mind. He had no need to strain for dignity, since it was apparent to the least observant onlooker that it was there. The charm, the attractiveness, the warmth, soon to be so much spoken of, were partly owed to this poise, this identity with all that was in the best way American and that carried others with him into a world of tradition at least as familiar as contemporary events.

Eleanor, too, possessed the same secure ease. She had shared his triumph with complete aplomb. I could see that when they moved to the White House, it would be as though they had come home after travel. They would know exactly what to do and how to do it. The years of stiffness, of awkward protocol, in that old mansion would soon be over; grace would return to fill the rooms again.

I realized that I had come to have a genuine respect for the quick and inquiring Roosevelt mind; also I was pleased with his concern that the country's face should be improved and its people lifted to new levels. He would be one of those Presidents who were the embodiment of the American model; very likely he would outshine the other Roosevelt in our history, as I knew he was ambitious to do.

Yet I recognized lingering doubts, not such anxious ones as were being expressed by my progressive friends, yet doubts that would not be banished. In this I was probably no different from others in our group, except that Ray seemed so intent now on campaign tactics as to have less time to consider what the end of them was to be. To Ray, the reverses we had suffered and the tacit rejections we had been forced to accept may not have seemed that at all; rather they were accommodations to the inevitable demands of getting ahead in politics. I did not think of this at the time. Ray was the one I complained to; he listened, he was friendly, but he was not disturbed. For Adolf, the experience may very possibly have been like mine, a mixture of disappointment and persistent but uneasy hope, but we did not exchange such confidences.

The source of my uneasiness was recognizable. Roosevelt, I knew, was originally a progressive; too much a progressive, perhaps; far too fixed in his orthodoxy.* In spite of his inquiring mind and experimental temper, the inquiring and experimentation were still confined—and rather strictly, I admitted to myself—within old boundaries, some of them obsolete and obstructive. I had a foreboding that this would limit his range. What he was in origin, I feared, he really did continue to be. If this was so, the policies he was likely to sponsor could be forecast.

Just such a progressive program, because it could not be implemented, and so never had been carried out, had frustrated several generations of well-meaning reformers. Meanwhile the economy had been transformed by a technology they refused to recognize and fiercely resented. The whole progressive agenda, if acted on now, would satisfy none of the new requirements we had to meet. It was mostly designed to turn back the processes responsible for our position in the world. This was a worry I was familiar with, but my present apprehension was to be explained, obviously, by my having hoped too much for logical adaptation to circumstances. There was no one to blame but myself.

I had begun to be afraid that the campaign months would produce no relevant debate. Below the surface, Roosevelt and Hoover were amazingly alike; they might just take to shadow-boxing.

* Cf. my article "The Progressive Orthodoxy of Franklin D. Roosevelt," *Ethics* (October 1953), LXIV, 1–23.

Within the week, Bob La Follette was to visit me with the same worry gnawing at his mind. What he wanted to ask—because he hardly knew Roosevelt—was whether we could expect something larger, freer, more daring when the time came and Roosevelt escaped his obligations to the elders. He asked whether Colonel House and the old Senate warhorses were going to control the campaign plans, and whether they would tell Roosevelt what to do when he had won. I had to say that what I worried about at the moment was that Baruch might be doing the controlling.

"Oh no," he said, "not that 'confidence' stuff again! That's Hooverism! I've fought it for four years."

I always felt closer to Bob ideologically than to anyone else. I would encourage him to make demands, and I arranged for him to see Roosevelt. He said he would push as hard as he could, and I hoped something might come of it. After all, Wisconsin—and Minnesota, where Floyd Olson was—were states that had to be won.

What I saw in prospect was what the La Follettes and Olson saw, and with the same growing dismay. Roosevelt had seemed to accept my argument that technical changes had so obviously altered the conditions of common living that they could not be overlooked. Politically, however, as well as psychologically, it was already apparent that he would increasingly recognize the utility of simply trying to reach the same objectives the other Roosevelt and Wilson had meant to reach. This was what I found so hard to accept.*

One practical difficulty with the economic program he was evidently going to adopt for the campaign was its similarity—as Bob pointed out—with that of Hoover. The most appealing argument of the progressives, since the days of populism—for that matter, further back in Jackson's time—had been attacks on "the money barons." These aspersions appealed to merchants, professional men, and farmers, even more than to workers, and often attracted votes no positive program for reform could have drawn. Every

* Cf. "The Compromising Roosevelt,' *Western Political Quarterly* (Fall 1953), VI, 2, 320–341.

debtor hated those primary creditors. The elder La Follette and his running-mate, Senator Burton Wheeler of Montana, had found populist progressivism good for five million votes as late as 1924; and their definition of that philosophy had been much the same as Wilson's New Freedom conception twelve years earlier than that. Unfortunately, an attack on Wall Street became one on "big business" and then almost inevitably—though without logic— spread to the whole system of large-scale enterprise, including scientific management and the entire technological complex. An understanding of the distinction between Wall Streeters and scientific managers seemed too difficult for demagogues to achieve, even progressive ones who had a largely economic program.

Most big businesses did have relations of an intimate kind with Wall Street, and abuses of power by the financiers and speculators in recent years had been too flagrant for challenging politicians to overlook as political material. Nevertheless, it was now still true, as I had been insisting, that the whole progressive preachment might be carried into action without bettering the economic situation in the least; and indeed I felt certain that its literal acceptance would worsen an already desperate crisis.

A passage in Ray's *After Seven Years* (pages 372–373) shows that his recognition of this difficulty was the same as my own, though I think he did not feel until later that the problem was urgent. He writes:

> It was easy to see that the early New Deal, with its emphasis on agricultural and industrial planning, was dominated by the theory of Concentration and Control—by the beliefs that competition is justified only in so far as it promotes social progress and efficiency; that government should encourage concerted action where that best serves the public and competition where that best serves the public; that business must, under strict supervision, be permitted to grow into units large enough to insure to the consumer the benefits of mass production; that organized labor must likewise be permitted to grow in size but, like business, be held to strict accountability; that government must cooperate with both business and labor to insure the stable and continuous operation of the machinery of production and distribution.

> . . . but there was a shift in emphasis . . . not in the form
> of a complete repudiation of Concentration and Control, but of
> an endless wavering between it and the philosophy advocated
> by . . . Brandeis.

Ray was right; this "wavering," so worrisome to me in 1932, did persist into the future and did confuse all economic policy for years. Roosevelt persisted in trying to satisfy both those who were convinced atomists and, at the same time, those who had accepted concentration and control as Bob La Follette had. I knew already that this was happening, but I did not know that he had no intention of resolving the contradiction.

Altogether, Chicago had been a sequence of strange experiences for me, and I was doubtless in a let-down mood after being so keyed up. My sophistication had been so largely pretense that it was a poor sustainer. Harry Hopkins had been a calming influence. I had met him for the first time in the rooms of Jesse Straus's Business and Professional Men's League for Roosevelt, where Bobby Straus introduced us. Harry had stopped over on his way to a vacation; unemployment, he said, interested him more than the outcome at the stadium. His remark actually was: "Hell, I don't know anything about politics except that unemployment is still going up, and if the federal government refuses to come across, there'll be riots that'll worry the politicians some." I recalled this as my train moved out of Chicago, and I thought how difficult it was at some times, and how unavoidable at others, to bring together political techniques and economic necessities. Perhaps we ought not to worry about anything but Harry's unemployed; all the rest might follow.

But apparently politics had its governing necessities too. This was illustrated by one of the happenings that had surprised me. Scarcely had the nominating vote been taken when there appeared in the Roosevelt headquarters the tall, lean figure of Bernard Mannes Baruch. This astonished everyone except, perhaps, Louis Howe, who may even have been expecting it. Being the purest amateur of the lot, I was aghast at Baruch's bland demand to see the speech Roosevelt would make when he arrived. His journey to the Roosevelt headquarters had been a short one. He had lately been in the Ritchie or Baker rooms, and before that, until all hope had departed, in those of Smith. He had only to take an elevator at each successive shift. We were told that he had been—with Raskob—the financial supporter of the formidable stop-Roosevelt drive. Was that to be ignored?

Apparently it was. The entry was on a party note. The fighting, said the newcomer, must now be considered to be ended and all must get together. We thought this came with strange grace from a man who had done so much to create bitterness along with dissension; but we learned something about practical politics from the sickly smile that Louis conjured up. Although Smith and his Tammany associates had walked out steaming and sullen, refusing any amenity, here was Baruch, his financial backer, prepared to ignore what to a thin-skinned man would have been an exceedingly embarrassing reversal—and expecting those he had fought to ignore it too. Even Raskob and Shouse had faded into the background, and neither Hague nor Ely had accepted humiliation but had gone home unreconciled. Baruch, however, intended to be identified with the winner. He obviously hoped to be called a good sport. Doc remarked that Louis was as gratified by Baruch's adherence as by the nomination itself. This exaggeration at least pointed up a reality of politics.

Baruch's was a history few people were familiar with. He had a way of being heard of quite often, but not unless it suited him—and also suited Herbert Bayard Swope, his public-relations adviser. Swope brought his client to the surface for giving portentous advice to public men whenever the signs were propitious, but only then. No sufficient part of the Baruch operations ever became visible at one time so that a record could be put together, but we were well enough aware that he was one of those epic speculators who did not so much deal in the momentary shifts on the exchanges as create the situations he took advantage of. We knew, too, that he had no hesitation in using the government for that purpose.

The train stretched out across Michigan and on across the Province of Ontario. I found some gratification in my recollections. Planning had, after all, had a certain recognition; so had agriculture as a national problem. The references to both in the acceptance had been real even if minimal. A whole speech, a little later, and possibly more than one, would have to be devoted to each; perhaps then much more could be said. The beginning had been made. Best of all, Roosevelt had actually suggested limitations on agricultural production.

The political conditions such proposals would have to meet could not be ignored. That is to say, remedies were valid only if they were, or could be made, acceptable. The conditions were even narrower than this; remedies must first of all be acceptable to Roosevelt himself, as ones he could put forward. He would judge their political possibilities. Even I could see that such decisions were delicate and involved considerations we might overlook entirely or not think important.

Planning was a good instance of this. The word had been given some content by such advocates as Bob La Follette, or such others as Gerard Swope. But evidently the party elders found it objectionable. They still stood on Wilson's New Freedom. Its agenda had never been carried out, and what they wanted now was simply resumption—more competition among small private businesses, enforced by government. At a minimum, planning required the identification of objectives and an indication of the sort of action needed to reach them. The politics involved in this was too complicated for my understanding, but I had had a few lessons now in the deference Roosevelt felt that he owed to his sponsors.

The outcome of these meditations was nothing remarkable. What we evidently had to produce for the farmers was a political promise, not an agricultural solution, and this required talents I did not possess. I resolved that the necessary exposition should not be written by me; Wilson or Wallace, or maybe both, would have to produce that speech.

My more serious meditations were interrupted by the recollection of pudgy Harry Byrd of Virginia being convoyed by a dozen screeching motorcycles from his hotel through indifferent streets to Convention Hall. Boss Kelly had put on that show.

Then there were *The Tribune*'s headlines offering the Democrats all the gratuitous bad advice its editors could contrive under what Roosevelt called "Bertie McCormick's whip" (Bertie had been a Grotonian too). I recalled too the single glimpse I had of Belle Moskowitz, Smith's right-hand woman, for whom I had devised an agricultural program in 1928. She had looked as sour as only an out-generaled manager could and had refused even to speak to me. It was still more amusing to recall Louis Howe showing unbrushed teeth while he sat on the floor, a telephone receiver at his ear, listening to McAdoo having his long-postponed revenge on Smith as he announced California's vote on the fourth ballot.

Next day was recovery day for me. The family home on the shore of Lake Ontario was a good place for that. It stood on an island within a harbor and was gardened under my mother's intensive supervision. I had never lived there; it was a product of my father's recent prosperity; but I had been coming there for the summers since I began teaching at Columbia. Everyone needs a place where his confused affairs can resume some sort of order, and this island had for years been that for me. Its grove of oaks, my mother's beds of perennials, the marsh where the same redwinged blackbirds always seemed so busy, and the lake beyond the piers—all these made up a world where growing things, natural sights, and old sounds predominated.

Unfortunately my perplexities refused to clear up. Would it really be believed, I found myself asking, that reforms in Wall Street, attacks on monopolies, or even drastic changes in finance would go far to re-establish industrial activity and cure unemployment? The question answered itself—for me, that is—but I was quite aware that this was what had been advocated, and partly carried out, in other such circumstances as we were in. It was what the populists had wanted, and then the progressives. They still believed its failure had been caused by Republican sabotage. The real question was whether disillusion with old solutions unsuitable for the present crisis had gone far enough. On the chance that it had, I would persist in offering something new.

I began to outline a proposal that would carry further the faint recognition of planning in the acceptance. The disorderly process at Chicago, the fact that the nomination had been traded out among the contenders, and my observation that very few Roosevelt supporters had shown any desire for drastic change—these signs were not encouraging. Yet I seem to have felt that such difficulties could be overcome and that we ought to be ready for much more.

What I had in mind was that a device for social management to establish stable relations might after all be used as campaign material. What we needed was not more competition, but less, so that co-ordinated elements might intermesh and function with relative ease, each complementing the other. There was no room in such a system for speculative businessmen who lived by creating uncertainties and friction. The volume of production must be anticipated, and investments must be allocated. How strange it was, I thought, that the old progressive program played directly into the hands of the worst enemies our system had. By calling for atomization, it multiplied the possible sources of uncertainty and made a paradise for speculators.

None of this was original, as I have tried to explain. The orthodox economists had always said that free competition, if it were forced into existence, would automatically regulate the relations among the forces and elements of our system. But I had long ago lost faith in this. There were—and had been from the first—others who pointed out that a system of competition always provided an advantage out of which there ultimately grew a monopoly, and that, when monopoly existed, competition was as much less free as the monopoly was effective. These others had sometimes been utopians or socialists, but sometimes they had merely believed in co-operation. We were at the present time a long way on the road to a system of monopolies. Ray, Adolf, and I had been insisting that we should allow it to evolve and should manage it publicly, rather than go back to a more primitive state where no social management existed. That primitive state was not only economically orthodox but was the political stock in trade of the progressives. It had, however, led us into terrible trouble, and persisting in it would not get us out.

I reviewed again the current considerable interest in planning and wrote a new memorandum, which I hoped might offset the demand for returning to the Wilsonian economics. I also composed a speech, or part of one. In it Roosevelt would say flatly that what the country needed was a government with such ability to plan and such powers to regulate as would approximate those set up during the World War.*

When my chance came, I argued that such an address would recognize the public spirit developing among business leaders and would begin the transformation of progressivism from its old atomic to a new collective phase. I hoped that Roosevelt, now safely nominated and legitimately hopeful of election, would make the venture. I was quite certain that he knew this to be an indispensable preliminary to much that would happen when he became President.

He listened, as he always would, to what I had to say, and even elaborated my ideas in an hour of brilliant improvisation. But I knew, when he had finished, that nothing would come of it. Something by now was telling me that nothing was going to come of the things we really cared most about until the campaign was over.

I could unburden myself to Doc, but he was further from being listened to than I. And Ray was running a speech factory now. Since he had been told to go to work, he had been casting about for experts who would give him material he could fit into those speeches he had to put together. He was very good at this. The only trouble was that it kept him from doing any thinking while it

* The memorandum mentioned here survived in the Moley files, thanks to the careful housewifeliness of Celeste, Ray's secretary. Passages from it are printed in an Appendix to this volume.

was going on—at least the kind of thinking I was certain ought to be done.

Roosevelt's entourage widened now, and our own relations with him could not be what they had been before the nomination. When I turned up at Albany for the first time—a few days after the convention—I was first stopped by a detective, then by a secretary I had never seen before. Until then, we had been used to the genial presence somewhere about of Carl Miller and Gus Gennerich of the state police, and of course to Missy Le Hand and the secretarial Tully sisters. There were strangers added now—not the Secret Service, which would take over on election night, but still new guards to get acquainted with.

The new factotum was Marvin McIntyre, whose cadaverous frame and skeletal smile were to interpose themselves between Roosevelt and his official visitors for years to come. McIntyre too was an old Navy Department man, whose services long antedated those of Ray Moley and even of Sam Rosenman and Doc O'Connor—but not, of course, Louis; he was, in fact, Louis' man in Albany, now that Democratic campaign funds were available to pay for such services. It was Marvin's business to save time and reduce contacts, a task more thankless with Roosevelt than, I imagine, with most other public men. Marvin did not take kindly to our informal comings and goings; he was irritated when they upset his schedules, justifiably, no doubt, and he and Ray never did learn to accommodate themselves to each other. Roosevelt pretended not to notice. It was our problem and compromise was taken for granted.

Our work, of course, was actually intensified. The campaign was to be strenuous; any Roosevelt campaign would be that. He intended, so he said, to reach by train or motor every part of the country—that is, every part he could get to within the time available. Had he never heard of radio? I asked myself. He enlarged for our benefit on what he had told Ray in Chicago; he would make a dozen big speeches on such subjects as agriculture, the railroads, power policy, tax reform, the tariff, and the like, as well as the cus-

tomary attacks on the current administration, and would speak
often—several times a day—from the back platform of trains or to
small audiences in many places, in whatever local accommodations were available. He made it plain enough, without saying so,
that his political talents were assets he intended to use. He would
exhibit endurance; his legs, swinging uselessly in steel frames from
his hips, would be a handicap only if they were allowed to become
conspicuous. There would be plenty of attempts to make something of his disability; they would make no headway if his audience
had the experience of seeing him speak and move.

It was heartbreaking sometimes to see him struggle with his
braces, or to be one of two lifting him into a car or down steps,
with him perhaps tickling or punching his helpers while it was
done. But he had long ago discovered the best defense. Ernest
Lindley had discussed this in his *Franklin D. Roosevelt.* After
describing the seizure at Campobello in August 1921 and trac-
ing its course, he had gone on:

> To everyone who goes through this kind of experience, there
> must come, one would imagine, periods of despair culminating
> in an awful moment of realization that there is to be no com-
> plete recovery. If Roosevelt ever had such a period, or even a
> moment, of depression, no one ever heard him mention it, or,
> so far as he can recall, ever senses it from his behavior.

But any man asking to be made President had to make a show
of manliness, and for a cripple it was much more necessary.

Anyway, our immediate work was laid out and Ray was the responsible director. It required exacting management. We must—
absolutely—make no mistakes, and we must develop the subjects
assigned in a way to impress even the most sophisticated listener.
The rest was for Moley—and Roosevelt himself. What to us were
memoranda, they had to make into speeches.

CHAPTER XXV

Candidate's Reception

Presumably the elders who had helped in Roosevelt's approach to the nomination were satisfied with him. He had accepted their platform in a ringing voice and had kept well within party understanding in making the deal for the vice-presidency. This ought to have made them happy. Still, they lacked the votes to win the election, and all concerned were conscious that this was so. Even with their organization mobilized and energized, they could deliver no more than the same minority of registered Democrats they had been losing elections with for many years. They had been out of power since 1921 and had only as many office-holders as local Democrats had been able to get appointed. There had to be a formidable accretion from other sources. They looked to Republicans and progressives. Sometimes these two sources of votes were identical, sometimes not.

The progressives, who had been complaining all spring, were as unhappy as ever with Roosevelt. Some of them, being Republicans as well as progressives, had not been at the convention; others, being easterners and Democrats, had clung to the hope that Smith would be nominated, and gone on clinging to it until disappointment turned to resentment almost matching Smith's own. Ray recalls that after the all-night session of the convention, when a third ballot had failed to start a landslide and everyone at headquarters was depressed, he and I made a visit to Doc O'Connor's quarters. He says that everyone there was earnestly—and picturesquely—cursing Tammany; and Doc and his congressman brother, John, were plotting vengeance. They were saying that even if all was lost, we'd still have the governorship for six months more, and that would be time enough to put the boys at the Hall on the rack.

I recall saying to Ray, at the same time, that most of our progressive friends would be pleased just to have Roosevelt beaten. They would be glad to tell us that he—and we—had got only what we deserved. His blanket endorsement of the platform would increase their dissatisfaction; they would see no reason to enthuse about a candidate who was not one of them any more—if he ever had been—because he was pledged to the elders.

This was not only true in the West. The New York progressives who had worked with Smith to enact the remarkable program of welfare legislation he had bullied the legislature into passing, and who had admired his skill as an administrator, had never been reconciled to Roosevelt as a successor. They had worked for Smith all spring, suspecting that he had been denied a second chance to run for the presidency by machinations they regarded as inadmissible. They could not believe what soon became as evident to everyone else as it was to William Allen White, that Al's friends in national politics were complete reactionaries and that he had no real power except in the corrupt city machines. Al's sponsor, Raskob, the DuPont executive, they found hard to explain, so they ignored him. They had a fixed irrational objection to Roosevelt himself and showed no inclination to explore the practical alternatives if Smith could not be nominated. They accepted the Lippmann line.

I have already quoted from Ray's account (in *After Seven Years,* page 30) of how we left the pessimists in our headquarters and walked to the stadium late in the day. (Doc and I had finished our draft of the acceptance.) Harry Hopkins was with us, and we walked some distance in a northerly direction before we caught a taxi:

> Rex and Harry, both thoroughly imbued with the prevailing pessimism, felt that the case was hopeless. . . . As we passed a newsstand I picked up a paper in which appeared the one column that is probably the best known of Heywood Broun's many and probably the one he would most like not to have written. I was still boiling with indignation over Broun's reference to Roosevelt as "the corkscrew candidate of a convoluting convention" when we got to the Stadium.

Progressives (or liberals, as they more often called themselves) of the Broun strain were determined not to forgive Roosevelt for winning; some were manifesting their disappointment by glooming about his certain defeat in the election. To this they intended to contribute. Since they could not abide Hoover, most of them said at once that they would support Norman Thomas, the Socialist. There may not have been a large number of these liberals, but they had some influence. I worried about them; they ought to have been Roosevelt supporters. If he could not win them over, there were only the disaffected Republicans to depend on. What he would have to promise those reactionaries I shuddered to think. It would have to be a more effective Hooverism, and I thought sourly that he inclined in that direction anyway.

It was, however, not only the progressives who were alienated because Smith could not win. There were also those who agreed with the fulminations of Henry L. Mencken. He had not been a Smith admirer, but he was a reactionary of determined bent; and being based in Maryland, he had clamored for Ritchie, who was exactly to his liking. He had no intention of being cozened now; in his rising choler, he almost equaled *The Tribune* editorialists in bending probabilities to his prejudice. What he wrote was this:

> . . . beating Lord Hoover and the Injun Curtis with Roosevelt Minor and the Texas Bearcat is not going to be easy. The betting odds tell the story. . . . At the time when the allies seemed to be prevailing, the Chicago sports offered 5 to 1 that Ritchie, if nominated, would defeat Hoover. But when the nom-

ination went to Roosevelt, they began offering 5 to 1 that
Hoover would win. Bookmakers of course sometimes err, just as
other varieties of mathematicians err. But in this case, their
guess is also the guess of the practical politicians.*

Mencken went on for a whole column reproaching the Democrats for their fatal mistake and using his unique command of in-
vective to ridicule all those involved in the last-minute deal with
the Garner forces. He came finally to Roosevelt himself:

> But Roosevelt won, and now the party begins the campaign
> with a candidate who has multitudes of powerful enemies and is
> far too feeble and wishy-washy a fellow to make a really effec-
> tive fight. Soon or late the voters of the country are bound to
> ask themselves two questions. The first is, In what way, pre-
> cisely, is he better than Hoover? And the second is, What has
> he ever done to justify making him President? These questions
> are going to be hard to answer.

He went on, however, to rumble viscerally about his own
doubts; he would regretfully have to accept the nominee after all;
but, he practically shouted, he didn't have to like it.

> Anything to get rid of Hoover and his Camorra of Republican
> blacklegs [he said]. I'd vote for a Chinaman to beat them, or
> even a Methodist Bishop. But I greatly fear there will be insuffi-
> cient Americans of like mind to re-establish and perpetuate the
> Roosevelt dynasty.

John Dos Passos also watched the proceedings with a novelist's
eye, but he came away with an almost nihilistic reaction, as though
what had happened in the stadium made no difference. Whatever
the result, no one would be better or worse off. As with Mencken,
prejudice controlled his comment, but unlike Mencken he was inconsistent. His account was factually unreliable, but his descriptive
talent furnished background and color.

> You come out of the Stadium [he said] and walk down the
> street. It's West Madison Street, the home address of migratory
> workers and hoboes and jobless men all over the middle west.

* *The Baltimore Sun,* July 5, 1932. Reprinted in *Making a President* (New
York, 1932).

Gradually, the din of speeches fades out of your ears. Nobody on the street knows about the convention that's deciding who shall run their government, or cares. The convention is the siren of police motorcycles, a new set of scare headlines, a new sensation over the radio. A man has got a job, or else he hasn't got a job, he's got jack in his pocket, or else he's broke, he's got a business or else he's a bum. Way off some place headline events happen. Even if they're right on West Madison Street, they're way off. Roosevelt or Hoover? It'll be the same cops.

. . . You go down a flight of steps, into the darkness feebly lit by ranks of dusty red electric lights of the roadway under Michigan Avenue. The fine smart marble and plate-glass front of the city peels off with exhaust from the grinding motors of trucks, is full of dust and grit and the roar of the heavy traffic that hauls the city's freight. When your eyes get used to the darkness, you discover that, like the world upstairs of storefronts and hotel lobbies and battles of the century and political conventions, this world too has its leisure class. They lie in rows along the ledges above the roadway, huddled in grimed newspapers, gray sag-faced men in worn-out clothes, discards, men who have nothing left but their stiff, hungry, grimy bodies, men who have lost the power to want. Try to tell one of them that the *gre-eat* Franklin D. Roosevelt, Governor of the *gre-eat* state of New York, has been nominated by the *gre-eat* Democratic party as its candidate for President, and you'll get what the galleries at the convention gave Mr. McAdoo when they discovered that he had the votes of Texas and California in his pocket and was about to shovel them into the Roosevelt band wagon, a prolonged and enthusiastic *Boooo*. Hoover or Roosevelt, it'll be the same cops.*

We were not much disturbed, Ray and I, by these comments, but I regretted those of Robert Morss Lovett, a senior colleague of mine on *The New Republic,* which appeared a week later, when I was still sore from other beatings:

The Roosevelt high command had originally reckoned on the advantage of a swift attack. . . . They had proposed not only nomination by majority vote, but the postponement of the platform discussion until after the nominations, following the precedent set at Baltimore in 1912. When they retired from these ad-

* *The New Republic,* July 13, 1932, p. 231.

vanced positions, the cause of their candidate seemed percep-
tibly damaged. Prestige was lost. A shallying between rashness
and timidity was exactly what the country had been told to expect of the boy scout in Albany. . . .

Governor Roosevelt's reception when he finally entered the
stadium was one of bounteous enthusiasm. His speech with its
engaging air of candor and realism would have been a success
between five and six. Between six and seven, it fell a bit flat,
with half of the visible audience departing, not too quietly. A
speaker under such circumstances, however, can always comfort
himself with thoughts of the unseen. Mr. Roosevelt outlined a
flexible campaign to be fought in the West and South on economic and social policies which are distrusted in the East, and
in the East on the repeal of the Eighteenth Amendment which
is a painful dose for the South. Threats of a bolt in either section may be dismissed. The Democratic party may be spilt, but
it can't be split.

This article was the subject of a conversation with Roosevelt. It
took me a little time to put this together with other appraisals in a
small sheaf of progressive-liberal pieces written by commentators
he had always respected as much as I. When the opportunity
offered—when we were alone—I showed them to him. I ignored
the Mencken diatribes, which had no political significance. We
dwelt on Lovett.

Roosevelt said thoughtfully that he didn't suppose he'd ever get
over being sensitive about this sort of thing; maybe he should say
"disappointed" or even "hurt." He really didn't think he deserved
such treatment. These were people who ought to be with him—
that is to say, they wanted what he wanted. Yet he expected this
sort of thing or anyway saw it coming. Walter Lippmann, he observed, had taken this line ever since he suspected that he, Roosevelt, might rise in the world; he knew what ailed Walter; but it certainly had taken hold, hadn't it?

He looked at several paragraphs again. Then he went on to say
that intellectuals never allowed a politician the least leeway; they
were positively afraid of being caught in an approving mood. They
ought to be sophisticated enough to know that if he had down-
graded the League of Nations, it had been merely a maneuver; and

that if he was elected, some sort of international organization would be more likely to come about than with any Republican. Why was it that such people demanded what was politically impossible? He sometimes wondered, he went on, how a few of them got into the Senate. . . . Cutting and Wheeler were as bad as my friend Lovett . . . or Paul Douglas, or John Dewey. . . . Maybe Dewey was the worst.

After some picturesque remarks about "my friends," he came back to it. There was one thing; if they kept on this way, no one would believe he was the radical demagogue Smith said he was. He laughed at his own conceit.

Thunder on the left? I suggested.

It had its uses, he said. But did it bother me?

I had to ask how it could help bothering me. These people, I said, were what a McDougall would call my higher audience. They were the people I had always most admired, I supposed, outside of some members of my own guild of economists and political scientists. They were his higher audience too, weren't they?

Well, yes, he said, but I should just keep in mind that he was not the nominee of the progressives. He was running on the Democratic ticket. . . . One Roosevelt had run as a progressive—it had finished him!

I did recall.

Then, he asked, did I think they would be happier if he went after the fat boys and spoke for the little fellows?

They ought to be, of course; that was the progressive line as well as the Democratic one. But I didn't know. I said to him that he'd already taken a crack at the wicked businessmen, and the unanimous progressive judgment seemed to be that he didn't mean it.

He laughed. Others would believe it, he said, plenty of them, especially the fat boys. I'd see.

It was in quite another vein that we noted how the business press regarded the political prospect when the conventions had made their choices. *Business Week,* published by the McGraw-Hill Company and having as its economist Virgil Jordan of the National Industrial Conference Board, was representative. Roosevelt watched it with us through July and August. Its editorials continued to labor an optimism by now worn pretty thin. For instance, it was the first to find reason for believing that a turn had come and improvement was beginning; it did ignore personalities, with fair consistency; it did not despair when Roosevelt won. It paid close attention to the legislation making its way through the Congress. The Wagner-Garner bill, first vetoed by Hoover, then revised to meet his objections, then finally approved, was found acceptable. Its assumption was that recovery must come through stimulation of private enterprise. Because both commercial and investment banking had nearly stopped operating, the government must furnish credit for expansion. This would result in more employment and thus in a start toward recovery.

In the issue of July 23, there was a summary of the congressional session as it bore on the economic situation, and there were indeed some interesting measurements. We were summarizing them for ourselves as background for the campaign dialogue about to begin. The magazine noted:

> The Reconstruction Finance Corporation had been established with $500 millions of capital and 1½ billions of borrowing capacity. It would make loans to banks, insurance companies, railroads and similar businesses. This was to prevent bankruptcies, support security values, and stop bank closings.
>
> The Glass-Steagall Banking Act modified the Federal Reserve System by allowing the Reserve Banks to discount more classes of paper as backing for Federal Reserve notes. This would help to prevent bank suspensions and stop the contraction of credit.
>
> The budget had been balanced by higher taxes and reduced expenditures. This would "be helpful in restoring financial confidence."
>
> Then finally, in an Emergency Relief and Construction Act, $300 millions had been added to R.F.C.'s borrowing powers so that it could make loans to the states for unemployment relief, $1½ billions to be loaned for self-liquidating projects, and $300 millions for Federal public construction. . . .

Hoover naturally was given credit for most of this; *Business Week* ignored his insistence on restricted appropriations and failed to mention several catches. Among these were the difficulty of determining what projects would be self-liquidating and the exhausted borrowing capacity of many states. On the whole, the magazine seemed to think that optimism was more justified than at any time in several years.

It must be said that *Business Week*'s own index furnished no argument for probable upturn. The trend, as it had been for two years, was obstinately down—with just a slight leveling off, perhaps; but nothing decisive.

One editorial (in the issue of July 6) could be looked back on later as foreshadowing a really famous pronouncement. Whether there actually was any connection, I have never known, but the following is so close to the famous sentence, "We have nothing to fear but fear itself," that it may have stuck in the memory of one of us, to emerge more dramatically shaped.

> Obviously there is nothing organically wrong. The country is full of people, the people are full of desire for a better standard of living, the fields are full of food, the mines are full of minerals, the factories are full of machinery, the railroads are full of rails, the roads are full of automobiles, the streets are full of labor, and the banks are full of safe-deposit boxes full of money. We have all the makin's of a mighty good time for everybody here in America, and it's hard to believe we are just too dumb to do anything with it.

Roosevelt took as seriously as the rest of us the possibility that an upturn might be starting and might be pronounced by election time. If this happened, it would lend weight to Hoover's claim that the measures already taken were the right ones and that a resumption of prosperity could be expected presently. If we had to contend with a rise of business activity and an increase in employment, Hoover's appeal, especially to the Republicans that Roosevelt hoped to persuade, would be much more difficult to counter. If the indices were still falling, they would make their own argument and it would only be necessary to underline the trend; that was what we had so far assumed.

The fact was that most economists had for some time been expecting an upturn. They reasoned, as Hoover did, that deflation "must have run its course." What this meant was that enough debts must have been canceled in one way or another so that borrowing could begin all over again. As activity was resumed, employment would increase, and with employment, the demand for goods.

We had several reasons for being skeptical about this. One was that agricultural surpluses were still immense and that, consequently, farmers had no prospect of increased purchasing power. Another was that the expansion of Reconstruction Finance Corporation loans to take the place of bank credit could hardly be felt for something like a year. They could protect the frozen assets until an upturn made them liquid again, but this was not a recovery measure. Then too, there was the low limit on relief and public-works authorizations in the Emergency Relief and Construction Act; $300 millions to be *loaned* to the states was not much more than was needed in New York alone—even if New York could have borrowed it. Also $300 millions had been provided for public works, but some study had convinced me, at least, that this was a remedy good only in quite a long run—say two years. Planning and organization for most projects was much more than one year's job. That would be too late.

So Adolf and I were not surprised that, at the end of August, we could say to Roosevelt that the depression was still in full course. Final decisions could not be delayed much longer; by that time most of the speeches of major character had to be got under way. What was surprising was to read *Business Week*'s editorial on August 31.

> Everyone is rejoicing at the signs of better times. Wall Street has been making whoopee, 1929 style. The newspapers, as if by concerted arrangement, scour the country for encouraging items and make first page news of the reopening of a button factory employing 15 men.

It went on to say, however, that even if the patient was on the mend and reimbued with that spark which is more important than any medicine, it was only kind to tell him that he was not going to be out of bed tomorrow. Moreover, real prosperity could not come without dealing with fundamental ills. True, a good start had been made at the recent Lausanne meeting to prepare the World Conference on these issues; but consider, the editorialist said, what this conference must undertake to do—deal with

> monetary and credit policy, with exchange difficulties, with price levels, and with the movement of capital; it must also find ways to improve conditions of production and interchange, with particular reference to tariff policy. Along this route runs the road to recovery; we can have—indeed we are having—improvement without dealing with the fundamental causes of our ills. But we cannot have real prosperity.

All this might be true enough. We had considered, among ourselves—in a preliminary way—what must be done internationally; we thought, however, that Hoover and the financial community were straining to explain the failure of the economy to show any real improvement. We thought it would be futile for him to ask Americans to look abroad for the explanations of their troubles; the causes—and the immediate remedies—were so obviously centered here at home. And when we studied the indices in the same issue of *Business Week,* those that, on July 13, had shown some sign of leveling off had again, in August, resumed their downward course.

We had no doubt that we were right to develop a strategy that assumed a continuing depression; to insist that much more drastic measures were needed to start recovery. We looked at some average prices. They were devastating evidences of paralysis. For instance:

> Wheat: $.47 per bushel in 1928 $1.25
> Corn: .20 per bushel in 1928 .75

And the productivity indices showed:

> Steel at 14% of capacity (five-year average, 64%). Building contracts at $4,784 (daily average in thousands); five-year average, $18,170. Carloadings: 58 (daily average, 1,000 cars); five-year average, 163.

Stock prices had indeed gained two points, but they were still thirty points below a year ago and sixty-eight points below the five-year average. What was the Wall Street whoopee about?

This pessimistic conclusion was, of course, no help at all in deciding how recovery could best be brought about. We still did not have any clear indication of Roosevelt's intentions. He seemed on one day to be considering greatly enlarged expenditures for relief and public works—the bolstering of consumers' purchasing power —and on the next to be making calculations about the restoration of confidence by balancing the budget.

Generally speaking, we were on one side and the businessmen were on the other. There had been some concessions. Now that the Recovery Act had been passed, the argument was somewhat different from what it had been before. The question now was whether relief should be given to the states as *grants* or as *loans*; also whether or not public works should be self-liquidating. This was progress of a sort, but there was still the annually balanced budget. This symbol dominated many minds other than those of the businessmen. It was not necessarily inconsistent with expanded relief, not if taxes were increased to pay the bigger bills; but if there was one thing more insisted on by the confidence theorists than the balanced budget, it was tax relief. Both were necessary to the return of an assurance that would encourage enterprisers to resume borrowing and lending.

This left Roosevelt with a choice we knew he intensely disliked. He wanted to do something for the unemployed, but without borrowing—just as he wanted to see farm surpluses cut down without making farmers reduce acreage. Also he was looking for some way to expunge the burden of debt without the wholesale bankruptcy involved in further deflation.

The domestic-allotment scheme offered a price-lifting device for farmers that would allow them to pay off their debts; but where was the comparable scheme for businessmen and home-owners? Was inflation on the way? Roosevelt was asking more and more questions about various monetary devices, trying to assess their practicality, and weighing their political appeal. Henry Morgenthau's continual effort to interest him in the Cornellians' theory that management of the price of gold would allow the government to fix the price level was getting at least some attention. Professors Warren and Pearson, being farm-management experts, had convinced themselves that this could be done more simply than any economist would have agreed was possible. All that was required, they said, was for the government to offer the right price and buy all the gold that was offered.

More, much more, was said among us about money as the summer progressed and we had to begin operating. But we had other matters to work at as well, and money was probably neglected. What Ray had was a directive to prepare speeches in first draft. He had been given an indication of their subjects; but other than his conclusions from our conversations, he had very little instruction about content. So far his efforts and ours had not resulted in a very clear focus on anything.

Talks were resumed after Roosevelt's return to Albany on July 5, and after the excitement of becoming a nominee had died down; but he was in such a euphoric state that he was not very useful for the job at hand. Perhaps this was true of everyone concerned. In any case, not much was being done.

Roosevelt must have had a wonderful July 4 as he progressed eastward. He had left Chicago on the night of July 3, so he entered New York State at Buffalo the next morning. The news of the nomination had created a demand for stops in Rochester, Syracuse, and Utica. The celebrating Democrats had assembled in cavernous train-sheds, with the crowds overflowing into the streets. This was his home country. Upstate had always been good to him; he was the only Democrat since Cleveland to whom that conservative region *had* been good. Evidently the bond still held.

We were told that even Louis Howe had expanded a bit. He still kept altogether quiet about his view of the tactical needs in the postconvention climate, but one element soon became visible. This was the same determination to demonstrate loyalty to the party that had guided his attempt to substitute his own acceptance for Ray's. He now demanded that Roosevelt's first speech should be still another declaration of endorsement. We were to hear about that in the first of the next week's meetings.

That was not all we would hear during the week, of course, because Ray was now actually faced with immediate campaign necessities and he was more inclined to insist on having instructions. The dozen drafts of formal importance he had been warned about in Chicago would have to be got ready at once. The task of setting up the Albany headquarters as well as preoccupation with campaign plans made everything difficult, but still no one doubted that the speeches could be got together. Our doubts were about what Roosevelt really meant to say.

This was something of an interval between more intense periods of activity. With the nomination won and the campaign strategy outlined (except what would be said about certain issues), Roosevelt himself was comparatively calm. There was turmoil, but even in the midst of it he seemed cheerfully detached. He had always been surrounded by servants and assistants. When it suited him they became completely invisible. This strange isolation fascinated me. I came to the conclusion that it must be a characteristic of the bizarre profession of politics, especially for one who lived year after year in its recurrent confusions. But then, of course, he had been reared in the purple, and that had something to do with a seeming indifference.

In our talks at the time, I had a natural hesitation about exposing my doubts and reservations. But I did expose them, and Roosevelt did discuss them with me. I was not always happy with the result; on the contrary, I was sometimes disturbed. I was becoming a sort of no-sayer about policy, as Louis Howe was supposed to be the no-sayer in politics. As long as I could argue and have a say, however, I found that I had no difficulty in accepting whatever decision was made. From the first, Roosevelt had felt confidence in my discretion. It was never mentioned between us, but it was understood that when he confided in me, or when he thought out loud, what he said was for my ears only. After some of those talks, I made notes, but almost immediately I destroyed most of them; if they were confidences they ought to be respected as such. Some I did not even talk over with Ray.

A potential President is supposed to be infallible, and Roosevelt was uncertain about several very important issues. He could not afford to have it known how painful the transition was from a governorship, after four years, to the presidency. I was quite convinced that every prospective President had to go through this learning period, and from what I knew it seemed to me that most of them had gone through it after, rather than before, their inaugurations. This accounted for the year or two of fumbling so often commented on by historians.

I came to the point of speaking to him about this very thing. He was more aware of it than I had realized. He said at once that he had no intention of wasting the honeymoon period. He must not. There had never been a time, the Civil War alone excepted, when our institutions had been in such jeopardy. Repeatedly he spoke of this, saying that it was enormously puzzling to him that the ordeal of the past three years had been endured so peaceably. Such reliance on the competence of leaders who did nothing but disappoint those whose miseries were greatest was very strange.

Speaking of the comment made by the *Business Week* editorialist—that we had "all the makin's of a mighty good time for everybody"—he said that this was the most sinister of all the indications. The country had been going on toward such a wonderful prospect, yet without any assignable reason, progress had stopped. We had begun to slip back, and no way had been found to stop the slipping. Everyone in charge of the system was helpless—worse, everyone was devoid of ideas about change and finally of any initiative. If that wasn't a situation calculated to lead straight to revolution, he could not imagine one.

He must not stay on center. He must offer something. He spoke again of Hoover, as he had before; of having known him and watched him with the admiration of a somewhat younger man. What had gone wrong? What was it that made so great a man so inept as a national leader? He had been forceful; he had worn a commanding air as of one who carried out the enormous tasks of administration. But when he had become President, he had hardly seemed the same man who had saved the Belgians and then the rest of Europe and Russia from starvation, had been so effective a food administrator during the war, and had then gone on to be the strong man in the Harding and Coolidge cabinets.

I told him I had studied Hoover's performance and had come to some sort of conclusion; would he tell me if it made any sense? But, I said hesitantly, the conclusion is fairly complicated, and there may not actually be any lesson in it.

Roosevelt thought a conversation about Hoover would be a good thing. He too was puzzled, and although he was generally confident in his own ability to emerge from tight places, the presidency, in the present circumstances, was a whole complex of tight places. Everything, almost, had to be reviewed and much had to be drastically changed. It must not only be done with a sure touch, but done fast. He really thought that the revolution he spoke of could hardly be avoided if another President should fail as Hoover had failed.

So we agreed to a talk when a quiet hour could be found. What he was thinking of, I knew. It was not Hoover; it was himself and his coming trial.

CHAPTER XXVI

Talk with a Nominee

❦ ❦ ❦

Than many pressing affairs were claiming the nominee's attention, in addition to all the routine work of the governorship. When I asked Doc why Roosevelt didn't resign from state office and leave himself free for the campaign, I received an enlightening answer. The best reason, Doc said, is that he's poor.

Oh, come off, I protested.

Doc laughed and explained: what he meant was that Roosevelt was poor for a Roosevelt. He had enormous expenses and an extravagant family. Not one of the lot ever thought of money except to spend it. He probably had a million dollars coming to him, if it hadn't disappeared in the depression, but however much it was, he wouldn't get it until his mother died. I might as well know, Doc went on, that the secretaries, the mansion, the cars, the state troopers, and all the paraphernalia he had were absolutely necessary. Roosevelt could never pay the bill himself. After the change-over in January, he just might have to borrow in order to get by.

Others had got by, I reminded Doc, beginning with Washington, who was wealthy in somewhat the same way; that is, he was land rich, but money poor. He had borrowed money to pay for his journey to the inauguration. What about the party, though; wouldn't it pay for all the campaigning?

Not for everything that went on around Albany and Hyde Park now, Doc said. Besides, hadn't I heard that the party was hard up? Jim would be lucky just to meet the payroll for all those people he had in New York City and running around the country.

There was another thing; this fellow had to have a situation, and until November the mansion was a good one. He could do a lot of things from it that he couldn't do from Hyde Park. That was an estate down there. He was Governor here; down there he was a country gentleman. The Albany establishment was the kind where small bosses came to call on the big one.

I accepted his teaching.

When, after Chicago, I arrived at the mansion and passed the guards, Roosevelt himself was, as so often in summer, sitting on the old-fashioned porch, its steps and railing thickly covered with blistered layers of green paint. There was a teacart beside him, and he was dealing with a large piece of cake, messy with frosting. He was licking his fingers and discussing the same subject as the first time I had seen him on this same porch—the Walker case.

This time Ray was not there. I do not, as a matter of fact, recall whom Roosevelt was talking with, but it must have been a New York politician because he was being urged to let Walker off easy. He told me, when his visitor had gone, that this advice was getting to be monotonous; even Farley and Howe were talking of ways to avoid having the charges aired. This he couldn't do. Walker was preparing an answer to Seabury. He would have to explain having an income several times his salary, and that he could never do; how could the whole thing be dismissed or even postponed? It just wasn't possible.

I had nothing to suggest, of course; he was only thinking out loud. Presently he dismissed the subject and I hurried to offer the project I had been working out over the weekend. Gradually he concentrated on what I was saying. I began by recalling what was being said by *The New York Times* as well as *The New Republic*; he was not being clear and forthright enough, and at this late time he had no right to be evasive about the crucial issues of a country in deep trouble.

I was certain that he knew much more than he ever said in public, and I thought he had his policies laid out. He expressed himself frankly enough to me about the imperatives of recovery; yet every statement we had prepared for him thus far had come out, when he used it, as something tentative and equivocal, as though he didn't really intend anything positive. In the acceptance, for instance, there had been hints of intention, but they were so slight that retreat from any of them was quite possible. It was obvious that he was trying not to alienate anyone. I thought the spectrum of appeal too wide. Not everyone could possibly be got to consent to what recovery would demand. He was in danger of avoiding anything positive.

It proved difficult to get his attention. He wanted to talk about his journey home. He had left Chicago on the night of July 3, after a day of meeting and greeting, he and "the missus" being almost the last of the conventioners to leave. The gatherings along the way and the local leaders' optimism had been beyond his expectation. . . . He had behaved before as though he were confident; now he really was. There was no hint of uncertainty.

All sizes and kinds of bosses had paraded into and out of the Congress suite on Saturday night and Sunday. They must have numbered in the hundreds. For each he had had some word intended to send them home prepared to do their best. This sort of performance, for almost anyone else, would have been unbearably exhausting, but he had kept it up through many hours with undimmed brightness. Each new face had brought a "glad to see you; tell me about Cedar Rapids"—or Fort Smith, or Missoula, or Atlanta. "Jim tells me things look pretty good. I hear you've got everything ready." And often the greeter forgot that he had meant to make a complaint, put in a request, or express doubts; he usually began to swell a little, to reassure, even to brag. The note was confidence, optimism, and good cheer. Delegates, tired from a week of wrangling and indulgence, heavy-eyed and sagging, came away braced and hearty again, as politicians should be. Doc and I had stood occasionally alongside or on the edge of groups, listening and marveling. Doc said, by God, he was going to keep close to this. I asked why and he said, damn it, he was a lawyer, and he might be called on to do something. But he wasn't.

Ray and I had left Chicago separately. I believe he went to visit his sister in Ohio. The day or two I had in Wilson, on the south shore of Lake Ontario, had been used to write the memorandum I hoped I could get Roosevelt to read. This was now a procedure with us. More often than not, the papers stayed in our pockets, and the real usefulness of writing them was that they made some issue explicit in our own minds so that we could outline more economically in talk what we had first put on paper. The encounter on the porch was interrupted. It was no time for serious talk. I gave up.

Missy Le Hand told me a little later that even though it was afternoon when he reached Albany after his progress across New York State, he had tackled the accumulated stacks of mail. Guernsey Cross, with Grace and Paula Tully, had already done most of the sorting, and the first job was to see that messages from important people were acknowledged; answering the rest in some fashion would take weeks. Even Roosevelt, Missy said, had been impressed with the enormous volume. He thought, though, that within a few days the business of handling the paper work would be organized. He laughed when he spoke of the signature-imitator Louis had produced so that replies could go out by hundreds instead of by dozens. He wondered, as a collector of stamps and documents himself, what dealers would do about this when they found it out. Apparently this was a recognized procedure, however, and there certainly could have been no other way of answering that seemed at all personal.

About this mass of communications: those having to do with political plotting or reporting went to Democratic headquarters, but those with implications for policy of all sorts were ours. They piled up until Bobby Straus could hardly see over the stacks on his desk. He made a game of it. Many of the plans, projects, and suggestions were too fantastic for serious consideration, yet some sort of answer had to be made. Others were evident attempts to be helpful, and most showed concern about the country's plight, but the infinite variety of American eccentrics was never better displayed. What most impressed me was the number of responsible people who had been worried about the condition we had fallen into and could not restrain the impulse to organize their thoughts and pass on their conclusions. These hardly ever fitted the Roosevelt scheme as it gradually unfolded, and there was nothing to do but answer sympathetically but vaguely that their contributions would certainly be considered. Bobby became expert at this.

Dinner on this particular evening was a gay but small affair—no business, mostly reminiscences about convention excitements and about the trip out and the one back. As Roosevelts always did, the family regarded politics as an ordinary business with amusing interludes. Even Eleanor's seriousness was lightened by the Chicago outcome, and the boys regarded the whole affair as a charade with their father as the principal actor. They had seen the convention in being as he had not, but they had seen only the surface. I wondered whether their father, back in 1904, had taken Uncle Ted's campaign in the same way. He had organized Harvard meetings and had become, for the moment, Republican. Uncle Ted's performance was, for other Roosevelts, fascinating in itself, not because it had any other significance; and that was how the new generation regarded Franklin's enterprise.

The young people competed in describing what had gone on. They had dozens of photographs taken by accommodating cameramen, and they commented acidly on each other's appearance. They were hazy about the speeches and they had not understood the maneuvering, but they had noted two highlights. One was Will Rogers filling in while the delegates were waiting for the platform committee to report; another was their visit to the Credentials Committee, where Huey Long had made an arm-swinging speech about the wickedness of his Louisiana enemies and had obtained a favorable vote. They were fascinated by his bravura performance.

Afterward, in the study, Roosevelt admitted lightly that he was not proud of the acceptance; still he thought it had done well enough. It was now seen to have been well received not only by the delegates but by the press. This surprised me. But I warned him that he would be less pleased by what would be said in the weeklies, whose writers would have been less influenced by convention excitement. He laughed at my reservations about the agricultural passages. What had been said was enough to start with; he would now get some of the farm leaders in and insist that they agree. This would be a new experience for them, but he thought that for once they would have to get together and acknowledge it publicly. I told him—what turned out to be the case—that they would demand an indication of his preference so that they could tell their constituents they had invented it.

We talked about this for some time; then I said I wanted a chance to speak to him about something else. He put me off until morning; he'd holler when he was ready.

About eight in the morning, he did call across the hall and I went in. He was wearing his old gray sweater and the newspapers were spread around. He'd been to the bathroom, he said, grinning, so I could go ahead. I did—for something like an hour. He let me talk first, and he really listened.

Ray had shown me the list of the speeches, I told him, and it seemed good—except for omissions. It was quite possible for him to make worthwhile suggestions about the railroads, about power, and about agriculture. Then I supposed he meant to propose banking reform. If he wanted to say something about economy in government, and even about reorganization, it would be a good thing to do if he was cautious. But, I said, the unemployment reference in the acceptance had been nothing to be proud of, and unemployment was the crucial issue.

He interrupted to mention the passage about work in the forests. We had talked a good deal about the enlargement of conservation work. This and the development of roads had seemed to us the quickest federal projects. I passed over his exaggerated notion of the number of men who could be employed in replanting forests; what I was more interested in was that he should acknowledge the cost of such projects. They would have to be paid for, and this made all the talk about economy—the obsession of the businessmen —dangerous.

He argued as he had before that economies could be found and would go a long way toward meeting the bill.

I objected. Economies, even if they could be made—and I thought he exaggerated them—meant firing people. That was unemployment. We oughtn't to fool ourselves or to try to fool the public. There would be immense costs for relief, and they could be paid for only by federal appropriations. He was stubbornly doubtful, but I insisted that the deficit involved in this would produce its own income if it led to increased activity. The spending would stimulate production, and taxes at the same rates would yield more income than they were yielding in a sick and halting system. At least this was the theory, and I thought it would prove to be true.

Even though there were complications about the financing that we ought not to say much about until we had done more studying, I reminded him again that he had made a firm commitment to provide work for all. This was likely to be a weak spot during the campaign. There were some thirteen million unemployed. To fulfill his promise of a job for every man was going to be impossible, and he ought to be careful about repeating. What he *could* promise was income for every family at once and increased employment later as public works got under way and as private production picked up.

Of these thirteen million—if we accepted Frances Perkins' estimate—not more than two or three million could be given public work within any short period. Money granted to the states—as the bill now being passed would provide—would result in the employment of one man for each thousand dollars during a year. That was only three hundred thousand men for three hundred million dollars. This was the hard fact. So there was no possibility that public employment could do much toward meeting the emergency in any short time; there would have to be handouts—a dole.

He balked at this, but after considerable argument and going over my figures he admitted that I might be right. Then I went on:

what we had to do was to get the unemployed back into those empty factories and mines, and back to running the railroads, rather than on to jobs provided by public agencies. This might not be easy or quick but it was what was meant by recovery. His strongest language ought to be used about this. We ought to be told at once to get busy on a speech or speeches, not on Ray's list, about getting things going again. It ought to be definite. And if its main theme was recovery, as I felt it must be, it ought to insist that unemployed men were unable to buy anything, and that if nothing was bought, factories would not have to produce and would not need workers.

Conversations of this sort seem to take on, as I write of them, an academic quality, but they were not like that as we talked. We never could really talk *to* Roosevelt; we had to talk *with* him. If we did not catch his interest, he would shift to another subject; if we did, it became a dialogue. Even when I knew that he was prejudiced against my ideas, that he believed I was being impractical, there was often emphatic response. It might be only when I thought it over afterward that I knew he had not been convinced. It was an exchange, but there was not often any conclusion.

His attention for theoretical discussion could not be kept very long now. His hours were too crowded, and some of the decisions he had to make had an immediate significance that plans for recovery still lacked. He could postpone these, and I had a constant nagging uneasiness about his evident intention to equivocate. Recovery was now actually in question. It would begin only when people had money to spend.

There were moments when the "confidence" of the businessmen and the "cheap dollars" of the Cornellians seemed to be materializing as personalized enemies. An easy and popular solution was still being sought, and there was none. It was a losing fight, and I think now that I should have known it all along. But all our talk was so fair and friendly that there was never a time when defeat was so definite that I finally gave up.

The Congress was about to pass a relief act, and although it had the modifications Hoover had insisted on, it involved large expenditures. I told him that when he talked about the problem attacked in the bill, he did not seem to be talking about recovery, but rather unrealistically about unemployment. Worse, he seemed to forget that it was most important to stress the theme of stability. He seemed to be forgetting now that this was what was meant by the "concert of interests"—producers making such bargains with one another that they could exchange goods (by means of money) without anyone's pinching anyone else unduly. Lack of organization for this was the fatal legacy of laissez faire to an economy that had unconsciously become collectivized.

I reminded him once again that imbalance had caused the depression, and that only restoration of balance could cure it. Management of relationships could prevent its happening again. This was the program—in three steps. I urged it as the central campaign theme—the one he ought to come back to again and again in its many implications.

He heard me out and seemed to catch fire; he expanded on what I had said much more eloquently than I had been able to do. When I recalled what he had been through during the past week, this dissertation, calling for concentration and ordering of his thoughts, seemed very nearly incredible. For the moment, I was encouraged.

Nevertheless, reluctant as I was to accept it, I was beginning to understand that his campaign speeches were to be muted. I knew by now that he was determined, persistent, and dedicated when his mind was made up, but it was not yet made up about recovery. He had no responsibility for explaining to me or to any of us. He was merely going to use what we brought him as it seemed best to use it at the moment. Meanwhile he was not being evasive, as Walter Lippmann and many others claimed; he was making up his mind.

We could see that he had to be wary about the demands of those who wanted to use him for their purposes. There were many of these. Nearly everyone who came to see him wanted assurance about something. His visitors argued for a cause, for an interest, for a group, or for themselves. He received them and was pleasant because this was political custom. Sometimes, when they had something to offer, deals were made. These were more often agreements than promises. Neither could be held to anything. Yet the exchange certainly went on. We heard echoes of it, not always pleasant.

We learned that this sort of upper-level trading in political life could only be relied on if both parties were professionals, and Roosevelt's visitors were not always in the trade. He had a way of applying his own rule of convenience. What it meant was that others were joining him, not he the others. The silent pledges bound them, but not him—not at least to the same extent—because for him to be bound was to put in pledge some other promise or policy. He obviously regarded himself as identified with something transcending any of these trading interests, and his loyalty was to that.

Having got so far, we asked ourselves what that interest or loyalty was. Lippmann and the other skeptics—some of whom were volubly dissident right through his approach to the presidency—said this was his will to power. They called it ambition and let it go at that. He simply wanted, they said, to become President. He had given no adequate reason why he should be chosen. He evaded every call for proof of competence, and even every profession of policy—until he could evade no longer. This had been true of prohibition, still an issue, if a fading one, until the convention. It had been true of the League of Nations. When pressed by Hearst, he had repudiated it, but at the same time he was telling others that what he said did not mean that he was against all international organization. Even worse, he was impossible to pin down on economic issues.

Presently, however, we began to see some purpose in the pattern—not very clearly, yet still unmistakably. We discussed it, but we could do little more at this juncture than to wait.

The progressives continued to find him as unsatisfactory as they had in winter and spring. I was self-conscious about this, perhaps more so because, relying on the Oglethorpe address and assuming that I had persuaded Roosevelt to make it, they thought of me as their envoy in the Roosevelt camp. This embarrassed me. A few individuals—Bob La Follette, Floyd Olson, and Fiorello La Guardia, for instance—could not believe that I had not written at least the first draft of the Oglethorpe address and kept asking me what had become of the theme. I told them that Roosevelt still listened when I argued for a collectivized progressivism, even sometimes mentioned it himself. But I had to admit that I was not happy. Collectivization, I kept saying, would have to include some device for management—that is, for determining what, in the public interest, industries must do—and would have to give them some reason for doing it. I thought this the most important of all the policies he could push as President, and I did not see how it could be done unless there had been a beginning during the campaign. We had been over and over this, and I was as worried as my progressive friends. The Oglethorpe position seemed to have been finally abandoned.

There were more discussions of progressivism. Roosevelt used a story to show, finally, why I should stop pressing. It was one that came from President Wilson, who had used it in talking with Roosevelt at some stage in the fight for the Federal Reserve System during the 1913–1914 battle when he could not marshal behind his legislation those who ought to be its supporters. The progressives, Wilson had said, could never get much done because they would not agree on detail and would not act together. They were individualists. Each had his own scheme, his own approach—and his own ego! If any two agreed on the problem—as they sometimes did—they disagreed on its solution. They fought furiously with one another. Compromise seemed to them cowardly. They would not acknowledge any leadership. Each valued his independence above any sort of loyalty.

In this, Wilson had gone on, they contrasted sharply with the conservatives, who were usually interested not in action, but in preventing it. In this they could be cohesive. They had leaders, accepted common tactics, and offered a tough opposition to any opponent.

Sitting at his desk in the small study of the Executive Mansion,

Roosevelt used his hands as, he said, Wilson had used his. The progressives, Wilson had told him, presented the same sort of striking force as a man would have if he attacked an opponent with the fingers of his hands extended. He illustrated. But the conservatives met the attack, he said, with sensibly closed fists. The progressives broke their fingers and retired; the conservatives held their own.

We were even worse off now than Wilson had been, Roosevelt said. Look at the list. There was Norris, that wonderful old man. Why didn't the progressive group accept his lead? His fight for Muscle Shoals had been wonderfully courageous, and look how he'd kept at it, but he'd never been able to get the others to agree on what ought to be done—yardstick power, yes; but beyond that, what?

There was Burt Wheeler, who thought of himself as La Follette's successor, thought too that he ought to have been nominated just now instead of Roosevelt. He had once left the party, so now he had no following, but he refused to join with anyone else. Then there were the others in the Senate: Cutting, an old friend, but he had held back from declaring support. Bob La Follette hadn't declared either. Bob should have done what some others out his way had done; but, no, he had to go it alone. Then take others like Floyd Olson in Minnesota and La Guardia in New York—real leaders, and on our side, but they were of no use except for attacking the Republicans. It was doubtful if they would agree to anything we shaped up even after a long hard series of sessions. Everyone else had to compromise a little, but not they; they'd never follow.

Hiram Johnson, he went on, would go along for a while. When he thought of what might happen in California, he wondered that he had the nerve to visit the state. It did suit Johnson right then to support him, but Johnson would never allow himself to be thought of as a Democrat. I'd see; he couldn't be counted on for long.

There was more analysis. I came away from the talk that included these remarks thinking I had seen some way below a surface that before had been bafflingly opaque; still, I felt that Roosevelt was hardly entitled to criticize the progressives on such grounds.

He was fortunate. He was the titular leader now, and so the pace-maker. Moreover, he had succeeded in becoming the front man for a major party. Now the elders—people like Cordell Hull, Key Pittman, Carter Glass, Claude Swanson, Jim Byrnes, Robert Wagner, Josephus Daniels, Thomas Walsh—were tied to him, and along with them came all the other old hands who were party regulars. His supporters formed a grave and steady group united by old ties, but there was not one of the progressives in the lot—and why should they be expected to overlook the omission?

What I got from my protest and my suggestion is mostly represented in the Columbus address of August 20. Roosevelt told me to get something ready and work with Ray, who would, of course, fix up the final draft.

He was at first somewhat vague about its intention, but some discussion brought out the preference for a speech about the depression. He was to state the view we seemed now to agree on about causes, and was to go on from there to a scheme for recovery. It was a job I could undertake with enthusiasm.

To make quite clear what I was to do, I noted a three-part outline and he approved it; but I was sure he gave Ray instructions too; it was Ray who had to do the writing. My instruction was to:

(1) Outline the causes of the depression.
(2) Attack the Republican position.
(3) Present an alternative plan for recovery.

When I look back and consider the possibilities for confusion, cross purposes, even jealousy in such arrangements, I still wonder why none of them appeared. Perhaps it was because Ray and I had so complete an understanding and each relied on the other's loyalty. I took some pains about this, and he must have taken some too. In spite of my increased number of contacts with Roosevelt, I think Ray never had occasion to suspect that I was trying to take his place. For one thing, I was no ghost-writer, but also he knew that all I wanted was to see my conclusions embodied in policy. Neither of us had any political ambitions. What I saw of political activity—and I was seeing a good deal—contrasted most unfavorably with my own position. We were, I thought, on a measurably higher level of human endeavor than any of those we were observing.

Did this include Roosevelt? We spoke of that, and Roosevelt himself, from his eminence as Governor and potential President, sometimes called us "Professors" in a derisory tone. He said, on occasion, that he was being a teacher on another campus, an enormous one. He spoke of the presidency, as he would some years later in an address, as very largely an educational effort. So we knew that although he might be puckish with us, there was a certain envy in it too. He would like to have had the academic distinction of Wilson. But he could never have written such a tract as *Congressional Government*. He knew it, and we knew it.

I was not aware then—I only found out years later—that he had started at least once on such an enterprise and had got no further than a first chapter. He had meant to write a different and more credible history of the United States than any he had read, but it was not within his powers. He had none of Uncle Ted's talent for exposition. He was not even a good phrasemaker.

But if he had no gifts as a writer, Ray had; and he used this very considerable talent during the campaign to write carefully composed addresses. Then he sat down with Roosevelt to see whether what he had written was approved. He had been given, in advance, only the sketchiest instruction. Now whole paragraphs and pages were sacrificed. What was really painful was to have Roosevelt reduce the quality of the writing to his own mediocre level. He was addicted to clichés that Ray would rather have died than accept if he had been given any choice; adjectives and adverbs that had no meaning cluttered up the text. Roosevelt dictated new sentences or paragraphs, saying things far less clearly than they had been said before, and these had to be substituted for Ray's own lucid statements. It was an ordeal for a skillful and meticulous writer.

Ray did what he must. He chose to think that the clichés and offending adjectives were a politician's judgment of what "would go over" with his audiences. At any rate, it was to be Roosevelt's speech, and he was entitled to have what he wanted. It was often possible to make it better by suggesting, by rewriting and resubmitting, by gently objecting; but this was a wearing process. I felt for Ray; but I was having my own problems and they often seemed more serious than his.

CHAPTER XXVII

Second Talk with a Nominee

🌿　🌿　🌿

We were learning now, if we had not known it before, that Roosevelt had a talent for adaptability. He was so skilled in taking advantage of openings that we worried because he depended on improvisation when there was no need for it and failed to allow time for careful checking. Nevertheless, the talent was useful when quick accommodation to some event in the news had to be made or when a challenge had to be answered.

The sudden inspirations sometimes turned out well and sometimes did not. One that was best forgotten was the inclusion in his acceptance of possible employment figures on work in the forests; I still think he got these out of his own head. They were wildly inaccurate, of course, as was his later estimate that the costs of the federal government could be reduced by twenty-five per cent. Considering the immense pains Ray took to check and recheck every such statement in the material we prepared, we felt he had some right to offer a protest. Occasionally he did, but it always got passed off with a laugh, and sometimes with a reminder that no votes had really been jeopardized.

Another favored tactic was one that gave us some worry but more amusement. This was confrontation—as when Roosevelt invited Hoover to confer with him concerning New York State's prior claims to power from the St. Lawrence River. A treaty was being negotiated between the United States and Canada, and the state was being ignored. The protest called attention to Roosevelt's long advocacy of public power and helped to make progressives feel that he was one of them. Not many people outside New York may have known the state had a publicly owned and operated power installation at Massena Point, but everyone knew it after the exchanged telegrams were published. Hoover replied disdainfully— he continued to be disdainful well into September—that no useful purpose could be served by a meeting before the treaty had been agreed to. He was made to seem indifferent and arrogant, as Roosevelt, of course, knew that he would be.

Advocacy of public power remained to be made more emphatic in a later speech in the Northwest, but the protest served its purpose; hitherto the progressives had seen all too few signs that Roosevelt was anything but the chosen candidate of the inner-circle Democrats who had made a deal with Hearst. Since loyalty to the elders was the impression that Louis had insisted on, and since Roosevelt had gone out of his way to confirm it, withdrawal by the progressives had been deliberately risked. The power issue was fiercely fought in the West, but New Yorkers also had been sensitized to it by years of contention with private companies. At this moment Senator Norris was so stirred that he volunteered for speaking. Roosevelt considered the Nebraskan an important acquisition. It was a beginning, he said, that could be built on.

Such opportunities could not be expected to present themselves very often. Opportunities of another sort were more frequent but could not always be taken full advantage of because on many questions the distinction between the Hoover and Roosevelt ideas was so fine; but Roosevelt was more willing than Hoover to expand governmental relief, and this served to dim Hoover's established reputation as the savior of Belgium. Roosevelt's conviction that unearned relief destroyed character was only a little less than Hoover's, but he had it under better control. He was not really more adventurous than Hoover about public expenditure; he was fixed on a balanced budget and still not at all persuaded that en-

larged spending in order to create consumers ought to have precedence over fiscal orthodoxy. On this particular point of oversavings and shortage of purchasing power, although he grasped the
concept, he did have to consider the general prejudice against governmental deficits; but we understood well enough that he shared
the prejudice. It is hard to imagine, in more enlightened times,
what strong emotions supported an annually balanced budget all
during the depression years. To suggest a calculated deficit was to
challenge a precious principle. The wanted balance was not to be
reached during the whole era, but the effort to attain it was unre-
mitting.

It was undoubtedly true that Hoover's soul was harrowed by the
suffering of the unemployed and their dependents. He might seem
cold and machinelike, but this was only his public appearance. He
was the same man who had given up his worldwide business affairs
to undertake the feeding and clothing of the war's victims. Lately
he had proposed a works program and assistance for the unemployed. He had, however, given the impression of heartlessness by
his insistence on the condition that advances to the states for relief
should be loans rather than grants, and that public works should
be self-liquidating. This last eliminated the readiest and most helpful projects. Then too, the setting up of the Reconstruction Finance Corporation to assist financial institutions and public utilities had made Hoover seem unduly responsive to the troubles of
his business friends.

The RFC was so necessary a device that it would be immensely
enlarged by Roosevelt when he became President, but the controversy about it confirmed the general view, by now well established,
of a President who was remote and unmoved in the midst of misery. It was said that he held to the "trickle-down theory"—that if
the big fellows were rescued, they would in turn rescue the little
ones; also that he allowed his precious principle of individualism
to prevent governmental action even in the nation's agony. His
"rugged individualism" was a bitter joke, endlessly repeated. He
was indeed vulnerable, but attacks on his policies would be difficult for one who differed with him as slightly as Roosevelt seemed

to do. It was fortunate that, in this instance, the controversy was mostly carried on by others.

The progressives in the Congress had, during the spring, intensified a battle now two years old. They had repeatedly introduced bills for relief and public works calling for much larger expenditures than Hoover would approve. Besides, the bills were based on a principle he repeatedly rejected—that welfare was a direct responsibility of the federal government and that federal funds should be granted, not loaned. This was obviously an opportunity, and Roosevelt took what advantage of it he could by saying repeatedly that every man must have a job, or if not a job, then some source of income. If it could not be done any other way, he said, the government must see to it. That he was being inconsistent and might have some embarrassing explanations to make did not worry him too much. It was we who worried.

The most publicized controversy about recovery had occurred as the RFC bill was being discussed and voted on. Garner, of all people, appeared in this as the hero of the progressives. He put up a strong fight for writing into the bill an authorization for loans to individuals and private corporations. Hoover demanded that these be deleted. He insisted that only public bodies should be made eligible to borrow. Since "public bodies" included banks and railroads (public only in the sense of being regulated), Garner could claim that Hoover wanted to save the big businessmen but had no interest in the little ones.

Since Garner, by the time it was over, had been nominated for the vice-presidency, the Republicans, with their newspapers happily joining in, set out to present the vice-presidential nominee as a radical threat to free enterprise. This caused amusement in Albany. To present Garner in this role was so enormous a distortion of his views that his embarrassment in Texas could easily be imagined. But it was one of the fortuitous events that could be regarded as providential. The Southern reactionary as a running mate would be less a liability than had been feared—if, from then on, he could be kept quiet.

On issues of this nature, Roosevelt's record was really unfortunate. It was well enough known, however, that as Governor he had tackled the welfare problem with commendable energy, using such resources as the state could muster, and this reputation was spreading without being advertised. We thought that a declaration in favor of assistance, regardless of its source or its budgetary effect, would have to be made. But one consideration always had to be kept in mind: Ogden Mills, Roosevelt's Hudson Valley neighbor, was Hoover's Secretary of the Treasury; he was resourceful and he knew Roosevelt's record thoroughly. He could be counted on to exploit any openings he was allowed. He was already campaigning. Roosevelt was wary of inviting his attentions.

It was only about a week after the Congress adjourned on July 16 that the Bonus Expeditionary Force (as it was called by its leaders) was routed by force of arms and driven from Washington. The outrageous handling of this incident had a tremendous impact, all of which was favorable to the Roosevelt cause. No Democrat was even remotely involved, and there was nothing whatever to do except to watch with incredulous gratification. If it had been planned by a political strategist, the affair could not have been more perfectly arranged. After country-wide publicity, the belief that Hoover was completely devoid of human sympathy was more than ever fixed in people's minds.

While the B.E.F. was being routed in Washington, there were other happenings in the farm states: Indiana, Iowa, Illinois, Missouri, and the rest. Easterners were shocked when the Midwestern farmers—the most conservative and solidly Republican of all Americans—began to demonstrate publicly against the authorities who were enforcing harsh eviction orders of the courts. The seething disorder was growing worse month by month. Sooner or later, I felt, Roosevelt would have to go beyond the vague promise in the acceptance and offer at least the outline of a more specific relief program.

All during July and August farm leaders were making pilgrimages to Albany and Hyde Park, and these were watched with intense interest everywhere in the farming regions. First came Henry Wallace, then M. L. Wilson. It was assumed that these trusted intellectuals were being listened to. Then came the farm politicians, the bosses of the big organizations. O'Neal of the Farm Bureau Federation led off, and the others, such as Holman of the Grange, followed because they must. O'Neal was a Democrat, but Holman was Republican, hard-shell and hostile. Still, he was brought into line reluctantly by the presence of competition.

Wallace and Wilson had some useful political suggestions, quite apart from their contributions to the program of action that must be formulated. Don't try to make Democrats out of Iowa farmers, they told Roosevelt; just get them to vote for you. Roosevelt's comment to us was that Jim Farley was going to love that. He accepted the suggestion for himself, but apparently he did not commend the tactic to Farley or Howe, who were intent on strengthening their party. Similarly, he said nothing to them of his intention to woo the progressives. He let them labor to energize the Democratic organizations in Wisconsin, Minnesota, Nebraska, and other farm states where Democrats had hardly ever been able to win. He himself, in his speeches and by receiving and greeting others, let it be known that votes from whatever sources were acceptable—and the implication was that they would be suitably rewarded.

This tactic began to get results at once, much as it annoyed the local party leaders. After the first month, even before Roosevelt began to make speeches, the drift throughout the Midwest was unmistakable—it began to seem that even Iowa might be won, if not for the state ticket, at least for the national one. Farley could see that this was happening; but he was so committed to the state bosses who had delivered votes in Chicago that he simply refused to follow. A curious situation developed. Since he had no direct instructions, Farley went on making the usual promises to his organization leaders. They naturally grew uneasy about Roosevelt's obvious fondness for the Olsons, the La Follettes, the Norrises, and the Johnsons. These were Republicans, even if maverick ones, and they were old enemies. It might be convenient for Roosevelt to have such allies, but what it meant to local Democrats was that their most dangerous opponents were being encouraged to think that the coming administration would be more sympathetic to them than to faithful party leaders. Patronage, favors, and influence were at stake, and the Democrats were resentful.

Because of this, the farm policy speech, set for mid-September, was even more important than it had seemed before. Everyone agreed that it must be devised with care, and the complicated nature of our early approaches to it reflected that concern. It would have been a more consistent and convincing statement if Ray had not had before him as he drafted it several memoranda, and if he had not been so impressed with the conflicting views he felt compelled to reconcile. I myself had backed away from responsibility since we now had such authentic agricultural experts at hand. My credentials, compared with theirs, were hardly recognizable. Besides, I had come to the conclusion that Roosevelt would not make the choice I felt he ought to make.

One of Ray's problems was that Louis had to be appeased with a platform speech, as compensation for his failure to get his draft of the acceptance used at Chicago. It was not enough that Roosevelt had made the "100 per cent" declaration. If the elders were to be reassured, there must be further evidence of loyalty.

Then the formal addresses determined on by Roosevelt had to be drafted. The subjects selected were agriculture (with a separate speech on agricultural credit), the railroads, the tariff, electric power, social welfare, unemployment, and, in a more general way, recovery. Besides these speeches, there was to be another having to do with my favorite theme of interrelations—the concert of interests; still another on the consequences of speculative fever during the boom; and at least one rip-roaring attack on Republican inactivity in time of crisis. Roosevelt determined to make another address specifically for the Business and Professional Men's League for Roosevelt. Finally, he consented to still another to appease Baruch and his friends.

At this stage of the planning, everyone had a say: the politicians, the businessmen, the farm leaders, and indirectly the progressives. This last came about partly through me. I was so close a friend of Bob La Follette, and he had such a lively sense of the possibilities if Roosevelt could be kept to the modernized progressive doctrine, that he made himself the communicator for the whole of the congressional group. It then consisted of some thirty or more representatives who acknowledged La Guardia as their leader and a half-dozen senators who looked to Wagner and La Follette. Wagner, of course, could speak to Roosevelt for himself. Their relations went back to their earliest days in the New York legislature, but Wagner had been unable to modify Tammany's stand at Chicago, and Roosevelt was not inclined to accept him as anything more than an ally for the occasion.

La Follette was different. A more modern and responsible edition of his father, he was just as intense and earnest, just as uncompromising, and just as devoted to a cause far beyond the fortunes of politics. He regarded that art as a way of reaching ends he conceived in apocalyptic terms. If drastic measures were not undertaken, he really believed we might not survive as a democracy. We might well become a dictatorship on the model he could see developing in Europe.

He had no certain faith in Roosevelt and was willing to concede him only as much as he must. But he did recognize the near certainty that the presidency was in prospect, and he felt it his duty to argue for his views with the man who was so likely to be disposing the presidential power. He was as serious and voluble about this as he had been for the past two years in the Senate, where he had sponsored one after another of the recovery and relief measures that had so embarrassed Hoover.

We had been like-minded friends before I had been summoned to Albany, and Bob had taken an almost interfering interest in my relations with Roosevelt from the first. I had not concealed this from Ray or Roosevelt. Both knew of my admiration for Bob and of our close relations. I must say Roosevelt approved them. He warned me once not to forget that campaigns were party matters, but this brought on an exchange that soon departed from the warning note he had intended.

I spoke of the future difficulty he was allowing to develop as Farley cultivated the Democratic organization and he himself encouraged the progressives. He tried to say that all he was doing was making it easy for anyone to vote for him, but this was easily refuted. In the first place, I said, he had been a progressive all his life, and in the second place his devotion to the elders was an expedient one. It was not even necessary any longer. The election was won now, in July, and, I said, he ought to be judging how far he could go in taking the party into progressive territory without incurring reactions that would lose votes.

There followed an hour of conversation I recall vividly enough; one, however, that I cannot pretend to reproduce literally. I made no note of it until afterward. It may be that, at the time, it seemed so intimate a revelation that I ought not to write it down. This had happened on other occasions. I cannot recall whether this was the reason, but the gist of what he said I have no hesitation in certifying.

I said I hadn't supposed that the progressives could command the strength he seemed to think they might develop. Would it follow from disturbances as the depression went on?

He replied that the hard conditions of the past years had softened opposition to welfare measures. It had been made quite clear that the government must intervene. That was progressivism, wasn't it? Besides, he said, the behavior of the business and financial people in allowing the depression to happen and then holding back about every suggested reform had created a climate different from any we had had before. They were no longer respected; they were discredited.

I remarked that he seemed to be speaking as a successor more of Bryan than of Cleveland. His father would have been shocked to hear such conclusions.

His father stood with Cleveland, he said, in an even less advanced position than Hoover was taking now. They stood there all through the depression of 1893 and after. They were wrong. But the trouble with Bryan, and with the populists too, who ousted Cleveland as party leader, was that they allowed themselves to become regionalized. That never worked in America. He'd learned that lesson anyway, he said.

I thought of the way he had established himself in the South and how he called Georgia his "second home." The phrase had meaning, too, because he really had a feeling for the Georgians he had come to know so well.

There would be enough of us committed to new schemes and new responsibilities, he said. We would get at least a third of the Republicans, and we'd get many more Democrats than would be thought now. That was where the La Follettes came in; they would lead the Republicans out of the party and into a new alliance—whatever it was called.

I said I was sure that Bob would ask nothing better, but Floyd Olson seemed to me too intractable. Floyd was a real radical, I said, and I should think a more likely leader in the Midwest. Wouldn't he go further than would be acceptable to any considerable number of the orthodox? Roosevelt had called attention to him by the important speech made in his city. It had been made quite clear that Olson was a friend.

He wouldn't be surprised, Roosevelt said, if Floyd Olson turned out to be his successor. That's what he thought of his political ability. Floyd couldn't be elected to anything beyond his state, or maybe his region, now; but in eight years it might very well happen. He had a strength that neither Bob nor Phil La Follette had, and all the others were too old. He stood out there on the northern plains like a great natural phenomenon. He would become less radical, of course, but what would give him his chance was that so many people would become more radical. He himself, he said, would be a stuffy old liberal by then.

A little later, I mentioned La Guardia. He was not too old, I said, and even the Western progressives accepted his leadership.

He'd be useful, Roosevelt said, and maybe he'd be the alternative to Olson. But Floyd had the stature and he'd grow. La Guar-

dia would be in our crowd, no doubt of that, a big man in his generation—but, of course, for President, he was just a little flamboyant.

I knew what he meant.

In spite of this glimpse of his usually guarded estimate of the
future, I thought that he might be underestimating the violence developing among the disaffected, both in the cities and in the country. It was in view of this sober conclusion that I was so puzzled as
the active phase of the campaign came on.

CHAPTER XXVIII

Diversionary Tactics

When our group came together again in Albany, early in July, and our discussions were resumed, they were mostly concerned with work to be done. But we could hardly avoid our first real embarrassment. There was no getting out of it, two mistakes had been made in the acceptance—but by whom? Ray and I were inclined to look for a culprit. Of course it might have been Roosevelt himself who made the blunders; probably it was; but someone else might have been responsible. We looked accusingly at Henry Morgenthau, who happened to be present at that particular meeting. Then we turned to Sam Rosenman, who had been with Roosevelt on the plane to Chicago and had attended to the last corrections. These, we said resentfully, had been more than touches. But Sam had been working under instructions and could hardly be blamed.

The mistakes had to do with agriculture and conservation, both of which had belonged to my special province, so I felt justified in feeling some annoyance. The agricultural blunder was actually the result of the introductory page that Louis had been allowed to foist on the acceptance. In that page Roosevelt had endorsed the platform adopted by the convention "100 per cent." Yet the platform said that the party condemned the "unsound policy of restricting agricultural products to the demand of the domestic market," and it also said that a Democratic administration would undertake to add to the price of staple products "the amount of a reasonable tariff protection." To make confusion complete, Roosevelt had gone on to say later in the speech that he was sure farmers would agree to reduce the surpluses and make it unnecessary to depend on dumping them abroad in order to support domestic prices. An editorial in *The New York Times* of July 4 had made the comment: "This looks as if he had not read carefully the Democratic platform."

As for the blunder about conservation, it was a much longer story. My own exchanges with Roosevelt on the subject, which included forests, water development, parks, and the like, had shown how much this sort of thing meant to him. He not only looked far back to his service as a legislator, besides recalling his recent actions as Governor, but also wove about the subject many of his hopes for the future. He felt a genuine responsibility for the national estate.

He knew how much there was to do if the resources of the remaining wooded areas, the valleys, and the wide plains were to be protected from despoilers, and how much more if they were to be made properly productive. In several of our conversations he had enlarged on schemes for using the unemployed in much needed improvement work—two purposes to be served at once. Brigades of workers could put the forests and parks in order, thinning, trimming, protecting from fire and pests, replanting cut-over areas, damming streams, developing lakes, making refuges for wild life and facilities for recreation. One of Uncle Ted's claims to a place in history that Roosevelt most envied was that of being first among the conservationists. He obviously meant to outmatch that reputation.

As deputy for this work in New York, he had chosen Henry Morgenthau, and Henry had set up the liaison with the colleges at Cornell and Syracuse. I had not known much about Henry's services until recently. In our early conversations, he had never been mentioned. When I did inquire about his activities, I learned that some of them seemed likely to conflict with my assignment to develop an agricultural policy. I went worriedly to Sam and was told not to give it a thought. Henry was obviously not taken very seriously by the others.

I had never actually seen him before that July meeting in Albany, and now I was curious about him because of what I had been told. He represented a family with a tradition of public service; his father had been Wilson's Ambassador to Turkey. He fitted somewhere into the plans we were making both for conservation and for agriculture, but no one, including Roosevelt, seemed to have anything definite in mind for him. In spite of warnings from the others to leave him strictly alone, I could see no good reason for not getting better acquainted.

He had been traveling through the farm states, interviewing farm leaders and reporting their sentiments to Roosevelt. How he had represented himself I did not know. He had called on Wallace and Wilson, and they inquired of me where he "fitted in." They had heard of his travels from others and they knew of his connections with the Cornell professors. Wallace warned Wilson that this was not a favorable indication for his domestic-allotment hopes; the Cornellians did not conceal their opposition to all such schemes. Was Roosevelt influenced by the Cornell agreement that only monetary measures were necessary? The question worried Wallace, but I could not give him a definite answer. What I did know was that Roosevelt had talked often about means for raising price levels. But I thought this was not, in his mind, a whole program. I could not even say whether he really intended to do any of the things being suggested by the experts.

Whether because he was hostile or because he was not asked, Henry Morgenthau had never before been present at our policy discussions. I was gradually getting used to men of wealth who were Roosevelt supporters, but Henry did not fit this description exactly; he was not a fortune-builder himself, and he was different also in having had a state job ever since Roosevelt's governorship had begun in 1928.

Sam, telling me how dour and unapproachable Henry was, also

enlightened me about an old rivalry between the Morgenthau and Straus families. For several generations each had had a member in public service and had supported one or another party with generous contributions. The Morgenthau ambassadorship was matched by a Straus cabinet position. Henry, Sam said, now hoped to attain the Roosevelt cabinet, obviously as secretary of agriculture. It was a close race, however, with Jesse I. Straus, who had headed the state's relief work and then gone on to organize the Business and Professional Men's League for Roosevelt, and who might well become Secretary of Commerce.

We were still discussing the acceptance. There was a passage in it that had been quite new to me when I heard it in Chicago. I had not asked Ray about it at the time because it had seemed merely a harmless interpolation. It had to do with what Roosevelt had called "common sense and business sense." This, as an introduction, should have warned anyone familiar with such productions —and especially with Roosevelt's style—that what was coming was to be suspected of being neither sort of sense. But what had followed had seemed innocuous and I could not recall whether it had been in the original draft or had been inserted when Sam and Roosevelt worked it over after Ray had left for Chicago. Ray enlightened me. The passage had been wholly strange to him too when he heard it read from the podium:

> We know that a very hopeful and immediate means of relief, both for the unemployed and for agriculture, will come from a whole plan of the converting of many million acres of marginal and unused land into timberland. There are tens of millions of acres east of the Mississippi River alone in abandoned farms, in cut-over land, now growing up in worthless brush. Why, every European nation has a definite land policy and has had one for generations. We have none. Having none, we face a future of soil erosion and timber famine. It is clear that economic foresight and immediate employment march hand in hand in the call for reforestation of these vast areas.

So much I myself might have suggested for the draft, but certainly I would not have let pass without protest what followed:

In so doing employment can be given to a million men. That is the kind of public work that is self-sustaining, and therefore capable of being financed by the issuance of bonds which are made secure by the fact that the growth of tremendous crops will provide adequate security. . . .

Yes, I have a very definite program for providing employment by that means. I have done it, and I am doing it today in the State of New York.

Several things about this evidenced a carelessness inexcusable in a state paper. We had been fearful all along of such lapses, and Ray had taken immense pains to avoid them. Yet here was an example, for one thing, of overparticularization about a subject that could not be reduced to defensible number without elaborate computation. No one could say offhand whether such a scheme could reasonably be expected to employ as many as a million men; it was all too evident that the figure had come out of the air. Then too, there was the affirmation: "I have done it and I am doing it today in the State of New York." There was such work going on in the state, but it was on so limited a scale that to draw on the experience as a national model was absurd. Further there was the argument that issuing bonds to obtain the funds was safe because of the "tremendous crops" certain to result. A person who did not know that forestry improvement was a contribution of one generation to the next, and that forestry income is never likely to equal the expense in any reasonable bonding period, knew very little about practical finance, and Roosevelt had been overseeing public work for many years and had paid meticulous attention to the details of its financing.

To make matters complete, there was the awkward use of words. By "self-sustaining" Roosevelt must have meant "self-liquidating," and by "capable of being financed" he must have meant "eligible for financing" or "susceptible of being financed." Ray never made such mistakes. We hadn't thought Sam did either. It was a last-minute carelessness that ought not to have marred such a paper.

Already it was becoming clear that an opening had been provided for the enemy, and of just the sort Roosevelt's detractors had predicted. We had only to look at the newspapers to learn that full advantage was to be taken of the unfortunate slip. The acceptance had been delivered on Saturday. The following Wednesday we read that the Secretary of Agriculture had something to say about certain passages and that what he was saying had resulted from "several visits to the White House." Anyone with the least political sophistication could visualize easily enough what had happened.

Secretary Hyde had called the Chief Forester, Major Stewart, and asked him if he had seen the Roosevelt speech. The Chief had laughed and said that it was all politics. Instead of being "common sense and business sense" it was a shot in the dark that had missed by a mile. Then the Secretary had said to the Chief, "Give me some figures." Assistants had been called in and some figures had indeed been given; a public-relations expert and several writers had been instructed; and by Tuesday a statement approved by President Hoover had been readied for the press.

It had been handed out with obvious relish; the tone was patronizing. It was somewhat overweighted with ridicule, but ridicule, next to charges of immorality, is the sharpest of all campaign weapons. We read it and shuddered. We knew that Roosevelt had read it in bed—he always read several papers before he thought of getting up. Had he shuddered too? The statement:

> The forestry program of New York, of which Roosevelt so enthusiastically exclaims, "I have done it, and I am doing it today," calls for reforestation of one million acres over a period of 15 years at a cost of twenty millions. It employs 72 men on a permanent basis and the equivalent of 272 others temporarily. The Governor's "Eureka" reduces itself to permanent employment of 344 men. . . .
>
> Forestry as a part cure for the depression is absurd. One man can plant 1,000 trees a day, so one million men could plant a billion. All the baby trees in the country today could be put in the ground in three hours.

There was a good deal more in the same strain. There was, the Secretary said, more to do than planting, of course; there was maintenance and fire protection; but he produced some figures about these tasks too, and they were devastating. Obviously the one public work Roosevelt had spoken of was ridiculously insufficient to be put forward as a cure for unemployment.

On the whole, Hyde's statement was an effective riposte in the manner we had been fearing. Doc muttered about that damned "farm" the Governor was always talking about, and said he'd always known it would get him into trouble with real farmers sooner or later. He was speaking for all of us. We had wondered how the frequent allusions to the Hyde Park operations and those on Pine Mountain in Georgia fell on practical ears—whether growing Christmas trees at Hyde Park and long-leaf pines on Pine Mountain would convince anyone that they were pilot projects for the immense enterprise of relieving unemployment. Doc, as we reminded him, was a little off the beam. Roosevelt had been talking not about his own properties but the state's. Doc thought it was the same thing. Hyde was right; New York was a small and hardly typical illustration.

Here, indeed, was that "well-meaning man without any practical sense" the critics had been talking about. Ray grieved; it would be assumed that he had furnished him with the figures, and so he was involved as well. Altogether, it was not a happy gathering.

When Roosevelt wheeled himself in, he looked around at the glum faces, threw back his head, and laughed. It was *his* mistake, he said; he had had that notion in the back of his mind and had written it in on the plane. Anyway it was not so far off. Besides, he said, people were sick of officials who could only think of reasons why nothing could be done.

The recollection I have of him as he offered this remark is a sharp one, perhaps because it seemed then, and has continued to seem, so characteristic. It summed up one of the political lessons he had learned in his long experience: Offer something and never worry about anyone's checking up on results. He transferred to an arm chair, lit a cigarette, inhaled, expelled a cloud of smoke, and said it in this way:

Yes, it was annoying to realize that you had let yourself go and taken in more territory than you should. It was still more annoying to get caught. But there was this: he was a candidate—and who knew Arthur Hyde? True, he'd overstated the possibilities. But Hyde was throwing cold water on enthusiasm people were waiting for. If he had been in Hoover's place, he'd have taken this on himself. Hoover was an equal. No one would expect Hyde to draw a reply. The thing to do was just forget this. It would lose no votes, not a single one. It would please some people who were against us anyway. but it wouldn't change anyone's mind.

I think it was Ray who asked what there was to do now. Roosevelt said he'd just told us: Nothing! But Ray was not happy, and I could not blame him. Considering the time and effort he had spent on being accurate—researching, checking, consulting—his grievance was just. For that occasion, this was all, but it does remain to be said that it never happened again. In making all seventy of the ad-libbed speeches during the next four months, and making quick and last-minute changes in the prepared addresses, he never again laid himself open to the charge of carelessness or exaggeration. So he was not after all beyond the need of learning. I gathered that there were always lessons and that politicians paid attention.

Some of the short speeches were trivial and trite—at least three of them would follow in that same week; but if they made us shudder, they seemed to please the people in the crowds that Roosevelt faced. If sophisticated commentators tended to sneer at folksy reminiscence and far-fetched allusion, they also tended to catch themselves up for being critical for almost no reason at all. What the commentators really deplored was his tendency on such occasions to say none of the things they hoped he would say. This was an item in our growing difference with our intellectual friends. They were annoyed when Roosevelt spoke to neighbors about old days in Hyde Park or to Albany crowds about being brought by his father to see Governor Morton. But it was not a defensible annoyance and they knew it. Even a candidate couldn't always be portentous.

As for ourselves, we had another and more serious worry, but one we gradually lost. We faced almost impossible difficulties of reconciliation, in regard to such contradictions as had already appeared in the agricultural and tariff issues, both in what Roosevelt himself had said and in the planks of the platform. We did our best, as we went along, to smooth over the contradictions and to suggest compromises. Such efforts found their way into several speeches. But that was our concern; it was not something that Roosevelt lingered over. Our discussions about coming occasions did not result in statements that all of us found appropriate. We had fairly violent disagreements about some of them. Usually the arguments came up or were continued in Roosevelt's presence. He encouraged that and liked to join in. The talk often resulted in repeated memoranda and renewed discussion. Naturally there was in the end some conclusion. After all the talk, Ray would write the speech that had to be made. He then had to go over it with Roosevelt. It was in those cross-table rewritings—and often not until then—that a choice was definitely made. At such times the rest of us were not there to object or suggest.

About the particular issue of the million men in the forests, I noticed that Roosevelt did not forget so easily as he recommended that we should. He explained to subsequent visitors for the next month in what way that number could be put to work. Wallace, visiting him on August 11, said afterward that he had hoped he would talk about other things, not go on with this hopeless argument. What he turned to in further developing the idea was the shelter-belt scheme we had talked about privately and he had asked me to look up. He explained over and over to others how this would not only offer tremendous benefits for the short-grass country but would be an immense field for public work. "A million men," he repeated, "easily a million!"

He did come back to the submarginal-land problem in the Topeka speech—the full-scale treatment of conservation for people as well as soil—but it was a different sort of approach, one we had worked out with care and with meticulous attention to wording; and no reference was made to development work as a field for the unemployed.

About the attack of Secretary Hyde we did nothing. But to the worried politicians Roosevelt said they might issue a statement: they might say that he was a candidate for the presidency, and under no circumstances would he make any answers to charges made by anyone except "his opponent." He knew this would infuriate Hoover, who continued to consider him so inferior as hardly to be taken seriously. But if Hoover had hoped to draw him into a controversy with his Secretary of Agriculture, he was disappointed. Also much of the edge was taken off the Hyde attack by an immediate response made by the American Forestry Association. It was a strong one, even a little unfair to Hyde, and it took us all by surprise. It rebuked the Secretary for "viewing forestry as nothing more than the planting of trees." The association was doubtless made up largely of Republicans, but recent administrations had neglected conservation, and the foresters were irritated.

Our politicians were more pleased when Congressman Marvin Jones volunteered a statement less strange to campaign controversy. Jones was the chairman of the House Committee on Agriculture. He said, through the Democratic National Committee, that the Secretary

> . . . understands more about politics than he does about agriculture. . . . Farmer Hyde has an apparent idea that reforestation consists of going to a nursery, buying a seedling and planting it. He overlooks entirely the problems of flood control, soil erosion, preparation of the soil . . . and drainage.

We did not understand and had not yet seen an example of Roosevelt's best emergency technique. He used it now. If we had taken seriously his admonition to forget what had happened and go on to something else, it was a mistake. He himself had not forgotten. But what he did to smother Hyde, and those who accepted Hyde's appraisal, was what in ordinary conversation would be called changing the subject, except that on this scale, and in these circumstances, that seems a most inadequate description. We did not at first recognize what we were seeing. It only gradually occurred to us that he was carrying out a massive diversion, one of a sort we would become familiar with in the future. He simply overwhelmed the news columns with interesting material. The Hyde attack was drowned in a flood of publicity about other matters.

That morning he had made the announcement that he and "his boys" were going to start next week on a cruise "they had long planned, whether or not he had been nominated," from Long Island Sound up the coast to Portsmouth in New Hamphire. They had hired a forty-foot yawl "because it was cheap," and they would be at sea for about a week.

This was a beginning. It did not altogether smother the attack, but it relegated the echoes to the back pages.

Of assistance also, in changing the subject, was a new initiative on the power issue that I have mentioned already. The Sunday papers published an invitation Hoover must have been very annoyed to receive: to confer on New York State's interest in St. Lawrence power. Federal negotiations with Canada, about to be completed, had indeed ignored the state, and the inference was that this was because New York's power authority was public rather than private.

If this did not suffice for diversionary purposes, there were three homecoming celebrations for the victorious candidate. Much could be—and was—made of these. The first was in Albany and was staged by Tammany allies, Dan and Ed O'Connell, who featured their Albany mayor, John Boyd Thatcher. It would be a torchlight parade and a gathering before the mansion. Since this represented the surrender of a significant segment of Tammany's strength even before the resolution of the Walker case, it had an immense news value. If it was something of an initiative to forward Thatcher's candidacy for the governorship, Roosevelt ignored it. He would take care of Thatcher in due time.

That was on Thursday evening. On Friday he drove down to Hyde Park, where there were two celebrations, one at the Moses Smith farm and one at the big house. The Moses Smith Association was composed of old neighbors, and the celebration made up in picturesqueness what it lacked in size, with the neighbors marching down the long drive with torches and a band. The other, on Saturday, was a gathering of home-towners from all over the old senatorial district: Putnam, Columbia, and Dutchess Counties. These were people who had started Roosevelt off by electing him to the New York legislature in 1910. They would now start him off for the presidency—or do what they could toward that goal—in 1932.

As if all that were not enough, he staged a party for all the headquarters workers in Albany and New York, who had, he told them in a graceful little speech, made it all possible.

These things accomplished, he slept for a night in the Sixty-fifth Street house; and next morning, early, he set sail on the *Myth II* up the Sound in a stiff breeze.

CHAPTER XXIX

Garner and the Deep Blue Sea

🏵 🏵 🏵

After the essential deals had been made in Chicago, it occurred to a reporter in Washington that he might inquire how Speaker Garner felt about the prospect of becoming Vice-President. The reporter went to the Hotel Washington and found Garner on the roof, a place he favored for his postprandial strolls because it offered him a panorama of the city and its many landmarks in the sweep from the Capitol to the Lee mansion. The evening was warm, and the Speaker was shirt-sleeved and in slippers. Asked how it felt to be relegated to second place after having bid for first, he replied, "Politics are funny, son."

He then disappeared down the stairway leading to his rooms, leaving the reporter to make what he could of the remark. Like many of Garner's pronouncements, it was intended to convey the effect of hidden profundities.

Behind the Speaker's façade there was a singularly restricted understanding of the events he was caught up in. He was involved at the moment in a noisy quarrel with President Hoover about the bill to enlarge the scope of the Reconstruction Finance Corporation. Suddenly he had become aware that proposals in the bill had something to do with recovery from the depression, but he was far beyond his competence and had no notion of what to do or say. As yet there had been no Democratic decisions, and so there was no official spokesman. He fell back on the safest gambit in political strategy. He spoke up for the little fellow.

It had worked, and while the bill was being fought over, he developed the theme. By convention time, he had become the determined defender of small businessmen against the Republican giants. To do this he had demanded that private as well as public borrowers have access to public loan funds. He made it appear that Hoover's insistence on confining the loans to banks, railroads, and other public and semipublic institutions was a special form of succor for financiers. Suddenly he found himself receiving strong support from allies quite strange to him. That he should be a hero to liberals was confusing to a lifelong reactionary. All he had had in mind was making rescue possible for his fellow businessmen in Texas. It had not occurred to him that government credit for businessmen was socialistic, but he was being reminded of it now by the amazed commentators.

It was apparent that he was floundering, but he was now officially second man in the party, and it was important to keep him from making mistakes likely to reflect on Roosevelt. If it had not been so late, someone might have been assigned to shepherd him safely through the short time remaining before adjournment. For the moment, however, the Speaker was on his own and was rather set up by the attention thrust upon him as a result of his effort to discredit Hoover. Even Louis had not seen the danger, possibly because he was so exhausted by the Chicago ordeal. The difficulty was that essentially Hoover was right. The RFC was indeed necessary, but it would be a mistake to have it take over the commercial banking business of the country. It was possible to think that credit facilities ought to be nationalized; some of us were quite prepared to argue for that, but this was not the way to do it. It would be competition for the commercial banks, not assistance for them and not an attempt to incorporate them into an integrated system.

Roosevelt was not very worried; he felt that whatever Garner said or did, attention was now going to be centered on himself as the presidential candidate. The Congress would adjourn before long, and with Garner back in Texas there would be less danger of his making some disastrous commitment. He was known to favor several policies that Roosevelt did not accept; he had, for instance, been loudly advocating a federal sales tax. Such a regressive measure typified his thinking, and it would be fatal to have it supposed that Roosevelt favored it.

As regards the RFC, it was quite apparent that Hoover would have his way. The Democratic majority was not large enough to overcome a presidential veto. In view of this, Roosevelt decided to ignore what was going on in Washington. He would keep to old party positions and, in the interval before he started active campaigning, work on the speeches already scheduled. About Garner, he told us with a laugh, he would pray.

Events were to prove, of course, that he had chosen the right path. During the next four months, he would easily manage to attract an attention that obscured Garner completely. That was in the American tradition, which decrees that Vice-Presidents are not to be taken seriously; but there were other situations, less traditional, in which Roosevelt insisted on having the spotlight. Whenever the possibility arose that attention might be directed elsewhere, he found something dramatic that called it back to himself. That summer he was aided by a series of events that gave him a central role. He spoke his lines and played his part with precise and effective finesse. He was dominant in every scene.

The cruise itself was a masterly performance, the more so because, although it was in the news, its significance was not generally appreciated. The shrewder political commentators saw that it was more than a vacation jaunt; they realized perfectly well that it was undertaken for wider purposes. When McGrath of Rhode Island turned up as a visitor to the *Myth II,* they understood that the preconvention stop-Roosevelt bosses were going to "get the treatment." There was still soreness among the Smithites; balm must be applied; it must be made easy for them to put party above faction and set to work for the nominees. "Aren't we all Democrats?" was Farley's plea.

The reporters were also aware that another exhibition of vigor was being made, like the ones displayed in the airplane flight to Chicago to deliver the acceptance speech and in the open house for delegates on the Saturday night after adjournment. Talk about the crippled state of the nominee must be smothered by showing that it did not affect his capability. It was rather prevented than smothered, in the end, with co-operation from almost everyone.

It was easy enough for sophisticated observers to see these intentions behind the ostensible vacation trip, but they had no real interest in conveying this perception to the public. Besides, it was not understood by even the shrewdest that this was the first indication of Roosevelt's competence as an actor on the immense national stage where he now performed. The picture of him that was formed in the public mind would, more than anything else, determine the outcome of the coming election.

Our part in shaping the picture might be small, but we felt a growing sense of responsibility. As his stature grew, it became more and more unthinkable that he should not be able to do what he was offering himself to do. At present the nation was unable to move. If he looked to us for ways of keeping his promise to make it move, we intended to respond. The confidence he radiated must be made good in speech now and in action later. Immediately, we might prevent any embarrassing disclosures of ignorance and avoid any more errors of fact. We might also contribute a mite to victory by showing a candidate who was versed in his lessons. What would clinch the victory would be the confidence voters would acquire, as a result of the campaign, that Roosevelt was preferable as a leader to the man they already had. Neither Garner nor the whole college of elders could have any but a sustaining role in such an effort.

During Roosevelt's voyaging, there were other matters of interest. On his departure, he shared the front pages with news of negotiations about the foreign debts; on the day of his return, he was relegated to inside pages by the adjournment of the Congress. So the drawing of attention to himself was just successful enough: it was not so obvious as to appear unnatural, yet no one could miss it. It was just a little spectacular for one in his position to sail from harbor to harbor in an open boat, but since it was something he often did, there was nothing to criticize in it. The time had not yet come to make any emphatic gestures. It was enough that he should be followed by an eager corps of reporters and that the events of every day should have suitable coverage. The projection was precisely what he wanted it to be.

If the reporters had written their accounts in a slightly different key, there might have seemed to be a false note in this father-and-sons outing. When the yawl was towed out to catch the wind across Long Island Sound, there were hundreds of onlookers. When on Saturday its dinghy brought them to the private dock of Randolph Coolidge at Portsmouth, Roosevelt drove at once to Little Harbor, where a motorcade was formed, and he was paraded to Hampton Beach. Crowds and parades are not a usual part of vacation outings.

In the meantime, each night while the *Myth II* swung on its anchor line, there were visitations. Local leaders were now competing for notice. They were of varied status, but all were anxious to connect with the new source of the power they respected. They made for the *Myth II* in every conceivable craft, shouting across the water, maneuvering to get within speaking distance, and hustling each other out of the way.

One aspect of the week that threatened to spoil its effect was the close pursuit of the Roosevelt party by a shipload of tycoons on the *Ambassadress*. This large yacht had been chartered by Jesse Straus, now functioning full time as director of the Business and Professional Men's League for Roosevelt. Coming and going on the yacht were such unlikely Democrats as Joseph P. Kennedy, the Boston-Irish speculator who was rapidly catching up with Baruch as a manipulator of stock and commodity markets, and who was climbing to new prominence by the use of his millions. There were such others as Will W. Woodin, Dave Hennen Morris, and Joseph E. Davies, all well up in the register of millionaires and not too credible as Roosevelt supporters.

These voyagers on the *Ambassadress* were, however, mavericks in the business world, not subject to the financial discipline that restrained the owners of smaller fortunes or of older inherited ones. Most of the mavericks lusted for the honors that making and having money never really win. They hoped for cabinet positions and would settle for embassies (as five of them did). The newsmen thought it slightly comical to see them ingratiating themselves with politicians to whom they would not ordinarily have given the time of day. For on the *Ambassadress* were also Jim Farley and Ed Flynn with certain of their satellite operators, who would surely have something to say about the distribution of the new President's favors.

Joining the party of tycoons a little late—at New Haven—was Eddie Dowling, who had been impresario for the lighter interludes at the recent convention. Eddie was an entertainer not quite in Will Rogers' class, but still well known; he helped to pass the otherwise tedious hours on shipboard. We heard—though we did not read in the papers—that the anxious millionaires found it hard to laugh; the competition was tough and strange. The reporters enjoyed all this, but knew better than to express their sardonic appreciation. Their publishers were tycoons too.

Not so prominent in the press accounts was another following craft, the *Marcon,* chartered for the reporters. An expedition of the sort might be thought of as an outing for them, but it was work too, for something like a column had to be produced every day. Their favorite subject, though they tried to find others, was Roosevelt's seamanship. It was obviously skilled, because the *Myth II* not only stayed afloat but came to its mooring each night in a safe and usually an appointed place. The technique of this, however, was outside their experience.

Roosevelt had learned the technique in the cold and chancy Bay of Fundy. As a boy he had helped to sail the small *Half Moon* until, as a young man, he had been given the splendid *New Moon* for his own. We had heard him speak of the *New Moon* as the most precious possession he had ever owned. His memory of the polio attack at Campobello was so sharp and painful that he had never gone back there, although it was now eleven years since that disastrous summer. The Campobello house stood empty, and the *Moons* were gone, but the lessons he had learned about coastal navigation were the kind that last. He sat all day at the tiller—captain, navigator, and executive officer—with the young men as crew. The boat acknowledged her master, and the newsmen wrote about this wonderingly. Having been raised on Lake Ontario, which was not an ocean but which offered a little of the same experience, I followed the newspaper accounts with appreciation both for Roosevelt's seamanship and for the political result. No actor could have given a more successful performance.

The *Myth II* had a fine first day. When she tied up at a New Haven yacht club mooring toward evening, Roosevelt stretched, and the boys busied themselves with tidying up and getting ready an evening meal in the galley.

> The quiet scene aboard the *Myth II* bobbing on the sunset waves in Morris Cove was in sharp contrast to the excitement of departure. . . . To the tooting of whistles, the cheers of a wharfside crowd and the roar of seaplanes overhead taking aerial photographs, the Governor at the wheel of the unpretentious yawl steered the craft out through the harbor mouth.*

Morris Cove was for a while disturbed by the arrival of the *Marcon* and the *Ambassadress*, then by the planes of the tycoons landing and taking off. The reporters got a shouted interview with Roosevelt, their stories were sent off, and finally, as darkness came, the cove lapsed into its customary quiet. Meanwhile the crew had a swim, cooked and consumed a steak, and, after satisfying the inquisitive reporters, settled down for the night.

Myth II got underway again early on Tuesday and that evening made Stonington. The *Ambassadress* offered roast duck from her ample galleys, and the voyagers accepted. The boys, being spared the chores of cooking and cleaning up, went ashore in the dinghy, seeking amusement. Jimmy Kieran noticed, however, that Roose-

* This and following quotations are from *The New York Times,* July 12–18, 1932.

velt did not spend the evening alone; suddenly he understood what
was happening.

> Dropping into this quiet harbor after an all-day sail, Governor
> Roosevelt extended the olive branch to Northeastern followers
> of Al Smith.
>
> As his yawl came to anchor in the sunset waters, he met J.
> Howard McGrath, Democratic State Chairman of Rhode Island.
> The Governor said, "I not only understood but admired the loy-
> alty of Rhode Island Democrats to our old friend, Al Smith. I
> am confident they will give me the same loyal support."
>
> McGrath was accompanied by Martin Flaherty, editor of the
> *Providence Tribune,* owned by former Senator Gerry. . . .

Next day, the *Myth II* failed to complete the expected run—
time was wasted in tacking against a northeast wind—and Roosevelt ran her into Cuttyhunk Pond. Then on Thursday anchorage
was found in Sippican Harbor after a day, satisfying to a sailor,
even if frustrating to reporters, in a fog on Buzzards Bay:

> Slipping into this blue-water cove tonight, Governor Roosevelt
> announced that he would ask Lieutenant Governor Lehman to
> take over his tour of the state institutions.

This was recognized as an indirect announcement that he meant
Lehman to succeed him in the governorship. The O'Connells in
Albany, having trapped him into opening their drive for John Boyd
Thatcher, were thus being warned. The trouble was that not only
the O'Connells but the Tammany sachems were involved. This
made it more serious, and therefore Roosevelt was not being belligerent; he was allowing them all to retreat and telling them they
had better. Whatever comes of the Walker case, he was saying to
the Tammanyites through the O'Connells, they had better not offer
a challenge. If they did, it would be met head on. His choice of
Lehman was a formidable beginning. If the Tammany chiefs did
persist, they would violate an elementary rule of New York politics; they would separate the Jews from the Irish—and anyone
who could count knew that the Irish would lose.

Next day the small auxiliary engine pushed the *Myth II* through
the Cape Cod Canal—with cheering crowds on all the bridges and

Roosevelt grinning up at them and waving his hat. All the reporters got that day was a shouted interview in the middle of Massachusetts Bay, with sails again spread and Boston's buildings in
sight to the southwest. Ships were passing on either side, and navigation needed attention.

The reporters would have liked to have answers to a number of
questions. The coming aboard, in the Canal, of Basil Manly had
caused speculation. He was a Washington representative for the
New York Power Authority, and his appearance signaled some action concerning the pending St. Lawrence treaty. Roosevelt, however, had said all he meant to say about that until after the treaty
was signed. Another question: The Congress was in the last days
of its session. Was there anything to be said about the Hoover-
Garner compromise on loans to the states for public works and relief, or about the Home Owners' Bank?

The white hat was waved. It was hard to hear. The candidate
was not going to make any serious answer to megaphoned questions. We were pleased to read about this, and even more pleased
to read about his speech on Sunday at Hampton Beach.

That was an exciting day, and he might have been stimulated to
make a mistake. *Myth II,* blown around Cape Ann by a fair wind
and coming smartly into Portsmouth on Saturday evening, had
been greeted by all the New Hampshire dignitaries, as well as by
Colonel House. They were ready to take advantage of their situation, having no history of opposition to live down.

The sailors stayed aboard that night—or Roosevelt did; the
boys, as usual, went whooping ashore with friends. On Sunday
morning the yawl was loaded to the gunwales with family, and all
of them were taken for a sail. That was the end of the cruise. In
the afternoon a parade was formed at Swampscott that drew practically all the New England leaders. The arrangements were made
by Robert H. Jackson, efficient as always, and the procession to
Hampton Beach was a triumph. When the motorcade passed Little
Boar's Head, Roosevelt had his granddaughter brought out to be
inspected. She was also the granddaughter of Boston surgeon
Harvey Cushing, whose home James and his wife Betsy were using

that summer. It was an expected visit and there were many to wave and cheer. The crowds approved; they were glad to let him know it in the summer sunshine. But everything was preliminary to the gathering at Hampton Beach, where "at least fifty thousand" came to see and, they hoped, to hear.

The New Hampshire Governor, expanding, said into the microphone that it was a fitting occasion. It had been a New Hampshire primary that had first indicated the party's choice. Now here he was in person to make the first of his campaign addresses.

If we had been present, we might have been suddenly afraid that Roosevelt would be moved to make an unfortunate ad-lib. We need not have worried. He had no intention of extemporizing about policy, and he pleased the crowd just as well by resorting to the irrelevant, and perhaps trivial, diversions he often used in conversation. But maybe they were not so irrelevant after all, we thought, reading *The Times*. For what he said was that in New England political speeches were not thought appropriate for Sunday. He would take their presence, he told the crowd, as a friendly greeting for a visitor just come into harbor from the sea.

Speaking of Sunday, and showing how New Englanders respected its decorum, he recalled that his Uncle Ted, when he had been Assistant Secretary of the Navy, had allayed civilian fears by sending a reserve squadron to Portsmouth during the war with Spain. Then, coming to inspect, he had been met by a young volunteer officer. T. R. had remarked that all the ships seemed to be in harbor rather than on patrol. The young man had seemed surprised. "Certainly," he had said. "It's Sunday, you know."

There was more in the same strain, all pleasing to the crowd, even if disappointing to the politicians. Then the thousands resumed their recreations, and Roosevelt went back to Jimmy's house for the night.

Meanwhile, the members of what was soon to be called the Brains Trust had more to do than merely read the papers. While the *Myth II* progressed from harbor to harbor in breeze and fog, while the Speaker and the President wrangled in Washington, while the St. Lawrence treaty reached the final stage of negotiation (it was signed on July 18, but was not to be ratified for twenty years), and while Jimmy Walker prepared his answer to Judge Seabury's charges, we were working on the dozen or more speeches that would constitute the statements of the candidate in behalf of the party.

I wrestled with paragraphs that would state in a simple way what was actually very complex. Before the campaign was over, I hoped that Roosevelt would have said that the depression resulted from the vagaries of an uncontrolled economy whose business operators were driven in individual self-defense—and in what was generally regarded as correct behavior—to ruin the economy and themselves with it. I wanted him to say that our industrial complex could no longer tolerate fierce and free competition among those who sought only to make profits from it, and that, in planning for themselves, they inevitably injured others. From this I hoped he would draw the lesson for his audiences that since we were an organic whole we must plan as one and behave as one.

To the Christian folk at Chautauqua, on June 11, Eleanor had said, gently but literally, that we must take seriously our commitment to one another. I hoped her husband would go further and explain, in economic terms, why this was so.

Not only Adolf, Bobby Straus, Taussig, and I had our assignments; Ray was trying to get useful material from several other sources. None of us was really expert about finance; we needed both academic and technical assistance. As regards insurance companies and railroads, so obviously on the verge of disaster, Ray must find those who could suggest a means for rescue. As regards tariffs, so entangled in both Democratic dogma and practical effect, we must find some compromise.

The hopeless disagreement between the Hull school of free-traders and the protectionists within the party was not the only conflict that embarrassed us. At the moment we were being told that business was improving. The press had long since taken to exaggerating the signs of change for the better and suppressing those reflecting the dismal truth. The signs of better times were false, and Roosevelt must not be misled.

We had Baruch to deal with. His obsession with confidence was rather more intense than that of most businessmen, and we knew he was communicating with Roosevelt, although we did not know with what effect on policy. As yet we had not the information we later acquired about his position in the party, and therefore could not know that one of the necessities was to fend him off without actually rebuffing him. How this was done would make a tale of political craftsmanship, if anyone knew the whole story. At the moment we were only aware that he seemed a sinister influence.

On Monday, July 18, Roosevelt motored back to Albany, arriving late because he stopped for some hours at Colonel House's estate in Beverly Farms. There he sat on the porch and gave ample scope to the photographers, thus underlining his connection with the last Democratic President and flattering the Colonel. Nobody was ungracious enough to recall that Wilson during his last years had exiled the Colonel from his household.

At the mansion in Albany, Baruch was waiting. He stayed overnight. What he and Roosevelt talked about that evening we were not told, but one result of importance to us was the gift to our group—accepted by Roosevelt—of General Hugh Johnson as a companion in our labors. Someone recalled that Johnson had come into Louis' room at the Congress Hotel just behind Baruch and that he too had looked at Moley's acceptance speech, but we had not noticed him then and had not seen him since. It took us some time to appraise the significance of the gift as related to economic policy.

We were learning, however, that politics *are* funny, though we had not yet learned *how* funny. It was some consolation that the author of the phrase was ending his brief time as Democratic spokesman. His greatest display of congressional valor had taken place on the same day that Roosevelt landed at Portsmouth and had received less attention in the press. Adjournment sent Garner home to Uvalde, deep in Texas, where he was heard from only late and routinely on the radio. What he said was carefully written for him to read.

With Garner out of the way—and not yet faced with General Johnson—we had been discussing the lessons to be deduced from the week's events. Our candidate had spoken hardly a word of politics, at least in hearing of the press, and yet the harvest had been immense. We learned from watching. We were not told, but it was clear about Roosevelt that—

1. In spite of his withered legs, he was an outdoor man, capable with a boat and knowledgeable about the sea.

2. He had big sons who liked his company and accepted his discipline.

3. He was the paramount Democrat, ready to receive the submission of all the lesser chieftains, even the formerly hostile ones—and they were coming around.

4. His ties with the old Wilsonians were unbroken. The agenda, interrupted by the World War, was to be resumed under his leadership.

5. He was a Roosevelt, and the parallel with Uncle Ted was underlined. The Republican progressives were reassured.

6. He was religious; he would not make a political speech on Sunday.

It was a good week's work. None of those characteristics or qualities was completely and permanently established in the public mind; the work would have to be done over and over in a variety of ways; but it was the right sort of stuff, pleasing to Louis. It is possible to think that the rapidly spreading approval, soon to become obvious, was given enormous impetus by the cruise. What had begun with the flight to Chicago and the unprecedented acceptance speech made to the convention itself had now a momentum that only inept handling of the Walker case was likely to slow down. We thought it was next on the agenda, but before it came up, we were forced to consider the effect of a new and unscheduled event.

CHAPTER XXX

The Bonus Marchers

❦ ❦ ❦

During that summer of 1932, which was not especially hot but seemed dreadfully long, there were matters without any obvious relation to campaign activities that nevertheless affected them. Some were lingering affairs, lasting for weeks or even into fall, nagging at Roosevelt's mind and demanding his attention. In this they resembled the Walker affair in a less important way. They provided party notables on both sides with worries. If the right attitude toward them was taken, they might in the end prove profitable. But what was that right attitude?

The most difficult problems arose out of the depression, naturally, since it was a sort of miasma that hung over everything. For example, there were strange financial events taking place in Europe; the weird mysteries of international banking plotted in directors' rooms of financial institutions were difficult to understand. Then business failures and massive unemployment in Britain and on the Continent were challenging authority through bands of Black Shirts and Brown Shirts shouting for demagogues, and governments were being overturned. The poisons from these violently bubbling volcanoes were spreading almost daily.

We had no time to study these events, but they portended something. Besides, they had a frightening similarity to occurrences here at home, and ours had begun to have the same immediacy. The weakened economy was collapsing now on people whose outcries were more readily listened to than those of the smaller fellows who had been the first to suffer. We watched the daily and weekly reports from the centers of trade with intense interest and analyzed every new indication for its possible meaning.

By now the millions who had no jobs were in a new stage of desperation. Summer was not so hard as winter; poor rags and work shoes did not have to keep out frost and slush. But food for a family was becoming harder to find; charities were by now practically closed down; public agencies were rationing their meager resources; and it was no easier than in winter to find another place to live when families were turned out of their homes.

What was different now was that the relentlessly progressing deterioration was squeezing many of those who had hitherto been nearly immune. Salaries were being reduced as wages had been, and managers at the secondary levels were being put on part-time. In city after city, public employees were being asked to take a salary cut of ten per cent or even more; in New York they were asked for a month's work without pay. People with debts had no way to pay them and had to resign themselves to the foreclosures of pledged collateral that might represent the savings of years. Graduates coming away from their campuses in May and June soon discovered that there were no jobs to be had and that there was not much they could do but join their fathers, who had nothing to do but sit around a house that was only doubtfully theirs or an apartment whose landlord was demanding overdue rent.

It was this pushing upward of the crisis into income groups hitherto untouched that rang the alarm bells in offices and board rooms. Forced official optimism and the patent playing down of bad news had little effect on the public. There was a darkness closing over the nation that Americans had not been conditioned to endure. Not even a lively campaign was likely to arouse people who had fallen into apathy; nor were promises likely to bring much cheer to people who were homeless.

Quite suddenly, in July, the Republicans became convinced that deflation had run its course and that an upward trend was starting. For a time their optimism seemed about to burst into jubilation. We ourselves were convinced, after intensive study by Adolf, that what they were relying on was no more than a flurry in the stock market, a false indicator of resumed activity. Frances Perkins hinted darkly that the upward flurry might even have been induced. She spoke of those who could still afford to spend something substantial if it would stop the loose talk of reform and reprisal that was being reported to them. Frances, just then, was having a heated controversy with federal officials about the number of unemployed. She had detected shady practices in reporting that resulted in underestimation by some millions. Much to Roosevelt's amusement, her challenge had received fairly wide publicity. It was really a challenge to Hoover himself, who stood sponsor for the figures. Nothing could be better than to have the high priest of figures and reports discredited by a New York State commissioner, and a lady at that. Roosevelt encouraged her; she was having much the best of the argument.

Continuing controversy over such depression phenomena was background for everything else. But there were other events and controversies that dragged along, further disturbing people's minds and adding to the prevalent confusion. Some were gradually concluded, but so many remaining ones were a discredit to Hoover and his Republican legions that we began to feel a furtive sympathy for one who lately had stood on so high an eminence and was now so generally reviled.

There was a corresponding change in the attitude toward Roosevelt. The general judgment that he was no great success as Governor and had shown no special promise of leadership was rapidly being revised. He was now being regarded with respect; what he said and did was being watched for indications of his policies, and even his record was being reassessed. True, *The Times* was not yet satisfied with his pledges, which seemed to the editorialists neither clear nor comprehensive. On some issues he was still criticized for being evasive. It was now generally understood, however, that he meant to do something about the prevalent misery, that he was well practiced in government, and that he had a far more sophisticated understanding of economic problems than had been imagined. This turn had taken place even before he had had much of anything to say except in the mutilated acceptance speech. Regard for him seemed to spread in some mysterious fashion that we tried to explain to ourselves.

Something that had a good deal to do with it, we guessed, was not really traceable to any efforts Roosevelt himself made to impress the public with his prescience; in fact, those efforts had hardly begun. It was more the projection of his personality. Now that he was being watched, he was assessed as a vigorous, mature, and competent public man, one who made no hypocritical pretense of not wanting office, but frankly asked for it, offering himself as an alternative to Hoover. Above all, he was not frightened by the country's plight, but regarded it as a challenge to American ingenuity.

Hoover, it must be admitted, had been Roosevelt's best asset. The judgment that his administration was a failure was strengthened with every passing day. The transfer of his presidential overlordship, the image of authority that Americans seemed to need, was already beginning.

When the false trumpeting of an imminent recovery was exposed by events, as it was certain to be, the confidence of the most convinced conservatives would be undermined. But the decisive failure—and, as I still believe, the symbolic end of his regime— was Hoover's mismanagement of the events associated with the bonus march. People suddenly saw their President as a hapless executive frightened into resorting to violent means when benevolent tolerance was obviously called for. Things had come to be more than he could handle, and he could no longer be relied upon to keep his head.

It was impossible to say how far disillusion with the incumbent government had spread, but a man in Roosevelt's position was bound to hear as much as anyone about the evidence. Tycoons and labor leaders, social workers and philanthropists, clergymen and newspaper publishers, farm organizers and officeholders—these last by the dozens—crowded the Albany mansion and his ante-rooms in the Capitol. The advice they had to offer was sufficiently high-keyed and alarmist, but it continued to be unfocused and diffuse. There was no agreement and actually not much disaffection that went beyond a call for Hoover's defeat. More than anything else, as Roosevelt said wonderingly, his visitors revealed a desire for leadership. Even people who held themselves out to be leaders wanted to be told, wanted to find an authority on which or on whom they could rely.

There were, however, mutterings from both right and left that tougher disciplines were called for. The rightists had taken to praising Mussolini for making the notoriously slack Italian train system run on time, while the leftists were pointing out that there was no unemployment in the Soviet Union. Fascists and communists alike offered order and security to people who were disastrously exposed to the risks of a free economy. Mention of the regimentation that was a feature of both creeds was usually omitted. The really novel feature of the situation was that anxieties were spreading with terrifying effect through the managerial elite. The real sufferers were strangely enduring even when their grievances seemed intolerable. True, the farmers were noisily disaffected, but their demands were for more equitable sharing, not for any deep changes. Such indignation as labor leaders felt was expressed only sporadically. It was now the well-to-do who were rejecting the daily doses of optimism administered by the press and who were growing more and more apprehensive. It was so evident that the unemployed had a grievance! Surely there would be mobs in the streets—and soon.

Against this background, the events—otherwise not so sensational—of the bonus march took place. They were a sort of test for the courage and competence of those in authority, and especially of Hoover himself. He failed dismally.

In other circumstances Hoover's calling out of the troops and their savage repression of the marchers might have brought him extravagant acclaim. Similar actions had done so for other Presidents in other times. When Cleveland in 1895—to mention one instance—had sent soldiers to suppress the Pullman strikers and quite unnecessary battles had followed in the streets of Chicago's South Side, he had been widely praised as the protector of law-abiding citizens. It had been one of the few occasions during Cleveland's second term when any considerable public approval came his way.

In 1932, however, there seemed to be some evil magic at work against Hoover. Even actions that citizens might have heralded as saving the nation from revolution brought him little but criticism. When the more conservative newspapers tried to present the rout of the bonus army as a heroic exploit, their editorials stuttered off into apologetics. Hoover had used a sledgehammer on a fly, and thus he had furnished perfect material for La Guardia, Bob La Follette, and other critics who, on this issue, commanded wide attention. Americans were uneasy, but they were not ready to believe that their government had been in imminent danger of being overthrown by a few thousand indigents who, not so long before, had been praised as its heroic defenders.

When the newspapers first started to carry accounts of the bonus army, late in May, it had reminded us inevitably of the similar march organized by Jacob S. Coxey of Ohio in 1894. That descent on the seat of federal power had petered out on the lawns of Capitol Hill, and Coxey himself had been jailed as a vagrant. Even the hoots and jeers that betrayed the relief felt by good householders had soon disappeared from the front pages. This time the newspapers seemed to hope that the bonus march would have a similar end.

The circumstances, however, were different. Times were even harder than in 1894, and W. W. Waters, the Coxey of 1932, had veterans of a more recent vintage in his army. They had been soldiers no more than fourteen years before. Now they were men in what should have been their busiest and most productive years, and their inability to find any sort of work was a grievance made more acute by recent years of rising prosperity. What they had come to ask for could be made to seem a reasonable request. In 1925 the Congress had "adjusted" the compensation for their military service and had authorized certificates that would be payable in 1945. The veterans were petitioning for immediate payment of an acknowledged but postponed debt; it was hard to picture this as an outrageous demand.

Commander Waters had started from Portland, Oregon, with a contingent of about three hundred men. They had made their way east by boarding freight cars, in the fashion in which tens of thousands of vagrants were traveling at the time. After a brush with railroad policemen in the freight yards at East St. Louis, Illinois, they had been written up in the newspapers, with the result that Waters reached Washington with about a thousand veterans. By that time almost every freight train that arrived in the capital from any direction carried a dozen or more recruits, who dropped off in the yards and began looking for their comrades. Soon there were two thousand, then five, and by July there were at least eleven thousand. They had established a large slumlike community on the flats by the Anacostia River and lived there under self-imposed discipline. When that first site filled up, the veterans found others, including half-demolished buildings on Pennsylvania Avenue, and simply squatted on them. Most of their camps had no water supply, none had more than primitive sanitation, and Washington's summer sun beating down on their tents and shacks produced, almost under the noses of congressmen, Hoovervilles that could not be ignored.

Having established a military chain of command, the marchers dug and filled latrines, served food in military kitchens, and buried their garbage. Other amenities in the camps resulted from the sympathetic efforts of the decent and kindhearted man who chanced to be superintendent of police in the District of Columbia. Pelham Glassford, who had been the youngest and one of the ablest brigadier generals in the American Expeditionary Force of 1918, chose to regard the campers not as tramps but as old soldiers fallen on hard times. He rode among them on his big blue motorcycle, offered them advice, and gave them what supplies he could procure from all the sources he could think of. He was easy and humorous. The veterans regarded him as a friend and protector.

They needed one, because their growing numbers were more and more regarded as a menace. The camp on Anacostia Flats and the smaller ones became more crowded, the days were hotter, and the outdoor plumbing smelled. Other camps appeared in empty lots and abandoned buildings; Commander Waters said that there were finally nineteen of these "cantonments." He also said that there were 23,000 or more bonus marchers, though Glassford thought that 11,000 was a more accurate figure. There was little crime in the Washington streets—much less than in the 1960s—but the citizens were becoming frightened. Bonus marchers were never called citizens in those days. The District Commissioners were not inclined to support Glassford's tolerance, and they finally ordered him to disperse the marchers by a date in the near future. The whole country was watching. It was an intolerable situation, and one that also seemed insoluble.

Only two of the persons in authority thought they knew what to do about it. They needed permission, of course. After an incident or two, which, it afterward appeared, had been provoked, they received the permission. The two were Secretary of War Patrick Hurley and Chief of Staff Douglas MacArthur.

Meanwhile the Congress had been considering the bill that authorized immediate payment of the certificates. It had passed the House in June, but in July it was rejected by the Senate. Members of the Congress then went home and left the problem to others. The marchers no longer had an excuse for staying in Washington, but most of them had no reason for leaving either, and now they had a grievance. Their number went on increasing.

Glassford thought that something more humane was called for than seemed to be contemplated by the federal authorities and the District Commissioners. He conceived the idea of reconditioning an abandoned army camp not far from the city where some sort of life for those who were quite homeless could be organized. Before he could make much progress, the infiltration of real radicals had begun. When John Pace of Detroit, known as an agitator, per-

suaded some two hundred of his fellows to gather outside the
White House, Washingtonians became as hysterical as Chicagoans
had been in 1895. Armed guards were set to watch the White
House, and hasty high-level conferences were held. The threat to
government became front-page news. Within a few days the whole
country was watching the President.

Hoover, harassed by advice from disoriented assistants and impatient generals, could think of nothing better than suppression.
On the morning of the 28th, MacArthur, in the full panoply of his
position, and with Major Eisenhower in attendance, deployed cav-
alry, infantry, and tanks on Pennsylvania Avenue. They systemat-
ically routed squatters from the buildings they had been occupying
along the avenue, then marched in column up Capitol Hill and
went on toward Anacostia. Arrived there, they unslung rifles, flung
tear-gas bombs, and then seized and carted away all those who resisted. The veterans and their families, many of whom had come
along, had to watch the soldiers raze and burn the poor shacks and
tents they had used for shelter.

The roads leading into Maryland were for days crowded with
refugees, herded and harried by Maryland police. Thousands of
them were loaded into trucks and driven first into Pennsylvania,
then westward on the Lincoln Highway. The Mayor of Johnstown,
Pennsylvania, a veteran himself, had watched the proceedings with
growing fury; he now offered a refuge in one of his city parks, an
offer vetoed at once by a fearful city council. Since this was the
only suggested haven for the refugees, they had nothing to do but
make their way to Johnstown, many quite literally starving. Hardly
anyone took pity on them, and soon they would be forgotten in the
press of other problems.

The week of these happenings, the last in July, had been one of
pressures and problems in Albany too. What we knew of the battle
in Washington was what we read in *The Times.* Such warmhearted
spectators as La Guardia, La Follette, Wagner, and many others,
outraged but impotent, told us in detail what had taken place. I
discovered that, despite other matters that would not wait, Roose-

velt had been told too, or had read *The Times* and drawn his own conclusions. On July 29, the expulsion occupied many columns, and there was a whole page of photographs.

On that same day, there was a report of Walker's reply to the Seabury charges, something that must have immediate study. It would be on Roosevelt's desk when he got there. Yet, about 7:30 a.m., when Roosevelt called from his bedroom and I went in, the page of pictures was open on his bed. They looked, he said, like scenes from a nightmare. He pointed to soldiers stamping through smoking debris or hauling resisters, still weeping from tear gas, through the wreckage to police wagons, while women and children, incredibly disheveled and weary, waited for some sort of rescue. In the lower right-hand corner, the victorious general—one of the few in our history who had led armed troops against civilians—stood nonchalantly by a fence, immaculate and smiling among the vagrants, drinking from a cup.

Roosevelt, spreading a hand over the picture page, reminded me that we had been going to talk more about Hoover, but, so far as he was concerned, there was no need now. He ought to apologize for having suggested him as candidate in 1920, although Hoover then had seemed just what was needed. No one else in sight had had so great a reputation. Hoover had run a massive operation; he had shamed generals and lazy officials; he had done what no one thought could be done. He was the world's most admired humanitarian. What hadn't been realized was that the man was actually a sort of timid boy-scout leader. Since he had done so much for people and on so immense a scale, he was supposed to be a kind of superman.

Roosevelt went on to say that the whole country had still admired Hoover in 1928; what he had done in the Commerce Department had been successful; by then he had become the Great Engineer instead of the Great Philanthropist, and that was just what the country needed. He had been the strong and honest man in the Harding and Coolidge cabinets. The contrast with the others in those administrations—except for Hughes in State—was obvious to everyone.

Even when the depression came along, it had seemed to be something that Hoover could handle. This was his specialty, economic management. No one saw the crash as the disaster it turned out to be. But from October 1929 to yesterday, when he had set Doug MacArthur on those harmless vets, Hoover had depended altogether on his business friends. He still talked about principles, and he organized charities, but actually he hadn't done anything that was nearly big enough. Now, said Roosevelt, look where he was. He'd surrounded himself with guards to *keep away the revolutionaries*. There was nothing left inside the man but jelly; maybe there never *had* been anything.

Roosevelt went on to say that his own political problem was smaller than he would have believed before this incident happened. MacArthur and the army had done a good job of preventing Hoover's re-election; if the battle of Anacostia had occurred a little earlier it might even have prevented his renomination. Anyway, the Republicans must know now that they couldn't win.

I made some objection. There were all those registered Republicans; they were pretty traditional. Wouldn't they vote the party ticket anyway?

He said no; this went deep. They wouldn't like to vote for a Democrat, but they would like even less to vote for Hoover now. And his own name was Roosevelt, still almost as much a Republican name as a Democratic one. If he did say so, it stood for energy, for action. He pointed at the pictures in *The Times*, reminding me, as he had done before—pridefully—that during his four years as Governor in a state troubled by depression he had never called out the National Guard. The fat cats had wanted him to, several times, when they were scared, but he never had. His answer had always been that suppression was not good enough.

They'd gone on suggesting that the country was in danger of revolution and that discipline was needed. I asked what he replied to those who said this. He laughed for the first time in that talk. He usually let them go on, he said; if he argued too much with them, they'd go away and say he was a radical, a dangerous fellow. A good many suspected that anyway, but now that Hoover had been frightened by a few poor, unorganized fellows, and the reaction had been against him, there was no need to say any more than had been said by the reporters.

I said I guessed he was right. There was a Hooverville bigger than the one in Anacostia down by the Hudson River just below Morningside Heights. The people there lived on scraps, in shacks built of bits and pieces. Their clothes were rags. But they were too beaten to be dangerous except to health. The difference in Washington was that this radical fellow from Detroit, Pace, had got some of them to march around the White House. Wouldn't people sympathize with the President? Wouldn't they consider him justified in using force?

Not in these times, he said. What Hoover should have done was to have talked with Waters when he asked for an interview. Then when those two hundred marched up to the gate, he should have sent out coffee and sandwiches and asked a delegation in. Instead he had let Pat Hurley and Doug MacArthur do their stuff.

He might even feel sorry for Hoover, he said, if he didn't feel sorrier for those people—eleven thousand of them, the paper said. They must be camping right now alongside the roads out of Washington. They must be sleeping cold. And some of them had families. It was really a wonder that there hadn't been more resentment, more radicalism, when people were treated that way.

Roosevelt smoked. Then he said that anyway they'd made a theme for the campaign.

He wasn't interested any more, he went on, in analyzing Hoover. The man had been turned inside out. Everyone could see what was there, and they wouldn't like it. Neither did he; he wouldn't feel sorry for him even in November.

If Roosevelt had had any doubt about the outcome of the election, I am certain he had none after reading *The Times* that day. But his last word was something to the effect that either Hoover had been very different in the war years or he himself hadn't known him as well as he thought. He was just a bit wistful.

CHAPTER XXXI

The Encirclement of Tammany Hall

❧ ❧ ❧

D uring the early days of August, Roosevelt was again preoccupied with the Walker case, which he felt would largely determine whether he was to carry New York State. Woodrow Wilson, in 1916, was the only presidential candidate since Garfield in 1880 to have been elected without the help of New York. Boss Curry in Manhattan and Boss McCooey in Brooklyn had the power—or so nearly everyone thought—to determine how large a Democratic majority the city would produce. It had to be something like half a million to overcome the usual upstate Republican vote. If it were cut by as much as two hundred thousand, the state might be lost—though after the rout of the bonus army Roosevelt was no longer afraid of losing the whole election. Tammany Hall, the Democratic organization in Manhattan, was quite capable of pursuing its own interest at the expense of the party and had often demonstrated that it was able to carry out its threats. The Brooklyn organization was almost as much devoted to its own special interests.

In the bargaining that surrounded the Walker case, Tammany relied on this complete self-interestedness. Roosevelt respected it, as any politician had to, but the dilemma it furnished was a constricting one, and the signs of his discomfort were apparent not only to those around him but also to the newspapermen and, through them, to such of the public as was paying attention. This accounted, in considerable part, for the insistent demands that he "make a choice." The accounts of his reluctance multiplied. That he would not stand up to Tammany now, the commentators said, was evidence enough that he would never confront his future problems with firmness and honesty. He would always allow his decisions to be determined by expediency.

This was serious. The demands, first of the New York press and then of the national magazines, that he adopt a forthright course on the issue expanded to the same demand on all the issues he confronted or might confront.

He had wanted to feel his way on several matters, such as prohibition and the League of Nations, and he had done so as long as he could, trying to reconcile the extremists with a moderate posture until an acceptable policy could emerge. The pressure for an immediate and irreversible choice came partly from those who were genuinely concerned and partly from those who saw a chance to embarrass him. He had been told that he must say without any equivocation whether he was wet or dry and whether he was for the League or against it. In both these instances, as in others, he had preferred to take his time, work out something new, find some compromise that would soften rather than exacerbate the dispute. He had not been allowed time or tolerance. When he had temporized, his explanations had been badly received, and each of these issues had been used as evidence that he was a trimmer.

That was a bad word in everyone's vocabulary. It was now being used with such effect that Roosevelt could not permit its further spread. He had to proceed in the Walker case as though under a magnifying glass, and no one on either side was disposed to allow him leeway. Either he would act or he would refuse to act. If he acted, he would mortally offend Tammany; if he refused, he would be selling out for the electoral votes controlled by Tammany.

That Tammany had so far been against him was hardly relevant. The question was whether it would sabotage the campaign now that Smith had lost and Roosevelt had won. Betrayal was possible, and Roosevelt, shrewd calculator, knew it better than anyone else; New York's vote might be at stake. It had been lost by Cleveland, another New York Governor, and in circumstances not too dissimilar. To the country, it did look as though he was caught. How could he present the picture of an upright and vigilant Governor and still hope to escape Tammany's vengeance?

The only possible resolution, Ray had concluded, was a full and public demonstration of Walker's guilt. That would close the alternative or, what would be better, force the sachems to admit that in their own interest they had better abandon Walker. This last seemed to be impossible. Tammany might be everything the reformers said it was, but internal loyalty was one virtue it clung to.

As this issue developed during the spring and summer, it had permeated the Albany air, poisoned minds, and diverted attention from important issues at a dangerous time of decision in the party and the nation.

I was instructed by my seniors in our group about the history of the case. It had begun in 1931, and what the public now saw was only its later development. The issue had a background that was determining, but largely invisible. Ray was the only one of us who not only knew all about it but had taken some part in shaping Roosevelt's position. Since he was the Governor's expert on the administration of justice, it was natural that he should have been consulted about procedures to be set up. The Governor of New York State could remove the mayor of New York City not only for misfeasance in office but also for unseemly conduct, and that made Roosevelt directly responsible.

Another difficulty was that the legislature was Republican and that the Republicans were desperate. If they could foment a quarrel among Democrats, it might affect the national campaign; it might even help to divert attention from the deepening depression. That partly explains why the legislature, in 1931, approved a resolution for a complete investigation of New York City's affairs. Samuel Seabury, respected member of the New York bar, had been appointed to head a committee of seven with comprehensive terms of reference. Already he was conducting an investigation for the supreme court of the city's judiciary, and another investigation of Roosevelt's malfeasance charges against the incumbent district attorney, T. C. T. Crain. Seabury was in the unprecedented position of representing all three branches of the state's government—judicial, executive, and now legislative. This established him in a conspicuous position and made him available for any position of trust. He was solid, able, and conservative; he radiated integrity; as a public figure, he represented impartial justice. Attention paid to such an individual, showing him day after day pursuing evildoers in public life, was bound to worry everyone with something to conceal. Also it might create a demand that he himself be a candidate for office.

It was quite certain that Seabury would find Walker's conduct improper, but would it be found that "the little mayor" had broken any laws? If so, everything would be easy. On the other hand, if Walker had done no more than neglect his duties and live a gay and careless life, there would be a difficult judgment to make. Seabury would not have to make it, but by piling up evidence he could force Roosevelt to evaluate and act on it.

What this meant politically had been made clear to me by a small incident in the summer of 1931. Walker, not at all deterred by the legislature's investigation, had gone on a characteristic "vacation" to luxury resorts in Europe. Each day's papers pictured him on one or another Riviera beach, or in Parisian night clubs and casinos. On a morning when he was reported to have been touring Monte Carlo, Cannes, and other resorts, I happened to board a bus on Riverside Drive. The conductor noticed that I was looking at the pictures and leaned across me to look too. With a rich Irish accent, he said, "Now look at that lad—right up there with them counts and countesses. Good as any of 'em!"

I remarked that a mayor of New York, faced with all the problems of the depression, might be home looking after his job. My criticism was badly received. Jimmy was a hero to New Yorkers —a majority of them—and in their eyes he could do no wrong.

I told Roosevelt this little story, and he acknowledged at once that it revealed what he had to worry about. The voters who followed Tammany would be quick to believe that injustice was being done to their Jimmy. Seabury would find that Jimmy had spent far more than his public income. Those many extended journeys to Palm Springs, Miami Beach, or wherever else his sort foregathered—and he took along a large entourage in special cars or trains —were beyond the means of any public official. But if he could show that the money came from friends—even though the friends enjoyed favors from the city—there would be no justifiable reason for dismissal. That was part of Roosevelt's dilemma.

It developed that Seabury had no trouble at all in finding the sources of the considerable sums that Jimmy spent. The question by now was whether they could be connected with city contracts. Walker was getting good advice. His claim seemed to be holding up: the money consisted partly of gifts from friends and partly of profits from their letting him in on business ventures. Some of those profits, however, seemed perilously close to being pay for favors. The publicity about them, beginning in 1931 and running on into 1932, gave added interest to the Mayor's doings. Whenever he went there were cheering crowds. His following grew, and his extravagance became more flamboyant.

Seabury and his assistants continued to dig. As a result of what he told the reporters, New York and the country were being polarized. Seabury too had developed a following; all the respectables praised him. He began to enjoy the image created by the press, and he had so many speaking engagements that it was hard to understand how he found time for his investigation. We often heard Roosevelt speak about his pomposity, his deviousness, and his ambitions. He was mentioned as a presidential possibility—an unlikely one, perhaps, but still the mention was calculated to dismay other aspirants. Prosecutors before him had become national candidates; in this particular venue, Charles Evans Hughes was a recent instance.

Roosevelt was right to be worried. Even if it had always been absurd to consider Seabury as a rival for the nomination, he was still in a position to make the Governor abandon any hope he might have had of postponement or conciliation. Now in August he was being forced to make a choice, and either way he would lose.

The cruise of the *Myth II* had brought the New England Democrats around; even Ely of Massachusetts gave in after some lingering sulks. Hague of New Jersey was persuaded by Farley to reverse himself, although it was a difficult reversal. Hague had said at the beginning of the convention that Roosevelt, if nominated, would not carry a single state east of the Mississippi. It was a threat of betrayal, and he had used it as the basis of his plea for some candidate with a chance of winning. When Farley, however, reminded him sharply that a professional owed his first loyalty to the party, he gave in, thus demonstrating that the New Jersey Irish differed from those in New York City, who acknowledged no loyalty except to themselves. Hague not only came round but did so handsomely. He offered to stage a good old-fashioned party rally at Sea Girt, so that Roosevelt could be formally blessed by the Jersey bosses and commended to the voters.

The situation in New York was more complicated. The party bond was publicly acknowledged by the leaders almost at once— that is, they "heartily" endorsed the Roosevelt-Garner ticket. The sinister overtones, however, were audible to everyone. The rumor was let slip that if Walker was removed, he would be nominated for the governorship. That would be an outright declaration of war—and no one seemed to doubt that if something like this were done, the state would be lost. Almost as bad would be support for Thatcher of Albany to oppose Lehman.

Seabury presented his charges. What was Roosevelt to do? Ray's suggestion of enlisting an Irish-Catholic lawyer of reputation to be the Governor's counsel was enormously helpful. Even if Martin Conboy was a Tammany member in good standing, he was disgusted with Walker and with Curry for supporting him. No better advocate could have been found.

A conversation while these preliminaries were being arranged made a lasting impression. We were supposed to be discussing matters germane to an immediate assignment: the speech to be made about the platform, the one Louis was insisting on. Roosevelt had some difficulty in concentrating; he could not abstract himself from the case of "the little mayor." He spoke of it as an "incident."

I asked why he used that word when the case might very well affect the election.

That was so, he said, but the case would hardly be remembered for a week if he got through it without a knockdown fight. It would be just another in a long list of Tammany betrayals. He said he had good reason to recall Wilson's appeasing habit with the politicians. It had been an unnecessary habit, too. He, Roosevelt, had got caught in one jam when he had run against Gerard in the Democratic primary for the Senate in 1914, and Wilson, being afraid of Boss Murphy, had refused to support him. The way I had heard it, I said, was that he, Roosevelt, had made peace with the sachems too after that. And hadn't Murphy supported him for the vice-presidential nomination in 1920?

Yes, he said, Murphy had certainly done so; but he must say that Murphy was a statesman compared with John Curry, his successor. The present leadership was quite willing to have Democrats everywhere else detest it—in fact, it would rather not be thought a Democratic organization except for convention purposes. The sachems had more power that way. To appease them, any national administration had to pay their price—give them all the New York patronage and risk the scandal that went with it. If Curry had any sense, he said, Walker would have been got rid of long ago. Instead Curry was going to raise the Irish, make the issue one that couldn't be compromised, and then have an excuse for knifing the ticket in the election.

Ray explained to me that the next step was becoming clear. It had to be made obvious that Walker was unfit—so obvious that if Tammany stood by him it would convict itself of protecting corruption. The Governor must be in the position of having absolutely no alternative to removal. Seabury had furnished the material;

Conboy must establish Roosevelt's duty so that everyone could see that he had no escape.

I had the nerve to ask, although it was none of my business, whether this corroding ulcer in democracy was really incurable. It seemed to have gone on, I said, for about a hundred years. For all that time, the same bargain had been demanded—patronage to dispose of for the organization's own purposes, which were oriented to graft and influence-peddling. Tammany's candidates would almost invariably be inefficient in whatever duties they had, and would likely be exposed for taking kickbacks from contractors, selling permits and franchises, and organizing bribery and blackmail. State and national administrations could protest, but the Hall, with votes to sell, could go its own way.

I said something of this, since Roosevelt seemed hopelessly preoccupied with his imminent problem, and we were unlikely to get on with our other business. I asked the obvious question: When he became President, would he be able to do anything about it?

As I recall, Ray intervened. In the drawl he used when he was feeling for the right phrase, he went back to his long study of and experience with city machines. I talked, he said, as though I'd never read Lincoln Steffens or Fred Howe or Brand Whitlock—or Tom Johnson himself. It was a built-in thing, just as all of them had said. The only answer was to keep exposing and reforming. Of course, a strong leader could force them to behave by going over their heads. They were not completely invulnerable.

The Governor had listened thoughtfully. He said hesitantly that after all they did live on patronage—that is, they placed their men so that they could squeeze contractors, businessmen who wanted favors, and even job-holders. But they used a lot of the proceeds to keep their voters in line. They didn't put it all in their pockets. Walker was a kind of exotic. Curious as it was to say so, he was only a front. As I had found out, the Irish loved him; so did a good many others. It was not because of anything he'd done for them; it was his defiance of the better people. He was one of them who had got ahead without being stuffy and self-righteous. His women, his Duesenberg, and his private railway cars—all his extravagances

—were thought of as getting the best of all the respectable people.

Then Roosevelt ventured that just possibly Tammany could be undercut by taking from it the responsibility for the unemployed. What would happen to the organization if handouts didn't have to be made, if it wasn't called upon to take care of Mrs. O'Toole when O'Toole was sent up for thirty days, or to do something for Clancy's boy who wanted a job, or to pay the rent and hand out a few buckets of coal when Scaletti was sick? Tammany might be ruined if relief was really organized. People on relief would have no use for Tammany's services. They'd be independent.

The talk ended on that note. I was too busy then or too much an amateur to realize the implications of Roosevelt's suggestion. We may have mentioned it again, Ray or I; but if we did, I have no recollection of it. I was supposed to concern myself with recovery.

What had been said was no less than a preview of Social Security. It was already lodged in the Roosevelt mind. There were, of course, other reasons for it than its effect in undermining Tammany's hold on voters. But that too was significant. The bosses did not know that their power was in jeopardy, but it was.

At the moment Tammany and the other machines, whatever their future, were an instant problem. Walker had to be dealt with. But Roosevelt was quite right; it turned out to be an incident. He could not have known that, and no one else could, as the drama unfolded during August. But when it was over, it was completely over. Tammany's September aggression—the attempt to defeat Lehman's nomination for the governorship—would fail. Roosevelt would carry New York State by about six hundred thousand votes, and Lehman would become Governor without owing Tammany anything.

The third act of the Walker case developed like a badly planned drama. The first act had been Seabury's investigation; the second, his presentation of the raw evidence to Roosevelt before the convention, and Roosevelt's rather testy request for actual charges; the third cast Roosevelt in role of judge and jury. His office was the judicial chamber, Conboy was his adviser, and John J. Curtin, another Irish Democrat, was his counsel.

Walker had submitted an answer. Russell Sherwood, a figure who had moved elusively in and out of Seabury's grasp, had by now vanished, and Walker was able to deny, without contradiction, that Sherwood had arranged the favors to be offered and had done his collecting as a mayor's fixer. Walker admitted having drawn a quarter of a million dollars from a trading account jointly held with Paul Block, the publisher; he had also sponsored the franchise of an unfit bus company; he had profited largely from a gift of bonds made by a concern supplying the city with traffic lights, and from the contributions of a firm interested in taxicab permits. All this, he contended, had had no effect on his official behavior. That it might have had, he said, was Republican slander intended to divert attention from the dreadful condition of national affairs.

When Walker was summoned to Albany for questioning, he left New York to the cheers of thousands of supporters, and he received a similar greeting in Albany from crowds assembled by the O'Connell brothers. He was escorted to the Capitol in a parade featuring banners with the motto "Walker for Governor." He acknowledged these evidences of popularity by shaking his own hands above his head in the manner of a professional fighter entering the ring.

In the hearing room, however, he was at bay. Roosevelt as Governor sat behind his great desk, cleared for the occasion. Within minutes after opening the proceedings, he took the play away from Conboy and began to ask probing questions that the subdued Mayor had obvious difficulty in answering. Walker had indeed lived carelessly and extravagantly and had spent for his pleasures many times his salary and allowances. Roosevelt pushed him on the ethics of his behavior rather more than on the possibility that it had been criminal.

At the end of this close pursuit, resumed on several succeeding days, it was obvious to everyone in attendance that Roosevelt was closing every avenue of escape and that Walker had no defense whatever. Removal became more and more inevitable. Tammany sought an injunction from the Supreme Court, requiring the Governor to show cause why he should not be prevented from going through with the expected ouster. The grounds alleged were that Walker was about to be deprived of property (his job) without due process (he had not been allowed witnesses or cross-questioning). This interrupted the hearings for a time, but it was ruled that the court had no power of restraint in such a proceeding, and the hearings closed with Tammany dismayed, the newspapers full of praise for Roosevelt's fair but exhaustive questioning and for his stern final reiteration of the rule—first enounced by Cleveland in a similar case—that public office was a public trust, not a bonanza for office-holders.

There was still the disagreeable final act to be got through, but, as it was being prepared on September first, news came to Albany that Walker had quit and fled abroad between dusk and dawn. Roosevelt closed the case without comment. Everything had been said for him; he had no need to gloat.

It was certain that Tammany was sullen and vindictive. Some New Yorkers would be disaffected, but it might well be that the Roosevelt performance had won more votes than it had lost. Tammany might cut into the city vote, but upstate Republicans might again go Democratic as they had done in 1930.

Jimmy Walker may have been only an incident forgotten in larger excitements, but it was one that had consequences (or so I believe) far beyond the considerations of the moment. It convinced Roosevelt that he must rid himself of the constant threat represented by Tammany. This conviction must have been growing in his mind for a long time. In past years Tammany had blocked him once (when he wanted to be the candidate for United States senator), made him knuckle under afterward (when he was Assistant Secretary of the Navy), and had then repaid him whimsically by sponsoring his vice-presidential nomination. Throughout the most difficult months of his approach to the presidency it had opposed him, embarrassed him, tried to force his submission, and it

had even gone on to challenge his leadership in the state by opposing Lehman's candidacy.

He would show Curry, Ely, Hague, Cermak, Kelly, and Pen-
dergast who was the paramount leader in the party. He would steal
their following, force *them* into subordination, make them *his*
henchmen. He had begun to see how it could be done. A nation-
wide system of assistance for those who were dependent on the
mean handouts of jobs, favors, food, shelter, or fuel would bring
the bosses to heel. They could no longer trade help for votes.

He would fix it in an institution so anchored in people's property
sense that no one could take it away. He would substitute security
for insecurity, and so he would defeat once and for all the system
fastened on democracy by free enterprise and its corollary, civic
corruption.

CHAPTER XXXII

The Platform Again

🏵 🏵 🏵

The emphatic preface to the acceptance speech, insisted on by Louis and received so enthusiastically by the delegates, was all very well, but we were certain that Roosevelt himself, and most others who spoke of "100 per cent" agreement, were merely pledging unity for the campaign to come. What, precisely, they were agreeing to they had not really understood. I was still convinced that Roosevelt had not studied the platform and that most others had not even looked at it. Moreover, they had not much cared, and this puzzled us.

We knew well enough that platforms in general were not taken too seriously, but these were special circumstances. The party was striking for victory after long Republican dominance; it had to attract those millions of votes from its adversary, and they would not come easily. It was a time to offer a thoughtful alternative.

Roosevelt's emphatic and comprehensive pledge had seemed unnecessary and even dangerous, and why he did not see it so we could not understand. We had hoped that his affirmation would be forgotten, and we hoped so more anxiously as we studied the platform. The policies we thought he must develop would be badly constricted if it should be taken seriously. Not only that; some of its promises were inconsistent with his expressed views. We were slow to gather that, despite the attempt that must be made to gather votes from the other party, the platform was not to be taken as a binding commitment, as we had feared. We were even slower to understand that Louis' insistence had a hidden purpose. He was still not satisfied that Roosevelt was identified as the elders' authentic representative. Smith had never gained that status, and the party's indifference and slackness in 1928 had been an impressive lesson. Louis meant to see that it did not happen again in 1932.

That neither Louis nor Roosevelt bothered to tell us why there had to be this sort of declaration was probably a fair indication of our position. Roosevelt probably assumed more sophistication on our part than we possessed and thought an explanation unnecessary. We had been concerned until then mostly with relief, recovery, and economic reorganization. There was still an assumption that the political proceedings could be kept separate from our assignment. He had said so to Ray in the beginning, and we had accepted the separation without question. It had seemed entirely reasonable.

That it was patently impossible in a campaign whose pronouncements would be gauged by their acceptability to voters still to be convinced had not yet become obvious. This involved promises; the campaign was becoming largely a contest in credibility, something not yet recognized by the political strategists. They assumed that Hoover was no longer believed or trusted about anything and that consequently Roosevelt would be.

Our situation was determined by what we were supposed to do, which was to produce parts of speeches or the materials for them, to be brought into shape by Ray, who had been around a long time and knew how the politicians thought about things. Roosevelt himself would then cut and add and ornament them to suit his ideas and his characteristic metaphor. The speeches would thus have dependable economic content because we would have done the research; they would, however, conform to the political plan. Roosevelt himself would make any necessary compromises and accommodations.

This scheme was so unworkable that it did not survive the first speech after the acceptance. This was the exposition of the platform, and its contradictions forced everyone involved to recognize that they would have to be dealt with. There were explanations, reconciliations, modifications, and extensions to be made. Ray would have to see that they were suggested and that Roosevelt did not ignore them—or if he did, that he did so knowingly and after deliberation. One of Ray's continual worries was Roosevelt's airiness about such matters. Still he had fair success.

The original mistakes to be dealt with had originated when Louis had conceded that the congressional group should prepare the platform, and when they had engaged the old Wilsonian, A. Mitchell Palmer, to do the drafting. The importance to the Roosevelt candidacy of the elders' support at that early time was considerable. It was notice to party leaders throughout the country, while Raskob was still chairman of the National Committee, that there was to be a change. The elders were leaving Smith for Roosevelt; this involved a separation from the city machines and a reaching for wider and deeper support. A South-West coalition was in the making; it was the needed strategy against such divisions as had disrupted the last two campaigns. They had their man in Roosevelt; they would prepare, and he would expound, a traditional platform.

This had been done to their satisfaction, and the convention had adopted the platform. It does seem a strange suggestion, but if either Louis or Roosevelt had studied it—or even seen it—before its adoption in Chicago, there was no evidence of their having done so. Doc was convinced that Roosevelt's only specification had concerned its length; it should not run to more than twenty-five hundred words. We concluded that this might well be accurate. Anyway, it was a pronouncement that somehow sounded vigorous and even novel without actually being either. Palmer, given the drafting chore, may well have been glad that brevity had been specified. A brief platform might avoid explanations likely to offend many of those who would accept simple declarations of principle.

Roosevelt, with Louis' help, and anticipating what the scheme would be, had made as much effort for unity as had the elders, and his concessions had involved real humiliations. True, the elders had had to come around on repeal of prohibition, so rigidly opposed in the South. This had been essential in extinguishing the issue Raskob and Smith meant to make much of. There were other differences too, such as the one about the tariff, but none that could not be smothered in ambiguous language.

Because his principal was still faintly suspected of collectivist tendencies, Louis was relentless in his insistence on their explicit and repeated repudiation. He had not been satisfied with the simple affirmation in the acceptance; he wanted more; the speech we now had to prepare, expounding the platform and vowing adherence to it, had this as its background theme. Ray's anguish, and especially mine, can be imagined.

It has to be said that the Howe strategy had so far got the results he wanted. The nomination had been extracted from a perilous preconvention situation largely because of closed ranks among the elders; everyone except the Smithites had been persuaded that the Democratic habit of staging a Donnybrook at conventions ought to be forgone in this year of opportunity. There was the best chance in decades to win. It ought not to be sacrificed to indulgence in mutiny.

The elders seemed to be well satisfied. No serious fights had broken out after the Smith-Raskob forces were routed, and now the party organization had been consigned to Louis' guardianship, with Farley as the outside man. It looked as though the campaign might be at least a Democratic ingathering, in contrast to 1928, when all the border states had been lost and even North Carolina and Texas had gone Republican. As things were shaping, no such defections were now in prospect; the local leaders in the West and South were adhering; they were even enthusiastic.

The city bosses were another matter; they still had to be won over. Aside from their support of Smith they had questioned the platform, mostly to make certain that the repeal declaration would be convincing. They knew that the Bible Belt delegates were reluctant about this, but even the western and southern professionals had recognized that a repeal declaration could not lose any votes, since the Republicans, meeting just before them, had already made such a commitment. Even Senator Borah, a sort of test individual, had already admitted that he would have to give in. But if he had not, whom would he support? Or if southerners, with the same reluctance as Borah, were annoyed enough to leave the party, they would have nowhere to go—at least nowhere that counted. (There was a Prohibition Party, but what that alternative amounted to could be measured by the number of votes it was likely to attract. In this election, it turned out to be about twenty thousand.)

Before the convention, and while it was getting organized, the Smith-Raskob forces had made much of the prohibition issue. They seemed not to have grasped the change in climate since 1928. When the convention, to their surprise, had quite cheerfully adopted a repeal plank, and they had no further excuse for remaining sullen and unco-operative because their candidate was unacceptable, they had resorted to the counterfeiting of tickets and the packing of galleries, as well as to blackmail. Repeal had been the grievance they had talked about, but the talk had been largely cover for their frantic effort to defeat Roosevelt. Even after all hope for Smith had vanished, they had persisted.

Despite inadmissible behavior running to refusal of the customary unanimous vote at the end, they had no genuine platform grievance. That being so, Louis had a compelling reason for insisting that Roosevelt reinforce the binding quality of the platform by pledging adherence. Even if Smith remained recalcitrant, his supporters might be lured back into the Democratic house. That was now Louis' aim.

We understood his motives, but we discovered at once, when we began serious study, that the document was certain to embarrass Roosevelt when he began to make public addresses. We set out to make the best we could of its more awkward declarations. Some could be explained away; some could be "interpreted"; some could be ignored; some could be made acceptable if they were enlarged.

At best, however, it was a disagreeable assignment and one Ray was not at all confident would be successful.

Any more of that "100 per cent" sort of commitment would be asking for trouble; that really would make maneuvering and modification impossible. The more we studied and discussed what had to be expounded, the more difficulties we saw. Ray remarked darkly that Louis' continued insistence must be the result of his annoyance that Roosevelt had not taken the whole acceptance draft concocted by him at the last moment. If another speech was to be made merely to appease Louis, perhaps an emphatic presentation of the difficulties might convince Roosevelt that he had better refuse. Without going into any strategic considerations, however, Roosevelt insisted that it had to be done and that Ray had to prepare the draft.

Ray was annoyed about this; otherwise, relations with Louis were improved. Louis himself was deep in preparations for the campaign, and besides, he appeared to be reconciled to having Ray take charge of the "writing department." His earlier fears that his strategy would be departed from were diminished by Sam's departure for the Supreme Court. This disposed of a rival and, as he seemed to think, moved Ray into his own orbit, a thought Ray took pains to encourage.

It is my belief that this particular speech was mostly Louis' production. This may have been because Ray was more interested in the later speeches and already so involved in shaping them, with help from varied sources, that he may not have cared much about the platform speech. Or it may be that my recollection is faulty. Perhaps Roosevelt, for his part, had come to see that he did face a difficulty—due partly to his own carelessness—but could think of nothing to do about it at the moment except to praise the spirit of compromise and emphasize the traditions of progressivism. It may have been that he thought the occasion could be used to begin trimming down some of the platform declarations. I never knew. If either was intended, the result was a crashing failure.

When we met to discuss the speech, he got from us at first a realistic appraisal of the contradictions and inconsistencies. They were so obvious, and the outline of policies he could not accept was so clear, that he would have difficulty in presenting even the most *pro forma* exposition. As I recall, we had reduced the list of contradictions to four:

1. *The Tariff.* The phrase, "a competitive tariff for revenue," achieved in four words the remarkable feat of adhering to two contradictory principles. The "fact-finding" commission, "free from executive interference," must be expected to equalize costs at home and abroad, or alternately, to increase revenues; there would have to be a choice, and the one would interfere with the other. That was not all; there were to be "reciprocal tariff agreements with other nations"; and this seemed to nullify both the guiding directives of competition and of getting revenue.

2. *Recovery.* The first promise about recovery was that there would be "an immediate and drastic reduction of governmental expenditures . . . to accomplish "a saving of not less than 25 per cent." This was to ensure an "annually balanced" budget. But further along, federal loans to the states for relief and public works were also promised, and veterans were to have "generous" treatment. Any assessment of relief—even to ensure minimum needs —would show how impossible an annually balanced budget would be, especially if "economies" were to be depended on for the revenue.

3. *Agriculture.* Farmers were to be aided in getting prices "in excess of the cost of production"; to do this they were to accept "effective control of crop surpluses" so that they might have the full benefit of the domestic market. In another paragraph, however, the Farm Board was condemned for its "unsound policy of restricting agricultural production to the domestic market."

4. *Money.* There was to be "a sound currency to be preserved at all hazards," but also an international conference was called for to "consider the rehabilitation of silver and related questions." How would this be regarded in the old populist country if the first was meant, and what would businessmen say if the second was really intended?

None of us believed, either, that the depression was adequately explained by saying that its "chief causes" were "economic isolation fostering the merger of competitive business into monopolies and encouraging the indefensible expansion and contraction of credit for private profit. . . ."

When we listed the means offered for bringing about recovery, it was hard to believe that they were seriously meant to be taken as a whole:

1. Federal economies amounting to 25 per cent
2. An annually balanced budget
3. A "sound" currency
4. Federal loans to the states
5. Public works "affected with a public interest"
6. The protection of investors
7. Reciprocal tariff treaties
8. Price-fixing for farmers, or getting them "the benefit of the domestic market"

Just the same, Roosevelt pointed out, there *was* a platform, and it could not be ignored or repudiated. We saw that he meant to begin, however delicately, the process of interpretation. As far as the specific issues were concerned, he was obviously not disquieted. He could present the document as a declaration of *intention to act* in contrast to the long Republican hesitation. Besides, he said, if we did not see by now that "a sound currency," a "reasonable tariff," and "unemployment relief" were changing concepts, we had not been listening to our own discussions.

He knew very well that Adolf and I were worried about the inconsistencies, but even more worried by what was left out than by what had been said. There was no mention of the measures we thought indispensable to recovery: massive bolstering of purchasing power and bringing the price structure into balance. Worst of all, there was no admission that large-scale industries were now established and that what had to be done was to make them operate in the public interest. It was an old-fashioned free-enterprise, balanced-budget pronouncement.

Opposition to the Oglethorpe tentatives had been fiercer, evidently, than we knew, although we had reason to suspect that Frankfurter had faithfully transmitted imperious Brandeis objections. Was Roosevelt a progressive or was he not? That was what Brandeis was demanding. Others were asking too—all those who belonged to the cult—and among them was Louis. We were not yet suspected of unorthodoxy. Frankfurter knew that the Oglethorpe speech had been drafted by Ernest Lindley, and as for others who knew about the origin of the speech, Lindley, as a reporter for the Republican *Herald Tribune,* would be identified with the big businessmen—the Owen D. Youngs, the Gerard Swopes, and the others who were writing and talking about industrial councils and planning. That he was following our arguments and was almost a member of the Brains Trust was not suspected.

Louis was still not even aware that a struggle was going on in Roosevelt's mind. He quite certainly thought that the Oglethorpe departure from orthodoxy was owed to carelessness; Roosevelt had let a couple of reporters write a speech for him and had not taken the trouble to correct it. Progressivism to Louis was what it had been in 1910 and on into the Wilson administration.

What resulted from several days of argument was a speech that was for us a defeat. It said much that should not have been said and very little that should have been said—and it set the pattern for the rest of the campaign. The explanation of the depression Roosevelt had discussed with us at such length was completely ignored. The beginnings made in the earlier speeches were abandoned. The Brandeis thesis was accepted and enlarged on.

However difficult it was to explain later, the fact is that we did not conclude that our usefulness had ended with this repudiation. For one thing, it was never stated, never brought into the open for discussion. We continued to argue, and we did have some small successes later on. For the present, however, we were nicely put in our place by an old man who was not yet even visible. It was humiliating, but we were learning to accept large compromises in the interest of having any influence at all.

In view of our objections, it is embarrassing to admit that the speech was generally well received and was regarded as a success. It began on a note that was disarming. "In the quiet of common sense and friendliness," the radio audience was told, "I want you to hear me tonight as I sit here in my own home, away from the excitement of the campaign." Roosevelt was, he said, weighing all the things he had learned from all his years in public service, and he reminded his hearers that those experiences had been many and varied. He had been a legislator in Albany; he had spent eight busy years in Washington and had visited all the states of the Union and most foreign nations; then he had become Governor of New York. He was saying that he was no novice, that he was well prepared for taking hold.

What might be expected to be done if he became President was, he said, outlined in the platform. There would be further specification, but, using the document agreed on by the Democrats at Chicago, he could "state the broad policies of my party." He then read the preamble, emphasizing the condemnation of present "disastrous" policies: ". . . economic isolation fostering the merger of competitive businesses into monopolies and encouraging the indefensible expansion and contraction of credits for private profit. . . ."

This—he went on quoting—represented "an abandonment of the ideals fought for in the World War." Moreover, it had "ruined foreign trade, destroyed the values of our commodities, . . . crippled our banking system, robbed millions of our people of their life savings, and thrown millions more out of work . . . and brought the government to a state of financial distress unprecedented in times of peace."

That all these disasters followed from "monopolization and the manipulation of credits" we would have thought incredible to most of his hearers; nevertheless, he read the indictment in his mellow tenor as though he believed it himself and expected everyone else to believe it too.

To make matters worse—for us—he went on with equal em-

phasis to speak of the alternative offered by the party. He did it as
earnestly as though we had made no objection. The promise was,
he said:

> An immediate and drastic reduction of government expenditures
> . . . to accomplish a saving of not less than 25 per cent. . . .
> Maintenance of the national credit by an annually balanced
> budget. . . .
> A sound currency to be preserved at all hazards; and an in-
> ternational conference to rehabilitate silver.

Nor was he satisfied to let it go at this; he went on to elaborate:

> Let us have the courage to stop borrowing to meet continuing
> deficits. Let us have equal courage to reverse the policy of the
> Republican leaders and insist on a sound currency.

Shades of the populists and all the Westerners! And how could
the Georgians accept this? It was Cleveland's gold democracy, long
ago abandoned. Were we to compete with the Republicans for
Wall Street's blessing? Why choose a battleground where we could
not win? The speech was not improved, either, by pious sympathy
for the unemployed. There might be sympathy, but there could not
be much relief if the platform was taken literally. Recall that "revenues must cover expenditures." It was true, said Roosevelt, that
the federal government would have a heavy burden, but it could
easily save in one place what it had to spend in another. The states
must be enabled to provide for "the needy."

This was some sort of gesture to those who clung to states'
rights; no one knew better than he, actually, that it was completely
unrealistic. *Credits* were no longer of any use because borrowing
power had long since been exhausted. *Grants* were imperative, but
evidently it was not yet time to say so. The strange thing is that
this position was the same one Hoover was insisting on. La Follette, Wagner, and others in the Congress were arguing for grants.
Where had Wagner, for instance, been when the platform was
being written? He was a good enough Democrat.

Roosevelt went on then to the tariff, and on this we seemed to
have made some impression. What he said made some sense de-

spite the platform: farmers and workers in other lands, who lived at lower levels than our own and so had lower costs, ought not to determine the prices of American-made goods. This was to a degree protective, but not to the extent of shutting off trade entirely so that our monopolies could exploit consumers. And it was suggested that about such matters there ought to be negotiation. If trade agreements were seriously sought, the negotiators could arrange for exchanges with mutual benefit.

This position was the result of a long discussion, one that had gone on to consider larger questions of economic relations among nations. Those questions were becoming more acute—although, as Roosevelt told us more than once, foreign policy was almost never mentioned in American campaigns. Still, if Hoover persisted in blaming other nations for the depression, Roosevelt would have to insist that its causes were to be found right here at home.

There was, however, a reference to war debts. Demand was growing more insistent that the Europeans pay back the funds they had borrowed in 1914 and after. It seemed a simple matter to most people; there were debts, and they should be paid. Most people found proposals for cancellation and postponement annoying; the moratorium recently arranged by Hoover had aroused resentment.

If Europeans could not sell goods to us, they could not accumulate funds to meet those debts. This principle of economics was, however, too difficult for the American public to grasp. That was something we regretted because the Republicans were vulnerable here. They had passed, and Hoover had signed, the highest protective tariff ever enacted—the Smoot-Hawley Act—and its effect had been to exclude the imports that might have paid the debts.

These matters might not loom large in the campaign, but they were serious issues and they ought at least to be stated. The paragraphs devised for this speech seemed quite satisfactory:

> The debts will not be a problem—we shall not have to cancel them—if we are realistic about providing ways in which payment is possible. . . . The Republican platform said nothing at all about this; but their position has been the absurd one of de-

manding payment and at the same time making payment impossible.

   This policy finally forced a moratorium as it was bound to do. Our policy declares for payment, but, at the same time, for lowered tariffs and resumption of trade to open the way for payment.

Perhaps I stress this satisfactory passage because the rest was so unsatisfactory, or perhaps because I recall so clearly the way it happened. We had closed an evening's talk without reaching a statement Roosevelt wanted to stand on. He had spoken of the feeling that, traditionally, foreign policy was not campaign material. I wondered whether he might not still have a bad conscience for having abandoned the League of Nations under Hearst's pressure. At any rate he gave us what seemed to be a quite unnecessary lecture about it. The old League, he said, deserved to be abandoned. It had become the agency for European imperialism. Nevertheless, an international organization was needed, and he hoped a new one would somehow be created. This, however, was not the time to suggest it. The national mood was isolationist; the center of interest was our own trouble, and that was what we had better concentrate on. This was especially true since we had Hoover over a barrel. We could insist that the depression was Republican and that there was no intention of doing anything effective about it.

   He would tell us one thing, he had said; if there was any issue the voters were unanimous about, it was that the French ought to pay their war debt to us. The feeling about the British was not so strong, but we still had to watch out for it. Cancellation was political dynamite. We mustn't touch it off.

   This had set me to thinking. I had got up early, and by the time Roosevelt was ready to talk in the morning—sitting up in bed, as usual—I had worked out the paragraphs that now appeared in the speech. We were against cancellation; we thought the debts could be paid, but they could not be unless we allowed the imports to come in that would pay them. It pleased him. It was neat, it was reasonable, and it was simple. He said to tell Ray it ought to go in just that way.

This shows how we had taken to working within the pattern of his judgment concerning what would be acceptable. We had started out to explain things and to deduce from the explanation what ought to be done. We were reduced now to something quite different. We were contriving ingenious accommodations to prejudice and expediency. We might not like it, but that is what we were doing.

There was nothing in this speech that even hinted at the causes of the depression we had discussed so thoroughly and, I am sure, had agreed on. There was nothing in it, either, that suggested the means for recovery we had worked out. The last paragraphs were a reading of the punitive clauses, calculated to focus the disillusionment of the voters on the monopolists and their allies in the government.

The suggested reforms were needed, and badly needed. What was dangerous was that they might get all the attention. The Brandeis group really believed that they were the answer to our economic problems; they would bring recovery, and they would maintain it once it had arrived. We had only to see that competition took place among enterprises strictly limited in size. The hidden hand of Adam Smith would provide that each was rewarded according to his deserts, and also that the consumer, the worker, and the investor would each have his just reward.

I had a shrinking feeling as I listened to the expounding of this doctrine. Roosevelt sounded sincere. I was torn between the hope that he was merely being expedient and the fear that, even if he was, the expediency would continue to prevail.

CHAPTER XXXIII

A Choice of Policy

❦ ❦ ❦

W hat we were justified in hoping was that the platform speech was not meant to be taken for anything more than an affirmation of loyalty to the elders. They had laid down policies, and Roosevelt had accepted; it was not appropriate that he should become assertive and take off on his own—not yet. Ray looked at it this way, fortunately, because practically all the comment and explanation he had assembled so carefully—except for the resolution of the tariff tangle—had been left out. The speech was not much more, he pointed out, than a reading of the document. If Louis had dictated what Roosevelt had read, why worry?

In any case, we had already gone on; we were deep in preparations for the next appearance—at Columbus—and, Ray said, this would tell us more of what to come. Since Hoover had now made his acceptance, contention would begin; first, we must study the pronouncement we had to counter.

It appeared at once that Hoover was going to be busy with apologies. There were disastrous events he had neither prevented nor found a way out of; he could not say much more than that he had done all any President could have done to meet the emergency. He could claim that it had been of overwhelming proportions and had arisen from unpredictable sources. He could say that he was not responsible, but that even so he had labored to fend off the results. Apparently, however, he meant to contend that these sources of calamity were foreign ones; this would be the reason he had been unable to forestall disaster.

Furthermore, Hoover was making great play about his fortitude in having stayed within strict American norms while he was striving to meet the emergency. If what had been done did not satisfy his critics, it must be because they had expected him to go beyond limits he felt obligated to respect, even if they did not. There was, after all, a moral order. "Come what may," he had said, "I shall maintain . . . the sanctity of these great principles under which the Republic . . . has grown to be the greatest nation on the earth."

There was a weakness in this: he was required to make an elaborate exposition of the guiding norms he held to be inviolate before he could establish credit for having persevered in respecting them, and people were no longer in a mood, we thought, for expositions of this sort. They were demanding credible plans for recovery. For beleaguered people the protection of free enterprise was less important, we believed, than checking subsidence into worse and worse economic chaos.

The limitations he had spoken of were not ones we felt Roosevelt need or should respect, even if they were important to Hoover. The President's acceptance speech had a succession of paragraphs intended to show how bold and vigorous he had been, and all began with the phrase, "in accordance with these principles." This, it seemed to us, weakened his whole argument. That he was thus bound opened an advantage for Roosevelt, apparent from the start; Hoover had already exhausted his possibilities. He could appeal only to those who had suffered in one way or another, or to those who feared that their interests might be affected by measures that Roosevelt would take to meet the emergency. He would show that he had gone as far as he could without adopting policies no decent Republican could approve; he bore down hard on what must *not* be done—even if miseries went on multiplying:

Measures taken should be of such character as not to supplant or weaken, but rather to supplement and strengthen, the initiative and enterprise of all the people.

Nor should they relieve individuals of their responsibilities to their neighbors, private institutions of their responsibilities to the public, local governments to the states, or state governments to the Federal government.

The Federal government must insist that all of them exert their responsibilities in full and that programs shall not compete with or replace any of them.

What this came down to was a determination that spending should not exceed income, that credit should be extended only when repayment was certain, that outright grants should not be made, and that "individual initiative" should continue to be relied on for recovery. His most eloquent paragraph was one eulogizing "individualism," and he came very close to claiming that his mighty efforts to encourage private charity, to save businesses from bankruptcy, and then to wait for deflation to be completed were all that anyone could have done without destroying the American inheritance. Moreover, they had been undertaken despite a tradition holding that governments could not be expected to furnish "such leadership."

This last he was entirely justified in saying, if anyone would listen. It was only necessary to recall the course of such depressions as those of 1893 or 1907 to understand that government was not really supposed to involve itself. Hard times, it was assumed, occurred in regular course; they were business phenomena, and businessmen would take care of them. Of course, all they had ever done was to sit them out. The banks had stopped loaning and waited for frozen assets to be liquidated; factories had shut down until they had orders. The unemployed survived or did not survive, meanwhile suffering incredible hardships. Investors lost profits or savings, but workers lost livings; they were the real risk-takers. Eventually bankruptcy, liquidation, and falling prices allowed a hesitant new start to be made; only slowly did activity pick up. It was the part of government to economize, reduce taxes, balance its budget, and worry about the soundness of the dollar. This program was supposed to reassure businessmen and to encourage the resumption of their operations.

Hoover certainly had done much more than this. It was quite true that he had gone beyond the recognized duty of Presidents. If what he had done had not sufficed, he could insist that the responsibility was located elsewhere and that things must not be made harder for those who had to find the way out. Whatever he did, he was obligated to keep business in mind. He recounted with evident pride his extraordinary efforts to help enterprisers through their ordeal.

Beyond this, he went out of his way to defend the protective tariff (he stood "squarely" for it). Then he spoke of himself as a worker for conservation and for peace. He reminded his hearers also that he had made recommendations for banking reforms. So he had, but this was the sort of claim leaders are never allowed unless something has come of it, and in Hoover's case nothing had. The final focus would be on the depression, and he was prepared to be belligerent in defense of his attempts to check it. He was forced to center on this; he had claimed credit for prosperity, so how could he hope to avoid blame for hard times? The cold fact was that, admirable as his principles might be, there had been a disaster just the same. If it was unfair to hold him responsible, that was what the voters were already doing. It might have been effective to blame "blows from abroad" if the country's mood had been a forgiving one, but it was no longer that.

He could see Roosevelt's attack coming, and to counter it he relied almost altogether on this theory of "blows from abroad." By now he had it well worked out. As Adolf said wonderingly when we talked about it, he seemed to believe it himself. We were slow to recognize how adamant his bindings were and how much he needed an excuse.

He insisted that we had been steadily gaining in prosperity after the war until "some of us went from optimism to overexpansion and reckless speculation." In this "mania" we had been like the rest of the world. Then retribution had come—a world-wide slump—no more than the normal penalty for a reckless boom. It

had happened many times before, but we ourselves had always recovered after a "short period of losses, of hardships, and adjustments." In fact, eighteen months ago—that would have been at the
beginning of 1931—a change had clearly begun. Just when everyone was anticipating the arrival of better times, there had been a
new series of calamities. The European governments, not having
economized as they should have done, began to pay the penalty;
one by one their financial institutions had failed, and presently
ours had been involved. Successive "blows rained upon us." Unexpected, unforeseen, and violent shocks brought new dangers and
new emergencies. Revolutions occurred among three-quarters of
the population of the globe; in all these places, dictatorships had
taken over to preserve "some sort of order." His own administration, Hoover said, had defended the United States from these hor-
rors with "the most gigantic program of economic defense and
counterattack ever devised." It was a matter of record that he
had:

> Maintained the financial integrity of our government.
> Co-operated to restore stability abroad.
> Paid every dollar demanded of us.
> Used government credits to aid and protect our institutions,
>   public and private.
> Made certain that none should suffer from hunger and cold.
> Created vast agencies for employment.
> Instituted measures to assist farmers and home-owners.

The recital ended, however, on the familiar note: we had maintained the sanctity, etc., etc.

The strategy indicated for Roosevelt was made more obvious
than ever by this recital. It was only necessary to use Hoover's
own words against him, setting out even more unmistakably his
line of justification and questioning sharply its legitimacy. By now,
that would be mostly a matter of recapitulating harsh comments
from sources other than Democratic propagandists. The New Era
Hoover had once spoken of was generally looked on now as having
been a preliminary to disaster. There were miserable millions who

found his claim that no one had suffered from hunger and cold a joke too grim for anything but sardonic rejection.

Charles Michelson might have been a holdover from the National Committee of Raskob's time, but he disliked Hoover unreservedly. Besides, he was a professional. He found that he operated much more happily with Howe and Farley than he had with Smith and Raskob, and his talent for starting rumor, together with the releases he fathered on various Democrats, produced a continual and devastating barrage. They pointed out every obvious weakness and discovered even more. They allowed none of the Republican excuses.

Michelson's operations were quite independent of ours. We were never consulted, but neither, apparently, was Louis or Jim. Assuming that Charley would do an effective job, they turned him loose to do it. We read the result in the papers, but since it was wholly critical and made no commitments to be honored by Roosevelt, it was not something to be concerned about.

It was still our responsibility to outline a consistent and constructive set of arguments, whether or not they were politically acceptable. Disparagement did not appeal to us much. Even if it discredited Hoover, it was no reason for electing Roosevelt. The indicated strategy for that, we still thought, was to state an alternative program for recovery and to give it a convincing clarity. It would be an extension of the theory, advanced in the acceptance speech, concerning the constriction of purchasing power and the consequent increase of debt as consumers tried to buy the products that, as producers, they were supposed to be making—until finally it had sunk the economy with its massive weight.

We could then go on to counter the "blows from abroad" thesis. This could be done by insisting that the surpluses our industrialists could not dispose of had, by Republican plan, been expected to find *foreign* markets; but since the Republicans' own protective tariff stood in the way of this, buyers in Europe were prevented from paying. Accounts could have been settled only by our purchase of imports now kept out by the Smoot-Hawley tariff. In the short run, of course, Europeans might borrow, and this they had been doing for some time at the rate of about two billion dollars a year. These borrowings were represented by bonds sold to American subscribers. But bonds were debts the Europeans would presumably have to pay; if not, they would have to be canceled— hence default and the moratoria; hence also the loss to our investors. In effect we had made a present of our exports to foreign buyers.

The alternative policy to be advanced by us was one of making it possible for *Americans* to consume the surpluses of our industry and our agriculture instead of presenting them to others. Our people were in extremity for lack of food, clothing, housing; they were unable to buy even these necessities, to say nothing of other goods that they might like to have and that we customarily produced. Furthermore, there was a vast accumulated shortage of public facilities—schools, hospitals, water systems, power plants, post offices, roads, and parks. There had never been enough of these for our expanding population, and there would be fewer if the federal budget should be reduced. Yet such amenities had been lavishly built abroad with funds furnished by American investors and now never to be returned.

Roosevelt, it seemed to us, ought to promise first of all that our idle factories and farms would be put to work and then that Americans instead of foreigners would be made able to buy the product. This in itself was a promise of jobs and of better living. Republican economizing had stopped activity; Democratic policy ought to show a way to start it again. Let us promise that and drive it home! Afterward, we could talk about reform and permanent reorganization.

Ray's organization of the attack on Hoover's theory of the depression was masterly. For two-thirds of its length the Columbus speech still seems to me about the most effective appeal of the campaign. He had Hoover's admissions and his untenable claims, and he had a reasonable alternative theory. Roosevelt made an inspired contribution when, catching the spirit of ridicule and using his expert sense of appeal, he manipulated the *Alice in Wonder-*

land passages suggested by Ray so that they caught the attention of his listeners—including reporters and commentators:

> It has been suggested that the American public was elected to the role of our old friend, Alice in Wonderland. . . .
>
> The poorhouse was to vanish like the Cheshire cat. A mad hatter invited everyone to "have some more profits." There were no profits, except on paper. . . . A puzzled Alice asked the Republican leadership some simple questions:
>
> "Will not the printing and selling of more stocks and bonds, the building of more plants, and the increase of efficiency produce more goods than we can buy?"
>
> "No," shouted Humpty Dumpty. "The more we produce, the more we can buy."
>
> "What if we produce a surplus?"
>
> "Oh, we can sell it to foreign consumers."
>
> "How can the foreigners pay for it?"
>
> "Why, we will lend them the money."
>
> "I see," said little Alice, "they will buy our surplus with our money. Of course, these foreigners will pay us with their goods?"
>
> "Oh, not at all," said Humpty Dumpty. "We set up a high wall called the tariff."
>
> "And," said Alice at last, "how will the foreigners pay off these loans?"
>
> "That is easy," said Humpty Dumpty. "Did you ever hear of a moratorium?"

When this sort of ridicule is happily phrased the effect can go on widening and deepening for some time. The *Alice* passages were quoted and discussed all over the country. It made the Republican defense appear ridiculous and ought to have warned Hoover that no one believed his "blows from abroad" thesis. Doc, for once pleased, said that if no other speech had been made, and if this passage had simply been repeated over and over, it could have constituted a campaign in itself. Cast unhappily in the role of Humpty Dumpty, and being insensitive to public moods, Hoover spent the rest of the contest trying ineffectually to climb the wall again.

The speech was one of the few read in preliminary draft at an evening meeting, and this particular passage aroused some misgivings. Perhaps because it was the first speech, and because we recognized it as one that might establish the tone for all the rest, every phrase was carefully considered. Roosevelt knew that in political appeals matters of style and tone were important, and the rest of us were catching on. Except for Ray, we were amateurs in this; although Roosevelt was not, he listened to our criticisms. Would there be a backlash from the Humpty Dumpty allusion? It was, after all, the President of the United States who was being ridiculed. True, the *Alice* allusion was far less derogatory than the ribaldry that was commonplace whenever his New Era was mentioned or, by now, his "rugged individualism." What made the difference was that Roosevelt was not just a man in the street or a news commentator; he was asking to become President.

The question to be considered was whether a candidate ought ever to risk such a close approach to humor. We had been told that this was one indulgence a candidate could never be allowed; its reception was too uncertain. And ridicule was humor's first cousin, intended to get laughs. It might offend—especially those wavering Republicans we needed so badly to convert. Someone also suggested that familiarity with *Alice* could not be assumed; there must be millions who hadn't read it. Ray argued that if they hadn't read it, they would now, and he thought it would grow on them. Roosevelt was pleased with the fancy and with its elaboration; he had no doubts. So it stood.

The quotations from Hoover, the next most effective passages in the speech, had been available to all of us. They could have been found in a pamphlet I had published that spring, putting together, in a much more academic way, Hoover's defensive claims. It had had a considerable distribution. After I had heard the *Alice* recitation, however, I realized that one short parable could be more effective than logical argument backed by the most elaborate compilations of evidence.

My misgivings about the platform speech were fading. I was immensely pleased now that we had worked out the formula Roosevelt was making his own, and pleased that it lent itself so well to political exposition. The quotations from Hoover's own speeches ran from his early failure to recognize the seriousness of the depression to his reiterated insistence that the worst was over and renewed prosperity was just around the corner. There stood in the background, also, his fatal formula that "we should interest ourselves in the development of backward or crippled countries by means of loans abroad." We were to pay for our own exports. They were gifts—not to the poor of Europe but to European bankers and merchants. This seemed to make the tariff even more offensive. We could do a lot with such an opening.

It was when Roosevelt and Ray sat across the table from each other, a few days or sometimes only a few hours before speeches were made, that Roosevelt's decisions hardened. Ray had been sent back, I believe, to rewrite the ending of this one and had been told what must be said. It was not as we had last seen it, but these final conferences were privileged times, as Ray had told us from the first.

Ray arranged adequate arguments; he gathered the needed material; he gave the man who had to make the speech and father its content ample opportunity to inquire. Now, in anticipation, Roosevelt saw himself facing his audience. What would he say, and how would he say it? Coming in upon him were the arguments we had advanced and the advice that came from the politicians as well as from the businessmen who had an interest in keeping him to their line. This was the time, too, when he summoned up his long experience of other such audiences and his knowledge of what was called for by the tradition he represented. The elders were figuratively at his elbow as he used his pencil. Then too, perhaps above all, this was another step in the process of self-projection. The model of himself that he meant to display was always in the back of his mind; every speech must help to mold the image.

No one, unless it might be Louis, knew even now what the model was, and Louis could only make a better guess because of the twenty-two years he had been associated with its creator. It was not Louis' creation, even though he might consider that it was; but, having seen it emerging slowly in one after another of Roosevelt's decisions, he must have known what shape it was taking. Louis' recent insistence on complete dedication to the platform was only a following-up of something begun long before.

Roosevelt had put Smith in nomination twice, in 1924 and 1928, and had supported his candidacy faithfully. When called on to run for Governor in a year of prospective defeat, he had complied even at the risk of ending his career. Afterward he had chosen party over Smith and had accepted the direction of its elders when they sought a return to an older tradition.

I reasoned, in disappointment, that when he now finally shaped the confrontation with Hoover, he was considering that it ought to represent this devotion to tradition; it should be above all one that the Democrats of the old, conservative school would approve. It was evidently not a time for adventure—not a time to say, for instance, that regardless of fears for the dollar, purchasing power must be massively increased. Quite the contrary; it was a time to say that fiscal responsibility was as much a Democratic intention as a Republican one. Nor could Hoover be allowed exclusive ownership of the individualism Americans were so certain they believed in. So, I gathered, his reasoning must have run.

In the last part of his speech, therefore, both principles were claimed for the Democrats; moreover, it was contended that Hoover's claim was fraudulent. The Republicans said that they believed in balanced budgets, in economical government, and in the freeing of individuals from governmental restraints so that they could act for themselves to bring about renewed activity. But it was easy to show that budgets had not been balanced, that government costs had not fallen but risen, and that the burdens carried by businessmen had become intolerable.

It was easy to show, too, that the "orgy of speculation" preceding the crash had been consistently encouraged. Coolidge, after having been the most enthusiastic encourager, had been shrewd enough to run away from the consequences; Hoover had foolishly boasted that poverty was about to be abolished. Worse, he had spoken of prosperity as a Republican invention; such wonders, he had said, do not just happen; they are planned. The truth was that nothing had been done to check the excesses of the speculators. No objection had been made, either, to bankers' use of their depositors' funds for their own ventures; they had mixed commercial and investment banking and had used the security markets as gambling places. This was the empty prosperity of the twenties, the Republican New Era.

The indictment was easy to make; it was also necessary; and reforms were called for. We all agreed on that. Adolf had furnished convincing evidence, and the conclusions from it were all too plain. But had this been the time for that indictment? Or ought it to have been a separate attack?

At any rate, Roosevelt did use castigation for the ending of this speech. My reservation, that he had started out by telling why the depression had occurred and had not ended by telling how to end it, I had had no chance to put forward. We had gone over the facts; yes, there must be reform, but every one of the indicated reforms could be made without moving the industrial engine off center. We ought now, after countering the Hoover argument, to have offered an opening to recovery. This had disappeared from the revised draft.

Something else about the tenor of the address made me uneasy. This, I had thought, was the opportunity to connect up the new progressivism with the old populist drive. Roosevelt was not a Cleveland Democrat, and the party was a later party—modernized—of farm rebellion and progressivism. Bryan and Wilson had not followed Cleveland in putting fiscal soundness ahead of welfare. They had never expected to be popular among the businessmen; they had never been concerned with "confidence." Balanced budgets and a sound currency were desirable, but in hard times welfare must come first.

Roosevelt was plainly attempting to appear more conservative than the Republicans, and it seemed to me an affront to the rural folk who were in the same sort of trouble they had been in when Cleveland had turned his back on them and Bryan had championed their cause. This policy had gained Bryan three nominations for the presidency from the party Roosevelt was now representing. He had not won, but if it was tradition we were thinking of, this was the authentic one for Democrats.

Roosevelt would have to choose, I thought, between two strains of Democratic philosophy; he could follow Bryan or he could follow Cleveland. I was afraid the elders were Clevelandites. They often huddled with Baruch, Owen D. Young, and such Wilsonians as Newton D. Baker and that stuffy survival, Colonel House. True, these might not like the threat of punishment for speculators, but they would applaud the firm promise of economies and sound money.

What Roosevelt was doing, I soon saw, was avoiding a choice and doing so deliberately. The final passages of this Columbus speech showed what that avoidance meant. He confronted the enemy on ground prepared by the free-enterprisers who wanted not institutional change but merely a purification of the present system. There had been no recognition by Hoover, he said, of unsound policies. No proposal had been made for protecting the investing public. Praise of individualism had been offered, but also policy in direct conflict with it had been followed.

The indictment he himself chose to make was that the individualism Hoover professed was an empty one, intended to deceive. In contrast, he proclaimed in the most resolute fashion that he was the genuine individualist. This did not mean that in the name of such a sacred word (yes, he said "sacred") a few powerful interests should be permitted to make "industrial cannon fodder" of half the population; it did not mean that the people should be "subjected to the ruthless manipulation of professional gamblers in the stock markets and in the corporate system." He went further:

> I dislike Hoover's individualism, not only when it is carried on
> by an unofficial group amounting to an economic government
> of the United States, but also when it is done by the Government of the United States itself.

He finished—I thought lamely—by saying that Hoover's ultimate crime had been untruthfulness. But his own "theory of the conduct of government," he said, "is based on what? On telling the truth." So he proposed a program under seven heads:

1. All securities must when issued carry disclosures of proposed use, of commissions to sellers, and of liabilities, assets, and earnings.
2. Federal regulation of holding companies.
3. Federal oversight of exchanges.
4. More rigid supervision of national banks.
5. The prohibition of speculation with depositors' funds.
6. The separation of commercial from investment banking.
7. Restrictions on the Federal Reserve System.

What had started out as a confrontation on the wide front opened by Hoover in his acceptance speech had ended by proposing reforms in Wall Street—nothing more! It was irrelevant, evasive, and untimely. I was deeply disturbed. I could only hope that I would be given an opportunity to protest again and to recall the centrality of recovery.

CHAPTER XXXIV

Progressivism with a Capital R

🌼 🌼 🌼

My concern was not altogether ignored. Roosevelt did take such pains with my further education as time and opportunity allowed, but I was not an apt student. It is true that I was supported by Ernest Lindley's criticisms, possibly franker than my own. He understood the political necessities better than I, but he still thought they were being given too much weight. Ray may have joined in, for he always encouraged me even when he regarded my objections as inexpedient; but he was so busy, what with speechwriting, liaison with Louis, involvement in the Walker case, and getting from Roosevelt the directions he needed, that I picture him at this time as harassed almost to exhaustion.

The rest of us were concerned enough about Roosevelt's journey to the West Coast, next on the schedule, but Ray was positively appalled by it. Serious statements of national policy would have to be made before immense audiences on subjects Ray had only recently become familiar with; his material had to be gathered from the various experts who were asked for contributions and, with some assistance from us, related to other issues; then it had to be put in political idiom. Finally his draft had to suffer hasty revision after Roosevelt himself had made his corrections.

The railroad speech, for instance, first drafted by Adolf after consultation with Joseph Eastman and James Mehaffy of the Interstate Commerce Commission, as well as with Ralph Budd, William Woodin, and Averell Harriman, had yet to be put in final form by Ray himself. All the material he gathered was no more than the raw stuff he had to work with.

Then again, in the Pacific Northwest, Roosevelt meant to make much of the demand for public power so important there. Ray knew very little about it, but others were available who did—James Bonbright of Columbia, for instance, who was a member of the New York Power Authority and a willing collaborator. Perhaps most complicated of all was agricultural relief. What would be said about this had by now become so confused that the speeches to be made in the Midwest had taken on the proportions of a major enterprise in persuasion. Besides these, the tariff must be dealt with in some fashion—we hoped with more logic than had yet been displayed; but since there were disagreements in the party that seemed impossible to reconcile, there were likely to be unpleasant repercussions whatever was said.

None of these issues, however, could compare with the difficulties surrounding the depression, with its accompanying unemployment and its intolerable dislocations. What was most important to be said about this, it was agreed, was what means for recovery should be advanced; still, beyond recovery, I was disturbed by the disorientation of economic enterprise that made any suggestion for merely starting up again in the old ways seem more and more absurd. I continued to wonder whether Roosevelt meant to stand on the shaky pronouncements of the Columbus speech. The irrelevant detour in the final paragraphs made everything more difficult. He had still said nothing about what could be done to end the depression or even about what should be done for the unemployed while it continued.

In his midsummer work, Ray had the help not only of Adolf and myself but also of Bobby Straus. Bobby, aided by Ray's pleasant paragons, Celeste and Annette, had taken over most of the letter-answering. There was the difficulty that most of the mail came either to Albany or to the political headquarters. Such of it as seemed to have more importance than could be acknowledged by a few neutral lines in reply was laid aside for us, and we had to devise answers, usually for Roosevelt's signature, taking care to keep everything bland and neutral. Bobby inevitably had a residue of suggestions, schemes, and complaints he felt ought to be passed on to Ray or me, and we had a few that Roosevelt himself ought to see. The stacks of various communications grew and grew as the campaign progressed. The attempt to reduce them occupied many hours that could have been better used in other ways. Despite everyone's efforts, the mansion in Albany became a vast litter of papers in piles that never seemed to grow smaller.

The Business and Professional Men's League for Roosevelt had its office on Madison Avenue. About this time, however, Bobby used the league's funds—which were being supplied mostly by his father—to hire a suite in the Roosevelt Hotel, and our New York operations were gradually concentrated there. Bobby went back and forth to Albany with us and was present at many of our evening meetings, behaving as a modest junior, but often making intelligent and useful suggestions.

Ray and I had spent the few days preceding the platform speech, and those immediately after it, continuously in Albany, and we were there too while the Columbus speech was taking shape. Despite the activities around us and Roosevelt's preoccupation with the Walker affair, there were occasions when we returned to the subjects we seemed never to settle. Roosevelt, it could be seen, was still turning over at some level of his mind questions having to do with the calamity of depression; they troubled him, as well they might, and in any case he could see that I was dissatisfied. At unexpected times he himself went back to the causes of depression and asked for further evidence or made some tentative suggestion. I recall several conversations even this late about oversavings and the shortage of purchasing power, theories we had discussed at length in the spring. Both Adolf and I kept talking about the massive numbers of unemployed and the inadequacy of the means being considered for relief.

Occasionally Roosevelt went back to the subject of disproportions in the price structure. He spoke with continuing curiosity about corporate concentrations and about the burden and distribution of debt. Adolf had been all too realistic about this, as about the frozen assets of the banks and the virtual bankruptcy of the insurance system. We kept saying, however, that everything depended on making a start toward recovery; it was the first consideration.

That he should have gone on exploring matters he had no intention of bringing into the campaign was evidence of his confidence in winning and of his realization that once he was settled in the White House these issues would be his responsibility, and his alone. He was getting ready—although we could see that he had not made up his mind where or how to begin.

It is perhaps overblown to speak of a struggle for his mind. Still, that is how we spoke of it then. We had made a good start during the spring, but all the signs seemed to show that the struggle was going against us now.

Ray was convinced that we were contending with Brandeis' influence. But there was not merely a choice between free competition and collectivism. There were other alternatives, and all had advocates with formidable claims on Roosevelt's attention. There was, for instance, the business solution, represented most intrusively by Baruch and Hugh Johnson, but often supported by other callers at Albany or Hyde Park, including Owen D. Young, Jesse Jones, and Joseph Kennedy. These financiers and industrialists continued to argue that confidence must be restored by economizing and by balancing the federal budget. (Confidence, in this usage, came to be regarded among us as one of the most annoying words in the language.) Then there was the advice that kept coming to Roosevelt through Henry Morgenthau from the Cornell agriculturists, Warren and Pearson. Their childlike faith in managing the price of gold seemed hardly worth serious refutation; yet it remained one of the proposals we knew was continually being urged on Roosevelt. The Cornellians were never visible in Albany. Roosevelt was conscious that if they had been, the inference that he meant to cheapen the dollar would be made immediately. But

even though Warren and Pearson were absent, the hungry look in
Morgenthau's eyes spoke of their readiness to rescue the nation
from its troubles.

I cannot now separate the occasions when talks about these
matters took place; there were several late conversations when the
coming and going had subsided and the mansion had taken on the
stillness of any other old house in summer, its windows open, the
heavy curtains stirring, and occasional night sounds coming in
from the street.

Once or twice Roosevelt departed from his rule and made at
least some explanation for my benefit. I am puzzled now when I
try to recall where Ray could have been. He was not usually there,
and I cannot tell why. Of course, in our more technical discussions, he was habitually restless. He was, as I have said, terribly
tired by now, and his attention was scattered among discrete matters that he must reduce to some sort of manageable order. When
we went on and on with our talk, he often dozed or went upstairs
to nap. Considering how remarkably well he put together a dozen
important speeches in the course of a few weeks, he must have
found a way of sorting out what was useful and what was not. This
concentration may well have diverted him from the further issues
we were intent on settling—the ones that went beyond the campaign and had to do with potential presidential actions rather than
with a nominee's appeal. On the other hand, he must have thought
they diverted us from labors more helpful in his immediate tasks.

Not until the campaign was virtually finished did he ask Adolf
to summarize and look ahead in a memorandum. This turned out
to be mostly unfinished business, an elaboration of suggestions already made but not found useful in the campaign. He did not need
a memorandum from me. I was always available—and always urgent, I am afraid.

I was never encouraged to think that what I had to say was the
only opinion he heard. It was consistently given some weight, however, by his knowledge that I did have some support. He believed
that I spoke for the La Follettes, Floyd Olson, and a considerable

number of other progressives; and it was true that I had discussed
with them more or less fully the same issues he must settle. He
continued to call them my "radical friends," but he did it with
affection. Of all his political contemporaries, I am sure that these
were the ones he regarded as most like-minded. He too had chosen
to be a progressive, and the years had confirmed the wisdom of his
choice. His liking for them was reciprocated; they always spoke of
him as one of them. They made complaints, but these were obviously about an erring brother. If he felt they could not be depended on as followers, he recognized that he could not have been
depended on either in similar circumstances.

I suppose the La Follettes and their collaborators might have
been called collectivists, taking collectivism to mean the opposite
of competitive enterprise. They believed, however, in proceeding
from where they were, not in starting over after some revolutionary change. They advocated, or at least favored, public ownership
of facilitating industries such as communications, power, and
transportation—and perhaps of banking, insurance, and the like—
activities long since grown beyond any limitations of state or region and, moreover, certain to be more efficient for their purpose if
allowed to find their optimum size. They were not doctrinaire
about this; they knew that if the railways were taken into public
ownership, the same people would have to manage them. The only
difference would be their freedom from the harassments of those
who shared Brandeis' objections to bigness.

I felt that Roosevelt, moreover, had generally accepted the in-
evitability of collectivization and that he thought the suggestions I
had made for the necessary devices and agencies would be a start
in an inevitable development. He had even improved on these in
our discussions. What I was doing was to make the best argument
I could when he seemed overcome by his instinct about the conservatism of public opinion and was convinced that he should go slow
in furnishing leadership. This was reinforced by the Brandeis arguments, and Brandeis had impressive credentials as a progressive.
To call him an antediluvian was to challenge a tradition. That sort
of challenge did not bother the La Follettes, who had left the tradi-

tion behind long ago. I always had to acknowledge that most of my progressive friends were not Democrats, or at least not ones accepted by the elders; and what I seemed to be arguing for was something that my friends were not eligible to press and that I could not say would be politically acceptable; very probably it would not.

This was a disadvantage, but it was not the important difference; there was something deeper, something that had emerged into the open in the Columbus speech. Roosevelt might have come to the conclusion that the nation must now be organized to function as a whole; I thought he had. Nevertheless, he drew back from it, whether from an understanding of the elders' conservatism or from an unwillingness to depart from the Brandeis imperatives.

He was certainly being told that individualism was so much the American tradition that no other basis for economic behavior could be taken seriously. This led to the persistent vision of a nation whose businesses were small. They would be forced to compete by enforced antitrust laws. It was assumed that smallness would keep them fairly equal in bargaining strength. Merging and meshing, guiding and relating, all called for in the collectivist scheme, and all difficult to manage satisfactorily, would simply be prohibited, and prohibition would be the only duty of government.

This was not what Roosevelt's mind told him must happen. He could see well enough, I was convinced, that the time for that sort of industrial disorganization was past, but he had beliefs that were inconsistent with collectivism, and he, like everyone, had to find a resolution for the war within himself. He considered that men's characters were involved in working for their livings and their families, and that it would be fatal if they found that they could live without this rule. Because of such attitudes, and the corollary assumptions about economic motivation, he found a collectivized society something to be anticipated with an emotional dread.

He never said this, exactly; on the contrary, he was able to—and sometimes did—make the case for collectivism with impressive logic; I might have been listening to Bob La Follette. More

than once I recalled my years with Simon Nelson Patten, the
teacher who had anticipated emergence from one era into another;
he had used the terms "deficit" and "surplus." When Roosevelt
had been learning from his Harvard professors that scarcity activated enterprise, Patten had been introducing me and my fellow
students to very nearly opposite doctrines at the University of
Pennsylvania; it was abundance, Patten said, that was being
reached for. I told Roosevelt of Patten's objection to the classical
theory—that it depended on bitter struggle, miserliness, unemployment, low wages, and long hours of work. He was intrigued; if he
had ever heard of Patten, he had forgotten it.

I told him how on one occasion Patten had publicly encouraged girl workers in Philadelphia not to save their pennies, as they
were advised to do, but to spend them for silks and satins and per-
fumes if those were what they most wanted. It was spending, Patten told them, that kept the economic system going, as well as giving the spenders satisfaction. The newspapers had made much of
his subversive talk, and the university's banker and lawyer trustees
had been so scandalized that they had forced the old man into pre-
mature retirement. But Patten had not retreated. Prosperity, he insisted, came not from saving but from the spending that sustained
production. When purchasing stopped, so did the economic machine.

Patten had not really been trying to instruct his affluent contemporaries. He had wanted to reach the young generation. A regime
of scarcity, where emotions and morals lingered, was one that
made penny-pinching a virtue; but this involved scamped social facilities and stifled research. Scarcity also justified Marx; wealth
had to be equally divided because there was so little of it. Marx
had never understood the dynamism of an industrial society. His
doctrines were extensions of classical English economics. I pointed
out that Hoover's views came from the same source, and that because of them his policies were appropriate to a vanished age. The
alternative was the acceptance of a new economics. He, Roosevelt,
ought to offer it; how could a dialogue be carried on if there was
agreement on policies? If there was agreement, Hoover would get

the best of it. Who would believe that he had been unfaithful to individualism and free competition?

I went on to argue that a punitive program for bankers was an avoidance of the lesson to be learned from the depression; indeed, it denied that any lesson was to be learned. People should be told that what they had was precisely the kind of atomized and risk-filled system speculators thrived on; it was one that could be kept off balance; it gave them opportunities for manipulation. Stability and continuity would make life hard for these gentlemen, but it would increase the security of those who were exploited. Why not expound this while so many were suffering from the hard times brought on by free enterprise? If the depression was not a conclusive argument for collectivism, there never would be one.

Of course, if he insisted that character was involved, if a man's morals and those of his family would be impaired by having an assured income regardless of his ability to get and hold a job, and if this was to determine policy, then no real change was possible. But also, if that was so, we could not expect to go forward into a world of increasing productivity. If the need to earn a living in a world full of risks was a necessary discipline, we ought to stop substituting power and machines for the labor of men. This was where progress came from.

Since he was evidently enjoying the discourse, I went on to explain Patten's theory that emergence from the era of "scarcity" into that of "surplus" was correlated with the conception that people moved away from pain and toward pleasure. These were terms borrowed from Jeremy Bentham, but that had been the language of his time. What he had meant was that we either accepted or did not accept the conditions for progress. If we persisted in holding to moral imperatives inconsistent with our productive technique, we would be unhappy—and crippled. Periodically, we would have hard times; we might even move backward toward the older society that relied on the need for misery. It would seem more virtuous.

Many of those who called themselves progressives, I argued, were actually—and literally—reactionary. They did want to go back to a time when there had been little shops and factories, little towns and independent farmsteads. People then had scrimped and saved; they were narrow and hard; they had grasped for profit; and when they had seen a chance, they had ruthlessly exploited their employees, their competitors, and the consumers of their goods.

If we wanted to go forward, we had to give all that up and accept its opposite. Most of all, people had to see that they could be free from want if they gave up believing it to be necessary. Continuous good times were possible not in a world of Scrooges but only in one committed to use of the surplus they were now able to produce. Men need not earn their bread by sweat; powered machines would do it for them. And they must not be told it was wicked to eat when they had not labored.

Roosevelt's comment was that the theory I was being so eloquent about was one that most of the people he knew would reject. We spoke of this at some length. I recalled Henry Ford's famous initiative in doubling the pay of his workers to make better customers of them. Yes, he said, but every other employer in the country had been furious for fear Ford's action would be used against them in their own wage disputes. As a precedent, it had largely failed. Most employers had gone on opposing their workers' ambitions, convinced that high wages would eat into profits and limit expansion.

What he said about general beliefs was true. It would be hard to find many workers who had any such view of the system as I was suggesting. They fought for wage increases only because they wanted to better their own situations, not to establish the conditions for continued prosperity. Unions even opposed unemployment insurance, old-age pensions, and other measures that would support the economy.

No, Roosevelt said, shaking his head, the exchanges in this campaign would be couched in well-understood terms. He himself had to be ultrasound; that is, he had to speak fondly of economies and balanced budgets, of work for all, and of rescue for bankrupts and protection for small investors. To my objection that these were what Hoover was claiming as particularly Republican virtues, he said that this was good because the claims could be shown to be false. The Columbus speech had begun to say that Hoover had not really economized, that he had even been extravagant, that he had not balanced budgets and reduced taxes—and this was the line Roosevelt was expected to follow. A candidate might surprise the voters, but he must not shock them.

I recalled an example he was fond of citing—the new Department of Commerce building in Washington. He had attacked Hoover for its extravagant size. Actually, I said, it was a very useful facility; more such appurtenances were needed, not fewer. No, he said, it was the sort of symbol everyone would recognize. It exposed the falseness of Hoover's pretense to prudence. It showed that he was no economizer.

On other occasions when I complained about his failure to persist in making a rational explanation of the depression, and said that because of this he could not offer any means for recovery that were believable, he said that I didn't understand about educating people; a campaign was not a dialogue or a program of adult education. It was a fight for office, and he meant a *fight.* A President, he repeated, could educate in the interest of his program, but a candidate had to accept people's prejudices and turn them to good use.

Hoover, he insisted, had left himself open, and it was possible to indict him in his own terms; that is, he had not done what he had promised to do. Four years ago he had been elected by that enormous majority because of those promises. Now he was vulnerable. Most people still wanted what they had not received. It wouldn't do to forget, he said, that a lot of Republicans had to be convinced that he would do what Hoover had not done.

He went on to say that all those people believed what I was saying they oughtn't to believe—in saving for rainy days, in being frugal and working hard, in every man's being responsible for his family. It took longer, he said, than people had yet had to learn the lessons of this depression; it was still the general impression that Hoover and his business leaders—the Republican elders—had mismanaged things and had not lived up to their own professions.

There was nothing wrong with the professions. People believed in them.

He did not stop there. Bob La Follette and Floyd Olson—yes, and Wheeler, Wagner, Costigan, and La Guardia—called themselves progressives, as I did. All of us, he said, might or might not make good our claim to the title, since we differed so much from the old breed. But if we did succeed, it would be because he had created a situation to be worked from, and because we had stuck with him. He might even get ahead of us, but he didn't intend to say so. There would be reshaping, but it would be slow, maybe, and not exactly to our plans, mine and the rest. He wouldn't be surprised if even Bob and Floyd deserted somewhere along the line; he'd even bet that they would.

But, he said, he would tell me one thing: "I'll be in the White House for eight years. When those years are over, there'll be a Progressive party. It may not be Democratic, but it will be Progressive." *

I still did not know what he meant by "progressive," although he evidently meant it to have a capital *P*. I thought afterward that maybe it ought to be given a capital *R*. It might be simply Rooseveltian.

Still, I recognized that he had made a sort of promise to escape from the elders in due time, to take possession of the party organization, and to turn in new directions. Whether he would return to his "bold experimentation" was not a settled matter, and neither was the question whether he would use some of the devices that we had been talking about. But I could hope.

---

* I have quoted this sentence because my recollection of it is precise. It made an indelible impression.

CHAPTER XXXV

Lessons in Politics

🏵 🏵 🏵

Before the speech at Columbus on August 20, there were many very important people on the list of Roosevelt visitors. Besides those who had been voyagers on the *Ambassadress,* there were others, equally well known to the financial pages and among the corporate reports, who were noticed by the reporters. Ray had some contact with them. When he needed information for speeches, the person who had it might be asked to come and see Roosevelt. Since it seemed more and more likely that he might actually become President—something until now hardly credited among the business elite, who had been estimating the odds about as Mencken had—pride was being swallowed in large doses and approaches were reluctantly undertaken. Some business leaders, if they were not invited, took the initiative themselves. They were well aware that Roosevelt was about to begin an exposition of the issues and make a statement of his intentions about them; they wanted to influence what he said.

An observer like myself could find amusement in these pilgrimages of the mighty. Roosevelt himself was inclined, in private, to be not only amused but caustic. He had been regarded very lightly by these same persons not long ago. Their attitude had been pretty much that of the *Times* editorialists, who had withheld approval until there was more than a suspicion that Hoover's discredit might have dissipated the Republican majority. Quite suddenly it became obvious that, unlikely as it had seemed, Roosevelt was marked for the presidency. Many of the mighty persons who now sought him out were known to him from the past, but they had shared Hoover's estimate of his abilities—or that of Ogden Mills, or again, that of Walter Lippmann. It was painfully evident that their capitulation was reluctant. But, as Roosevelt remarked with a grin, it was now beginning to be mentioned that he had had respectable business and legal connections.

Associates at Carter, Ledyard and Milburn, the Wall Street law firm where he had been a clerk until he had left to run for the state senate, Langdon Marvin, whom he had joined as a partner in 1921, and such officers of the Fidelity and Deposit Company as Van Lear Black—all were individuals no one could find objectionable. All were staid and conservative, and more was made of this, suddenly, than was warranted. Roosevelt's rather bizarre adventures in business just after his defeat in the campaign of 1920 seemed to have been forgotten; anyway, no mention was made of those escapades; nor did anyone recall such gubernatorial policies as his support of public ownership of electric power, once taken to betray a socialistic tendency. Roosevelt remarked that there was a lot of wishful thinking in the upper class. It amused him to receive its emissaries, and of course he treated them as old friends.

Our Roosevelt roared with laughter when he read that Theodore's widow was annoyed by confusion among the voters. She was getting a fair number of letters indicating that the Oyster Bay branch was not clearly distinguished from that at Hyde Park, and that Franklin was thought to be a nearer relative of theirs than he was. She had a son, Theodore, Jr., who might aspire to the presidency as the legitimate successor to his father. He had already made a creditable record in Puerto Rico and the Philippines. True, he had not held any elective office, but he had more claim to one than Franklin. Take it all together, the Oyster Bay branch was infuriated by the Hyde Parkers' replacement of themselves. It was illegitimate.

This bothered the Republican politicians too. They had the widow make a public announcement that Theodore was neither father nor uncle to Franklin, but only fifth cousin, and had her state that she and her family intended to vote for Hoover. Plans were made for her to appear at the notification party and be introduced to the assemblage. The distinction was to be made plain.

Still, if the Hyde Park branch had not yet produced a president, it could hardly be called disreputable. James, Franklin's father, had been a promoter and capitalist himself, and the family fortune was mostly invested in the securities of the railroads James had shared in promoting. Franklin might not be safely conservative, but to call him a radical was to judge that he had repudiated not only his family tradition but Groton, Harvard, and the Columbia School of Law—not to mention Carter, Ledyard and Milburn, the Department of the Navy, and the Fidelity and Deposit Company.

Except for the twinges caused by his power policy, men of importance had had no reason for alarm because of his behavior while he was Governor. His efforts to help the farmers, his recommendations about conservation, and even his welfare proposals had been no more than a continuation of Smith's policies. When he had needed a director for his Temporary Emergency Relief Administration, he had chosen the head of the Macy empire, Jesse I. Straus, who, in accepting, guaranteed the soundness of the Roosevelt attitudes, and who later found a good many generous contributors for his Businessmen's League. They were men of wealth who recognized the inevitable somewhat earlier than their contemporaries. If disillusion with Hoover had seriously eroded Republican support, it would only be prudent to ensure against change as Straus had done. The later-comers had given up only *in extremis,* but men who claim to be practical are sometimes actually that. These were. They had not suddenly seen how admirable a statesman Roosevelt would be; they simply made a practical accommodation.

Roosevelt was acutely aware that if he was to be President he would be dependent on the operating organizations of the economy. Steel had to be manufactured, railroads had to run, commerce had to flow, and consumers had to be served. Even the power companies could not be taken over and run without the present managers, since there were no others who had the capability. Even if the properties should be expropriated, that would still be true—as he pointed out to us, pretending, for the moment to be an expropriator.

He had a deep annoyance with the bankers, especially those with international connections. This extended more or less to the whole financial fraternity. He thought that much of our trouble could be traced to the financiers. He knew a good deal about this from his own Wall Street experience and was finding out more. What Adolf dug up, and laid out so lucidly, confirmed his own more haphazard—and now out-of-date—information. The heart of the managing complex in New York, the place where capital was gathered and distributed, where values were registered and price policies determined, had been seized by well-dressed bandits who recognized no responsibility beyond that of quick and large profits. They had speculated with other people's money. They had exploited the greed and the hopes of those who trusted them because they were big, powerful, and ruthless. This he believed.

He believed also that all this was known or at least suspected now by the millions who had lost so much in the resulting debacle. Most of those who were now coming to see him could be assigned only minor blame in these operations; many were also critical and recognized that reforms were overdue. Some had said so. What they feared now was a general overhaul directed at the business system itself, rather than at those few who had insinuated themselves into its managing complex and taken advantage of its opportunities for profit. They hoped Roosevelt saw it as they did and would be "reasonable." They were trying to find out what he intended, and they hoped, as well, to be the men who gave him advice. One of their handicaps, the most serious one, was that they had no suggestions to make that were consonant with the magnitude and complexity of the crisis. Sticking to "confidence" threatened to become ridiculous. The notion that "confidence" would suffice had already been contradicted by Hoover's strenuous measures, especially the Reconstruction Finance Corporation—although, to be sure, Hoover himself still talked of initiative and self-help. That was all very well for a beaten politician, but any sensible businessman could see that changes were inevitable.

Most of the mighty came away encouraged from their talks with Roosevelt. He had a great deal more actual knowledge than they had been led to believe by commentators who had been picturing him as a dilettante. His appreciation of the complexity and delicacy of business problems surprised them. He knew that there had to be a means of gathering and distributing capital, and he knew that the productive apparatus could not be managed by amateurs. It was absurd to suppose that he had the wild notions attributed to him by the Republicans.

His way of dealing with mighty persons was to enlarge on their own suggestions. Because he would listen, interrupt, and then run away with the conversation, they were apt to think he had agreed with them when he had only meant to indicate that he understood. Some, when interviewed after seeing him, interpreted his views in this way. This misunderstanding had its dangers. As time went on, more and more of them thought they had been deceived and were filled with angry resentment. Sam Rosenman expressed the wish that he could warn the pushy ones; they should be told that what seemed like consent was only a pleasant conversation. Sam had had more experience with the Roosevelt method than the rest of us, but all of us were catching on.

I noticed, if no one else did, that those who were the first to come and the most eager to co-operate were those who had for some time been talking about planning, about general or overhead direction, about reducing the risks of competition, about order and system in industrial affairs. Many of them already had their own mutual arrangements, and the Oglethorpe speech had opened the prospect of legal authorization for such arrangements, now very doubtful. Some realized that understandings among industries for reducing competition would have to have governmental supervision. Roosevelt could talk with them knowledgeably because of his experience with the Construction Council; he knew all about trade associations and expressed some wonder that they had not made more progress during Hoover's presidency.

What he heard from certain of those who came to see him—especially such prominent businessmen as Henry I. Harriman, president just then of the United States Chamber of Commerce—was much like what I had been saying. This was not strange, since I had had some exchanges with Harriman myself. These had had more to do with the domestic-allotment scheme for agriculture than with the organization of industry. Harriman was one of M. L. Wilson's enthusiastic recruits; he was quite convinced that recovery would have to start with the rehabilitation of the farmers' fortunes—but the general principles involved were obviously the same. We had gone on to talk of an adjustment mechanism for industry, and he was eager to join in devising one.

Not only Harriman but also Gerard Swope of General Electric, Fred I. Kent, the banker, the presidents of several railroads, and some other industrialists saw that business had dug the pit into which it had fallen. It was not Hoover's "blows from abroad" and not the "aftermath of war" that had to be blamed. These were, after all, circumstances that should have been foreseen and provided for. The management of investments had borne no relationship to their supposed function, but only to the gaining of individual and temporary profits. There must be changes in the economic order of the sort called for by the national interest.

In a few instances I was present at these conversations. Ray, because he was digging for information, sat in on more of them or talked separately to more of those who were consulted. I had some reason, I felt, for encouragement. There was a strain of collectivism in the exchanges that seemed to point in the direction I wanted Roosevelt to follow.

Roosevelt certainly saw a fairly representative roster of those who directed vast industrial organizations with headquarters in New York, Chicago, Philadelphia, and Detroit. Some of these visits were reported by Ernest Lindley, James Kieran, Charles

Hurd, and other reporters assigned to Albany and Hyde Park, but a good many were missed because of precautions taken by visitors uncertain about the approval of their associates.

This sort of thing, coming to the ears of others who had the deepest suspicion of Wall Street or who had made a political career of attacks on just such people, produced very strong reactions. I heard from Olson, La Guardia, the La Follettes, and some of the others. Roosevelt heard from them too, but, as he said, none of the protesters had ever run anything but a political organization; put them in a factory or a bank and they would be as helpless as children. He was going to need some practical advice.

On most weekends he went down to Hyde Park, as he liked to do. These were brief visits, but long enough so that new adherents of this sort could come to see him in semiprivacy. Some came on Sunday afternoon, after the services in the small church to which he was so attached and where he had been so long a vestryman. Some escaped the reporters' notice altogether.

Every appearance in public—even his travels—I now understood, was calculated for its effect. In a way it was the man Roosevelt I was watching, but in a more important way it was the Roosevelt who for years now had been Governor of the Empire State and was about to move on. Albany was an anteroom to the presidency. He was progressing in due and regular course to the place of power, and now he had to face his responsibility. Such an expectation, or at least such an ambition, had been held by many hopeful politicians. If matters arranged themselves favorably, they succeeded. In spite of the grossest ignorance of presidential duties, both Cleveland and Uncle Ted had moved up from the governorship, Cleveland at a time when Republican postwar corruption had opened the way, and Uncle Ted by the accident of McKinley's death. Others had failed, lacking the necessary skill or having no luck. Franklin had the skill; it looked as though he was having the luck. He meant to be a better President than either Cleveland or Uncle Ted. Meanwhile, he had to appear vigorous and trustworthy.

The parallel with his successful predecessors was developing very well. When Uncle Ted was yearning toward Washington, the way had seemed blocked and he had been forced to maneuver through the vice-presidency. He might have been permanently sidetracked if it had not been for an assassin. He had not been favorably regarded by the powerful of his party, and his vice-presidency had been intended to get him out of the governorship and into the well-fenced environs of the Senate. When McKinley lay dead and T. R. was being sworn in, he had affirmed that he meant to submit to the party elders; he had learned by then that to go on he had to make a show not of Rooseveltian drama, but of loyalty, even humility. If he was to have a nomination of his own when the time came, he would have to overcome the dark suspicions of such McKinleyites as Mark Hanna, who had said to his confreres that now they had done it—that damned cowboy was in the White House!

Franklin, I knew, was letter-perfect in the lessons of T. R.'s career, and I understood that by careful cultivation of the powerful, and the even more careful assumption of loyal attitudes, he had made progress toward a presidential posture. But the compromises needed to get the nomination had been damaging; the Walker case had so far been hurtful; and he had given no reason for confidence in his ability to meet the complex and demanding tests of national leadership in a time of terrible strain. This was what he had yet to achieve.

It was in this that we were meant to be of use. He must display a knowledge of the national economy that explained its breaking down, and he must promise reactivation. But also he must lead people to believe that he knew how to make the economy work when it was reactivated. If the banks were failing, it was because they had been mismanaged; if the farmers were in trouble, it must be shown that he understood where the trouble came from and how to cure it; if industry and the facilitating services were paralyzed, he must offer plans—not merely ideas—for getting them going again and keeping them in motion.

He had worked at his exploring job now for some four months in the midst of incredible distractions. It remained only to make the final decisions and to shape the discourses that would explain and convince. We knew now what we were supposed to contribute. It was not what we had thought at the beginning, or what many of those who might have been included in our small circle would approve. Some had withdrawn because of this; they had found they could not dictate policies. More had simply not been asked for further help because they failed to grasp the limitations of "advising." We had remained because, under Ray's tutelage and with advice from Doc O'Connor, we did come to understand and to accept. If we continued to press a point of view, it was one that we had reason to think he was willing to consider further.

In my case it was something more than this—a good deal more—and in the months of this spring and summer I had come to recognize it. The fondness I had for all the scenes and circumstances in which my life had been passed, the respect I felt for the institutions shaped by the generations before me, the democratic faith I had been bred in—all this was for me, as for so many others, symbolized by the presidency. I was fascinated by it and wanted nothing better than to improve and enlarge it. Roosevelt was moving toward it. For me, withdrawal was impossible.

Even if I now had become much more aware of the contrivance and maneuvering that made Presidents, I still held the office in awe. Hoover was certainly not a Grant or a Harding. He was indeed an admirable man, but he had refused to use governmental powers as they must be used in crises. He had even delegated them—following Republican tradition—to those who had no claim to share them and who would not use them for the general good. What this meant to me was that I was obliged to help in Roosevelt's cause.

Still, I could not so quickly give up the habit of my profession. I watched with the most intense interest phases of the developing campaign that I had little to do with. The policies Roosevelt was moving closer to—that is to say, the policies necessary for getting the largest possible number of votes—were all very well, but I still fought rearguard actions. I had softened—though not, I must say, unconsciously—but I was, as I can see now, ready for the lesson I was about to be taught, the most important, I suppose, of my experiences in the spring and summer activities.

I mention a particular journey of Roosevelt's to Hyde Park because I can see now that it helped to prepare me for that lesson. I did not go with him, but I saw him go and was there when he came back. Although these comings and goings were kept informal enough, the ceremonial quality could not be quite extinguished by his boisterous manner. The limousine with its several motorcycle outriders—state police—waited in the driveway. The reporters made a watching circle, along with others who had been with him until the last minute. He was wheeled down the long ramp, calling gaily to the reporters, saying what a beautiful summer evening it would be going down the Post Road along the river, telling them he would see them when he got back, but not in Hyde Park tomorrow—he was staying only for the day.

Gus Gennerich, almost his shadow, was there, but Earl Miller, the other familiar watcher, was not. Roosevelt beckoned, and I helped Gus lift him into the right-hand corner of the open car; he settled his old Stetson, allowed Gus to arrange the admiral's cloak over his shoulders, whispered to me that next time I must go along, waved, and was gone in the sharp clatter of the motorcycles. I guessed that one reason for these trips back and forth was that he escaped for a couple of hours, passing through a countryside where he knew every hill, every wood, and every house. Each bend would open out a landscape that pleased him, and when he came to the gate at Springwood, the long driveway would run through the fields he had played in and the trees he had climbed as a boy. His oldest and closest associations were all around him then. He had enlarged the house, some years before, to provide a more spacious setting for his anticipated responsibilities. He had been remarkably right. From a house, it had been transformed into a mansion that befitted a pretender to high office.

The reporters, most of whom had been following him for much longer than we had, were familiar with his effort to emerge from a state to a national role. They were almost part of the family, and the effect made by the dramatic going and coming, the touch of flamboyance in the admiral's cloak, but only the merest touch, the circumstance of the big black Governor's limousine with escorting motorcycles, were background for their Albany and Hyde Park dispatches. This was democratic royalty proceeding on its occasions in seemly ways. They were as moved as I by its fittingness and by the courage behind the gaiety.

Roosevelt came back to Albany again, as usual, in the evening of the next day. There was time to talk after dinner. It was then that I was taken further into the mysteries of political strategy. Why he thought it worth while, I did not know, but I supposed it was that he no longer felt any need for a veil between us. If there was a reason, I guessed it might be because of my intimacy with the active progressives whom he was, at the moment, deliberately neglecting.

It went like this. There was something, he said, that he wanted me to see. I was following, as I should by now, what he was working out. I was trying, he said, to make him accept two commitments that he couldn't make. I wanted him to go further with the Oglethorpe beginning. It was true that we had the outlines of a device; it seemed to be a workable one. But we had to put it back in the closet for now.

That was one. Another was the business about confidence. I realized that he knew what nonsense it was. That was why I wanted him to repudiate it and say that whatever must be done would be done. It would unbalance the budget—that damned sacred budget. It would call for higher taxes, much higher—either that or printed money in quantities that might cause inflation. This he simply had to be equivocal about. What the "better people" still wanted was reduced governmental activity and sound money. They wanted a cure for unemployment too, but they thought it would come when businessmen began to expand their operations and hire more workers. He knew, as he told me, that this was not the way to start, but he was not going to say so.

"Now hear this," he said. He'd told me before, and I hadn't

really taken it in. Unless he was elected, the things I wanted and he wanted could not be done. *"I'm going to keep my options open."* He would not say that we were going in for planning or managing the economy, but something of that kind might be possible. He would not *say* that we would do what was necessary to bolster purchasing power, but he was sure something would have to be done—something big.

He went on: I thought, or he thought I thought, that I had a workable device. He must say that he thought so too. But we'd better be a little modest. He hadn't worked in Washington since 1920; I never had. These adjustment mechanisms had to fit all around, and neither he nor I really knew what "all around" meant. We'd risk being ridiculous if we got to talking specifically. It was something that literally "had to be worked out." Besides, it had to pass tough critics and high hurdles. In other words, it had to become law—several laws, probably. He'd have to take what he could get of what he finally decided to go for. Now what kind of material was that for campaign speeches?

One more thing. I considered myself, I had said, an experimenter. Then why did I insist on closing opportunities for experiment? He must get to the presidency free, or as free as he could. He must get people to think he had the ability to handle the job, so that during the honeymoon he could ask a lot of the Congress and get it, or most of it. He'd ask a lot, all right, but he was not going to say now what he intended to ask—not in any risky detail.

Generally speaking, he was going to experiment—try and see what worked—but that was just no way to campaign. The voters liked a man to know his mind. But he was not going to make any real commitments. Oh, he'd promise action, speak of recovery and reform in traditional ways, just as the platform did, and present a clear alternative to Hoover's awkwardness, but there it had to stop—until he had the responsibility.

I can only say that I was convicted of naïveté. His carefully guarded forecasting had taken me by surprise. I suddenly realized how hard and inappropriately I had been pushing. I went to bed in the enormous, overdecorated room, not far from where he was sleeping, a contrite helper. I was that now—rather than a demanding advocate.

Just as I was going to sleep, I found a sudden thought so amusing I could have laughed out loud. It concerned Walter Lippmann, who, more naïvely even than I, had undertaken to smoke out a Roosevelt program, and who was so certain that, because he could not, Roosevelt was vacillating and weak, with ambitions and no abilities. Walter was due for an awakening too. It would come later than mine had and, because his effusions had been so widely circulated, would be much more embarrassing. I could keep my humiliation to myself.

CHAPTER XXXVI

The Second Most Dangerous
Man in the Country

🏵 🏵 🏵

R oosevelt's rebuke had not only softened my objection to compromise but had mortified me; I ought not to have needed it. Anyway, it prepared me for the next lesson that came along, after his talks during another weekend at Hyde Park with several VIPs. It had to do with their suddenly assiduous cultivation of him and with certain other related issues.

There was a fairly typical Albany family luncheon that day. Present were Eleanor, Missy Le Hand, and, I think, the Tully sisters, Grace and Paula. We had been talking about the bonus march. It was over now, and the "dangerous elements" were scattered into the countryside from Maryland to Indiana. Pennsylvania state police had stood at the roads running north from the Lincoln Highway and—without making arrests—had prevented all but a few hundred of the evacuees from reaching Johnstown, where the Mayor had seemed friendly and they had thought they might be welcome.

Roosevelt was saying that even the people he had been talking to had done some head-shaking over the savage expulsion—or, he amended himself, more likely over the public reaction to it. General Glassford had become something of a popular figure, and the

Hurley-MacArthur performance was now being pictured not as heroic but as burlesque, an overdisplay of muscle. A desperate drumfire of statements was issuing from all concerned, making out that the marchers had not been veterans at all, but a crowd of malcontent communists and shiftless tramps. A threat to orderly government had been suppressed by necessary measures. The explanations went on and on. Hoover himself, unable to escape, had made a series of such assertions, and MacArthur in lofty prose had handed down the opinion that a revolution had been in the making and that only courageous action had served to avert it; the President, in fact, had cut it very thin; a day's delay would have been disastrous.

One of the stranger reported remarks referred to by Roosevelt was that of Pat Hurley, Secretary of War, who had said that he could not afford to make any heroes just now. It was Roosevelt's guess that his comment was caused by MacArthur's showy performance and suggestion of competition. That, he said, was the most likely interpretation. Pat knew how MacArthur's ambitions vaulted.

The official explanations were not well received. Now that the threat had been averted, all those involved, including the excited news commentators, were ashamed of their panic. There was some wonder about the fate of the eleven thousand refugees, but even more about what would happen if the hundreds of thousands of others in Hoovervilles all over the country—not too different, many of them, from those in the camp at Anacostia—should be dispersed in the same fashion. People like Owen Young, Will Woodin, and Averell Harriman, men of sensibility—Roosevelt was saying—knew that something other than repression was called for. They might not like what it would be, but the time was past for temporizing. There must be a policy, and it could not be this sort of savagery. If revolution was feared, this was not the way to avoid it.

He had heard from others whose views he regarded as appalling. They had said that the Hoover-MacArthur action was just what was needed to restore order and discipline. These gatherings of shiftless irresponsibles in dirty camps where there was no rent to pay, and where food and clothing had to be cadged from impoverished charity organizations, were a menace. Begging on the streets, lying about in doorways, sleeping on park benches or in jungles along the roadsides, and riding aimlessly about the country on freight trains showed a defiance of authority that had to be controlled. MacArthur had proved that he knew what to do. Concentration camps far from cities would have to be substituted for Hoovervilles. Only the army had kept its sense of duty and its respect for order.

Roosevelt spoke of these views as something he had by now become familiar with; he had heard them repeated over and over by the most surprising people, many of whom were otherwise humanitarian and some of whom were well-known philanthropists. Lately their irritation had been more insistent, and the publicity about the bonus marchers had given it a new intensity. There were others—important people in the business world, too—who found these suggestions repugnant, but who had been infected with the prevalent fear and had no practical alternatives to suggest.

Business and financial leaders, he said, persisted almost without exception in their demand for the restoration of "confidence." It was easy to see why. Government, following their prescription, would have fewer duties and would cost less to run. The changes they feared, and the higher taxes being talked of, would not be necessary. He was not so sure that they really believed all this. They were beginning to see that relieving business from the freeze it was in would not relieve the massive alienation and, of itself, would not bring about recovery. The business leaders were sticking to a formula they had once thought sufficient. There were some, it was true, who were worried now about the rumors of induced inflation. That was typical. They knew what they did *not* want done.

Admonitions to do nothing foolish were evidently being pressed on him more insistently as the odds on his election became more favorable. When he pointed out to the business leaders that the balanced budget they thought necessary to the resumption of investment was hardly consistent with large expenditures for relief and public works—an argument I had not thought that Roosevelt himself had accepted—their answer was that the government's bureaucracies were overblown and largely unnecessary, that economies were possible if a real effort was made, and that these savings would take care of emergency expenditures.

I remarked that I was delighted to hear these comments from him. I had never thought that in hanging on to the promise of making large economies he had been doing more than conciliating the Democratic conservatives. But economies were implied in the platform, even though it did refer sympathetically to the unemployed. The simultaneous emphasis on sound fiscal policies and relief for millions of unemployed was as bad in the platform as in the talk he had been hearing. Even if it was admitted that the understood political habit was to say something pleasing for everyone, this was playing with dynamite. As things were, it seemed downright irresponsible.

I must have noticed, he answered, that Cordell Hull, for instance, was the one at the platform committee meetings who insisted that the paramount issue, the one that must not be avoided, was the depression and its consequences in unemployment, bankruptcy, and general disruption. Cordell, he went on, was no young radical; he was an old professional who knew that something had to be done and that it must be drastic, but he was not for admitting during a campaign that it might include the unlimited printing of greenbacks and deliberately unbalanced budgets. The inconsistency in this, he said, had to be accepted for the present.

This led to some discussion of my alternative proposal: taxes that would capture the immense incomes that were really sterile, the ones that did not help to support the economy. Levying on those being hoarded, used for speculation, or sent abroad, would go a long way toward providing the needed purchasing power. He admitted it was a possibility that we had not really explored as we should.

Indeed, we had not explored it, but nevertheless I had suggested it several times when Roosevelt himself was still clinging to the notion that twenty-five-per-cent reductions would meet the bill for relief. The discrepancy here was now becoming obvious; larger and larger promises were being made, and as yet no adequate means had been suggested for making the promises good. What was likely to happen was that the funds would be provided, but not provided *for*. The government could always print the money it gave away. But that way lay inflation, which was all too likely to take away much of what it gave, and generally from the wrong persons.

It would not be fatal to provide limited funds without also providing the revenue, but this ought to be a temporary device, and the end should be kept firmly in mind: the funds appropriated ought to be such as would result in the increased productivity that would yield more taxes. It would be much safer, and would be no brake on activity, to increase tax rates on the sort of incomes I had mentioned. I knew what the objection would be: confidence would be impaired. But those who talked of confidence were worrying now about inflation. They could not have everything.

I had urged that purchasing power must be restored. Now I was having second thoughts. Had I said too much, and to one who had a weakness for "easy money"? At any rate, Roosevelt was at last admitting that we ought to explore ways to provide purchasing power. The deepening depression was impressing everyone with its massive size and its explosive possibilities. We could thank the bonus marchers for the heightened concern.

Roosevelt remarked, thoughtfully, that we could talk about soundness and balanced budgets all we liked, but the only real soundness, actually, was full recovery. I thought the argument that savings would pay the bills for relief had proceeded too far already. He admitted that it was all right to talk about bureaucracy, for everybody disliked bureaucrats, but there would be an awful howl if anything was really done to cut off services to business or agriculture, reduce appropriations for the navy or for MacArthur's army. Reducing pay might be possible, but it would not help much. He could see that.

I said satirically that I supposed it would be all right to cut down on expenditures for conservation; such reductions would cause no loud outcries from injured interests. Roosevelt winced. Anyway, he said, there wouldn't be much saving in that; Republicans hadn't been spending much on conservation anyway. I pointed out that the way he felt about conservation was the way others felt about the postal service or about public roads. He had a real problem, I said, if he meant to follow the money-saving line —that is, if he was going to say anything more about it. The inconsistencies were just too glaring, and the choices were too hard.

I should have guessed, he answered, that retreat would be possible from any position he took. One of the frustrating things about most of the problems we'd been discussing was that even when it seemed pretty clear *what* we would have to do, it was not at all clear how it could be done or how far we would have to go. Hoover had let government get too big; it could be cut down. That would please a lot of people. Bureaucrats had some power of resistance, and most of them had political supporters, but still the economy argument had weight. Anyway, a lot could be said about it without later embarrassment of much account.

I asked, "Research too?" I meant to be sarcastic, but he refused to react. Yes, he said, we'd talked about this before, and he knew I shuddered about it, even more than he did about conservation. But he'd had experience and he was sure that all through the government there were hundreds, maybe thousands, of research projects started that never came to an end and never would. He'd seen so much of it that he was prepared to be tough. The universities did it better; it could be left to them. He laughed at my scandalized expression. But it was an old argument by now and I did not pursue it further.

We had finished with lunch and Roosevelt was moving into his wheelchair—he had appointments—when the steward came in and whispered in his ear.

Yes, he said, he'd take it at the table. The phone was put down beside him. He said to all of us that this would be good; we should listen. Then he spoke into the mouthpiece: Hello, Huey, how are you?

The shrill platform voice of the Louisiana demagogue instantly began what could only be described as a tirade. God damn it, Frank, he ended his first outburst, who d'you think got you nominated?

Well, Roosevelt said, you had a lot to do with it, Huey.

Huey refused to be placated. He shouted, You sure as hell are forgettin' about it as fast as you can. Here I sit down here and never hear from anybody, and what do I see in the papers? That stuffed shirt Owen Young comes to see you. Then there's a regular parade of others just like him.

Oh, I see a lot of people you don't read about, Roosevelt said. The newspaper boys only write up the ones their editors like.

We won't even carry these states down here if you don't stop listenin' to those people, Huey protested. You got to turn me loose. Things ain't going good at all.

What d'you mean, turn you loose? You don't need anyone to do that. You *are* loose.

That Farley, said Huey, that's what I mean, and that Louis. They keep tellin' me to wait. They won't give me any money. I can't win elections without money. They liked it well enough when I dug 'em out of the hole they were in, but now they don't know I'm livin'.

Everybody appreciates all you've done, Roosevelt said. It's just not time to start yet. It's better to wait till election is nearer and people can remember what's been said. I'm not going to start out myself till the middle of September.

You comin' down here?

No, I don't need to; your country there is safe enough.

Don't fool yourself, Huey warned. It ain't safe at all. You got to give these folks what they want. They want fat-back and greens and they ain't getting any unless they raise 'em and it takes help even to do that. Nobody's tellin' them they're goin' to get any help. They'll believe me if I tell 'em. Maybe I can't make good, but that's something you'll have to figure out.

That's about what we're going to tell everyone, Roosevelt said. But we're busy figuring out how we can deliver. Give us a little time.

You're makin' a big mistake, Huey said (with some picturesque additions). We got to get started. You tell that Farley I need money and let me get goin'.

Just be patient for a while, Roosevelt told him. Let us work out some plans.

Hell with plans, Huey said. Don't need any plans. I'll carry this country for you, but I can't do it without money.

You never needed money before; why do you need it now? Roosevelt asked.

Damn it, you musta been born yesterday. Huey's voice rose; he could have been heard out in the street. I know where to get money when I'm running for myself. But this ain't the same. I'm runnin' for you, don't you know that? We not only got to have money down here; we got to make a lot of promises, and Farley won't tell me I can make any. You better take care of things yourself. You mind what I tell you; stop wastin' time seein' those Owen Youngs. Let me come up there. People are goin' to feel a lot better if they see me comin' out of that big house than those crooks that got us into this mess in the first place.

I'll see you get asked, Huey, Roosevelt said. You keep your shirt on. It'll be all right.

Did you see what that fool Hoover did to those bonus boys, Frank? Huey was calmer.

Yes, said Roosevelt. Things like that are going to hurt him. Don't you think so?

Damn right, Huey said. But we got to treat 'em different. There's a lot of that kind around, and they've got friends. Somethin's got to be done for 'em.

We're working on it, Huey.

You ask me up there, Frank. I'll give you some schemes that'll bring in the votes.

Roosevelt hung up. The steward took the phone away.

He turned and said, after a minute (and I remember the exact words): "You know, that's the second most dangerous man in this country."

He elaborated: Huey's a whiz on the radio. He screams at people and they love it. He makes them think they belong to some kind of church. He knows there's a promised land and he'll lead 'em to it. Everyone'll be rich; there'll be no more work, and all they have to do is vote the way he says. He'll throw all the wicked Wall Streeters into a pit somewhere and cover it up. Then he and his folks can build their paradise. It's a time for that kind of thing. It's spreading.

What Huey claims about Chicago is at least half true. He horned in on the proceedings before Jim knew what he was up to; then it was too late. When the crowd voted with him, Jim didn't know what to do. He was in a corner himself, you know. Those other votes were still not in sight, and it would have been wonderful if he could have rested on the simple majority he already had.

Still, Huey needed us more than we needed him. His delegation wouldn't even have been seated if our people hadn't supported him. He'd have had to sit and watch his enemies from down home represent the state. Besides, his two-thirds business backfired. That rule will have to be changed some time, but it couldn't be at a time like that. As it turned out Huey's motion didn't actually do much harm, but it might've got a serious reaction.

When anyone eats with Huey, it'd better be with a good long spoon. But we can't let him go. I'll have to speak to Jim.

This thinking out loud was something I had never heard Roosevelt do before. He had often made tentative excursions into unlikely schemes when we talked in the evenings, but they usually had to do with the problems we had to solve and not with ways to proceed. What I had just heard made an impression. I thought, What a job! He had to use explosive allies and figure how it could be done with the least damage. Huey was not the only one either; there were some others I knew about—Father Coughlin, for instance, and jumping jacks like Milo Reno and John Simpson out in the farm states. There must be a dozen or more of these characters.

And then there were the conservatives with their ready advice and their tough resistance to anything novel. . . .

Roosevelt showed no sign of actually leaving the table. I ventured a vagrant question that somehow occurred to me: "You said Huey was the *second* most dangerous person, didn't you? Did I hear it the way you said it?"

He smiled. You heard all right. I meant it. Huey is only *second*. The *first* is Doug MacArthur. You saw how he strutted down Pennsylvania Avenue. You saw that picture of him in *The Times* after the troops chased all those vets out with tear gas and burned their shelters. Did you ever see anyone more self-satisfied? There's a potential Mussolini for you. Right here at home. The head man in the army. That's a perfect position if things get disorderly enough and good citizens work up enough anxiety.

He went on: I've known Doug for years. You've never heard him talk, but I have. He has the most portentous style of anyone I know. He talks in a voice that might come from an oracle's cave. He never doubts and never argues or suggests; he makes pronouncements. What he thinks is final. Besides, he's intelligent, a brilliant soldier like his father before him. He got to be a brigadier in France. I thought he was the youngest until I read that Glassford was. There could be times that Doug would exactly fit. We've just had a preview.

No, if all this talk comes to anything—about government going to pieces and not being able to stop the spreading disorder—Doug MacArthur is the man. In his way, he's as much a demagogue as Huey. He has as much ego, too. He thinks he's infallible; if he's always right, all people need to do is to take orders. And if some don't like it, he'll take care of them in his own way. He has good officers. You saw that at Anacostia. There was a fine parade down Pennsylvania Avenue. There'll be order, all right.

He wheeled himself away. He had a long afternoon and evening ahead of him.*

---

* I report this conversation verbatim. I made notes about it that afternoon, but afterward tore them up. It remains so vivid a recollection that I am willing to stand on its accuracy.

CHAPTER XXXVII

More about My Radical Friends

❧ ❧ ❧

On a day in August—it must have been about the tenth—when Roosevelt was worrying over what was to be done about Walker and Ray was distractedly busy assembling materials and interviewing experts, I had one of those tea talks, with Eleanor present, that sometimes proved more interesting, because more intimate, than those in the evening when we were supposed to consider some matter of business. This one proved to be preliminary to others on the same subject; the whole could be said to constitute a series, although it was late in our association and came at a crowded time.

The bountiful teacart, with its heavy polished silver and its fine china, loaded with sandwiches and cakes, had been wheeled out to the green-painted porch, and all of us were gathered around. I was prepared for a needling that several thrusts in the past few days had warned me to expect, and I had got ready defenses of a simple sort—very simple; nothing more, in fact, than current copies of *Time, The New Republic,* and some other publications, all to be held as a reserve. There were two items from *Time,* one a diverter, the other a story headed "Third Parties."

The diverter was a montage of newspaper headlines showing how general the feeling was that recovery might at last be under way. The implication was that if business was now let alone prosperity would not be long delayed. It might just be, I said to Roosevelt, that if it went much further, this wave of optimism might have to be countered. I pointed out the top line. It read, "Chicago Wheat Scores Third Straight Gain," and beneath, "Business Pulse Beats Faster." The next said, "Boom Awakens Textile Plants in New England." Others proclaimed, "Revival in Trade Gains Momentum Throughout East" and "Bright Spots Grow on U. S. Business Map."

I knew he was concerned; we had spoken about it several times. People were so weary, so ready for the least glimmer of hope! Also, the press was so eager to find good news of this kind, and its proprietors so well aware of the political implications, that everything possible would be done to find any sign and to exploit it. "Camden Gives Jobs to 900 Long Laid Off" might not be much to build on, even if true; but, put together with the stock-market rally we had been watching, it would have an exaggerated effect on the attitudes of those whose votes Roosevelt had to capture.

He asked if I was suggesting that many people could forget their troubles between then and November. Eleanor answered for me. From her talks with all sorts, she thought they would like to forget if they could; they certainly wanted to believe that the depression would cure itself, and very few wanted anything done to bring about a cure that would make a change in their own situation—that is, their situation of a year or two before. They still hoped nothing serious was wrong. If it could be made to look as though recovery might come without the government's taking over the banks or other businesses or even raising taxes to provide relief, they would strain to believe it. Eleanor had been listening as well as making speeches.

She had made observations of undoubted value, but her husband was doubtful of her conclusion. He was sure, he said, that by now most people knew things could not go on as they had been going. After all, the depression had been getting worse for nearly three years. Stories about stock-market news didn't reach the workers. If Frances Perkins was right that there were thirteen million unemployed, then at least ten, or maybe twelve, million would still be

unemployed in November; re-employment faster than that could
not be imagined. He would bet anything, he said, that Hoover
wouldn't even mention revival in his acceptance speech. He would
know better. What he'd say was that things were awful, but that
Democrats in the Congress had made it impossible for him to do
what he had wanted to do about it; if he were put back in the
White House and given a Republican majority, he'd know how to
start up activity. Then unemployment would disappear, and those
two chickens he used to talk about could be put in every pot every
day. No, Roosevelt didn't think the Republicans would even try to
claim that business was recovering on its own.

I was not so sure. I said that what businessmen had been urging him, Roosevelt, to say, amounted to the same thing: when they
were certain that government meant them no harm, they would
take over responsibility for recovery and soon everything would be
moving. That was what Hugh Johnson was relaying from Baruch.
I suspected, so I told him, that he was impressed too—not by the
argument, but by the number of his supporters who would be
doubtful of his regularity if he didn't accept it.

He let that drop. From preliminary discussions I already had
reason to think that the Columbus speech might be weak about
this. Actually I was afraid the conclusion that business had dug itself the hole into which it had fallen was something no one wanted
to hear, and that, since this was so, politicians would not speak of
it.

To change the subject, or so I suspected, Roosevelt spoke again
of the "radical" crowd; they were the only ones, he said, who were
receptive to the notion that the business system had to be over-
hauled; everyone else reacted to such suggestions as skittish horses
reacted to tractors on country roads. He'd noticed that Norman
Thomas had been endorsed by the Dewey-and-Douglas crowd.
Thomas wanted to do some revoluting, and they approved. *They*
would vote for him, but how many votes did I think that amounted
to? It was the least of his worries; even if all of them were sub-
tracted from the Democratic total, it would be a trifling loss.

If that was so, I said, why mention it? Wasn't it because he was unhappy about their disapproval in spite of his disparagement? Anyway, I had brought along a summary from *Time* to show him that Thomas rated high for honesty. He might not get many votes, but he was doing a good job of educating a lot of people. Another thing: I hated to tell him this, but practically all *my* close friends —and maybe a lot of *his,* the nonpolitical ones—would vote for Thomas if a more believable program than they had yet seen didn't appear. They intended to, as of then, and they'd carry out that intention if something didn't change their minds.

I was pretty sure he'd already seen the same things in *The New York Times,* but he pretended not to know what I referred to. His pretense provided the opportunity to use my small round of ammunition—the "Third Parties" piece—and he did read it carefully. If he had seen it before, he still did not let on.

The story described a picnic at Ulmer Park, a "big, bare plot near Brooklyn's Coney Island." It was the start of the Socialists' campaign. There were about twenty-three thousand of them. They had brought their lunches and had sat around in fraternal content, the women gossiping, the children using the swings and patronizing the hot-dog stands. The young men were playing soccer, and occasionally a band struck up. But the highlight of the day was to be a speech by Thomas, who, when the time came, quite simply climbed the steps to a wooden platform and began without introduction. They listened with obvious approval. In the course of his remarks he had produced the year's Socialist slogan: "Repeal Unemployment!"

His speech was described as having flowed easily, without reference notes, and with total neglect of the abstract doctrines so dear to the older generation of immigrant party members. He had relied on plain talk about what he would like to see done. He wanted relief to be given, he said, not as the other parties proposed, but "by means of production for public use rather than for profit." He spoke movingly of ten or twelve million unemployed, of men and women searching garbage cans for food thrown out by those who could afford it, of men competing with rats and cats for those leavings. He had exclaimed, "That's how the celebrated law of supply and demand works under capitalism." Next winter, he had said, offered no hope. No hope, "unless we declare war on poverty with the energy with which we warred on Germany or . . . sought to repeal the Eighteenth Amendment."

He had outlined the Socialists' plan; they intended to subsidize consumption instead of letting the subsidies all go to producers seeking profit. . . . The federal government should make emergency grants every week . . . thinking in terms of ten billions. . . . If necessary an issue of government money, to be retired by stamps on its circulation. . . .

Roosevelt was intrigued, said it might work at that, then asked, What else? There were other proposals: taking over unused factories to be run by workers; much higher income and inheritance taxes; a five-day week. . . . He said these were not so practical; they were reaching for the moon.

It was a decent account, fair and full. I turned back and showed him the picture of Thomas on the cover. Now why, he asked, did I suppose Henry Luce had given Norman that publicity? While he thought about this, I read him a few sentences of description:

> Through this frolicking crowd in shirt-sleeves moved a tall, lanky figure extending a friendly welcome to all. His smooth white hand shook many a horny fist. Outwardly he was with the throng but plainly not of it. His blue coat and grey trousers were wrinkled, but he wore a necktie. His hair, above a high, intellectual forehead, was a silky grey, but his pale blue eyes were young, fresh, benign.

Let's see, Roosevelt said, Norman had been running for office since the early twenties. The Socialists had finally nominated him for the presidency in 1928. He had got only about a quarter of a million votes; Debs, back in 1912, had got a million; that was not such a fancy showing. It looked as though the Socialists were losing, not gaining.

I reminded him that 1928 had been before the depression, and that when the Socialists had joined with La Follette in 1924, the vote had run to nearly five million. Norman Thomas now had doubts and downright hardships going for him, and he offered at least something. I didn't think he would like to be pushed on detail; his specific suggestions weren't impressive, but he did put the central problem first. He saw that the prospect of unemployment was a terrible worry, even for those who still had jobs, and that for those who hadn't, calamity was closing in.

After leaving Thomas we went on—or Roosevelt did—to John Dewey and Paul Douglas; they were on his mind. He asked if I really considered that they were behaving like grown-up politicians. I said I didn't see why that mattered. Their league's recent meeting in Cleveland had found Thomas acceptable because they were not persuaded that he, Roosevelt, meant to do what needed to be done. I hadn't been there, of course, but I had heard about it from those who had been. And Dewey afterward had written an article for *The New Republic* describing it. I had the article. I read the final sentences:

> I came away . . . more encouraged than at any time in the past. The constituency is waiting; the response is waiting. Work and organization are the agencies needed to effect the creation of a strong new party, which will, moreover, become more than a party of mere protest.

To be honest, I told him, I had to report the comment about this in *The Times*—by the fellow, whoever he was, who wrote the political editorials: "Most of us—and majorities are said by some advanced thinkers to be always wrong—will surmise that *the League is waiting* and may have a long wait."

That was a dismissal Dewey probably expected, I said, and I was sure Douglas did. But most of the people I knew who were going to vote for Thomas were neither Socialists nor members of Dewey's league. They just did not credit the Democrats with intending to offer anything that was likely to do any good. They felt that even if he, Roosevelt, did propose something and got himself elected, a Democratic Congress would turn it down. I wouldn't estimate how many felt this way, but even if they were few, they were vocal and were being listened to. In fact, I thought and wanted to say that, as things were then, Thomas, not Hoover, was the real opposition he ought to be meeting. Hoover was dead; discontent was alive.

What did that mean? he asked. It meant, I said, that the depression had defeated Hoover. So he, Roosevelt, would be elected, but in winning he would not have won the minds he would most like to win. They would stay with Thomas. I didn't say, as I might have, that he had to choose between the intellectuals who were looking for something more substantial than he had offered and the businessmen and financiers who were afraid he would do something disturbing. I did insist that neither group would decide this election. What worried me was that he was being much more considerate of those who were afraid of change than of those who wanted it. The truth was that those who were scared did not really have more votes than those who wanted to do something drastic. If it was a matter of votes, how did he explain this?

Very simply, he said: party! If, as I argued, the Republicans were being licked by the depression—and it did look that way, all right—then he would win. Hoover's loss would be his gain. He still had to reassure the party workers who would have to get out the votes; they could persuade wavering Republicans not just to stay home on election day. It was always on his mind that Democrats were a minority, and that they had been one for generations —since the Civil War, really. Cleveland and Wilson, the only Democratic Presidents, had never had a majority; they were minority winners. Besides, since 1920—twelve years—the party had been out of office. He hoped he wouldn't have any such cliff-hanging decision as Wilson had had in 1916, or even in 1912, when he had been elected only because Uncle Ted had made Bull Moose of half the Republicans.

If he had an impressive majority, he said, and if the regular Democrats worked for and with him, then he could really do something. Otherwise he'd be checked as he had always been in Albany, able to propose a lot of things but not to get many of them done. Even the honeymoon would be unproductive.

I thought about that. But, I asked, wouldn't he have to do what the elders wanted, not what he himself wanted, and wouldn't they refuse to go along with him unless he conformed? He would have to conciliate Garner, for instance, and Cotton Ed Smith, and any number of other immovable reactionaries. If that was so, it didn't look promising.

That, he said, would depend on the situation; we weren't likely to get to next March in any but crisis conditions. There would have been a fourth winter of misery, and the banked-up discontent would be tremendous. Emergency, emergency measures! They'd have to be improvised, of course, when the situation became clearer, but that's what we'd been discussing these past months, and we were beginning to see what might have to be done. I insisted on thinking about it as something to do with the campaign, he said, and it was not. Nothing said in his speeches should make what he might have to do impossible, but also not much of what we guessed might be necessary should be exposed. It might very well be ridiculed; if not that, it might be repudiated by Democrats all over the place because they didn't understand it, or because it seemed to threaten some interest of theirs, or because it just seemed outlandish. What they expected from him was reassurance—neither Huey Long's revolution nor Norman Thomas' Presbyterian socialism. He would talk about specific issues—including the tariff—and would denounce Republican neglect, but he wouldn't say what he intended to do except in the most general way.

Somewhat later, after thinking over what he had said, I asked several questions about possible consequences. One originated in something I recalled. He had spoken of Wilson several times, and since he had served in Wilson's administration for more than seven years, some of them confused and difficult, he must have learned lessons useful to him now. When I asked him, he said that was true. He added, however, that he thought he had learned more from Wilson's mistakes than from his successes. For instance, Wilson had made poor use of his honeymoon period because of concentration on one measure, the Federal Reserve Act. As a result, nothing much else on the progressive agenda had been converted into law—only that one thing. Wilson's relations with Congress had never been good. The insiders who had wanted Champ Clark, then Speaker of the House, as the Democratic candidate had never forgiven Wilson for winning: they were conservatives anyway, and could only have been got to support him if he had compromised, and he was no compromiser. So not very much actually got done.

He explained. The Federal Reserve struggle had taken most of the precious first year and just about all the credit Wilson had. At first he had been unwilling to have patronage managed by a party man and had tried to apply strict merit standards. Later he had admitted defeat and turned that job over to Burleson, a Texas politician who was Postmaster General. Then things had gone better, but many months had been wasted. If Wilson had simply held on to the available jobs and said they would be distributed after the legislation he wanted had been passed, it would have gone much faster and ended with better feeling all around. As it was, he had had to give in and had gained nothing from yielding.

What about the *campaign* of 1912? I asked. Wilson had begun making mistakes right from the first. He had disliked to consult anyone. He had written his own speeches on his old typewriter, and usually no one had seen them or discussed them before they were made. He had concentrated on becoming the head of the party, and he wanted followers, not allies. For years before his nomination he had been making a second career, besides that of being Princeton's president, of lecturing all over the country, mostly to conservative audiences, and mostly, therefore, to Republicans. It was not even known that he was a Democrat, and in a sense he was not; he had never done anything for the party, never even voted.

He had been made Governor of New Jersey by the local boss for personal reasons, not for party ones. There were only a few Democrats anywhere who felt that he was one of them. They

thought they were being used, and they were. Wilson had no intention of consulting party people; he was going to make his own decisions. The truth was that the campaign of 1912 had been a miserable one, and Wilson had won only because of the Bull Moose
defection. Taft, the Republican candidate, had finished not second
but third. It was a wonder Wilson, when he became President, had
got anything at all done. If it hadn't been for Bryan, Daniels, and
Burleson, the professionals in the cabinet, he would have been a
complete failure; it was these party men who got the Congress to
act.

I asked him if what I had heard was true, that political leaders
actually learned very little from the experiences of their predecessors. He said yes; but he himself hadn't had to learn about Wilson's methods from reading; he had been close enough to watch.
He would have been pretty dumb not to have drawn the conclusion
that Wilson's way of operating was not one to be copied.

Was that the reason, then, I asked, for his own insistence on
being regular, cultivating the old hands, letting them write the platform and, in effect, guide the campaign? His reply was a question.
Did I really think he had lost control to that extent? It was not the
answer I expected, but I recovered enough to say that I was troubled by his conciliating of the conservatives. I couldn't help thinking that they were blocking what he ought to be saying and would
block whatever he might want to do. It seemed too that this could
only be offset by his own popular support.

He had said to me once, he reminded me, that he could normally expect two terms in the White House, and that when they
were over, there might not be a Democratic party but there would
be a Progressive one. Yes, I said, and it had bucked me up when I
was discouraged. I didn't wholly understand what he had meant,
though, and I had been wondering ever since.

What I had to understand, really, he said, was what a President
could and couldn't do. He had to accumulate what power he could
and hoard it, spending it grudgingly. It wasn't something he was
endowed with; it came from support built up over a long time. If
he had the people with him—if he had a majority like his own in

New York in the 1930 election—then the legislators would be inclined to accept his suggestions; even those who didn't like him would hesitate to oppose him openly. Also, the private interests, so influential with legislators, would be respectful. He could gradually inch into a position of leadership. But he had to prepare the way for what he intended to do and prepare it carefully. He had to overcome the opposition of those who were sore. On the other hand, if they stayed sore, and were extreme and reckless enough, they would make useful enemies. There was nothing like a noisy opponent to convince people that a politician was their friend.

If his majority proved to be slim, he would have to be cautious. Cleveland and Wilson, with their weak popular support, never had been able to discipline their Congresses. If that seemed to be the prospect, a candidate had better make himself without any question the party candidate, cultivating a kind of father-son relationship with the elders. That was something neither Cleveland nor Wilson had done.

He was beginning to think he might have a safe majority, but it was still not certain, and how the campaign went—and how the presidency would go—depended on whether that big vote developed or didn't develop. Anyway, he had to go after it.

He brought the lesson to a close by pointing out that my continual reverting to the need for a mandate, and therefore the need to spell out what would have to be done, might be all right in case he himself was going to do the winning—that is, if he got in without owing too much to the party. In that case it was possible, and probably good, but in the present instance it would be risky—too risky.

He went on at some length about Cleveland. I recalled his telling me that his father had taken him to see Cleveland both in Albany and in Washington. On that last occasion, the bulky man in the frock coat had patted him on the head and advised him never to become President.

Cleveland had had a hard time, he said; he had not been a war veteran, and he had even bought a substitute, the worst thing he could have had in his record. Besides, he had hardly any friends in the party, even in his own state. He had been mayor of Buffalo only two years before, and at that a mayor who was noted for punishing the regulars for favoritism and graft. He had made the same sort of start as Governor. The first thing he had done was to provoke a bitter fight with Tammany, and the hostility of the sachems had lasted through his governorship.

Cleveland had been known hardly at all outside New York State, but it just happened that the country was sick and tired of the corruption that had begun with Grant and run on through subsequent presidencies. When the Republicans had nominated Blaine to run against him, Cleveland had had his lucky break. It was disillusioned Republicans who had given him his narrow victory. There was nothing like that to count on now, but there was something just as good—Hoover's failure to deal with the depression. And that was what must be worked on.

It had to be done in two ways. First, Hoover must be attacked for his failure; then Roosevelt himself had to persuade the voters that he would do something and do it fast. He mustn't talk much about specific or drastic changes, but he must promise to get results. Actually, he had to stick to the platform. That didn't mean that if there should be a real crisis and drastic things should have to be done, he wouldn't be able to do them. It meant that they must be done only when there was an overwhelming demand for them. The Congress would then have to go along.

He should have been a teacher, I told him. He replied that these were professional secrets, not to be found in the textbooks. Anyway, they wouldn't work if too many people knew them. Voters were cynical enough about politicians, he said, but I might have noticed that once a politician got to be President, he was thought of in an entirely different way. No matter how he got there, when he *had* got there, he was almost invulnerable, at least in the beginning; he had to have a very bad accident, such as had happened to Hoover, or be a weakling—a Buchanan or a Harrison—to lose the enormous respect Americans had for the center and head of their whole system. A President could count on being thought a statesman.

As a result of my tutoring, I took a different view of those friends I knew to be leaning toward a vote for Thomas, the preacher who had become a Socialist. He was doubtless a good influence in the community; he turned people's minds toward virtues and away from vices; he asked the question whether, in a system of competitive enterprise with profits for incentive, we could possibly live up to the professions we made about mutual assistance or even about simple decency in dealing with one another. His answer was, No! With the depression for an irrefragable example, he had only to outline the alternative: a system run for use, not for profit.

That our pluralistic arrangements were inconsistent with his socialism and that the sources of initiative would be closed, Thomas did not mention. Roosevelt wanted to keep open those springs of American progress. More earnestly than Hoover, however, he meant to channel them and limit their effects on those who lacked the instinct for profit-making or who had borne the risks of competition. Thomas would not persuade any considerable number of Americans that it was necessary to adopt the sort of system he advocated, but his criticism was devastating.

Even though my friends had endorsed him, I could not believe that they wanted to see his monolithic economy established. They were simply disillusioned with the business system, and it was easier to advocate a complete alternative to the system than to consider whether its virtues might be salvaged from those who had exploited its vices. I thought to myself that Paul Douglas might some day regret his simplistic political judgment. Dewey, the philosopher, would not care, for he would never run for public office; but Paul was obviously ambitious, and he might not have a party to affiliate with when he needed it sometime in the future.

I myself might have been an earnest member of the league along with my friends. I had felt about as they did no longer than a few months before, and I might well have voted for Thomas and thought myself quite justified. I had to admit that it was only by accident that I had been given a chance to work instead of talk and to learn some lessons not yet in the academic manuals.

CHAPTER XXXVIII

Trouble in Agriculture

🎖 🎖 🎖

The farmers of the country, especially those who grew crops for export—cotton, wheat, corn—had fallen into an abyss of vanished markets as soon as the war had ended. Hoover had not been blamed at once, as he might have been (it was he who, as food administrator, had urged the expansion of production), but when, as Secretary of Commerce and later as President, he had persistently opposed the measures that the farm bloc was fighting for, responsibility had begun to lodge where it belonged. Especially as the farmers' troubles extended through the twenties and Hoover refused to be moved, he was more and more identified as their enemy. In 1929 and after, when the agricultural depression was made even worse by the industrial failure, disillusion with his leadership had become universal.

It was not fair to say, as many of his critics did, that he had done nothing at all. He had sponsored expansions of agricultural credit and had recommended the Marketing Act of 1929, which established a Farm Board with broad instructions to find solutions. Hoover was well aware that the agricultural decline was deeply involved with the general depression, and he would have liked to do something to relieve it. Here again, however, his preconceptions got in the way of his practical sense. He would not entertain any

448

solution that interfered with ordinary marketing processes or the freedom of individuals to do as they liked. In practice this meant that any governmental action he regarded as permissible was so limited in its scope as to be virtually useless. There were some twelve million farmers, and unless they acted together under the aegis of government, no general improvement was possible.

The congressional bloc, harder and harder pressed by constituents, demanded something much more immediate and promising than was being offered by the Farm Board. The board was authorized to make loans, but only to co-operative associations; through these associations, farmers were to set up marketing facilities and also, if necessary, stabilization corporations to buy up surpluses. Senators Norris, Walsh, Norbeck, and others from the wheat and cotton states tried to get approval for their favorite schemes for dumping the surplus crops in foreign countries. Hoover would not accept any of the devices, and the Congress, still having a Republican majority (until 1930), did not override his objections.

From 1929 to 1931, the Farm Board struggled with its task, under the chairmanship of Alexander Legge, former president of the International Harvester Company. It did establish and finance enormous co-operatives for marketing, and finally, when its export efforts failed, it used its stabilizing powers to buy and store surpluses. But what could be done with them? By 1932 every available warehouse had been filled with deteriorating grain and cotton for which there was no market. A late statement by the board admitted that only crop-control by government would be effective. For this it had no authority, and so for all practical purposes its operations came to a dead stop.

Midwest farmers, traditionally Republican, were reported to be in a mood to accept even a Democrat as candidate if he should promise some kind of relief. Of course, it had better be within their accepted ideologies, but M. L. Wilson thought that these were not so militantly defended any more. The farmers might even accept subsidies under another name, and he was sure they would join in an effort to reduce surpluses.

There were half a dozen farmers' organizations, some large and country-wide, some small and regional. They had expanded immensely during the period of protest and had pushed persistently for federal legislation. The lobbyists they maintained in Washington had an influence respected by all politicians. Roosevelt, for instance, recognized from the first that disaffected farmers were one of the richest sources of converted voters, and he had every intention of trying to attract them.

There threatened to be serious difficulty with the thorough and demagogic agricultural politicians as they competed for his support. Their prestige was deeply involved in their own schemes. They had campaigned to get and extend their membership. In vehement language they had prescribed what they considered to be remedial measures, and they were now persuaded that their members strongly agreed. To demand of them, after a decade of such agitation, that they accept a device put forward by a competitor—or any device they had not themselves invented—was an intolerable threat to their pride and perhaps to their positions.

Roosevelt was more and more acutely aware of this, as he was of the mandate that every leader felt was imposed on him to reject crop reduction. They said that there was a deep revulsion among farmers against reversing the first tenet of their occupation—making the land produce to its utmost. Roosevelt was disposed to accept this notion, and although the platform gave him some freedom, he was still impressed by the vehemence of visiting leaders.

This was the problem, and it seemed awfully like a dilemma. The hope that the domestic-allotment scheme might be a way of escaping it was not encouraged by his visitors. There was no denying that domestic allotment was a device for crop control. M. L. Wilson, of course, agreed that it was to be a voluntary one—meaning that it permitted farmers to decide whether or not they wished to co-operate. If they did, they would be paid for allowing their land to lie idle; this would limit supply, reduce surpluses, and raise prices. If they did not join, they took their own chance in a paralyzed market.

But most of the farm leaders who were coming to see Roosevelt during July and August, some on their own, more brought by Mor-

genthau, were either ignorant of or stand-offish about domestic allotment. Some were fiercely opposed. Edward A. O'Neal of the
Farm Bureau Federation insisted that the McNary-Haugen Acts
must be revived. Others expounded their own solutions. The most
extreme was John Simpson of the Farmers Union, who raucously
demanded that prices be fixed by law.

Most of the others, like O'Neal, clung to some scheme for subsidizing exports. This somehow seemed to promise that foreigners
could be made to solve the American problem by consuming the
surpluses of cotton and wheat. That this was a false promise, and
that even if it worked foreign consumers would in reality be supplied with cheap food and fiber by American taxpayers, were facts
they simply ignored. The fight for subsidized exports had gone on
so long that arguments against them seemed not even to be heard.

This was a conspiratorial avoidance of inevitable consequences
that I could not sympathize with and was even at a loss to understand. I was certain that if Roosevelt gave in and used the promise
of subsidized exports for campaign purposes, the subsequent disillusion would be hard to deal with. My frustration occasionally
brought me to exasperated protest. When no one seemed interested
and Roosevelt blandly put me off, I gradually withdrew. He was
listening and waiting, learning about attitudes, not about the work-
ability of proposals.

Another complication for me was Henry Morgenthau's gnawing
jealousy. Having so long been Roosevelt's liaison with farm leaders, he could not tolerate a seeming rival. He could not encounter
me without glowering. Since my participation was beginning to
seem like a contest I had no desire for, I began to avoid agricultural discussions. I felt lost among the acrimonies and demands of
politicians calling themselves farm leaders. I had no interest in
their maneuvers or in making any sort of choice among them. If
Roosevelt wanted anything more from me, he would let me know.
He was holding off the farm leaders, letting them talk, and giving
them opportunities to make a show before their constituencies. If
they went back to their meetings and said that they had laid down
the law to the Democratic candidate, he would not contradict

them. He had a natural sympathy for politicians who had gotten themselves into embarrassing fixes, but it was a tenderness I did not share.

The last thing he meant to do was to admit publicly that he favored any scheme. He was saying and, as I could see, meant to go on saying that *something* would be done; but so far as he could, he would avoid any specification that implied one or another project. He would obviously have to mark out some objectives, but he meant these to be the ones that were least offensive to the greatest number of farmers.

I knew well enough, and I knew that he knew well enough, because we had discussed it many times, that eventually some means would have to be found of reducing the flood of staple products that could not be sold either at home or abroad. Then, as a more permanent solution, means would also have to be found of establishing substantial equality between agriculture and industry as equal halves of the economy. Since this commitment had even been acknowledged in the acceptance speech, I could not understand his retreat from it; but it was a subject on which I did not make myself a nuisance.

Among the leaders whom Morgenthau brought to confer was Henry Wallace, but I had no chance to see him while he was in Albany. This was true of others; I heard of their visits after they had left. On July 19 Roosevelt treated an assembled group of farm leaders to pleasant questioning—as I read in *The Times*—and I believed what was reported: they went away without knowing any more about his intentions than when they had come. It was said that they seemed to be gratified by the invitation, but it was also said that they were not given any satisfaction. I heard about this particular meeting from Roosevelt himself, who, on occasion, recalled that I might be interested. He had done no more, he said, than say to them that they must come up with a proposal, one they could accept and would support. I asked if this implied a commitment on his part to adopt whatever they agreed on. He said no, that when the time came for action instead of talk, they would have come around to some reasonable plan and would have to support it, but they needed time to make their compromises.

I noticed that M. L. Wilson had been ignored by Morgenthau, so I arranged myself for him to come. His meeting with Roosevelt was most agreeable, and their private conversation went on for some time. I had considered that Roosevelt judged Wilson's scheme to be one that met most of the tests, even the political ones; sure enough, after this visit I heard him several times make a very clear and, I thought, approving explanation of domestic allotment to visitors of various sorts. I was quite satisfied that however ambiguous his public statements, and however tender he was with the farm leaders, he now had in mind the plan he would finally adopt as President—if not as candidate.

He understood how important it was that the plan should be "voluntary," that is, participated in by farmers themselves. He knew too that for participants there would have to be compensation roughly equal to a fair price for the products they agreed not to grow. Calculations made by Wilson resulted in an estimate that his method of compensation—a tax on the first processing—would yield somewhat less than a billion dollars. This would not make farmers riotously prosperous, but it would be a start. Its disadvantage was that the billion dollars would come from increased prices to consumers. If, however, it was accompanied by relief benefits and public work for the unemployed, it would be tolerable. Since these were now inevitable anyway, defense of higher prices for farmers could be explained as fair exchange. The unemployed would have incomes; workers would have more employment because farmers could again make purchases.

When I was satisfied that Roosevelt really did see this as the most effective solution, I considered that my own responsibility had been fairly well met. I was not entirely excused from helping with the speeches, especially the important one to be made at Topeka, but Ray and I had agreed that the first draft might well be prepared by M. L. Wilson. I warned Wilson that he would have trouble with Morgenthau, who would be wanting his Cornell professors—Warren and Pearson—to be recognized, and that he would have to handle this as best he could. I was quite sure he would find Morgenthau fiercely opposed to the domestic-allotment idea and just as fiercely an advocate of monetary manipulation. It was quite plain that Morgenthau had not been told anything by Roosevelt that served to stop his aggressions. He would, moreover, be briefed by his Cornellians, who would tell him that Wilson and I were urging something "socialistic."

This sort of nonsense only amused Roosevelt. He spoke to me about it once after a Morgenthau visit, and his expansion on the theme could only be called hilarious. Perhaps he felt that by then he owed me an explanation. I must realize, he said, that Henry wanted to be Secretary of Agriculture so badly that he was hardly responsible for his behavior. It wasn't possible; the secretary would have to be somebody from the Midwest. Henry and the Cornellians were regarded with suspicion by all the farm organizations except the Grange. They did represent that, but it was reactionary and Republican through and through, so much so that he could not hope to move many of its members and would not need to give them any concessions.

I thought it would have been kinder to relieve Henry's obvious anxiety by telling him not to hope, but Roosevelt evidently did not mean to do that. Henry was not going to defect under any provocation. And the Cornell professors, I thought to myself, would be there if they were ever wanted. I had some suspicion even then that such a time might come.

I passed on to Ray the permission I felt Roosevelt had given me to retire from this field; we never kept anything from each other, and Roosevelt never expected it of us. I was thinking by now that Ray might have trouble from a source he was not alerted to—from Hugh Johnson, Baruch's man. He was not much aware of Johnson's interest, or of Baruch's, in agricultural matters. Because of Johnson's facility in writing, Ray was finding him agreeable. I felt I must tell him what I knew and what I suspected, and I did, at some length. Strangely, this is something he did not recall when he was writing *After Seven Years,* but it seemed important to me.

As things turned out, it had consequences running on into the future.

The intimations were plain enough once a few relationships were understood. The processors of agricultural products—the meat packers, the wheat and cotton millers, the farm-machinery manufacturers, and the speculators on the commodity exchanges —were probing industriously for some means of influencing Roosevelt. They were relying mostly on George Peek, then president of the Moline Plow Company, the agent who had captured Al Smith for their purpose in 1928. Peek's business associate for a long time had been the same Hugh Johnson who was now a recognized member of our Brains Trust—delegated to us by Baruch and accepted by Roosevelt.

The same considerations, I suppose, that caused Louis Howe to receive Baruch with exclamations of welcome just after the nomination in Chicago were the ones that brought Johnson into our midst. He was advertised to us as an economist, an experienced administrator, an expositor of the business community's thoughts, and a ready writer. He was to "help." Roosevelt did not say all this; he merely invited Hugh to sit in on our conferences; but we got it from everyone else.

There had been manufacturers of farm machinery on Hoover's Farm Board; one of them, Alexander Legge, had been its president. A prosperous agriculture was good for their businesses, but they were by nature opposed to any scheme that would give the farmers increased bargaining power. They did see that farmers' prices had to be raised, but they shared the business community's fear of inflation. Their allies in the processing trades were reluctant to see acreages—and crops—reduced because they profited from larger and larger volumes. Also, they were hesitant about passing on higher prices to consumers, who, at some point, might become balky, but on this they were beginning to feel they would have to compromise; it would be better for them to raise prices than to have government do it.

They, more than the farmers themselves, had been responsible for the monopoly enjoyed by export-subsidy schemes in a decade of agitation for farm relief; no others had really been considered. Their lawyers had done the preliminary drafting, their lobbyists had worked industriously for the bills, and their congressmen had made supporting speeches—written by their publicity men. Actually, the agricultural bloc belonged less to the farmers themselves than to the processors, who were almost scandalously influential, too, in the Department of Agriculture. There the bureaus were largely staffed with determinedly subservient civil servants; lobbyists even used the departmental offices as headquarters.

If there was to be legislation after election, the processors did not mean to surrender the advantages they had established in many years of cultivating human relations. They did not much care how exports were increased as long as machinery buyers were kept solvent and the surpluses were moved through warehouses, mills, and packing houses for the profit of themselves.

They had seen the possibility, however, that they might control matters through "marketing agreements." This meant that they themselves would accept the responsibility for paying farmers higher prices. But this would not be bad; they would pass on the increases to consumers. They were beginning to argue that the arrangement would make farm relief simple for the government. In return they asked only one favor: exemption from prosecution under the antitrust laws. They had hoped for this during many years, of course, while the scale of their enterprises was growing and competition was disappearing. This might be a way to get it.

I heard about this and told Roosevelt what I knew. He saw at once how it had come about. The relation of the processors' ideas to businessmen's suggestions for co-operation and planning was quite obvious. It made a good deal of sense, he said, if, in administration, the processors could be made to accept proper disciplines; we would have to see about that. But he laughed when we discussed it, and said never to mention it to Louis, who saw middlemen in all his worst nightmares. Exempting them from antitrust prosecution would be a betrayal of Louis' dearest principles.

Roosevelt knew that Baruch and Johnson were opposed to domestic allotment, and when I recalled for him the way Smith had gone in 1928 he understood why that was. He had not known that I had anything to do with such matters in 1928.

Smith had felt in 1928 that Peek was more practical than a Columbia professor, and his advice to promise the subsidizing of exports had been taken. On one hand, this device had the advantage, politically, of having been vetoed by Hoover, Smith's opponent; on the other hand, many farmers had already lost faith in it. Smith did very badly in the farm states—not altogether for this reason, it must be said. The fact that he was so obviously a Tammany product, and Catholic as well, had much to do with his losing the farm vote, but certainly his farm-relief offering had not helped to overcome his handicaps. Besides being disillusioned about dumping, farmers could not believe that their traditional enemies really meant to help them out of their trouble.

The situation was the same now, except that Wilson's scheme was further developed than mine had been. I would have had Roosevelt state the proposal—very generally, but still recognizably. He was, however, getting contrary advice from others, including Johnson. Their advice, he evidently felt, as Smith had felt—although Roosevelt did not say so to me—was either more practical or more politically acceptable. My warning about Smith's similar acceptance made no impression, or so I feared. At any rate, Peek was in business again, Johnson being an old associate of his, and behind them both stood Baruch.

I had hoped that Roosevelt's support for domestic allotment would be made easier by Clifford Hope's introduction of legislation embodying its main features. In fact there were two such bills, one offered in June and another in July. Domestic allotment had become well and favorably known among the farm-bloc congressmen because of Wilson's missionary work.*

I had been told—not by Roosevelt—that Baruch had by now become the most generous angel the party had. He seemed to associate very little with Jesse Straus and his league members, but he

---

* Clifford Hope of Kansas was chairman of the Committee on Agriculture for the House of Representatives.

had bought his way into the Businessmen-for-Roosevelt circle with larger contributions than those of Kennedy, Davies, Harriman, or any of the rest. It was not so much this, however, that earned him the respect of the insiders; that came from the generosity of his contributions to the local campaign funds of many senators and representatives. These beneficiaries, if my informants were to be believed, ran to a considerable number, but no one knew, or would ever know, exactly how large it was.

Even if Baruch's involvement was no more than half what was rumored, it was still huge, and he was expanding it because it appeared likely to pay dividends. The Democrats were going to win, and the party's angels would be in a position to cash in. It was fairly obvious, even to an amateur like myself, what this cashing in would consist of. He would want to become a member of the cabinet—Secretary of State or of the Treasury. This would seem fitting enough to the public, since he had been one of the best known of Wilson's war administrators. The professionals would think it advantageous to the new President because such a party supporter would have an immense influence in the Congress. With some bitterness I meditated on this horrifying weakness in our system. I did not count enough on Roosevelt's superb ability to use troublesome people without ever really conceding anything.

There was one immediate difficulty for Baruch: things would have to come out as he had planned. Still, they appeared likely to do so. The processors of farm products were not his only allies; he was a speculator on a scale achieved by very few predecessors. Joseph Kennedy was perhaps getting into his class but he was far from having reached it yet. It could be guessed that, having made immense gains by selling short, Baruch would make greater ones by buying long. But he had to know what was going to happen or, even better, be in a position to make it happen and then take advantage of it. Friends to whom I confided my fears about this sinister influence in our midst were inclined—most of them—to say that I was seeing things in the dark. But I was not consoled. The campaign was certainly being influenced. What had begun as an attempt to reach the grass roots seemed to be ending in appeasement of the processors—while the representation was being made that farmers' welfare was the first consideration.

Still, during my last talk with Roosevelt about agriculture, he asked me to make a draft of a bill embodying domestic allotment. I recalled to him that this had already been done. Congressman Hope's latest bill might need recasting, however, and this I promised to study with the help of friends I could count on in the Department of Agriculture. Perhaps all was not lost after all. Wilson thought not, and if he felt that way, it might be so.

CHAPTER XXXIX

Scant Harvest

🌿 🌿 🌿

As the active campaigning came on, Roosevelt seemed to me more and more concerned with pleasing the "practical" people. However glossed over, this was a crude business; they were making large contributions and so were allowed influence. Of course it was nothing new; they expected, and were expected, to dictate policy. There were congressmen who sometimes seemed no more than their servants, and in the departments, their lobbyists in Republican years had been the mentors of numerous well-placed bureaucrats. They knew very well that a change impended, and their allies were numerous in the Roosevelt entourage, especially in the New York headquarters and in Washington. This was bad enough; but it seemed outrageous to have had them infiltrate the Brains Trust. I was conscious of my amateur status, but I was stubbornly certain that more was being lost than could be afforded.

I protested in somewhat high-flown language that this was consorting with the enemy; unless I was altogether wrong, a purge affecting these same people would have to precede reform, even the minor reform that was promised in the Columbus speech. I probably made myself a nuisance.

Johnson by now was offering a draft speech for nearly every appearance Roosevelt was to make. These did not stand as written any more than mine or Adolf's did, but Ray made use of them as he made use of ours; the difference was that he sensed Roosevelt's tenderness for the businessmen's approach and relied more and more on their representations. The shadow of Baruch hovered over all the preparations now. We seldom saw the man himself—during part of the summer he was in Europe—but Johnson was always present, always condescending to those of us who were "theorists," and always voluble. However glowering he was with us, he was colorful and entertaining when Roosevelt was present; he had been sent to please, and he worked at it.

It has already been noted that when Baruch had come into Louis' room at the Congress Hotel before the demonstrations had died down, Johnson was following just behind. It was he who had really read Ray's acceptance speech and briefed Baruch on its harmlessness from their point of view. I remembered how Ray's temper had flared when Baruch asked to see the speech and how the approval had quieted his annoyance.

We did not know it then, but within the hour Johnson had wired Peek: "We will get what we want." Peek had been skeptical. What he had wanted was unequivocal agreement to an export-subsidy bill. Johnson counseled patience; Roosevelt, he told Peek, could be persuaded. At this time, it appears, neither knew of domestic allotment, or at least of Roosevelt's acquaintance with it; but Johnson soon heard about what had gone on in our discussions and alerted his friend. This made it certain that when it came to shaping the agricultural pronouncement at Topeka, Wilson's draft would have against it all the processor forces headed by Baruch, as well as those represented by Morgenthau and the farm leaders. We did not sort all this out at the time, and Ray was not much concerned anyway, but I was only too well aware that what had seemed a clear and workable policy was falling into unnecessary confusion.

The speech in Columbus, of course, had been delivered more than a month before the agricultural pronouncement at Topeka was due. While the Brains Trust was lining up on the new issue, we—or at least I—had to manage an accommodation to the Columbus retreat. What made it so difficult was that the speech which had offered such a lucid statement of the causes of the depression had also included a wholly unconnected attack on Wall Street, and that it had given not even a hint of recovery policy. Unlike the agricultural compromise, there was no confusion about the reason for this retreat; it was the result of Brandeis' demands—his first show of force. It had been completely successful, and we were impressed, not to say dismayed.

But it was not until the Pittsburgh speech, on the nineteenth of October, fairly late in the campaign, that a complete commitment to confidence for business would be made. In that speech Roosevelt was to attack Hoover for extravagance and to promise a large cut in government expenditures. Until then no one could say for certain what the recovery policy would be. During this time our discussions were unreal and indecisive. Roosevelt was listening and trying to find his way through a jungle of demands. In some despair, we judged—and I had his own word for it—that he meant to stay in a position of such indeterminateness that he could make whatever moves he found feasible when the time came for action. All might not be lost, but there were dismaying signs that our position was weakening fast. Baruch and Brandeis, who at least agreed on free competition, even if for different reasons, were now the main contenders. Collectivism was no longer mentioned; Oglethorpe was forgotten, and we were being pushed to the side. Roosevelt was as pleasant as ever, but during September I had almost no intimate conversations with him like those of the preceding weeks.

I continued to think that his ultimate objective was a concert of interests. However indirect the methods, however devious the means, he meant to make the country one, really one. This, however, appeared to be a much more complex endeavor than anyone could have realized who was not actually involved with political persuasion at this highest level. I had glimpses of the whole, the strategic intention, but no more than glimpses. A few times we talked briefly about it. When we did, I was pleased by the shapes, however dim, that seemed to be materializing. At the same time I was distressed by the apparent difficulty of bringing the intentions into the political dialogue. When I said so, Roosevelt reminded me again that this was *his* problem, and that he did not yet have a *commission* to solve it. He was still a candidate; wait till he was elected!

When we had finished our conferences about speeches, and when Ray had finished drafting them and preparations were substantially complete for the campaign trip to the West Coast, some of us had a furlough from active participation. The travelers would be gone for three weeks, and the manuscripts were as ready as they could be until they were about to be used. Ray, of course, would have to do the final drafting with Roosevelt. Both would be descended on, in transit, by all sorts of people who had demands to make or advice to give, but this was something neither seemed to dread.

In *After Seven Years* Ray described this experience vividly. Even a few hours before Roosevelt placed a manuscript on the podium before him, improvised a few words of introduction, and then began to read, his speech was not really completed. Although the original subject and its treatment had some time since been outlined and agreed upon, Ray could not be sure until he heard Roosevelt begin that there would be no more alterations.

While the train rumbled from one city to another, Ray might be told to consult with some prominent person—a politician usually, but often a newspaper proprietor or a businessman—about what would be appropriate. That meant showing him what was to be said, and this, only too often, prompted objections and mollifying changes. It might be almost too late to make them and get mimeographed copies ready for the reporters, but Ray had to try. The prevailing atmosphere was one of irritating emergency. It made well-constructed exposition almost impossible and was something that even so talented an expositor as Ray found it hard to cope with and still keep an amiable appearance.

The confusion had been serious enough during the two weeks after the Walker case was settled and before the long journey into the West began. It became infinitely worse when the journey was under way. Ray then had to see that Roosevelt finally did sit down across the table, behind a closed door, and actually did use his pencil on the draft put before him, though he was often interrupted by the coming and going of politicians. The train was also crowded with reporters, who were constantly being aggrieved by changes of which they had no warning, and their importunities were an added irritation.

Those of us who were left at home still had some small chores. In the Roosevelt Hotel headquarters, Bobby Straus and his associate John Dalton labored usefully. It was arranged that they would set up a watch, when the train departed, for calls from Ray. If plans were changed, if facts were lacking, or if something had to be looked up or verified, New York was to marshal its resources.

I cannot say that I was reconciled to what I had deplored in the scheme I had seen taking shape. I had substantially failed, and I regretted that I had not been more effective. There was also a lesser failure, apart from defeats about policy. Ray's knack of writing for Roosevelt was one I did not possess. As a partisan in what lately had seemed much like a battle with those who, as I saw it, either had a reactionary bent or meant to take advantage of opportunities for exploitation, I was downcast. It was something I now had to keep out of. True, I had lost my commission only for the present. Roosevelt had asked me to get ready for the next phase, but for the moment I was unemployed. What I feared was that the ground being given temporarily would turn out to be a permanent loss. While the Western expedition made its way across the plains and mountains, I went away for nearly two weeks. The torments of frustration were made worse by the onset of hay fever, my old enemy. I defected.

Recalling, these many years later—years? decades!—the weeks of hectic preparation for the expedition that would take Roosevelt to the far Northwest and down to California before coming back to the East, and reading the speeches again as they are printed in the *Papers,* I can see why they served his purpose effectively. They made no enemies and won him many supporters, as they were intended to do. At the time, I deplored the continuing inconsistency, the incoherence, and the compromises, besides being unhappy about what I regarded as a setback if not a defeat for my plans for recovery.

Now, however, I can see that the exposition of several issues—power, railways, farm credit, the tariff—gave the impression that he was competent to tackle the problems of the presidency. They were serious and knowledgeable addresses. They left open solutions still not so easily detailed, but familiarity with the issues was so evident that they held the attention of vast audiences to whom the matters discussed were vital. It seemed at the moment that they sometimes went beyond the average person's ability to take in what he was talking about, and the argument in a few of the speeches, I should have thought, could have been understood only by specialists. It was, however, a time for earnest exploration, and Roosevelt knew the West and the Northwest. He got a patient hearing and was approved even by the hostile press.

It has to be remembered that Hoover had enjoyed a reputation for being overwhelmingly competent in such matters, and indeed in everything having to do with large management. But the reputation had been weakened by his feeble handling of the depression, and it is possible that an irresponsible promiser of good things for everyone might have collected a majority in that election. There were several of that sort operating in their various strident ways, and they had followings of some size; Huey Long was the best-known example. Roosevelt preferred another way. If some speeches were not well constructed and were dull in whole or in part, they gave the impression he wanted. Especially the Northwest addresses were counterthrusts against a formidable opponent. They were an obvious success.

When the campaigners departed from our midst, there was leisure for calculating the position more carefully. Behind Roosevelt was an already shaped career; he had had administrative as well as political experience. It was a record with passages he would rather forget, but none likely to be really embarrassing. I told myself that various things he had said to me were sufficient indications that in the future he would make his own policy. Neither Brandeis nor Baruch, nor anyone else, including the elders, would be followed.

Even now he was giving no one any conclusive satisfaction. Everyone was getting something, but not much. In spite of disappointment, I had to admit that I had been privileged—as much, almost, as Ray—to have been involved in his final strike for the presidency. I could even conceive that my own relation with him was a more intimate one because I was *not* useful in the way Ray was; my chores were less demanding, and I could be more detached. He needed someone of the sort. Doc was such a person too, but we had different capabilities. Doc, by the way, was on the train, unobtrusive but often helpful. We frequently talked; it was from him that I got most of my reports.

I was a stand-by for speech-writing, as, of course, was Sam. If something had happened to Ray during those preparatory weeks, or during the rowdy confusion of the journey, I should be sent for. It was understood that I was on call. There are two reasons—at least two—why I have always been glad that nothing of the kind happened. The most important was that, as I have confessed, I was an incompetent ghost-writer. I might have compelled myself to improve at this, perhaps, if I had really been forced to try, but I was glad not to have the duty. There was, however, another reason: I found it difficult to communicate with the ebullient politicians who had to be dealt with every day. My difficulty was not political. Most of my progressive friends were thorny, charismatic professionals. La Guardia was a prize exhibit of the species. Wheeler of Montana was another, and even Floyd Olson, for whom I had an affection almost as warm as for Bob La Follette, never needed to make an effort with me; we got along very well. Besides, I was country-raised and I understood such people. What disqualified me was that I was so ardent an advocate of a point of view.

Roosevelt, like those others, must have recognized that my ultimate commitment was to the same ends as his. I knew now that he meant to become the strategist for the whole nation in the service of those ends. I told myself that I must excuse almost any use of the political arts if they resulted in his attaining the position of power that he needed as a base for moving toward the objectives he meant to reach.

I was always fully aware, as Ray was too, that our work with Roosevelt was exceedingly tentative. We had had a chance to see, Ray even more than I, how ruthless a man must be in the service of his ambition. That ambition might be—Roosevelt's was—a mixture of concern for public policy with furtherance of a career. To be kept in his service, everyone who had proved himself to be useful in some degree must continue to be useful. The helper could not count on much tolerance or any gratitude. He must, besides, be in some degree pleasing to those on whom Roosevelt depended for support of one sort or another—not to all of them, because there would be *some* objection to everyone. Generally, however, he could not be obnoxious.

This was something helpers of our sort must accept. If it was too serious a trial, we could drop out. Most of our Columbia colleagues could not make the adaptation. I still do not know for certain how we qualified—or how we endured. But in my own case, I think it must have been the unspoken encouragement, amounting to signs of confidence, which did once in a while come my way—that and my somewhat impaired but still hopeful belief that Roosevelt's policies as President would be in the pattern of collective progressivism.

So I did not really envy Ray his closeness to the events of the campaign as it moved into its later, intensive phase. Some of the productions he had to be responsible for I would not have wanted to acknowledge. Not that I was critical of him; someone had to do it, and I wanted to see it done, even if there were more compromises than I thought necessary.

When the speeches dealt in sober and decent detail with problems that must have answers, they surprised me, I am afraid; I did not consider them characteristic. I was right about that, but I belatedly discovered that the idea was to show forth a responsible administrator who could compete with the Great Engineer. For that the expositions were excellent. As for the speeches that came out a mishmash—like the one dealing with agricultural policy—it has to be admitted that even they succeeded in their own way—the political way.

Looking at them afterward, I could see how they did make that sort of sense. Evidently the most persistent intention was to keep away from commitments. This might not have been acceptable in other circumstances; there might have been further taunts of evasiveness; but the country was in such bad shape now, so desperate for rescue, that, contrary to the opinion of a good many knowing critics, a promise of this vague sort was sufficient. Roosevelt's virtual admission that he did not know what would have to be done about everything, that he did have some ideas for change but realized that they would have to be tried and perhaps modified, was regarded as honest and realistic. To the astonishment of the Eastern professionals, he returned to Albany with an enormously enhanced reputation. He had made none of the mistakes they had prophesied and had left behind him a swell of good feeling. They had anticipated disaster in the West, but they had underestimated Roosevelt's sure knowledge of that strange region.

He had professed a liking for small businessmen and farmers, but had given the impression that he distrusted big men in either occupation. He had been moderate about tariffs; that is, he had not advocated free trade; he merely pointed out that the wrong people got the most protection. Even about power, he did not argue for a wholesale take-over; public ownership was for yardstick purposes. He talked sensibly about credit; he merely wanted to expand all the institutions of most use to ordinary businessmen and farmers, and to ease distressful situations for the owners of farms and homes.

On the large issues he was evasive, but he was not faulted for that as he had been earlier. It bothered me, but apparently almost no one else. About getting out of the depression, for instance, there continued to be no apparent connection between what he evidently conceived to be its causes and the measures he hinted at as cures. As to the unemployed, he spoke of jobs for everyone, but slighted the means for furnishing them; true, he made promises of relief and of public work, but these were not connected with recovery, as I thought they must be. He still spoke of rescuing people from misery and injustice, not of supporting purchasing power to reactivate the economy. I would have thought this open to the old charges of evasion, but it did not seem to evoke them.

Putting the whole together, and wondering about the popular approval that developed so rapidly during September, I could see that he had done very effectively what was essential to his present purpose: he had offered something to everyone, not in specific terms but in general ones, so that they could read into what he said much more than was actually there, and do it according to their preferences. More than that, he had said nothing that would alienate any considerable number of voters.

It is true that he continued to speak harshly of speculators, bankers who betrayed their trust, but these were so generally discredited by now that his attacks on them echoed a common resentment. The time was arriving, or had arrived, when it was scarcely respectable to admit any connection with Wall Street. The opportunity was too fortunate not to be exploited.

His nomination of a group such as this to be pilloried was no novelty in politics. Having enemies is, for a candidate, almost as essential as having friends. They had better be persons who are already on the defensive and who are, moreover, few in number. For this Wall Street was ideal. Bankers neither had many votes themselves nor could at the moment influence large numbers of others. As targets they were set up for him by the events of the depression, and they were quite as vulnerable as those Cleveland had taken aim at, or, further back, Andrew Jackson. These predecessors had been Democrats too, and he made something of that. The party had a tradition of enmity to exploiters. He meant to enlarge it in circumstances that called for enlargement.

This contrasted interestingly with the consensus strategy so long available to the Republicans, especially in recent campaigns—the simple assumption that there were a few guiding principles a statesman ought to symbolize, principles that were generally accepted by the majority and could always be relied on. This rule necessitated a candidate of such stature that proper pride in him could be taken by every good American. Ever since the Civil War, with a few exceptions, the Republicans had succeeded in convincing the electorate that to be against their nominee was somehow to disparage American institutions. They had, moreover, shamelessly claimed to monopolize patriotism. Grant, Hayes, Garfield, Arthur, and McKinley, all weak, were all Civil War veterans. Their weakness was a constant invitation to corruption, but it had taken twenty years for the promise of a clean-out to counter patriotism successfully as a campaign slogan. Cleveland was elected as an honest man, but after him the patriotic racket had worked again for the Republicans until Theodore Roosevelt had split the party in 1912. Even after Wilson's war, and despite Harding and the Teapot Dome scandals, the Democrats were suspect; their loyalty was not quite beyond question.

Now hard times had undercut the authority of the Republican elite, and they were in real trouble. The Democrats could claim victory in another war and so had finally scotched the Copperhead insinuation. The Republicans, besides, had to bear responsibility for a depression they could not cure, and this was a denial of every appeal they were accustomed to make.

Democrats had never used the consensus strategy; since the Civil War, it had never been available to them. Minorities have to attack, to climb, to grow; they cannot stand still as majorities can, complacently refusing to acknowledge any need for change and relying on identification with accepted moralities and institutions as the foundation of their support. Republicans considered that they still had the impregnable majority they had possessed for generations. True, their unsophisticated military heroes had been the dupes of smart businessmen, but they had presented bland and confident fronts for their backers. Democrats were rebels; they agitated for cheap money; they were unstable; they offered as candidates draft-dodgers like Cleveland and crackpots like Bryan. To stay respectable it was still necessary to vote Republican. So they hoped.

Careful as the Democrats were not to say so, the depression was actually the most fortunate thing that had happened to the party since Wilson had won in 1912 solely because Theodore Roosevelt had defected with half the Republicans. Of course there were dis-

advantages. Some infuriated Democrats were left from the acrimonious struggle at Chicago over the nomination. Although most
of the contenders were by now reconciled to the result in the manner of professionals, Smith and his supporters continued to be resentful. Roosevelt, however, understood something about city machines that even the Tammany bosses, who had the most cohesive
machine of all, seemed not to have learned. The Tammanyites
were not above conspiring to defeat their own party's candidate, a
disposition they had shown again and again. But this was not true,
or was much less true, of leaders like Ely, Hague, Kelly, Pender-
gast, Conners, and others less powerful in lesser cities; they stood
to gain more from winning national elections than Tammany,
whose amicable arrangements with the local Republicans had ensured for a hundred years that they would be about as well off in
defeat as in victory. So the murderous mood of Tammany did not
spread, or rather tended to dissipate as Roosevelt's prospects improved.

With Doc's help I could understand all the political folkways,
and I cultivated the learning attitude appropriate to my position.
But about the recovery gap I continued to be aggressive. Whenever
there was the slightest opportunity, I urged concentration on this
issue. My persistence had some result, even though I had granted
that Roosevelt's desire for open options must be respected; I
thought the issue could be exploited without offering dangerous
specifics. As a general rule, things did not go my way, and presently mine was the only dissenting voice in a rising babble of anticipation. Washington was to be Democratic after all these years. In
the euphoria, talking about the possibility of disaster seemed absurd.

The manuscripts Ray had taken with him had been remarkably
varied. There were speeches for Westerners, concerned with public
power, the railroads, and the credit system; there were speeches
for the Midwest—at Topeka about general agricultural relief, besides those that dealt with credit and farmers' other needs; there
were speeches demanded by Baruch and the businessmen, emphasizing confidence; there were speeches expressing the wishes of the

elders, professing loyalty to the platform and its principles, and discussing the perennial tariff issue; there were also speeches for the Brandeis progressives, threatening an expeditionary force to subdue Wall Street, while promising to enforce the antitrust laws and thus re-establish self-regulating free competition.

There had once been a speech drafted for those of us—Adolf, the La Follette progressives, myself, and the business leaders I have quoted—who insisted on the need for planning in a society become collective, but this was not in Ray's bundle when he departed. Oglethorpe was not to be repeated. Perhaps we had failed. If, however, we had more hope than would have been thought credible from anything Roosevelt said, it came from his persistent refusal to make any definite repudiation. If this did not seem sufficient, still it was something. The concert of interests still shimmered in the future, and I could not believe it to be a mirage. Bob La Follette hooted at my optimism. We were licked, he said, and we might as well admit it. As far as he was concerned, Roosevelt was a complete washout. Floyd Olson, telephoning, was positively raucous in his denunciation. The hell with it, he said; he was going fishing.

CHAPTER XL

Roosevelt's Way

❦ ❦ ❦

I have often reproached myself, as Adolf must have done too, that I voiced no objection to the Columbus and Pittsburgh speeches; they were foolish beyond calculation. Even Roosevelt's formula of attracting support without surrendering his freedom of action does not explain them. They were not the familiar evasions; they amounted to commitments he would have to reverse. As I recalled them later, I could excuse myself only by thinking that I was too much influenced by the lessons I had been absorbing from Roosevelt's unexpected pains as teacher. I must have said to myself that if this was how he calculated the impression he must make, and if he was sure it ought to be said in this way, it was justified as an effort to get the majority he needed, and beyond that, the accumulation of presidential power on which our system depended. He could go on then to the bold experiments he had mentioned only once in public.

There was no reason to doubt that Roosevelt had accepted the explanation of the depression's persistence, and of agriculture's part in it, that we had for months been elaborating. The decline of purchasing power relative to production, which accompanied, paradoxically, our advances in technology, was perhaps not a concept easy to use in a campaign, but we had made it fairly simple. There was the difficulty that it charged business with appropriating the gains from the efficiency being achieved year by year since the war, but this charge he had not hesitated to make. There was also the fact that the remedy was a hard one. Prices would have to come down, profits be narrowed, and wages be increased so that consumers and wage-earners would have more purchasing power. That was where hesitation set in.

The Columbus speech offered reform of the banking system as a sufficient remedy and avoided all talk of unpleasant discipline. The test seemed to be whether the voters were impressed—the millions of wavering Republicans who were disillusioned with Hoover but still wanted to believe that they themselves were exempt from discipline. They would be delighted to have someone in the White House who would give the economy a new start, but not if business had to make any sacrifices. Bankers would be scourged, but not small enterprisers, admired by themselves if not by their employees, or farmers, who had been as greedy as anyone without making any return in co-operation.

As Roosevelt prepared for his long journey into the far West he was gay and confident; there would be a special train; there would be plenty of what he spoke of as "political malarkey." The prospect was for tonic days. The Walker crisis, one way or the other, would be behind him. Speeches, yes; there would be crammed briefcases of prepared or half-prepared ones, but plainly they were not the first consideration. He would show himself, lift the spirits of the local bosses, and lend them prestige by inviting them to ride with him from station to station. The numerous newsmen would report his reception by the trainside crowds, who, he believed, would respond to his high humor and find new hopes in his promises. It was something he could do superbly. He was anxious to be free of everything else.

While we were watching from New York, Ray began at once to have troubles, and we might have been more sympathetic, perhaps, than we were. On the first journey, for instance, a newspaper proprietor in Minneapolis—Frank W. Murphy, who owned the *Minneapolis Tribune* and was also a politician—took exception to parts of the draft for the agricultural speech. He insisted that it must be changed. Ray refused to give way, taking refuge in the shortness of time; the text, he said, had already been distributed. Since the objections involved some of the statistics, he wired for confirmation; having got it, he paid no further attention to that particular matter; there was enough else to do.

Ray had other embarrassing encounters, not all of them with outsiders. He told us about one with Charles Taussig, who showed up in San Francisco and announced that Roosevelt had asked him to travel east with the party. This annoyed Ray, who felt that Taussig had added nothing except irrelevancies to our preparatory conversations. When he discovered that Taussig, supposedly one of the wealthy businessmen, had made no contribution, he was more resentful than ever. Baruch, he noted, had paid for *his* participation with a sixty-thousand-dollar gift; even Raskob, despite his having been replaced summarily as chairman of the National Committee by Farley, had sent in twenty-five thousand, and Kennedy had honestly bought *his* place on the campaign train—he was always somewhere close—with big money. All the members of Straus's Business and Professional Men's League had made substantial gifts. But Taussig!

Roosevelt, however, had somehow accepted him as a stand-in for Hull, and in the summer, at Roosevelt's suggestion, he had been sent on a mission that Ray had considered harmless. He was to visit Hull, get his ideas in order, and make suggestions about presenting the tariff issue. Ray soon realized that this was a mistake; the differences were deeper than he had realized, and the compromises would be more embarrassing. References to the issue would be more frequent than he had foreseen or than Roosevelt had anticipated; whether it was agreeable or not, Hull was a powerful Democrat and had to be mollified.

The question was whether the free-traders, of whom Hull was the long-time representative, would be able to prevail over the Westerners—Senators Walsh and Pittman, for instance—and those of us in the Brains Trust who were convinced that in order to work out our problems of recovery and reform we would have to be insulated from European interference. We were, I suppose, nationalists, as opposed to internationalists. Of these latter, Hull was only one; there were others in Wall Street who sold foreign securities to American investors and dealt in the exchange markets. Hull was rural and traditional; the financiers wanted to speculate as they liked and therefore objected to national economic fences. The alliance was a curious one, but nevertheless too strong to be ignored.

It is true that our early arguments about the tariff had been prolonged and sometimes almost acrimonious. Taussig had duly gone to see Hull and had taken it upon himself to act as Hull's representative. He had worked out a formula for compromise involving a moderate reduction, and since this was so traditional, Roosevelt gave very little attention to it. He was presently to regret not having taken the issue more seriously. The contradictory phrase in the platform, "a competitive tariff for revenue," would, he suddenly realized, have to be dealt with; that is, he would have to decide whether the policy was to "equalize competition from abroad" or to maximize revenue. They were irreconcilable, something I had tried to tell him earlier.

We had gone over it, recalling the time, in Cleveland's administration, when tariffs had produced enough revenue to support the whole government. That was the origin of the phrase in the platform. Then too, older Democrats had not forgotten that Cleveland had been a mighty fighter for moderation, that he had, indeed, lost an election to Benjamin Harrison on the issue. Moreover, the Smoot-Hawley Act (signed by Hoover, and now being defended by him) was ultraprotective, and in fact had been written by and for manufacturing and mining interests. It imposed an indefensible burden on consumers and left the farmers altogether out of consideration.

This last was one reason why Peek and his crowd were turning to Roosevelt although their every instinct was Republican; they wanted somehow to give agriculture benefits equivalent to those given certain industries by the tariff. "Tariff equivalent" was a locution they had taught Al Smith to use in 1928, and Roosevelt had picked it up from the newspapers. He still used it, to my annoyance, ignoring my protest that it was meaningless. It was silly to talk of protecting products that were not imported anyway. To give farmers the "equivalent" of tariff protection must mean, if it meant anything, that they were to be paid prices for their products that were somehow artificially raised to equal those of industry; either that or they must receive some sort of benefit payment. In either case, how was the subsidy to be calculated? It was much more realistic to compare the price levels of agricultural and manufactured goods at home and abroad and devise ways for equalizing them. But what on earth, I asked, had the tariff to do with it?

I knew M. L. Wilson did not agree; that is, he did not object to Roosevelt's using this language. Farmers, he said, were high-tariff folks; never mind why. All they wanted was to get incomes as large as others were getting. It was only political realism to accept their notion and make use of it; no harm would be done.

Hull had always argued reasonably that lowering tariffs was necessary because it would open foreign markets to farmers' products. If Europeans could pay with their goods, they would buy ours. The manufactures farmers must buy, including machinery, would also be reduced in price if they had to compete with imports. This did not at all suit Baruch, Peek, and other businessmen, who found themselves in the dilemma of wanting protection for industry as well as wanting prosperous farmers. Their way out was to insist that if processors were allowed to raise prices, then consumers could be made to meet the bill.

This curious scheme, once seen through, was so obviously self-serving that Roosevelt was not inclined to give it any attention. But, being assured by Wilson that the farmers were thoroughly indoctrinated, and feeling that there had to be tariff speeches, Roosevelt decided to make two. One was to be at Seattle on September 20 and the other at Sioux City on the 29th as he came back from the west coast. The first was to advocate the solutions we had been calling "reciprocal tariffs," meaning that rates would be fixed not in rigid schedules but in flexible ones worked out in bargains with other nations. Each could determine what its interests required and concede enough to get trade going. We felt that this at least got the party out of the worsening controversy between the free-traders and the protectionists. It was duly set forth in Seattle:

> . . . tariff by negotiation means to deal with each country con-
> cerned on a basis of fair barter; if it has something we need and
> we have something it needs, an agreement should be made that
> is agreeable to both parties. That, of course, avoids a violent
> and general shake-up in business. . . .

Ray, in *After Seven Years,* was to cite this issue as a flagrant instance of Roosevelt's irresponsibility; he was airily told to "weave
together" two totally inconsistent views. This was doubtless regarded by Roosevelt as no more than a necessary means of avoiding an issue on which he preferred not to take a stand during the
campaign—something which, as I have noted, seemed to be the
rule about other issues as well.

As might have been anticipated, neither the Hull nor the Baruch
faction was satisfied with the Seattle statement. Hull made his annoyance known; he wanted reductions; and Baruch, briefed by
Peek, began a series of intrigues intended to put pressure on Roosevelt in the interest of the processors. Roosevelt considered that a
clever compromise had been found, counting on the "Yankee trading" phrase, but the adverse reaction brought him, in the midst of
his journey, to the necessity of saying something more definite. He
had come to have considerable respect for M. L. Wilson as an in-
terpreter of farmers' reactions, and he listened to the warning that
the sentiment for protection, however unreasonable, was as strong
as ever throughout the Midwest. Moreover, Wilson said, it would
be wise to give farmers the assurance that whatever was done,
their commodities would be protected. This might seem ridiculous;
but they had been told over and over by the farm-organization politicians—mostly Republican—that there was danger of their markets being flooded with foreign commodities, and they believed it.

So a contest began. Retiring to Santa Barbara for a few days,
while the other travelers politicked in northern California, Ray,
with the help of Senators Walsh and Pittman, set out to do the
weaving Roosevelt wanted. The date in Sioux City would offer an
appropriate occasion.

The speech already in Ray's briefcase was acceptable enough to Walsh and Pittman. They were sensitive about being protectionists in a traditionally free-trade party; it was a conspicuous singularity. Our Albany draft, leaning heavily on the reciprocal formula, but also defending moderate protection as against wholly free trade, was something they could swallow; also, it somewhat relieved their embarrassment.

Taussig, however, as Hull's stolid emissary, insisted on another version that argued for immediate and drastic revisions downward. Walsh, who was irascible anyway, was irritated by Taussig's persistence and, in effect, dismissed him, saying coldly that there was no further need for his services. Taussig at once disappeared, to be seen no more during the journey, and the senators had their way. What resulted, however, deepened Hull's annoyance. The weaving did not suit him. It was true that ironic reference was made to the excesses of the Smoot-Hawley Act—it was called "the Grundy tariff," referring to the notorious Pennsylvania lobbyist—and Roosevelt had hoped this would serve for appeasement. Smoot-Hawley, he said, had erected unscalable walls without the slightest calculation that retaliation by other nations would be inevitable.

The Democrats, Roosevelt was made to say in the speech, intended to adopt a different scheme. Protection would be given, after factual study, to every legitimate American interest; cheap foreign goods would not be allowed to outsell decently produced American ones. Still, there might be room for reciprocal arrangements. Here he repeated his defense of "Yankee trading," claiming that this would increase trade rather than block it:

> I do not have the fear that possesses some timorous minds that we should get the worst of it. . . . I ask if you have no faith in our Yankee tradition of good old-fashioned trading?

If Hull was dissatisfied with this, so were Midwesterners, since there was nothing to guarantee equality for agriculture. Later speeches, in consequence, had to protest several times that there was no intention of exposing farm products to foreign competition; moreover, farmers were promised "benefits" equal to those given

protected manufacturers. Hoover quite rightly assailed this inconsistency and demanded clarification, but since he stuck stubbornly
to protectionism pure and simple, the issue was probably not so
important in the end as had been feared. There was not much to
choose.

This was the most annoying issue Ray had to deal with during
this journey. It was not, however, so difficult, really, as a later one
that caused the most heated argument of the campaign, finally involving everyone, including Roosevelt himself. It occurred in the
interval just before the New England tour at the end of the campaign and had to do with the speech to be made in Boston on October 31. There would remain, after this, only the final visits to the
home precincts, particularly to New York City, where nothing new
need be said. Roosevelt had at last determined that the Boston
speech should firmly state a commitment about unemployment and
outline a plan for recovery. These, after all, remained the inescap-
able issues. It was late, but not too late to make a record.

By then he had promised in Pittsburgh to reduce the budget and
restore confidence. I was still sensitive about having let this go
without protest. It might easily have been toned down, but for
some reason it had not been, and it left Roosevelt open to the attack from Ogden Mills which he had been so afraid of earlier in
the campaign. An effective riposte was now inevitable, and it was
likely to be devastating, since Mills was the most agile and intelligent of Hoover's campaigners and had a formidable knowledge of
federal finance. Most fortunately, by now no one was listening to
anything offered by the administration's speakers.

Adolf and I had continued to argue that something ought to be
said to extend Roosevelt's earlier remarks about recovery. To do
this, of course, he would have to reject the politicians' insistence
that, since the campaign was already won, nothing controversial
should even be mentioned. We could think of no way to counter
this advice, but it occurred to us that what the professionals were
saying gave us instead of them the best of the argument. The forecasts—including the private ones made by Emil Hurja for the

Democratic National Committee—did show that there was a land-slide in the making. We said this offered a wholly new opportunity. Vote-getting could be ignored.

Ray, by now, had been consorting with prominent Democrats for more than a month. Until lately he had been accepted in these circles only as a necessary nuisance. But in the writing of the speeches to be given in Baltimore and other places, Byrnes and other Southern senators had asserted their right to be consulted, as had Pittman and Walsh in the West, and Roosevelt welcomed this new evidence of the elders' affection. So Ray had become their—as well as Roosevelt's—amanuensis. The Baltimore speech, next to that of Pittsburgh, was certainly the worst of the campaign; it was pure political hokum.

In *After Seven Years,* Ray was to recall this final disagreement among those of us who had worked together for so long. His account differs from my own recollection, and it seems to me to make no sort of sense. His defense was that now he wanted to end the campaign on a note of serenity and statesman-like dignity. The rest of us—meaning Adolf and myself—wanted to go on attacking and, besides, to make more and more radical proposals that would have stirred up controversy.

Actually, what we pressed for was a credible discussion, at last, of what was needed for recovery. Even the familiar *Times* editorialist, by now become tolerant, still felt forced to point out this lack. Others were even more insistent. Theirs, we felt, was a justifiable demand; in all the many set speeches there had been no proposal looking realistically, and with some specification, toward the reactivation of the economy. A good deal had been said about helping the unemployed, although I still could not see how there could be much consolation in a promise to do no more than use the savings from governmental economies for relief. Taken literally, this was a meager prospect.

"Restoration of purchasing power" had also been spoken of, but there had been no explanation of how the restoring was to be done. The subject had been dropped so quickly that it could hardly have been thought to be seriously meant. Adolf and I, not being so caught up in the excitement of the last weeks, were appalled by the prospect of the coming winter, which was certain to be even worse than the last two, with no possibility of any change until March. At the very least the millions in trouble were entitled to something substantial to hope for. So far there had been nothing—not if the pronouncements of the campaign were carefully examined. Every realistic appraisal, every calculated proposal—except that the budget would be balanced—had been eliminated or, at best, so moderated as to be noncommittal.

We urged that Roosevelt now say something to the unemployed. We thought the politicians ought to be put on notice that changes were coming whether or not they were agreeable. True, some unpleasant forecasts for businessmen were involved, the small ones as well as the large. But why not? If it was true that victory was now certain and Roosevelt was really going to be President, he could lose nothing by preparing the way for what he knew well enough would have to be done.

We were reluctant to conclude that Roosevelt himself remained unrealistic about the "purchasing power" he still spoke of. How could he really mean to try for a budget balanced at once, hoping that, together with enough economies to pay for unemployment relief, a subsequent business pickup would cure unemployment? It was incredible.

As I gradually took in what was happening, I did not hide my disappointment that Roosevelt was allowing Baruch and Johnson to draw him into their axis. It was a bitter defeat. This was what the late-campaign controversy was about, although Ray would explain it differently in *After Seven Years:*

> Berle and Tugwell were for a detailed elaboration of the industry-labor program and a sharp attack upon those in government and industry who had countenanced the abuses that existed. Pittman, Byrnes, Johnson, and I were for a more moderate approach. We felt keenly the weariness of the public as the campaign drew to a close. By all the signs, we felt, Roosevelt was as good as elected. The time had passed for sounding the tocsins. This was the moment for the dignity and conciliation that befitted a President-elect.

I have always felt that Adolf and I might justifiably resent this passage. Besides, it was made worse by Ray's saying in the next paragraph, "Happily, Roosevelt concurred." Adolf and I were certainly not asking for "a sounding of the tocsins." We were contending that since the caution appropriate to a doubtful outcome was no longer necessary, preparation ought to be made for what must come next. Education at long last ought to begin.

Above all, we thought the many soft promises of the last months ought finally to become hard. We would have liked Roosevelt to say, as he now seemed more inclined to do, that since the signs of recovery had faded again and the depression was still deepening, heroic actions would have to be taken. Funds for relief and public works; increases of funds for the Reconstruction Finance Corporation; expanding loans to home-owners; benefits to farmers—these, it ought now to be said, would have to be immensely larger than had so far been estimated.

Ray certainly put a more defensible interpretation on his consorting with Pittman, Byrnes, and others of the conservative elders than I would make. If he gave in to them, it was not because toward the end of the campaign it was a time for Roosevelt to be "statesman-like." It was because he had allowed himself to become far too impressed with these insiders. They had dominated the campaign and frustrated our hopes for a realistic setting-forth of the nation's problems and the means for their solution. We did not think now that this was what had brought about the likelihood of victory. Republican futility more than the prospect of Democratic action had done that.

The fact is that Roosevelt rejected the politicians' advice at this stage. The Boston speech, compared with what had gone before, was notably forthright and not at all "conciliatory." Not everything it said was defensible, but it did outline the first steps to be taken. It spoke, for instance, of restored purchasing power: "Grim poverty stalks through our land. . . . Against this enemy every ounce of effort and every necessary penny of wealth must be raised as a defense."

This was still general, too general, but it freed him from com-

mitment to economy. The Hoover conferences back in the twenties
and their reports were cited in some detail to show that there were
known means for combating depressions. These had been waiting
all summer to be used. The exposition did not go on to say, as we
would have liked it to do, that there must be an organization for
national planning and for co-ordinating productive operations; but
there was a genuine and patently sincere undertaking that the federal government would accept responsibility for a balanced economic system. That went far beyond the promise of an immediate
rescue operation.

I am afraid I have to say, with all due reservation, that Ray was
beginning that long journey with the conservative compromisers
that would end, to my sorrow—because of my fondness for him—
in a position so far to the right as to be quite inexplicable.

Roosevelt, however, had begun preparation—too late and too
meagerly—for the hundred days after inauguration. There should
have been several Boston speeches, and they should have taken
back, or straightened out, much of what had been said at Pittsburgh and Columbus. But it was something to have got as much as
we did.

CHAPTER XLI

Mission to the Progressives

🏵 🏵 🏵

Before the Brains Trust began to disperse as the campaign neared its end, there were occasional calms in the eye of the storm, and I had several other conversations with Roosevelt. What I recall most clearly about these is how familiar the subjects had by now become, and also that although the discussions were no more conclusive they did include some new intimations of policy.

One of those talks was in the familiar surroundings of the drawing room in the old mansion. Traffic through the halls had stopped for the night; there was a wood fire, and Roosevelt, who was never ready for sleep before midnight, was in an unusually meditative mood. Others of our group had gone their ways. I was staying over, and no one else was present. The last journey would soon begin—against the advice of all the professionals, who were urging him to stay at home. They admitted that they had been wrong in the past about the value of his travels, but, as Roosevelt said with a big laugh, they were willing to be wrong some more. He was like all politicians, he guessed, always greedy for more votes. Besides, even if the votes weren't needed for the election, they would be useful later on.

I remarked a little sourly that he had listened to the professionals about everything else and that some day he would be sorry for it. But, he said, what he had listened to them about was how he should campaign, and that was something they were expert in. I replied that there was not so clear a distinction as he had tried to make. He had let them tell him to avoid most of the hard problems, but this did not mean that the problems had gone away. He would have to face them as President, and then he might be sorry that he hadn't seen the campaign as something more than a mere election.

He was offended by the word "mere," and I admitted at once that I shouldn't have used it. Election was the first business, but, as everyone acknowledged, it was as good as won; he could now look beyond it, and what he would see was more frightening than ever.

Things between us were so much easier than they once had been that such reservations were permissible. I thought this might be because of, rather than in spite of, my continued disapproval of his decision to avoid the difficult questions. I was implying that he had not been frank. He knew how I felt. Several times he had answered my criticism by pointing out how carefully he was reserving his freedom to move, but that answer was no longer true. Obviously his Pittsburgh speech had been a definite commitment and one sure to haunt his administration.

That, however, was where our argument stood by now. He had made choices as he felt he must. He knew my reservations. But I had been unjust about the word "mere" before "election." I guessed that he might already be having second thoughts, now that his election was fairly assured, but the assurance was not a trivial achievement. I said so, and he accepted my amendment, saying, O.K., Professor, we'd get to the issues in plenty of time, and I'd see how free he was to make choices.

Why, when he knew I was a dissenter, should he have gone on allowing friendship to develop?—for that is what it amounted to now. As far as my usefulness was concerned, he was still expecting me to contribute some of the devices that must be got ready; but usefulness was one thing and communion was another. Thinking about it, I realized that although he was surrounded by all sorts of people, there was no one he could really rest easy with. That seemed to be a peculiarity of political life; everyone within call was either subordinate or somehow not quite right for trying out his still amateur and tentative conclusions. Even Ray did not share many of his interests or hopes. Dependable and capable as Ray had proved to be in helping to shape Roosevelt's public image, the elders, sure now of victory, were leaning over his shoulder.

Every day there were evidences of widening approval, but what was responsible for this, it seemed to me, was the travels and speeches that had so worried the professionals. It was nothing he actually said. All of this continued to be unsurprising; it was what the professionals were so used to hearing that it did not make them prick up their ears. This avoidance of controversy gratified the elders; furthermore, to put it crudely, the big contributors were in an approving mood. They felt that they were aiding a candidate who would be a grateful winner, and this prospect led to more generous subscriptions, so that Howe and Farley were floating in the euphoria peculiar to politicians when they are paying their way in a winning race. Time ended for them on election day, and everyone who had helped was a friend. It did not matter that there would be other sorts of debts to be paid.

Roosevelt in this had drawn ahead of the professionals around him and was far into his future responsibility. He understood that I too had discounted the victory, and since I was not of much use any longer in immediate matters and was brooding over his problems, there was something between us that he valued. He had come close to saying several times that he shared my view of recovery and even my conviction that some insurance of permanent fair-sharing must be found. Now he occasionally discussed it as though all that remained was finding a way to proceed. That took him to his presidential power—how much he would have, how he could use it for what must be done, and what it was, more precisely, that must be done.

I recall that after a while, during this evening, he got around again to my "radical friends"; they were worrying him. This time, however, he spoke of them with a different twist. He had lately been accused by the Republicans of having radical associations himself. He had not answered the charges, but Hoover was desperate and was becoming accusatory. Roosevelt chose to pretend that this annoyed him and that I was much to blame.

It pleased him to include among "my friends" not only the Dewey-Douglas group (the League for Independent Political Action) but still others who were making what noise they could. These people constituted a band of literary revolutionaries who had recently issued a manifesto under the heading *Culture and the Crisis,* proclaiming belligerently an alignment with "the party of revolution." Only the communists, they said, understood that capitalism had degenerated until it had finally caused its own doom. The old parties would try to save it, and in doing so they would lend themselves to further exploitation of the masses, putting off the inevitable end. The communists promised a wholly new system. The international party was the image of the future. Its time had come.

The signers of this manifesto included, in addition to others less well known, John Dos Passos, Edmund Wilson, Malcolm Cowley, Granville Hicks, Sidney Hook, Lincoln Steffens, Matthew Josephson, and Lewis Mumford—all names with prestige in their own world, but some, it appeared, not known to Roosevelt, and if not to him, then not either to the political fraternity. But they were getting the attention they craved, and it was even being said that Roosevelt was preparing the way for the take-over they saw in prospect.

He spoke of them half-jokingly, but in some wonder, remarking that they would have a morning-after feeling when they sobered up and realized how alienated from American tradition they had allowed themselves to become. Of course, they could afford this complete irresponsibility; it was even less likely that any of them would have to answer to voters than that my friend Paul Douglas would. Still, he said, they were going to squirm when the economy was righted and they had to find a way back home from Moscow.

The disquisition was, however, really an aside. What he was concerned about, because after all he belonged to the American elite, was not this tiny coterie, so eager to abandon our institutions and so willing to forget the wreckage caused by revolution. He showed real concern about a third group now being identified in the press. These were professed supporters of his own cause who had met recently at the call of Senator George Norris and had organized as a National Progressive League. Producing a clipping that described the meeting, he called attention to the names. Besides Norris, there were Bainbridge Colby, Amos Pinchot, William Draper Lewis, Francis Henry, Ray Stannard Baker, Felix Frankfurter, and Harold Ickes, with Frederick C. Howe as secretary.

He pointed out that the list included several old city reformers of muckraker days, some of whom had left the Republican Party to follow T. R., while others had been Wilson liberals. It was an honor roll, he said, from old wars. This fellow Ickes, he had heard, had tried to persuade them last spring that they ought to endorse Gifford Pinchot for another third-party presidential run, since the Democrats had shown no interest in the progressive program and were about to nominate a man they could not in conscience support. Nothing had come of it; most of them were disillusioned by now, knowing that victory by any third party was most unlikely. But there were some with Republican backgrounds who intensely disliked supporting a Democrat. They had been joined by Hiram Johnson, Burt Wheeler, Ned Costigan, Bronson Cutting, and the La Follettes, and all of these had made public declarations.

These last, and a good many others, were experienced politicians, not literary radicals. They had won elections, and some could swing a whole state. I said it looked as though, without being one of them, another Roosevelt was splitting the Republican Party. Yes, he said, most of the progressives had been Hoover people not long ago, but Hoover had offended them over and over— uselessly, it sometimes seemed. The trouble was that they might desert the Republicans without joining the Democrats. He knew well enough that most of them were unhappy about his campaign.

He went on to say a good deal more about the old progressives—"your progressives," he called them. They were wonderful people, but they did have the general characteristic of complete unreliability. They were individualists who never really granted leadership to anyone. Because of this they had never been effective as a group, and naturally they had never been able to keep a party going; even Uncle Ted had not been able to hold them together for more than one campaign. They could agree neither on a leader nor on what progressivism consisted of. What it said in *The Times*—he referred to the clipping—was that they had gone to this Washington meeting at Norris' call, and that the Senator reported for them, when it was over, that what this country needed was another Roosevelt in the White House. He would be happier about that, Roosevelt said, if he didn't recall that when there had been a man of that name in the White House, the progressives had found him unsatisfactory, or many of them had. They could never be counted on for support. Besides, the bonds holding them together were weak.

He asked me to look at the list of proposals they had issued. He read it aloud: relief; a farm-market program; reduction of farm taxes; revision of public-utility laws; reform of the courts; reforestation; public power.

That, he said, was not a list they ought to be proud of; look what they had left out. Nothing was said about recovery, about the tariff, or about financial reforms. It wasn't worthy of Norris; the old man was so taken up with his Muscle Shoals fight that not much else seemed important to him these days. He was a grand fellow, and he'd stick better than the others, but he really didn't have a program. Only Bob La Follette did—with Wagner going along—but Bob was too young to be a leader in this crowd.

Did I know why the important issues had been left out? It was because they couldn't agree on them—just what he'd been telling me. Still, these were people he wanted to please, maybe not for election but for what would come after; they were excited about the real issues, however little their manifesto showed it.

When the progressives had followed T. R. out of the Republican Party in 1912, he went on, it had been a typical performance; they were always willing to quit something, and they were apt to become haughty and high-minded about it. When it came to giving anyone who represented them the leeway he had to have for maneuver or compromise in getting something done, they were almost sure to make a virtue of demanding more. They were the best standers-on-principle we had. But the principle always turned out to be whatever happened to interest them as individuals—or maybe as politicians.

He was well started now. We had talked some, he and I, about ends and means. Any political leader, and above all any President, had to have tolerance for making deals that would build and keep public support. That was in fact the nature of his power. The progressives, when such deals had to be made, deals that might be vital to something they themselves wanted, were quite likely to defect in moral dudgeon. Yes, that was the word, dudgeon. They insisted on dictating means as well as defining ends; they'd sacrifice the cause if the strategy happened not to please them, and they would be noisy and accusatory.

He wanted to remind me, as he had before, that Wilson had trouble of this sort (in fact he had reminded me of this several times). How well he recalled the treaty fight! Most people now would say that old Lodge had been the responsible leader of the "willful little group" of senators who had refused to ratify the peace treaty, but Wilson had been much more hurt because the elder La Follette would not come around. La Follette wanted peace in the world, all right, but he refused to accept the League of Nations as a way of getting it. He said that was because the other members couldn't be trusted. Actually, it was more because Wisconsin was as sick of hearing about Europe as all the rest of the Midwest and had reverted to isolationism. It was simply good politics for him. That was the way Wilson was repudiated; all his fair-weather friends deserted—including the progressives.

I objected. The La Follettes, I said, had always opposed foreign involvements. Also, they had deplored armaments, and they had never liked the war. It was nothing new for the elder La Follette. Incidentally, young Bob would be the same way.

He admitted this, but he went on to say that when Bob defected he would remind me of what he had predicted. All those German sympathizers out in Wisconsin had made it easy for a politician to oppose Wilson's war, and young Bob would find it convenient to stand by only as long as Wisconsin approved. Then there was another thing. Old Bob had been burned up by the acclaim Wilson had got all over the world. Senators simply couldn't stand presidential popularity, and all these progressives were senators.

Wilson had told him, he said, that even before the war he had been quite likely to read in the papers a furious denunciation from one of his progressive supporters about something he had said or done, and the outburst would come without any warning. In the circumstances of war and the negotiations for peace, it had been impossible to consult every one of the progressive group and there had been no one who could speak for them collectively. But they had acted as though every single one of them ought to have been consulted.

It did have to be admitted, he said, that Wilson, besides being exhausted, had seemed to become arrogant and self-righteous and had felt more and more that he ought to be allowed to speak for the nation. All Europe had hailed him as the voice of his country —but not the progressives, and not the Lodge Republicans. To them this was a usurpation of power. They had to assert themselves.

He expected, he said, to have the same problem; he could never hold the progressives' approval for eight years. The elders of the present would be gone by then, and the party might have a very different look. Who could tell?

He had noticed, he continued, that I had no filial feeling for the old war horses—I showed it clearly enough. Didn't I realize that as President he would have to begin his work with them and through them? They were not like the progressives; they would suffer almost anything to hold this party intact. They would try to shape policy as they would like it to be, but they would compromise to keep things peaceable.

He spoke again about jeopardizing the election with strange ideas and novel suggestions, even those urged by progressives in conclave. What, he asked, did I suppose Robinson, Byrnes, Pittman, Harrison, and Hull thought of young Bob La Follette or the rest of his group—Burt Wheeler, for instance, who had left the party to run as vice-presidential candidate with Bob's father on a third-party ticket? Everyone knew that the progressives took pains to distinguish themselves from the Democrats more than they did from the Republicans, not because they didn't often want the same things, but because they themselves, many of them, had Republican origins and depended on Republican support. No, he could not count on them. Didn't I see that they were a good deal like the farm leaders? They disliked one another more than they did their common enemies.

I asked if this was why he had kept himself a regular Democrat. He replied that I should have learned that much this summer, if I hadn't learned anything else. I said I had taken that lesson to heart; a political leader had to begin by belonging. I saw that he must have people he could call in and say that such and such must be done and ask them how it could be managed, not what they thought about it. I was still puzzled about his way of deciding that what he would have to pay was not more than the end he had in mind was worth. He must expect to run into hard bargainers, in addition to those whose motives were questionable and whose demands were unreasonable, and those who had inflated legislators' egos. Once in a while he would run into one of the sort who had tried to impeach Andrew Johnson. Weren't these the ones who nursed a grudge against all Presidents, who thought the Congress should make policy and the President should merely carry it out?

In answer he merely said that I hadn't done so badly as a student, considering where I had started in the spring.

Taken as a whole, this was more of a disquisition than I had thought myself capable of. Some of what I understood of professionalism I had found hard to swallow; still, I had pretty well got over that revulsion. That is to say, I accepted—perhaps as fully as any of the others—the necessity for staying in accord with the elders. I had not agreed and still did not agree that Roosevelt was right to avoid saying what recovery required. I thought he underestimated the reaction there might be to the drastic actions he would be compelled to undertake as President. I ventured to say again, as I had done so often, that he still ought to think seriously of a frank warning.

He spoke now more approvingly of such a venture. He had had good reason up to now for not explaining the dimensions of a necessary program. It was still true that such frankness would startle the elders and would also divide the progressives. Now, he asked, if he made the decision, where *would* he look for his support?

I pointed out that in going so far in commitment to the Baruch notions he had practically made the essential enlargement of purchasing power impossible. The commitment would have been intelligible if he had not known that vast expenditures would have to be made and that they would alienate the businessmen. But he had known that all along, since our first talks. It was as inevitable as anything could possibly be.

He objected. I would see, he said, that apart from economy, this businessman's idea could be turned into something of the sort we had been discussing. Baruch, after all, had run the War Industries Board and could hardly oppose a new version of that. As for himself, he still thought that funds could be found for relief and public works without levying new taxes or resorting to the printing presses. If only business could be got going, the unemployment problem would diminish like snow in a spring thaw.

He was fooling himself, and I told him so. He had said too much about economy and budget-balancing; the sums he would have to spend were simply not there. And the resumption of activity would not come with confidence. Roosevelt was not ready to concede, but I could see that he was shaken. He knew well enough what the winter would be like.

One thing I learned from this talk—our last really confidential one—was that since he did not wholly accept our forecast of what the situation might be when he took over, he was more than ever convinced that he had better be cautious about any specifics. What might happen—the businessmen were telling him—was that, as in other depressions, an upturn might follow liquidation, and liquidation might by now have run almost its full course. There were

economists who were saying that it had, and Hoover had proclaimed the signs that he, and they, professed to see. These, so far,
had shown themselves to be false; some of the unemployed had
found seasonal summer work, but the number was pitifully small;
businesses were still failing and banks were still closing. But opti-
mists were interpreting these facts as evidence that the depression
had reached bottom and that activity would have to turn upward.

I found no reason whatever to think that recovery was imminent. It seemed to me that if conditions did not get better during
the coming winter, while Hoover was still responsible, Roosevelt
would take over at a time of dreadful discouragement. If he had
nothing planned and ready, he would find himself making excuses
just as Hoover was doing. I had thought a good deal about this,
and we talked about it. He acknowledged that it might happen that
way, and that if a crisis had to be met he would need to act quickly
and boldly. But, he thought, there would be no trouble about acceptance if that happened. Everyone would be in a panic. As to
preparing, there would be four months for that, and we already
had some thoughts, if not actual plans.

Four months, he admitted, was not too long. At least two things
were needed by way of preparation. First he must make up his
mind what measures could be taken if things went on as they were,
or if they got even worse; and then he must arrange for the acceptance of those measures by the people who had to approve them.
He went back to the progressives. They had argued with Hoover
for years about the means for recovery. The question was whether,
when the time came, they would support a new President who had
plans of his own.

I said it seemed to me more likely that they would support him
than that the elders would when they found out what would have
to be done. Did he really think they would allow him the freedom
he must have?

If I was right, he said, they would be in a panic, and that would
give him plenty of freedom. I could forget any worry I had about
the Democrats. If there should be a crisis on March 4, it would
have to be met immediately and by drastic action. Did I think the

progressives would accept his version of what was necessary?

I threw up my hands. What was he saying? I asked. He was going to become President despite having ignored the first problem he would meet. Why should they trust him?

March, he replied, would be at the end of another winter, and that might be like the end of another century. Who knew what would happen? He was saying that if it should be the worst we could guess at, nothing he had said, or anyone had thought, would stand in the way of action. But the progressives might prepare the way.

We talked a little about that, but there was not much more to be said, really. I saw perfectly what he meant, looking ahead from where we were, or where we would be when the election was over. It was of no use now to complain about the past, about the campaign I thought so misleading. It would be won, and there was a terribly critical future to be thought about.

He went on to what he had in mind for me. He really distrusted the progressives, but he knew that some of them thought pretty well of me—better, right now a whole lot better, than they did of him. Bob La Follette had been telling him the same things I had been saying, and he imagined we were pretty much in cahoots. Bob didn't come around any more, for he was suspicious, and there were at least a dozen in his group. They normally wouldn't stand up under much strain, but they might be needed. They were where they could do the most good. If they were cultivated they might be firmed up.

He was right about Bob, I told him. Bob was not only a friend of mine, but a think-alike. He'd left the old clichés a long way behind; he was now a collectivist and a practical one. I went on to say that I knew him better than I knew any of the others, except perhaps Fiorello La Guardia; but Fiorello, as he knew, full as he was of good impulses, had never been remarkable for consistency or practicality. The others I met occasionally—through Bob, mostly—but if they had some reason to assume that I came from a future President they would certainly talk to me and let me talk to them. They might be suspicious, but they were thoroughly frightened by what they saw ahead.

All he wanted, he said, was for me to keep talking to them. It was left there, as so many of our Roosevelt commissions were left, tentative and indeterminate. He had not told me to do anything, but he had assumed that I would do what he suggested. Other such directions had not always turned out well. All of us had been given jobs to do that, when done and reported on, he had forgotten all about, or affected to have forgotten, we never knew which. He leaned very heavily on the assumption that we wanted the same things and that we would work for them with no other reward than the prospect of getting them done under his leadership. It was he who would say what should be done and when. And it was our part to wait on his arranging, meanwhile not asking questions about how the arranging was being done.

This was my compensation for being shut out of the current proceedings. I could tell myself that what I had to do was important, if not very exciting; anyway, I do not recall any twinges of self-pity. I suspected that he had not said all he had in mind. The progressives might be undependable, but they were inventive and they knew how to carry on a dialogue. They were not talking to him any more, but they might go on talking to me. While the Democrats were winning and occupying Washington, they might be the only ones in the whole country who were considering without self-interest what was called for in the nation's extremity.

CHAPTER XLII

Hoover on the Hustings

⚜ ⚜ ⚜

Roosevelt had started out in genuine awe of Hoover, and with some apprehension about the sharp intelligence of his neighbor, Ogden Mills, who was Secretary of the Treasury. His respect was hardly less for Henry L. Stimson, Secretary of State. The others who might campaign actively—Hurley (War) and Hyde (Agriculture), for instance—he hardly considered at all. Hyde's belligerence over the forestry employment issue, rude surprise as it was, had been blunted successfully; he was in such bad repute that nothing he said was likely to draw attention, and besides, he had no credentials for coping with farms or forestry; he was an automobile dealer.

Hoover himself had for years dictated agricultural policy; differences were with him, not his Secretary, and Roosevelt kept them centered there. The failure of the Farm Board was so notorious that in this, as in so much else, Hoover was on the defensive. He could not say much more than that he had done his best "within American principles," an explanation he was by now using as a general excuse. It was apparent when he made his acceptance speech that his devotion to principle was something he supposed the voters would readily accept as an excuse.

This obtuseness was an advantage for Roosevelt, and when he saw that it was part of the Republican reliance on consensus that had been the bulwark of the party since the Civil War, he knew how to use it. The consensus had to be broken into. The Republicans' two losses, to Cleveland and Wilson, had been caused by temporary desertions at times when they had become corrupt and reactionary. But the deserters had returned to the party, and through Harding's and Coolidge's administrations the Democrats had fallen further behind. The public had overlooked even Teapot Dome, and Smith's defeat in 1928 had ended any hope of successful challenge within the foreseeable future. He had carried only eight states and his electoral vote had been 87 to Hoover's 444. To have predicted at any time before the spring of 1932 that this showing would be almost exactly reversed by November of that year would have seemed extravagantly unrealistic. No professional on either side anticipated any such outcome, and certainly no Democrat.

Nevertheless, the Democratic leaders were quick to sense a change, and the bitter contest for the nomination, even after a majority of the delegates had been accumulated by Roosevelt workers, showed how generally recognized it was that suddenly there was a chance, even a good chance, that another wholesale Republican defection was in the making. Myopia about hard times in 1929-1932 had shocked loyal Republicans much as had corruption in 1884 or reaction in 1912. Hoover, being surrounded by unusually sycophantic associates with blunted perceptions, was kept in ignorance about the Republican defection; besides, he was not himself sensitive to opinion.

In fairness it should also be said that he was laboring through troubled days and nights, and that he had become more and more withdrawn from those who might have warned him. His trusted associates, Mills and Stimson, belonged to a disdainful elite. Neither had ever been elected to office, and neither ever would be. The professionals in the party, who might have given him better advice, had never been able to involve Hoover himself in their efforts on his behalf. Even in the approaching disaster of this summer he continued to rely on his own defective judgment. It was reported that he was writing his own prolix and inept speeches without asking anyone with political skill for advice.

Watching the Democratic proceedings from his withdrawn en-
clave—when he found time to watch them—he had been relieved
to learn of Roosevelt's nomination. He must have read Lippmann
or the editorialists and been convinced that the Democrats had
chosen the weakest candidate of all those in the running. Roosevelt
commented at the beginning of September that this must be the explanation of Hoover's evident determination to be as little as possible involved in campaigning, which he apparently regarded as
unbecoming for a President—especially for one who had conducted national affairs with unexampled competence. The voters
must surely recognize and reward his faithful stewardship. His associates would call attention in a dignified way to the record of
their administration, and the Republican majority could be trusted
to respond at election time. Roosevelt could hardly believe that
this was what was actually happening. The mistake was so colossal
that he was for a time needlessly worried about attacks that must
still be in preparation.

It is amusing to recall how Hoover's self-satisfied reliance on his
vanishing majority affected Roosevelt. It seemed to amaze him as
a politician, and it was a little humiliating for him to realize that in
Hoover's judgment the American voters would not regard him as a
worthy substitute for so seasoned a statesman. This irritation was
an added incentive for actively attracting voters. Roosevelt had
several weeks to convince them that Hoover was actually a hollow
image and that he himself was a desirable alternate, and he meant
to use them.

In a passage of his three-volume *Memoirs* (1951–1952),
Hoover would explain at length why, a month before he plunged
into campaigning, he had judged that he need not undertake it seriously. Even when looking back after twenty years, he was still
hurt, still convinced that the voters—or at least the Republicans
among them—had been ungrateful. In retrospect he was no more
willing to admit mistaken judgment than he had been when he took
to the road in October 1932 and began to instruct Americans in
their duty. The reasons he then gave for his re-election were so

convincing to himself that their rejection would always be utterly incomprehensible.

Roosevelt spoke wonderingly a number of times about the indications that his opponent seemed not to realize his situation. Could it be the recollection that he, Roosevelt, had been no more than a minor official in the Wilson administration when Hoover had been a major one with an international reputation? Or could it be a judgment that in time of national crisis governorship gave no claim to the presidency? Hoover, after all, had been involved in greater affairs than those of a single state. It was quite possible, Roosevelt said wryly, that a man standing on such achievements might believe the estimates he had been reading in the press and hearing from Stimson and Mills.

I thought I understood Hoover's position better than Roosevelt did. The fact was that Roosevelt's speeches before the nomination—the ones at St. Paul and Oglethorpe—had not really made a nation-wide impression. The "concert of interests" and "bold, persistent experimentation" had not taken many headlines. They had been commented on briefly, but both themes had been muted in later talks because the professionals disapproved, and since the nomination nothing more definite had been forthcoming. If Hoover had not taken alarm, it was no wonder.

Information about Hoover's scornful attitude and his reluctance to take any active part in the contest continued to filter into Roosevelt's widespread net of information. However much it puzzled him, it was accurate enough. If from nowhere else, the information would have come from Louis, whose firm alliance with the elders brought him floods of professional estimates. Besides, that shrewdest of publicists, Charles Michelson, knew where to look for the signs of success and failure, and he was certain that Hoover was doomed.

When these clever calculators became convinced that Hoover was making a fatal miscalculation, they took it as the most useful indication for further strategy. For them, as for us, it was easier to believe what seemed to be happening than it was for Roosevelt

with his rather exaggerated respect for his adversary. Hoover's estimate of himself in comparison with Roosevelt was credible
enough to Michelson, who had been watching him closely for
years. He—and Louis—could imagine Hoover in his White House
stronghold asking himself what Roosevelt had to offer and finding
the answer to be "practically nothing." In contrast, see what he
himself, the President, stood and stood boldly for—American
principle! He was its unshaken defender.

As far as the depression was concerned, Hoover considered that
he had acted with immense energy and effectiveness; he had recognized it as an enemy and had mobilized every permissible weapon
to defeat it. True, "blows from abroad" had frustrated his efforts
just when they were beginning to succeed, but surely that would be
understood, and he would be trusted to overcome this obstacle as
he had overcome others. He had taken his stand on the declaration
that he had met and was countering the new threat that everyone
must be aware of. He had explained what was happening, and that
ought to be enough.

But most to his credit, he felt (as he explained afterward), was
his refusal to compromise the most strongly held beliefs of his fellow citizens. Even in the heat of combat he had not consented to
the undermining of individual responsibility, nor had he jeopardized the traditional rights inherent in free enterprise. Still, without
giving way to panic, he had found a way to succor the unfortunate.
This was nothing new; he had done it throughout his long career,
and surely no one could claim to have a compassion for the
stricken more sincere than his own.

All things considered, it was understandable that he simply
could not credit the rumors he was beginning to hear that defections were becoming serious. He continued in this state of disbelief
until Roosevelt was on the road. Suddenly the news of his opponent's progress began to pre-empt the front pages, and the impression he was making invaded the editorial columns. This was a matter of weeks after the Democratic professionals had correctly estimated Hoover's disposition to stand pat on his presidential
accomplishment. Until about this time, Roosevelt had not been

certain that he could attract the millions of Republican votes he would need. As the weeks passed, however, and Hoover did not come awake, Roosevelt began to accept what was more and more obvious. When he began his journeys he had reached the tentative conclusion that it was already too late for Hoover to repair the damage.

This reappraisal meant that he himself had a different situation to deal with from the one he had anticipated. A landslide was in the making—not yet a full avalanche perhaps, but stones were already rolling that might well set the slopes in motion. Every report that came to headquarters from the local leaders reflected a growing confidence that victory was in prospect. Since this was so, campaigning need only be directed to holding a present advantage, not to finding new ones.

Roosevelt, pondering this change, had to conclude that the fighting canvass he had planned was not now necessary. Senator Key Pittman gave him typical advice: take it easy, make no mistakes, offer no surprises. Pittman opposed the plans for travel into the Midwest, the South, and New England. He added, however, when he spoke of it to Ray, that he knew his advice would not be taken. Also, he remarked wryly, he had been wrong once and might very well be wrong again. He was beginning to see that Roosevelt was no ordinary campaigner and never seemed to make mistakes. But the same advice, often urgent, came from other old-timers not so shrewd as Pittman, who also underestimated Roosevelt's persuasive talents. The battle was won, they said; why jeopardize it? Even Louis, well as he knew his protégé, opposed taking further risks and wanted to stand on Hoover's weakness.

Roosevelt was unmoved by all this sophisticated pressure. What they did not know was that he had a good deal more in mind than simply winning one election. Everything, moreover, was encouraging the enlargement of his plans. He could now begin to implement the ambitious scheme he had all along been contemplating. He could press toward the permanent realignment he thought the country was ready for.

First, it was necessary to accumulate the power that would free him from party obligations. The elders had to understand that he was winning a personal victory and that his debt was no longer to them but to the people. If this election was already decided, in effect, he could start looking forward to later campaigns. Even Louis—not to mention the other professionals—seems not to have guessed what was in his mind. They watched with foreboding as he risked what they estimated as a sure thing. While he traveled, they sat shuddering in the Eastern headquarters, or they rode in his train sweating with apprehension.

As for the traveling, he was obviously confident that he could get through all its hazards without making mistakes, at least any of such proportions as would affect very much the tidal drift now gathering volume. Also, he was much more impressed than others who did not know him well by the need to answer the whispers about his disability that always began to spread during his campaigns. Jim Farley was assigned to denounce them, and he did it with evident sincerity, but Roosevelt knew from experience that only personal appearances would be really convincing. When he did appear, if only for two minutes on the back platform of his train, his son James, who was a towering six feet five, was always beside him; so were Betsy, Jim's wife, and Anna, his blond daughter. It was an argument more effective than any words. The opposition could not match it. Hoover, in contrast, when he finally took to the road, was revealed as a high-collared recluse who wore a weary and sourish smile and was accompanied only by a far from glamorous wife. Altogether the contrast was a sorry one.

Curiously enough, Roosevelt's appearances were undervalued by the professionals, probably because of their acute fear of mistakes, but also because they had no intimation of what he was reaching for in the now changed circumstances. Even when Walsh, Byrnes, Pittman, and others of the senatorial coterie joined his train and began to scrutinize every speech, they continued to be more apprehensive than confident. Roosevelt, as the old-timers had not realized, possessed a special brand of what Doc—who was much more realistic in his appraisal than even Louis—called "hokum." He almost always recalled a former visit, giving the impression of familiarity; he then offered a few comments on the weather and the crops and on his pleasure in seeing his old friend, the local leader. He always managed to call attention to his "little boy, Jimmy," evidence of potency and, by implication, of vigor; and when the train pulled away as though without his consent, he left the impression he had meant to make. Contact had been made, trust established, faith that he would *do something* implanted.

None of this appeal was open to Hoover, who, even if he was a dedicated worker for "the people," was hopelessly unable to communicate with them. He was so taken up with his pressing problems that he could not see the yearning for reassurance in the faces turned up to him in the crowds marshaled for trainside greetings or for party conclaves in meeting halls. Roosevelt knew how to reflect enthusiasm; if the feeling had been synthetic in the beginning, it soon turned genuine; he created response. Hoover dampened any incipient gaiety; no one went away inspired to labor.

I had taken no part in this progress toward victory. I went on none of the trips, and along toward the last it occurred to me that I had never seen Roosevelt in action even when he was making speeches that I had worked on with the others. I had been in the room when he made two radio addresses, but that was all. What I had to go on was what I heard from Ray or Doc. I never talked with Farley, with Howe, or with anyone else at political headquarters. Still, for some reason I was not clear about, Roosevelt had certainly talked to me in ways that he could not have talked with the others, because if he had, we should have compared experiences.

Even in the busiest weeks there were interludes, and it was during these that he sometimes found me handily present and talked in a way he seemed not to have done even with Ray—although this is probably only seeming, because in order to do his drafting, Ray must have had the same intimations of what was to come that

I had begun to sense. In *After Seven Years,* however, Ray was to reveal surprisingly little understanding, as I would define it, of the Roosevelt plans for the future.

Ray also did not estimate Hoover as I did, and he may not have understood that Roosevelt never really gave up his regard for his predecessor. On the other hand, Hoover's failure to do anything curative about the depression had shaken this respect, and the incident of the bonus marchers was evidence of an insensitivity that seemed almost incredible. The public servant, once so greatly admired by the younger man who had now become his rival, was no longer so admirable. It was not until the October speech in Pittsburgh, however, that Roosevelt gathered the courage to attack Hoover directly as the responsible author of the country's ills. The attack was made with a text furnished by Johnson, Baruch's man, and so presumably approved by the business community. He might not have relied so easily on one of our productions.

About the middle of October, Hoover suddenly awakened to his danger, came out of his corner, and at once began swinging wildly. His sudden panic, after his former indifference, was attributable to several happenings. The July indications of recovery had faded; Roosevelt had made his long trip to the West, and the reports of his favorable reception were unanimous; and Maine, of all places, had gone Democratic in its September elections. Possibly Hoover discovered also, what was quite evident, that none of his associates was being very well received even by carefully mustered audiences. With all his calculations thus upset, he made the worst mistake he could have made; he undertook to direct his own campaign and to insist on ratification of his recovery efforts as its central issue.

His acceptance speech had been effective enough. He had recited, even if at tedious length, his many achievements, including his vigorous efforts to stem the decline into stagnation of the national economy. In later appearances, however, his labored explanations were notably unconvincing. He relied most on the one we had hoped he would emphasize—that all he had done at home had been overwhelmed by "blows from abroad." Again and again he recited the phrase, not realizing that each repetition counted against him. His other favorite explanation was that the July upturn would have continued if businessmen had not suddenly begun to be suspicious of Roosevelt's intentions; in consequence, he said, they had withdrawn all plans for expansion. This was an appeal to fear, always a favorite device of conservatives, but in the present circumstances it was hopelessly inappropriate. What more could the millions of unemployed lose? How much further into bankruptcy could farmers and businessmen fall?

The man he trusted most gave him advice to which he should not have listened. Ogden Mills, being Secretary of the Treasury and in touch with the financial community, assured him that Roosevelt was determined to induce an inflation that would cheapen money and jeopardize everyone's investments. It was incredible to Hoover, therefore, that Roosevelt should attack him as the man responsible for overblown budgets and generally weakened finances. He could not believe that anyone would be influenced by so outrageous a suggestion.

The reversal of roles was infuriating; so too were Roosevelt's repeated attacks on his indifference to the desperate situation of unemployed workers and bankrupt farmers. Hoover considered that he deserved the country's thanks. He had indeed rejected suggestions that he consent to a federal dole, but he could not believe that he would be widely blamed for this; on the contrary, he expected credit for his stalwart refusal. At first, he had some reason for the expectation. In Des Moines, for instance, his argument seemed to carry and be approved. But he was now weary almost to collapse, as well as being overcome by the sudden knowledge that his regime was in jeopardy; he noticed how cold the crowds were at the whistle stops and along the streets as he went to and from the meeting halls where he spoke. Like all candidates, however, he tended to forget that the cheering crowds inside were captives, required to be there by local leaders and officeholders. That theirs was a whipped-up enthusiasm was easy to overlook. The gatherings were large, and they were suitably loud and loyal.

Republicans had been in office since 1920, and the number of those whose jobs depended on Hoover's continuance in the White House was immense. This was assessed realistically by the Democratic strategists as another handicap to be overcome, and probably it was counted on by Republican professionals, but seemingly Hoover did not appraise it realistically. He must have noticed that support from this source was about the only real encouragement he was getting, but if he did, it was not apparent. What came home to him finally was that every poll, every regional report, and every estimate of political reporters concluded that Roosevelt was running further and further ahead.

The effect of this on the indignant and self-righteous Quaker President was to make of him an uncertain and irrational pleader for a cause he hardly knew how to defend because it was so obviously just. His late appearances, particularly one in Detroit after he had spoken in Ohio, were political disasters. The crowds in the streets were hostile to the point of booing and hooting. This was not only an offense to him as the Republican candidate; it was an inadmissible affront to the President of the United States, who was being exposed to almost treasonable indignities. By going on the hustings as President, Hoover had risked a prestige that ought never to be thus eroded. He was desperate, but now there was no possibility of retreat.

In the final days he was a stricken man, disoriented and very nearly incompetent. His speeches were more and more crammed with figures and complex economic arguments, all defensive. He dug and scrambled among the facts he knew so well and found them useless as he put them together. In the grip of his panic he did not hesitate, at the end, to intimate that American institutions were in actual jeopardy. What Roosevelt intended about the tariff alone would cause "grass to grow in the streets" of the cities. Still worse, there were irresponsible radicals around Roosevelt who not only would institute free trade but also would destroy the gold standard, bring on inflation, and jeopardize the whole future of the nation.

It was in Madison Square Garden, October 31, that Hoover delivered this desperate attack. Roosevelt was making his Boston speech a little later that same evening. He had not intended to listen to Hoover, but Ray and other friends turned on the radio in the sitting room of his hotel suite, and Roosevelt heard part of the speech through the half-open door of the bedroom. He was furious at being pictured as a revolutionary. For the first and only time he was discomposed and disposed to react with some violence. That his loyalty should be questioned was something he could not let pass. It was only with considerable difficulty—Ray has written—that he and the press secretary, Marvin McIntyre, persuaded him not to interject angry rebuttals but simply to continue in the calm and confident tone of one who was ahead.

Except for this one instance in which he deferred to the judgment of others, I am quite certain that Roosevelt decided on his strategy for the final stages of the campaign without consulting anyone. Louis had his own ideas, and these had been represented by the Pittsburgh speech, but after that quite a different scheme appeared. Hoover was attacked for a while, without much spirit, since the arguments had already been presented, but soon Roosevelt was trying to reach a higher level. The opportunity seen by Adolf and myself for a really constructive and soberly educational ending was not quite accepted. He read and discussed our memoranda, and what he decided did somewhat reflect our urgings, as I have noted in discussing the Boston speech, but he made his own adaptation.

Anticipation of victory was freeing him from the elders, and in these weeks he was finding a new orientation. Through New England and New York he spread optimism, but not many specific promises. There was not much in the last Eastern speeches for which he needed a Brains Trust; a skilled speech-writer was sufficient. That, of course, was still Ray, who takes credit for having counseled the rejection of our plans and for supporting those of the professionals. I was willing then—and I still am—to yield him this claim.

When it was all over, Ray notes having spent a quiet evening with him at Hyde Park before he came down to New York for the election returns. They talked, Ray said, of how it had gone, but apparently not of how it would be. Whether Roosevelt spared a thought for the loser, I do not know. He may have done so, although he had been enraged by the aspersions on his own loyalty. By then he may have come to understand Hoover's exhaustion and near-hysteria.

Hoover had decided at the last minute to vote in California as an acknowledgment that it was his home. On the way, he felt compelled to make more speeches. One particularly, in St. Paul, was an incredibly unbalanced performance. He thanked God that there was still a government in Washington capable of dealing with a mob, a remark following the cry that the Democrats were the party of that mob. To anyone with our history in mind, this sounded much like Hamilton's observation in an unguarded moment that the people were "a great beast." There was obvious and audible resentment even among the Republican faithful. Reporters said that Hoover was unnerved, that he swayed on his feet, repeatedly lost his place in reading, and looked as though he might collapse at any minute.

Next day, as his train rolled across the plains, he went on working, this time on the final broadcast he was to make on election eve. The train stood on a high-plains siding that evening while he warned Americans once again over the radio of "destructive forces" that might affect the welfare of generations still unborn. William Allen White, editor of the *Emporia Gazette* and a faithful Republican, sat with him for a while and said afterward that his voice had become tired—"infinitely tired"—and that his words were hollow and sad "in disillusion."

The nation he cared about so deeply was being handed over to a man whom he distrusted and who he felt would listen to those who counseled policies he had spent all his public life in combating. He was not only exhausted, he was convinced that his beloved country was endangered.

CHAPTER XLIII

End—and Beginning

❦ ❦ ❦

The labors of the Brains Trust had begun on a spring evening; they ended gradually on fall evenings in the same room, in the same house, in the same city. Albany had been shabby and disheveled at the end of winter; summer greens had partially hidden its drabness; when they were gone, the ugliness again began to show.

The drawing room and the mansion were losing their place in our lives. For months the house had suffered the careless occupation of a political army intent on an objective more suitably sought in the usual temporary quarters of politics. The workers had worn its carpets and stained its plush, and now its colors had faded to an even sicklier brownish yellow. As I look back after so many years, an obsolete mansion in a run-down city seems to me a strange place in which to have contended about the rescue of a nation from a three-year sickness that had begun to seem chronic.

As argument went on in those weeks about the content of his last speeches, Roosevelt could hardly be said to be involved. He had lost interest in the present, I presume, and was thinking about what was to come. His indifference may have been why discussions among the Brains Trusters verged for the first time on quarreling. Some acerbities of our association were showing too clearly for concealment now. I was smarting from defeat, and I no longer had Doc O'Connor to hold my hand. Neither he nor Sam Rosenman was active any longer; both had lost touch with the dialogue they had once followed so intelligently—and so critically.

Whereas Adolf and I were agreed on one last thing, that we wanted Roosevelt's final appeals to forecast a program with genuine promise, Johnson wanted more reassurance for business. His intention, it seemed to me, was to commit Roosevelt to a line favored by Baruch. The Brandeis crowd wanted commitment to *its* line and was pressing just as hard. By now, apart from a difference about punishing wicked Wall Streeters, the Brandeis followers were curiously close to those of Baruch. Ray, under the spell of the professionals, wanted everything kept serene, serious, and friendly. Actually, everything was coming apart. Roosevelt was falling into absurd inconsistencies and would not choose.

There was a certain euphoria among the hangers-on. Because victory was in plain sight, I realized—as the others must have done—that what we had left to argue about was how Roosevelt would emerge as President-elect. What, we asked, would he really have held out as his promise for the future? The voters might realize only that he had promised action, but those who were pressing in on him meant to control that action in their own interest.

Since there was no more need to win votes, the professionals might have been expected to lose interest as Roosevelt seemed to be doing. Actually, they were as insistent as ever that coasting to the end was the strategy to be followed. They had no novel suggestions to make, and they seemed to think, as Hoover had done, that the depression would quietly go away. This had been their attitude since the middle of summer. I thought Louis should have known better than to demand—and finally obtain—both the Columbus and the Pittsburgh pronouncements. They clearly contradicted each other. Columbus had caused such consternation not only among the Wall Streeters but also among businessmen generally that in the Pittsburgh speech Roosevelt had offered appeasement amounting almost to repudiation. Johnson's draft of that speech, promising everything required for the re-establishment of confidence, had been intended to make the large contributors happier; perhaps it had, but it had infuriated the progressives. Roosevelt knew well enough that these included influential political figures in at least eight states, but he had begun to act on a theory he would follow for a long time—that he need not please them because they had no other leader. Generally speaking, the compact with the elders had dominated the middle part of the canvass just as it had the beginning. The victory was to be a party one; Roosevelt was the inner circle's man. Louis had his way. Inconsistencies could be resolved after victory.

Farley, for his part, had an accomplishment of enormous importance to his credit: the surrender of the city bosses. This was something with true political irony; it would eventually react on his career and eliminate him altogether from sharing in the power he was now doing so much to create, but "eventually" was a long way off, too long for a professional to foresee.

From the harsh denunciations of Roosevelt by Hague and Ely at Chicago, and the machinations of Kelly, the machines had swung around to a respectable show of support. Even Tammany had not dared to hold out; Farley had got at least nominal support. The coming-around was grudging; Walker was still too recent a martyr; but the Hall was effectively neutralized. The professionals reminded themselves that it was nowadays a Manhattan organization, regarded with jealousy in other boroughs; it could no longer swing the vote of the city, to say nothing of the state.

Years before, Roosevelt had captured the Bronx by making its potent boss, Ed Flynn, his secretary of state. As can be understood from Flynn's own account, in *You're the Boss,* not only was he able to dictate in his own borough, but he was one who thought sometimes of the party's—if not of the public's—welfare. He had worked hard as Farley's second during the campaign. His influence in bringing around the organizations in other cities had been considerable, and Roosevelt was grateful. When one added up contributions toward the end, Farley and Flynn had to be credited with the capitulation of the old Smith cabal, and Louis with the continued support of the elders.

It might be that we too deserved some credit—in this case for the emerging Roosevelt, the Roosevelt now being visualized by the voters. At least they now regarded him as competent in several important technical matters, and they had the impression, it seemed, that he would really tackle the problem of recovery. They must have come to this conclusion more because he had exhibited a muscular and lively personality than because he had said anything consistent and convincing, but the fact was that even the skeptical press had given in. By now even the Brains Trust was being given more recognition than we knew ourselves to deserve. The prospect of victory was making everyone generous.

Adolf and I, though we might not have agreed on precisely what ought to be said in Roosevelt's last speeches, were generally on the same side. Having lost the last engagement in the Albany drawing room to arguments that we forced into the open but could not counter successfully, we were really through. The Brains Trust returned its commission to Ray, our principal. We had served our purpose.

The rest of the campaign was pure charismatic appeal, more than a little low-flown, repetitious, sentimental, innocuous—all the sort of thing that Doc called "hokum" (when he wasn't using saltier epithets). Doc watched its absorption by vast crowds with hardly concealed contempt; he was not a good democrat. He conceded that the condescending aristocrat had been accepted in this role, despite all probability, but this did not make him think that the acceptance was something to be relied on for long.

Very late in the campaign Roosevelt had gone south, against all advice, and had experienced one of his gaudiest receptions in Atlanta. He had even gone to Warm Springs, having a yearning, evidently, for a unanimous vote in that small village. (He would not quite get it; there was to be a lone unconverted dissenter about whom he was afterward lingeringly curious.) At the very last, looking to the longer future, he had toured New York City. If Tammany had thought anything remained of its ability to obstruct and undercut, the shrieks of Manhattan crowds dispelled the illusion. Obeisance to the new boss was now the alternative to futility, even for a sachem.

Since this is an account of my involvement and not a history, it is enough to say that I had no part in the further proceedings. After that acrimonious last meeting of the Brains Trust in Albany, I did not see Roosevelt or, as I recall, Ray until it was all over; the nature of the last speeches was such that Ray's composing skill was enough. No more novel suggestions were to be offered, and, as no further research was needed, I imagine Adolf was also suddenly an outsider.

We were both teachers anyway, and the fall term had begun. The excitements of the campaign were muted by the demanding routine of our occupation. Naturally I watched with a more informed interest than I should have had a few months before; besides, I was still not entirely reconciled to my various defeats. When I went to vote on Claremont Avenue and met colleagues on the way, I said I supposed they were casting some of the few ballots Thomas would get. Most replied that they were; none, I think, had been converted to Roosevelt. I had told him this would happen, and I was not surprised. What I was less able to understand was why some five or six million of the twenty million who were going to vote for him were converts. Later I talked to Doc about it. He advised me not to be a damned fool; they weren't voting *for* Roosevelt, he said; why should they? They were voting *against* Hoover. For the moment I had forgotten that this was what Roosevelt and the professionals had been counting on; it was all the party managers really wanted.

The result ran with the prediction. Actually, the count for Roosevelt was 22,815,539, and that for Hoover, 15,759,930. The vote for Thomas did not sustain John Dewey and Paul Douglas—or my several colleagues—in their hope for a substantial showing. His count was 885,458. That was more than could have been produced from the campuses—more even than could have come from the old-line Socialists—but it was not much more. If Tammany had a new boss to contend with, so did Thomas; Roosevelt had already begun to erode his following. He was right; they had no other leader to follow.

I heard the returns on the radio. There were fairly vivid descriptions of Roosevelt's early evening descent on the Biltmore headquarters, his retreat with pencil and paper into a secluded room, and his emergence, when Hoover's telegraphed concession had come, to stand gaily before the crowd of elated party workers on a platform in the ballroom and thank everyone. Ray may have felt just a twinge of neglect when Roosevelt, his arm over their shoulders, said that he owed his victory to two people—his old friend Colonel Howe and Jim Farley. Ray got no credit.

As a matter of fact, Roosevelt had done his own thinking, his own planning, and his own sorting out of our suggestions, however urgently they had been made. It was a political victory. We did not know it then, but our usefulness had not yet had its real trial; that would come later. But it was as individuals, not as a Brains Trust, that we would go on.

Bobby Straus, when I asked him many years later what he recalled of that night, wrote:

> I haven't the vaguest idea where you or Moley were; all I can remember is where I was. I was sitting with my mother and old Mrs. Roosevelt. I watched her with great interest when the moment came and she knew her son had been elected President of the United States. I don't think she batted an eyelash and I felt at the time that she really didn't approve all these rather crude goings-on. . . .
>
> My other recollection was seeing FDR waving to everybody in the hall as he went to the elevator. I thought to myself "just like the Harvard-Yale game—as they carry the winning captain off the field. . . ."

I probably would have seen the celebration in much the same way if I had been there. Hearing it over the radio, interpreted by excited commentators, I gained from it even less awareness of the consequences than Bobby felt, and there was certainly no solemn dedication to future responsibility. There were only the whoops and hurrahs of victory.

As I reflected on the months just past, I thought that at my age I ought not to have been so unsophisticated about political processes. My economic conclusions, fully accepted as they were, had not proved to be political possibilities. Still, I was stubbornly unconvinced. They should have been, and I resolved to find out why they had not. It would be just as interesting—and evidently more useful—to one who cared what happened to his country.

About Roosevelt's situation as he became the president-elect, it still seemed to me that grave mistakes had been made and unusual opportunities wasted. I thought he would be in trouble before long. One mistake was the promise to reduce expenditures and balance the budget, something not only manifestly impossible if he was to make good his other promise of relief for the unemployed, but also a departure from his determination to talk of ends but not specifically of means. Unfortunately, as I had come to realize, we had not really cleared his mind of the fallacies he had gathered during the years of separation from intellectual disciplines. For instance, he still clung to the concept of the nation as a family—a large one, but still having all a family's characteristics. This led to the conclusion that when expenditure rose above income and debt was incurred, bankruptcy must be imminent. That was the basis of his belief in the annually balanced budget. He still held to this common-sense image; nothing we had said had shaken it.

That was one fallacy. I had a fairly long list of others I still hoped to argue before he became President. But it was not a very lively hope. I was afraid he was concluding from his political success that his economic policies were sufficient.

The most important of the wasted opportunities, I thought, had to do with failure to follow up the Oglethorpe beginning. I continued to wish that he had asked the voters to support a movement into the collective economy of the future instead of reverting to a competitive order whose confusions and imbalances had caused this depression and would cause others. Baruch and Brandeis, taken together—although each detested the other—had smothered our arguments. Especially toward the last, Roosevelt had gone over completely to an oil-and-water mixture of both. At the same time that he was telling me he meant to keep himself free to experiment, he was encouraging those who would oppose experiment to the last gasp.

It was all very well, I thought, to say that the electorate must be persuaded and not pushed. I could accept that. But he had not been persuasive. He had encouraged the victims of the depression to think that their miseries were attributable to a few wicked individuals who had transgressed some moral rules. That the trouble was with the moral rules themselves was something I thought he must realize, but he had not even hinted at it during the campaign. It was politics, perhaps, but was it statesmanship?

His lessons in the realities of candidacy had so impressed me that I had very nearly given up urging the remedies I felt more certain than ever were the only ones that would save the situation. What so depressed me on election day was that he had not kept to this rule but had succumbed to the urgings of those who wanted to fence him in with commitments. If he should fail, I said to myself, a memorial plaque in that stuffy discussion room in Albany might very well read: "In this place, Franklin D. Roosevelt lost his options."

Nevertheless, I voted for him; in that way, at least, I shared in the victory. Besides, I still had a report to make—if he and Ray had not forgotten—about agricultural legislation. More important, there was that vague mission to the progressives. I wondered what I could say to them now. Still, I had that deep and ineradicable commitment to the presidency that had sustained me all along. If there was anything I could do I knew well enough that I would try.

🏵 🏵 🏵

If we thought we had done with Roosevelt's business, now that the election was over, we were mistaken. Before long we were involved—especially Ray and myself—in his preparations for assuming the presidency.

We might have anticipated this. Perhaps Ray did, although when we spoke of such matters in November, it was about the campaign in a reminiscent way. I had indeed been given the commissions I have spoken of, but by now I knew better than to take Roosevelt's requests too seriously. Probably others had been similarly instructed, and quite possibly he had forgotten.

It was certain, however, that there were sinister signs of further troubles. What he had not been willing to suggest during one summer he would have to think of for the next one. The winter between them would inevitably be the most distressful the nation had ever known. By December that was already evident. Cold was being added to hunger, and the two were pressing in on more families every day.

It was being said—and Roosevelt had special antennae for what was being said—that the Democratic victory had given the depression a push downward instead of upward. Those who disposed of capital were less willing to risk it, suspecting they would not get it back in money as valuable as the money they had loaned. This was the rumor; if it was not true, the deflated Republicans were disposed to make it seem true. What was fact, as anyone could see, was that Hoovervilles were spreading, that bread-and-soup lines were stretching around whole blocks, and that no smoke was coming out of factory stacks.

Sure enough, when Roosevelt got back from a short rest, there began a renewed but quite different association lasting until inauguration in March. It was a time of study and discussion about what should—and could—be done. Roosevelt had to choose the members of his administration, too, and this took a good deal of his time. While this was going on he saw and talked to all sorts of people. Everyone was available to him now. There was power to be shared, and even the most unlikely people thought they ought to share it. But also, those who were most fearful for their own interests were eager to offer advice. Most of the hopeful sharers were unsuited to Roosevelt's purposes, and most of the offerers were obviously meaning to warn against drastic change. It was safe, and sufficiently serviceable for his purpose, to make use of us instead.

Ray, Adolf, and I had the same virtues Roosevelt had seen in us before. We were disinterested, reasonably knowledgeable, and willing to assist without talking about it. Actually Ray, with me helping, was again most depended upon. Although other economists were consulted, and Wall Streeters—some of them old Roosevelt acquaintances—were often talked to, it became more and more apparent that my anticipations of near-disaster were moving nearer to realization. The take-over on the fourth of March, after the terrible winter, would be in the midst of crisis. Roosevelt was fully aware of this; if he had not believed me, then he heard it from his frightened friends. But he had to choose among the plans for recovery, and this involved weighing and consulting. As before, his mind was inclined toward my drastic remedies; also as before, the politicians were conservative and the financial people were reactionary. I was pretty much alone.

By then we knew one thing about Roosevelt that those who had elected him did not know: he was already familiar with Washington and the presidency, and he knew the possibilities and limitations of presidential power. When March 4 did come, after what seemed like an endless winter, the desperate situation had in fact arrived. For my reforming plans it was too desperate. There had to be emergency makeshifts, and they were fairly well accepted; what was necessary for permanent reform never got done.

As in the campaign, I began this period hopefully in Roosevelt's confidence and ended it by being outside. In the end Ray assembled for Roosevelt a collection of experts in financial affairs, mostly those who had been running things before, and they patched together a rescue operation. The new administration began with that.

I had learned some discipline, at least, and some resignation as well. Throughout the period I did what I could, but I also said what I felt I had to say. Whatever Roosevelt decided, he usually admitted that I was right, then said that what I felt was needed could not be done. He was good-natured about it, and I knew better than to insist.

There were to be some occasions in the future when I would find it hard not to say that I had told him so. Sometimes he said it for me. But what I mean to indicate in this note is that the campaign I have written about was not the whole of my Roosevelt service, but only the beginning. It was, however, quite typical. I was always urging something he would not or could not do, and he was always discussing it with interested attention. Sometimes a little of it came through, but not much. The New Deal does not deserve the reputation it has gradually gained. Roosevelt does. He was one of the more remarkable Presidents, and I have never regretted my frustrated attempts to convince him that he should do what he readily admitted ought to be done.

We had always tried to ignore the spreading tendency to zero in on us as a Brains Trust. As time passed and we were more in evidence, that sort of publicity became more and more difficult to evade. But we did serve somewhat the purpose indicated by the locution. It was not because we were superior in any way to many others who might have been used; it was because we interested

Roosevelt with our concern and our inventiveness, and because our loyalty was something he knew how to value. What happened after we moved on to Washington is another and longish story. Here I shall say only this: we did go on with Roosevelt for a time, and it was an interesting time.

Appendix / Index

APPENDIX

Proposal for an Economic Council

(Presented to Roosevelt after nomination)

🏵 🏵 🏵

The present crisis in economic affairs has taught us one lesson which we ought to have known before. This is not our first depression and it will not be our last unless we accept its obvious dictates for the future. Integrated industrial planning is necessary if we are not periodically to suffer from inflation, wrongly directed productive efforts, waste of capital resources, and consequent periods of stagnation for the redressing of past mistakes.

An industrial enterprise today which undertakes a program of production has no assurance that all of its efforts will result in the making of goods which can be sold. Its factories have to be planned far ahead of demand; its raw materials have to be assembled, its labor force gathered in anticipation that somehow customers will appear. At the same time other enterprisers may be making similar plans or new products may be entering the field. It is a result of this that surpluses are built up during failing demand and that excessive advertising budgets are maintained in the futile hope of persuading consumers to buy.

There is one way out of this impasse and only one. The average of demand must be gauged in advance by experts, co-ordinated production programs must be based on them, and it must be made certain that the amount of goods flowing into the markets is proportional to the purchasing power of consumers. Otherwise, periodic depressions will occur. It is not sufficient for industry to undertake this co-ordinating task for itself. Only nation-wide monopolies, with definite contractual relations among themselves, could cope with the task; and the dangers in such a scheme are obvious. Industries in pursuit of profits would limit their production to profitable quotas, prices would outrun purchasing power, and all the difficulties we now suffer would again show themselves.

There is needed a Federal Economic Council attached to the Executive, and operating under his direction to secure the needed co-ordination. It ought to be made up of economists and representatives from industry. I suggest a council of twenty-one with the following divisions:

(1) Statistical, with the duty of gathering and interpreting information relative to current production, distribution, capital issues, monetary supplies, domestic and foreign trade, and consumption;

(2) Production, with the duty of planning the national output of staple goods, agricultural and manufactured;

(3) Consumption, with the duty of estimating future needs of the population;

(4) Domestic trade, with the duty of estimating the ability of distributive resources to care for the streams of commerce;

(5) International trade, with the duty of formulating policies with respect to our international economic relations;

(6) Prices, with the duty of watching and advising concerning the general and specific relationships among various prices for the preservation of balance;

(7) Capital issues, with the duty of encouraging or discouraging the flow of capital into various industries;

(8) Natural resources, with the duty of estimating the rate of use and the efficiency with which resources are used;

(9) Finance, with the duty of co-ordinating the work of the Council with that of the national banking system.

With such a council set up, the federal government ought to press for a reorganization of industry somewhat on the model of the Federal Reserve System in banking. The antitrust acts can be repealed and each industry can be encouraged to divide itself into suitable regional groups on which will sit representatives of the Economic Council.

The Economic Council ought to be set up, at first, as an advisory body to the President. Its powers would be restricted to advisory ones, at least in its experimental stages. It might be necessary later to implement its powers by constitutional change and enabling legislation. But first, we ought to try the efficacy of reasoned planning and expert persuasion. If our plan were executed with sufficient care, if it were carried directly to the executive levels of industry, American business would have had the opportunity, at least, to sink its own differences in a national program of expansion and stabilization. This it has not had under Republican auspices in spite of that party's pretensions to the service of business.

The Democratic party met one great crisis in the Nation's affairs with administrative imagination and skill which was the admiration of the world. It substituted persuasion and planning then for the use of force. In another great crisis, I now propose that it follow its own historic precedent. If business continued to display the divisive policies of self-interest in spite of governmental co-operation and administrative leadership, then it might be necessary to resort to compulsion in the public interest—but not till then.

Not all of what is suggested could be achieved at once, nor even, perhaps, very quickly. A nation like the United States, however, with our vast resources and our badly balanced system for exploiting them, ought to look forward to something of the sort. It is not proposed to have the government run industry; it is proposed to have the government furnish the requisite leadership; protect our resources; arrange for national balance; secure its citizens' access to goods, employment and security; and rise to the challenge of planning that concert of interests of which I have spoken before. It is not possible for anyone, in advance of extended and expert study of the difficult and complex problems involved, to be certain of having discovered the most effective machinery for securing the desired results.

Something of the sort indicated is obviously needed. There are administrative and constitutional difficulties to be overcome. If they seem to you burdensome or costly I would remind you that something like thirty billions of national income has been sacrificed annually now for three years to the gods of chance.

I propose that we offer no more sacrifices of this sort; but that we accept the role of men, assert our mastery of these historic forces, and move on to our destiny of well-being undismayed by any burdens less costly than those we carry now, or any difficulties which we, as men, ought to confront.

I propose to invite a group of economists and industrialists to consider the problem of co-ordination and the avoidance of depression, and to devise an economic council which will meet it. I propose, so far as I can, to put their recommendations into effect. It must not be said that the party of Democracy shares the complaisance of its rival in the face of national disaster; we must show our willingness to go the whole way necessary to cure the distresses of unemployment, insecurity, the dwindling of national income, and the inequities of an uncontrolled industrial Moloch which threatens, under Republican policies, to ruin all of us.

INDEX